RAIN over
BAGHDAD

BOOK SOLD
NO LONGER R H P.L.
PROPERTY

RICHMOND HILL
PUBLIC LIBRARY

JUL 2 9 2014

CENTRAL LIBRARY
905-884-9288

rh

BOOK SOLD
NO LONGER R H P.L.
PROPERTY

RAIN over
BAGHDAD

Hala El Badry

Translated by
Farouk Abdel Wahab

The American University in Cairo Press
Cairo   New York

RICHMOND HILL
PUBLIC LIBRARY

JUL 2 9 2014

CENTRAL LIBRARY
905-884-9288

First published in 2014 by
The American University in Cairo Press
113 Sharia Kasr el Aini, Cairo, Egypt
420 Fifth Avenue, New York, NY 10018
www.aucpress.com

Copyright © 2010 by Hala El Badry
First published in Arabic in 2010 as *Matar ala Baghdad*
Protected under the Berne Convention

English translation copyright © 2014 by the estate of Farouk Abdel Wahab

All rights reserved. No part of this publication may be reproduced, stored in a retrieval system, or transmitted in any form or by any means, electronic, mechanical, photocopying, recording, or otherwise, without the prior written permission of the publisher.

Exclusive distribution outside Egypt and North America by I.B.Tauris & Co Ltd., 6 Salem Road, London, W2 4BU

Dar el Kutub No. 13679/12
ISBN 978 977 416 588 7

Dar el Kutub Cataloging-in-Publication Data

El-Badry, Hala
      Rain over Baghdad / Hala El-Badry; translated by Farouk Abdel Wahab.—Cairo: The American University in Cairo Press, 2014.
      p.   ; cm.
      ISBN 978 977 416 588 7
      1.   English fiction
      823

1 2 3 4 5   18 17 16 15 14

Designed by Adam el-Sehemy
Printed in Egypt

My thanks and profound appreciation to Iraqi researcher in sociology and political science, Dr. Sadiq al-Ta'i, for his meticulous review of facts and social and political events.

To the people of Iraq

Three Knocks

December 1979

Disappearance

Where has Anhar Khayun disappeared to suddenly from Baghdad and why?

I inquired about her at the Iraqi News Agency where she worked during the day as an editor in the culture section. Her boss Abu Lu'ay said to me, "Hello, Sitt Nora Suleiman. Anhar has not gone on leave, has not called in sick, and we don't know why she hasn't come to work yesterday or today. Tomorrow is another day and who knows, maybe we'll have news."

I sensed tension in his voice as he answered my questions, knitting his brows, looking me in the eye as if trying to find the reason for my asking even though he knew that she worked with us in the Baghdad bureau of the Egyptian magazine *al-Zahra* after her day job at the agency.

I called her at home in the evening. Her mother's tearful voice said, "Please, Nora. I implore you: if you find out anything new about her, let me know. I'm going crazy. She hasn't come back since she went to work the day before yesterday. Her father, her brother, and the husbands of her sisters all looked for her in the hospitals, police stations, at her friends' houses, everywhere. We've asked everywhere. Please, if you hear anything. . ."

"By all means, Tante Fatma. God willing we'll hear good news soon."

I asked Abu Ghayib, the doorman at the Sheikhaly Building who also cleans up and runs errands at our office, if Anhar had come to the office earlier and left when she didn't find either of us.

"I haven't seen her since she finished work at the office the day before yesterday," he said.

I don't know why we're so worried about what could have happened to her. It's only been two days since she went missing. Why are we all so pessimistic?

On the third day, when Anhar did not call or show up at the office, the anger of the bureau director Hilmi Amin, turned into that sort of tension that lies midway between vexation and worry. I expected he would contact his secret sources, who I guessed were comrades in the Iraqi Communist Party or Palestinian or Egyptian friends with close connections to the Ba'th Party, who could help him figure out complicated situations. Today he was in dire need to know where Anhar was, whether Security was behind her disappearance, or love, or whether she had been, God forbid, the victim of an accident.

When Hilmi Amin opened the door for me on the fourth morning of her disappearance his red eyes told me at once that he hadn't slept for some time. I grew apprehensive and asked him if he had any news about Anhar.

"No one knows anything," he said despairingly as an almost spent cigarette dangled from the corner of his mouth. "Do you have any news?"

I said, "I stopped by at the Agency as usual and got the morning bulletin. I noticed that a journalist friend, Imad al-Bazzaz, totally avoided me, returning my greeting in a faint voice as he headed for a distant room and closed the door behind him, and that Abu Lu'ay looked as if he had put on a wooden mask as he answered my question without taking his eyes off the newspaper he was reading, saying, "We don't know anything, Sitt Nora," then adding curtly,

"We don't know. When we find out, we'll let you know. In other words, don't call us, we'll call you."

Hilmi Amin said, "I expected that. None of the comrades know anything about her whereabouts. Usually news of detention is confirmed only after a few days, when one ends up in a specific detention camp."

A week after her disappearance, when we received no news of an accident or her being the subject of an interrogation or detention, we came to the conclusion that she had disappeared of her own free will, whether that was inside Iraq or somewhere abroad.

I said to myself that it didn't make sense that Anhar did not think of hiding in her native village, built on sixteen hundred kibashas, or islands, in the Ahwar, or marshes, north of Basra, a lowland area located in the southern basin of the twin rivers, the Tigris and the Euphrates. The houses there are constructed of reeds and matting and from a distance would appear as if they were nests of mythical birds flying over the water's surface. During the flood season when the dwellings are submerged the villagers build more permanent islands or 'dibins' of layered reeds, mud, and buffalo dung, each big enough for one small house and a few buffalos. These dibins could be pushed and moved around in the marshes. Anhar could hide in one of them and keep moving in the midst of bulrushes in the secret mazes of the marshes. How could anyone tell the difference between her and any of the marsh peasant women if she put on that long black dress and that turban with tassels on the sides? Anhar lived in that area the first ten years of her life before coming to Baghdad with her family and the Khayuns have retained their influence and could give her shelter there. Yes, she must have thought of that just as we are thinking of it now and just as Security also is thinking of it. It is a place that seems open and transparent on the surface with its expansive stretches of water covering thousands of acres, but under the cover of deceptive fog, it plays host to a myriad of mirages that provide fantastic means of escape, waiting for time to decipher it. Finding one's way in it without help from its own

3

people and without some kind of betrayal is impossible. And Anhar knows that very well.

I found comfort in that line of thinking and when I shared it with Hilmi Amin I saw him murmuring softly, hoping that that was what happened, that Anhar was out of danger, if she had chosen to get away from him of her own free will.

June 1975

A Wedding

I put on my white bridal gown and veil and got into the car on my way to the airport, followed by several cars carrying my family and friends in a morning bridal procession to join Hatim, who had to go to Baghdad ahead of me. I had not yet taken my finals in college when he signed a contract to work in Baghdad. We arrived at the airport at the last moment: eleven o'clock, just one hour before departure. I found my father waiting for me, having taken care of the ticket and weighing the bags. They took me running from the car to passport control. I said a quick and distracted goodbye to my mother as everyone kissed me. Loud ululations of joy erupted accompanied with grains of salt showered on me as my father extricated me, saying calmly, "Say goodbye. Seventy kilos? What did your mother put in your bags?"

I smiled. My mother had insisted that I take in my carry-on bag a box of bridal cookies with sugar and another box in which she had put a roasted duck, two squabs, some shish kebab, and kofta, and rice with nuts and raisins, saying, "This is your nuptial meal. I hope they will let you take it with you."

I said, "Father will see to that. As you can see, he has enlisted everyone at the airport to make my trip go smoothly. It is getting it into Baghdad that is problematic."

She said, "Do what you can, anyway. They'll understand these customs of ours."

I said to my friend, Salwa, "It doesn't matter what rung of the social ladder the bride comes from. They'll say she is from Sayyida Zaynab or Shubra and not from Zamalek!"

My family had a reception last night for the extended family and a few friends, a sort of henna ceremony, without the henna or the ceremony, in which the women, away from men's eyes or ears, exchanged stories and experiences of the first night. My aunt nudged me in the thigh, saying, "Be a good girl. Don't make a scene and don't be afraid."

I said, "Why should I be afraid? I've never heard of a bride dying on her wedding night."

The other women caught the drift of the conversation and mother said to my aunt in a soft voice, "Who are you advising?"

My mother had taken pains to keep me from visiting any bride the morning after the wedding night. I remembered that when I heard my grandmother saying, "Who will take care of her first morning after? Oh, my dear Nora!"

My cousin came in with a large platter of hot mumbar, saying merrily, "I know it's your favorite dish. Take some of it with you in case you crave it."

Salwa said, "Don't they have mumbar in Baghdad?"

"Not like ours, of course," my cousin said.

My other cousin said, "Of course. Our mumbar is bigger and harder, like iron rods!"

My aunt said, "If they see it at the airport they'll say the bridegroom is no good and the bride is bringing a spare instrument!"

All the women present burst out laughing. I remembered the day my cousin Mona, in tears after visiting her sister, Hind, on the first morning after the first night when she said to my mother, "He savaged her, Auntie. Her face and whole body are covered with wounds." Then, after catching her breath she added, "He's an animal!"

My mother chided me and motioned me to move away when she discovered that I'd heard those comments. I watched Hind closely as she was wrapping a shawl around her hips and happily joining my women friends in belly dancing. I asked myself, "Where have the wounds gone?"

They played Hurriya Hasan's beautiful wedding song about the zaghruda ululation that rang out in the house and gathered all the neighbors to celebrate.

They let me go to sleep at 3:00 a.m. and slept on mattresses spread out in every room of the house. Their whispers continued and I could make out bits and pieces about pinpricks and rubbery hymens. I got up at six in the morning to find my mother, moving on tiptoes, having made a light breakfast for me and Salwa. After breakfast I went with Salwa to the beauty parlor which had opened early especially for me.

I told Salwa, who was studying medicine, that I had my period a few days earlier for the first time in my life and that it had ended only yesterday. "Can you imagine, in the midst of thinking and preparing for the wedding, traveling, the heat, my period, and all this worrying?"

Salwa said it must have been the excitement. "Thank God you purified yourself yesterday."

I said, "Mom told me to recite the shahada again while bathing in the morning."

Salwa smiled and said, "Mothers!"

I couldn't tell her that my mom had dealt me quite a blow in the afternoon. I had opted to use halawa to remove hair by myself at home before going to the beauty parlor on henna night. I took a shower and wrapped my hair in a large towel. I poured glycerin and lemon juice all over my body, trying to avoid thinking about giving myself over to the massage and the Moroccan bath, wondering why I had to bare myself before women who were complete strangers. I heard some knocks on the door and my mother's voice asking if she could come in.

"I haven't put my clothes on yet," I said.

"Put a robe on and open the door," she replied. I let her in, wondering in astonishment what was so urgent. She said, "Sit on this chair and raise your arms and stretch them out."

She placed her palms on my armpits and felt them. Then she said, "Spread your legs." She turned me over while I was in total shock, telling her, "Everything is fine."

She said, "I refused to let a professional do this. You are a bride and we have to be absolutely certain that you're one hundred percent intact."

She raised my legs to inspect me below the abdomen. I screamed. She said in a commanding tone, "We are not going to let you disgrace us."

Her fingers parted my labia. She was not looking for a hair here and there that may have strayed from the halawa. She was looking for God's seal.

She let me go. Other hands would complete my makeover. I didn't exchange a word with her until I got on the plane. I put on a smiling mask, but my happiness with the warm feelings of my friends and family was diminished by my mom's insulting behavior, a behavior I couldn't do anything about. I believe the insult will remain with me forever.

My eyes welled up with tears. My father said, "Hatim is a beautiful human being and he will take good care of you."

I smiled. He got on the bus with me. The bus took us up to the ladder of the airplane. The passengers made way for me and let me go ahead of them. My father kissed me and gave me a paper bag that had two bottles of whiskey and one champagne bottle, saying, "A gift for Hatim."

The steward took the bag and I wrapped the long train of my dress around my arm and got on the plane. The passengers cheered and hurriedly climbed the ladder. My eyes filled with tears.

I must confess that I was going to Hatim without fully comprehending my confusion. I was like a bird with its feet tied, unable to walk and unable to fly. I had met him at the birthday party for my neighbor and childhood friend Salwa. He had just returned from Germany where he had studied engineering. He was a friend of her fiancé, Hashim. When he saw me he said, "I left Germany for one reason: to marry an Egyptian young lady with brown skin and honey-colored eyes and brown hair like you. Would you believe that I've just found her?"

I said, laughing, "But I only met you a few minutes ago. Most Egyptian women have brown skin, honey-colored eyes, and brown hair, even if it were dyed."

"Don't underestimate my intuition about people."

A week later I saw him standing in front of me at the Faculty of Arts. He said, "Sorry for not being here sooner. I had to travel to Maghagha. My mother was sick and I didn't want my younger brother to handle all the responsibility by himself."

I said to myself, "A Sa'idi with red, frizzy hair and freckles all over his face. Maybe he is a Sa'idi from Holland!" I held myself back from laughing at the thought and took him to the cafeteria to drink some tea.

I found myself caught up in his life. He bombarded me with details, saying, "I am a practical man. I face the whole world in an impartial way, but I am partial only to you."

After a few months we announced our engagement, then he went to Baghdad.

I sat next to an Egyptian engineer who worked in Iraq. He wished me success, then fell asleep. I couldn't sleep in spite of staying up very late and waking early. Throughout the flight I didn't think of the marriage or the unknown I was about to encounter in my new life, leaving behind my friends and family and my writing job at *al-Zahra* magazine. I'd had the job during my years in college and now my boss told me, "Send us news and features from Iraq." I busied myself with the details of the trip, placing my full trust in Hatim. The new city, Baghdad, would be full of excitement. I never suggested to Hatim going back to Germany, which he loved very

9

much and always remembered with great longing. When he got two job offers, one to Saudi Arabia and the other to Iraq, we both decided without hesitation to accept the Iraqi contract offer even though its pay was half that of the Saudi one. Our thinking was that life in Baghdad was more natural and more civilized. We thought of *The Thousand and One Nights*, of Harun al-Rashid, Zubayda, al-Farabi, Hammurabi, Enkidu, and Ishtar.

The stewardess brought a cake and an Egyptian woman who sat behind me ululated. After a few minutes I found myself facing the open plane door to the scorching heat of a June day at four in the afternoon. I felt I had suddenly stood in front of the open door of a bakery oven. The airport employees deliberately took their time finishing my arrival procedures as I moved from one window to another; each officer held on to my passport, smiling. As I slowly made my way to the exit, I saw Hatim in the midst of his Egyptian and Iraqi friends, waving to me.

On the way to our house his friend, Adel, asked me, "Don't you have a sister?"

I said, "No."

He said, "I want to marry your sister or cousin or even your friend, anyone close to you."

Hatim said, "Today I alone get to make all the requests."

Adel said, "She's ours until we arrive at the house. I beseech you, for the Prophet's sake. I want a bride."

Whenever Adel visited us afterward, he persisted in his request. One day, a few months later, I welcomed his bride at the airport. His mother had chosen her for him from the girls of the family. He introduced her to me, saying, "This is Nahid."

October 1980

Destruction

"Al-Dora Refineries and Baghdad Power Company Bombed. Today at 12:00 noon, the Baghdad Power Company and the oil refineries in al-Dora were bombed heavily by the Iranian Air Force. This led to power outages in most neighborhoods of the city, several injuries among the workers, the destruction of the nearby residential neighborhood, the martyring of a number of inhabitants, and the wounding of many, some in critical condition."

I stared at the television screen and the Cairo TV announcer. I saw the wall of my house lying in ruins and on fire right in front of me. I said to my father, who was listening attentively to the news, "Father, my house in Dora is burning." He said, "Thank God that you've arrived in Egypt safely. War is nothing but destruction!"

My mother said, "Who's there now?"

I said, "I don't know. Titi and her two children are here in Cairo. Most of our Egyptian women friends have left Baghdad with their children, leaving behind the men in their jobs. Her husband, Mahmoud, is at work in the factory right now. I think the floor I lived on is still vacant and nobody would be at home at that time except by chance. Perhaps Abu Maasuma, the gardener. Only God knows. The war broke out nine days after I left Iraq. I'll call Titi in the evening to inquire about Mahmoud. I'll also call Tante Fayza to make sure that Ustaz Hilmi Amin is all right."

I remembered Umm Samira and Umm Tayih, my neighbors in Dora. I had friends in all the neighborhoods of Baghdad. I remembered Anhar and wondered whether she had returned to Baghdad. I remembered the Egyptian peasants in the Iraqi village al-Khalsa and the Murabba' Café and al-Rashid Street.

Titi's voice on the telephone in the evening was sad. She told me about the devastation that her husband Mahmoud described to her on the telephone. Tante Fayza said that Hilmi was fine but that the situation in Baghdad was bad.

Titi and her two children returned to Baghdad a few months later, having made sure that calm had returned. I remembered the letter that she wrote to me as soon as she entered the house:

In the name of God, the Merciful, the Compassionate. My dear beloved sister and friend, Nora, my dear son, Yasir, and my brother, Hatim:

I write to you from Baghdad. I hope you receive the letter in the best of health and happiness. Dear sister, I would like you to know that I arrived in Baghdad on Saturday 2/5/81 in the morning after waiting in Amman airport for approximately nine long hours. When I arrived at the house I was totally surprised by what had happened to it. The house was badly hit and one side of it was burned down. You can't imagine the look on my face when I saw that and imagined how anyone would have fared if they were at home when it was bombed. Of course they surrounded the whole neighborhood and evacuated everyone. They did the same with Abu Gamal's and Abu Nidal's houses. Anyway, Nora, it was a harrowing scene. They paid Mahmoud the sum of three hundred dinars for all of our losses. Can you imagine all of the boxes in which I had packed all the household items so that

Mahmoud would ship them if we decided to return for good? The living room set, the fridge and the washer and a vacuum cleaner that Mahmoud had bought and a rug. Mahmoud also said that his monthly salary was in his suit pocket because the house was hit on 2/10/1980. Anyway, nothing really matters so long as we are all alive. They compensated the owners of the house by paying them two thousand dinars, a small sum since the house is old. Not a single window has any glass left. And of course whenever I sit down and look around, I wonder what would have happened to us if we were all there when it happened. My friends saw fire all the way from the Mechanic neighborhood. My colleague, Hizam, remember her? She told me that the flames of the fire extended all the way to the Muthalath area at the beginning of the Mahdi from the direction of the Sayidiya. That was one reason why Atef, the engineer, did not take lodging with us and—can you imagine? - he's thinking of resigning and returning to Egypt: Sawsan is pregnant after Duaa. Her daughter is quite a darling, just like your daughter, God willing.

I've talked too much. You must be tired of reading by now.

Dearest Nora, I went to the market for the first time yesterday. I found a baby outfit for one dinar, would you like me to buy several for the coming baby? I found some baby shampoo for 850 fils and Johnson powder for 650 fils and a heater for nursing milk for 4.5 dinars. I also found Shiku pacifiers for 420 fils each. All baby clothes are about one dinar each. I would like you to know that when I arrived, Ustaz Hilmi Amin was at a conference in Tunis and came back only a few days ago. I have given him the stuff I had and reassured him about Tante Fayza and the girls. The house still needs repairs. I am using only one room on the second floor. I hope that you are well and that the pregnancy is progressing in the best of conditions and that your features get published regularly. Unfortunately we don't receive *al-Zahra* magazine.

At the end of my letter, in which I have gone on for so long, I send you greetings from Mahmoud, Madu, and Amani. Please convey my greetings to Yasir and Hatim until we meet again in another letter. I hope to receive your reply to make sure everything is okay.

Your sister, Titi

First Text

Three knocks on the door of memory restored life to days that were lingering as they turned toward disappearing forever. I tugged at the end of the thread of time that used to tame mountains and humans. The days broke loose and came tumbling down on my heart. I tried to stop their ruthless flow and pay attention to what was happening around me, but I couldn't. Inside of me there was a rush seeking to recapture the flow of the days and once again feel the pleasure of the pain that didn't contain the moment. I was carrying my suitcase to the airport on my way to Baghdad, not believing that I had indeed left my six-month-old son with my mother-in-law in Maghagha, two and a half hours away from Cairo.

My mother said, "They're going to forget you if you keep declining invitations to travel like that. Accept the invitation to participate in the conference. Five days will not turn the universe upside down."

I said, "I am still breastfeeding Haytham. How can I leave him?"

"Take him with you," she said.

I called the Secretary General of the conference and asked about the hotel where we'd be staying and the possibility of daycare for my infant son during the conference sessions.

After some hesitation she said, "Al-Rashid Hotel, in front of the Hall of Conferences. Yes, we can provide daycare."

I don't know how she conceived of the idea. I relied on her consent to convince myself that it was possible for my baby to accompany me. I searched in my memory for the location of daycare centers close to the hotel. I knew the city quite well. I had worked in it as a correspondent in *al-Zahra* magazine bureau for

14

five years. I visualized the program, the panels I would have to run to attend, the official lunch and dinner invitations I would have to go to. I asked myself, "When was I ever able, during a conference, to return to my house at midday or even midnight? Where would my son be?"

I thought of hiring an Iraqi nanny to come and live with me in the hotel and take care of him in my absence. I liked that solution, but once again I found myself thinking, "Where would such a lady come from all of a sudden? Should I, before the trip, ask for the help of my neighbors, Umm Gamal and Umm Tayih? Or my friends, Rajaa, Ilham, and Titi?" Between my reluctance and acceptance I started writing my paper about educating women after teaching them how to read and write. I asked myself: "What do mature women who have just learned how to read need?" I thought of offering them a program closely relevant to their lives. I thought, "Would the Iraqis accept models from non-Iraqi thinkers?" I remembered the battles I had to go through in discussing with them the absolute necessity of Arab unity before adopting socialism and how I was not at all convinced of the possibility of a union of countries that had not achieved freedom. I wrote a preliminary program on several levels convincing women that knowledge was of the utmost importance.

My life was filled with competing tasks: running to finish my magazine features, taking care of my son, Yasir, who was now going to school, and Haytham, who got a meal of yogurt while I was away from the house. I didn't need the added responsibility of writing an important paper for a conference organized by the League of Arab States and the Iraqi Women's Union. Haytham's laugh was sufficient to settle the competition between writing my paper and taking care of him. And of course he was the winner.

My daily program began at 5:00 a.m. with his first feed. I would go to him in his crib and change him, then leave him to sleep and wake up again at 8:00 a.m. During his nap I would run the washing machine and the dishwasher, cut up the vegetables, prepare breakfast for the whole family, get Yasir ready for school and send him on his way, put lunch on the stove, then run a warm bath for Haytham in a plastic tub. A spoonful of honey or tomatoes and a good breastmilk meal were quite enough to fill him and give me a sense that I had carried out my duties, for the time being at least. He would protest noisily against my abandoning him in the crib, then would calm down and begin to observe me, his eyes following me so long as I was in his field of vision. When I went out the door he would summon me with real tears and sobs. I would rock him until he slept or sang "Da, da, da." My getting absorbed in writing without talking to him was always met with revolt and protest. I would say to him, "Clean and full up, what do you want?"

I would stop to play with him a little, then go back to writing. Sometimes he would totally refuse my ignoring him, at which point I would have no choice but to carry him on my thigh while reading or writing, turning him over from time to time or rocking him on my legs until he went to sleep and I went back to what I was doing. When he refused to go to sleep, I would leave him on my leg and try to create a balance between the sentences running away from the blank page in front of me and the pupils of his eyes, which followed my face, wanting me to be his at that very moment. I wanted to belong to him but also to my work and to those women who wanted to catch up with what was happening around them in the big world. It is the child who enslaves the woman, not the man.

I came to when I heard Hatim's voice as he was driving us to the airport. I smiled. He laughed and said, "Where did you go? Don't have any fear on Haytham's account: Thank God his problem has been solved. Take care of yourself and say hello to everyone in Baghdad." His pats on my shoulder reassured me and led me to images chasing each other in my mind's eye.

My mother and I were visiting my mother-in-law one week before taking off for Baghdad. I had bought the plane ticket for Haytham and added him to my new passport. I closely watched

16

Fattum, my mother-in-law's maid, whose round, very kindly face was constantly smiling as she walked swaying from side to side like a duck while carrying her daughter. She sat in front of the kitchen door and took out her breast that was swelling with milk to feed her daughter.

My mother asked her, "When are you going to wean her?"

Fattum said, "I've gotten tired, Ma'am. I swear I'd like to, today rather than tomorrow. She eats all kinds of food but gives me a heartache all night long."

The child hit her on the face as she was trying to move her breast away, which was hanging down to her belly, so she could put it back in the galabiya to take out her other breast, but the girl had no patience until she held onto it with both hands and we could hear her regular slurping sound.

Fattum added, "I was afraid to wean her so that I wouldn't get pregnant again while she's still an infant, but I had my period and she is getting close to two years. So I figured, it's a boon from God for her, so why should we deprive her? But, I swear, I got tired and the doctor told me, 'Come the fifth day of the period and I'll fit you with an IUD.'"

My mother said, "Postpone weaning her for two weeks and nurse Haytham. Nora will go to Baghdad for a week. What do you say we leave Haytham with you until his mother comes back?"

Fattum said, "I'd do anything for Umm Yasir. No one is dearer than her. Two weeks is not that long."

I said, still taken by surprise, "Haytham is used to you and he loves you."

Hatim's sisters showed great enthusiasm for the idea and said, "Leave him here. Have no fear. He'll eat and sleep."

My mother-in-law said, laughing, "The land raises the child."

I said, "What will I do if my milk dries up?"

My mother-in-law said, "You have a breast pump, of course. Just pump the milk at times of feeding as you would when he has a tummy ache."

I said, "I can pump the milk for a day or two or even three, but a whole week? I am afraid the milk will dry up and so I would be doing Haytham an injustice. This way we'll lose both worlds."

My mother said, "Have no fear on Haytham's account. Just make sure you pump the milk out on time and make sure your breasts are totally empty. Each drop of milk you leave behind you will lose."

Haytham did not understand my tears. He burst out crying. He thought I was mad at him. I tried in vain to laugh as I said goodbye to him, but it was no use. My mother took him and moved away until he stopped crying.

Yasir confidently said to him, "Don't cry, Mom will buy you a big toy from Baghdad."

My husband carried my bag, urging me not to tarry so as not to miss the plane. My mother said, "Take a heavy coat. You can't trust how cold it will be at the airports at night."

I checked my travel papers: the passport and the ticket. I opened the conference invitation.

Yasir said, "Mommy, the airport."

I said, "I know; you are a good boy and I love you very much. I'll call you on the telephone whenever I can because telephone service in Baghdad is difficult."

He said, "Say hello to Madu, my friend."

Members of the Egyptian delegation started arriving. We waited until most of us were there, then we made our way to passport control. Direct flights between Cairo and Baghdad had stopped since relations between Egypt and Iraq were severed because of the signing of the Camp David agreement. I looked at the large number of women colleagues in the delegation: journalists, members of the Women's Unions of Egyptian political parties, members of the People's Assembly and the Shura Council, women activists and business women, and some artists and writers, a mix of different age groups and ideological affiliations. It was my first time in such a large official Egyptian delegation. Usually I would be waiting for their arrival and welcoming them in Baghdad. We waited in the VIP lounge. Nuha, a young lawyer and daughter of a famous lawyer sat next to me. She asked me, "You think our lives are in danger on this trip?"

I said, smiling, "No, the Iraqis would never arrange such an event before taking everything into consideration, even if they had to reach an agreement with Iran to protect us."

The group sitting nearby laughed and we got into a group discussion of the circumstances of the war. I noticed that they were not well informed about the situation, but I didn't comment. The journalist Siham Fathi asked, "Were they really able to erase women's illiteracy up to the age of forty-five or is it just propaganda?"

I said, "They actually succeeded. I followed the project's progress and wrote about it. It was a good program and they implemented it over a three-year period. May it be our turn!"

I remember them waiting together close to their houses for the group to be complete before going to school together. The 'erasure of illiteracy school' in the mid-afternoon turned into a compulsory opportunity for the women to leave behind all family responsibilities and to go out. Joy replaced fear and they experienced the whole episode as if it were a long, beautiful picnic. Once again they were young women full of hope. I remember a road trip that Hatim and I took in the company of a group of these women. They were laughing and making fun of Rashid, the leading man in the literacy campaign textbook. They made up different sentences to express candidly what they thought of men:

Rashid drank thirty bottles of beer.

Rashid came back from the tavern at two in the morning.

Rashid sold his mother's and his wife's and his sister's gold (ha ha).

Rashid rode the Toyota and left his wife working in the orchard.

I loved those women and I learned a lot from them. They deserve some sacrifice on my part, but Haytham?

Time passed. The plane did not take off on time. My breast filled up and the sensation of the milk rushing kept creeping gradually until I feared it might gush forth and soak my bra. Where would I find an opportunity to pump the milk out if I left Cairo airport? I hurried toward the restroom and took the pump out of my handbag. There were several sinks in a line facing toilet stalls. How would I take off my clothes in front of the other women passengers and the attendant? I entered a narrow stall where I could barely stand. I started pumping the milk, which took a long time even as it was gushing out of the nipple. The whole process is designed for a baby to suck as much as he can. I finished pumping my left breast, with which I nursed Haytham first because it is closer to the heart, and I moved on to the right breast. The minutes passed slowly. I heard the voice of the attendant outside calling out and asking, "Do you need anything, Ma'am?"

"No, thanks," I said.

She could hear me moving about and sitting down and standing up and couldn't understand what was happening inside. A few minutes later she asked me again if I needed anything. I said, "I am pumping my breastmilk. I am traveling without my baby."

"I feel your pain, sister. Why did you leave him behind? It must be work, also. Who is comfortable in this world? Neither the poor nor the rich. Come out and empty it in the sink. We are all women and there's hot water here."

"I am almost done."

"Take your time. If you need anything, just call me."

I finished the job. If I started doing it in a hurry the first time, what am I going to do every three hours? And during the panel presentations and discussions? I adjusted my clothes and came out wondering what Baghdad was like. What has changed in you since I left, almost two years ago? I looked forward to visiting my house which I missed very much after my return to Cairo. I remembered Anhar Khayun. Would I find someone in Baghdad who could tell me where to find you, and solve the riddle of your disappearance?

I opened my handbag to take out a cotton handkerchief with embroidered edges. I still like them despite the widespread use

20

of tissues lately. My fingers hit my keychain. I still have the key to my house in Dora and the key to my office in Bab Sharqi and a third key for my mailbox at the Rashid Street post office. This is a letter from Basyuni's family to him. His sister gave it to me yesterday after making me swear by all that is holy in all religions to contact our friend Fathallah Hasan and his wife Maha, for they were the only ones who knew where he was. They were also the only ones to whom he would listen. She said, "Please see him and convince him to come back to Egypt. He got entangled in the Iraqi army unnecessarily." I promised her to try. I remembered my first and only meeting with him.

A beautiful Iraqi winter morning. I began it, as usual, by going to the Iraqi News Agency to get their morning bulletin. In *al-Zahra* magazine bureau we have no telephone and no ticker. We conduct our business the old-fashioned way. I arrived at my office in a good mood because of the soft rays of the sun, which I loved after a rainy night. I found a young man sitting with Ustaz Hilmi Amin, the director of the bureau. He couldn't be more than seventeen. I imagined he was one of the Egyptian students who had begun to go to Iraqi universities. Ustaz Hilmi introduced him to me saying, "Basyuni Abd al-Mu'in, one of the detainees of the January 1977 incident. He came with a recommendation from al-Tagammu' to look for work."

I said, "A detainee? Is it possible? He's just a child."

I realized what I was saying without thinking when I saw the young man's face turn pale. I went on to say, "I am sorry. I didn't mean it that way. I just calculated in my mind: two years ago, you would have been fifteen most likely. So do they detain boys now?"

He said, "I am eighteen now and they did detain me. I was as big then as I am now. They imagined I was one of the university students who were demonstrating. So I was taken to the detention center and inside I got to meet the leader of the political struggle and the big names about which you hear. They became my friends and cell mates." He laughed and blushed. "Then I got into politics after I was released and joined al-Tagammu' political party."

21

I asked him, "Didn't you finish school?"

He said, "I studied in a vocational school and specialized in auto mechanics, but I haven't obtained my diploma yet."

I said, "Why didn't you stay in Cairo until you finished? Do you want to study here?"

"I want to get a job. Unfortunately life here in Baghdad is difficult because of the millions of Egyptian workers who have flooded the market. Getting a job without a diploma has become almost impossible, except in construction," he replied.

I asked him where he stayed.

"In a small hotel in Shuhada' Square."

I said, "I think most guests there are Egyptian workers."

He said, "From my village alone, I found between eighty and ninety young men. I felt I hadn't left Egypt or my village, but when I went to the hotel I couldn't stay there. I must find some other place, quick. They put a foam rubber mattress, designed for one person, for three people to sleep on. I am not used to this kind of life. I would like to start working right away so I can move to a place where I can feel comfortable, otherwise I'll go back to Egypt. The hotel reminds me of the prison experience, so why should I go back there of my own free will? I won't stay there one more moment. One of my colleagues got in touch with me and told me that Fathallah Hasan was in Mosul. I'll go there. Do you know his telephone number or address?"

Hilmi said, "Give him Fathallah's telephone number, Nora. Right now he is at the factory and his wife is at the university. Wait until the evening and call him. Come back here tomorrow, I'll have arranged something with him."

I found out that Fathallah was very happy when Basyuni contacted him and told him to jump in the first available taxi going to Mosul. I never saw Basyuni after that but I asked Fathallah about him on his first visit to Baghdad afterward. He said, "I appointed him to work with me in the roads and bridges department for a large salary. Now everyone envies him. He is working on a project extending paved roads from Mosul northward."

I asked him to give me more information about these projects and said that I might write a feature about them. He said, "We are now extending the roads between Mosul as a big city and the regions where Kurdish Yazidis, who have been neglected for a long time, are now living. These roads will enable them to build hospitals and factories and to reclaim nearby land for use. This would help them build a better world and a higher standard of living."

I said, "This is what is happening to Kurds throughout the north."

He said, "Well, not really. These belong to a different group of clans who are not followers of Mullah Mustafa al-Barzani and they don't like Talabani and they believe both have sold them out to the authorities."

I asked, "On what route does Basyuni work?"

He said, "The Mosul–al-Sheikhan route. He comes to Mosul once a week. The department has set up good and comfortable camps near the work sites. Basyuni has made many friends among the Kurds and sometimes he prefers to travel to their villages and spend his days off with them. This is quite rare, the Kurds don't usually let strangers into their homes. He's won their confidence rather quickly." Then laughing, "Quite a little devil!"

My colleague, Salwa al-Attar, an editor at *al-Zahra*, asked me, "Are you still in touch with Hilmi Amin's daughters?"

"Yes, of course," I replied.

"What a tragedy! We'll have time in Baghdad to speak a lot. I want to make sure they are all right. One gets distracted. He's a life-long friend," she said.

I said, "I know and he was my friend, too."

Anhar has taken up residence in a lofty place in my memory. It is difficult to hear Hilmi Amin's name without remembering her and remembering her disappearance, which is still a riddle puzzling everyone. It's a riddle that Hilmi Amin with all his contacts and acquaintances couldn't solve, as he could never arrive at any

23

real information about her. I thought to myself, "How do you know, Nora? Maybe he's found out, but for one reason or another hasn't told you, either for fear for her life or to keep his own pride intact." Despite the noise created by all the women sitting there and their laughter and loud voices, I remembered my first meeting with Hilmi Amin. I had known him by name only by following his articles and I also knew a few facts about the history of his political struggles.

When I returned to the Cairo offices of *al-Zahra* after a year in Baghdad, carrying my first articles on Iraq, I met Latif Girgis, who said to me, "We've sent Hilmi Amin to open a bureau for us in Baghdad. Have you heard of him?"

I said, "Yes. I've read his coverage of the Afro-Asian writers' conference."

He said, "You're lucky. He's here on vacation. Here's his number at home. Call him."

I called him. I said, "I am Nora Suleiman. I live in Baghdad and I write for *al-Zahra* from there."

He said, "Welcome. They told me you're great. Let's meet in two days at the office at 10:00 a.m. Our address is Sheikhaly Building, Mashjar Street from Saadun Street, the eastern entrance. Take an issue of *al-Zahra* magazine with you to the Ministry of Information in Tahrir Square."

I said, "God willing, I'll do it."

I knew Saadun Street well. I kept asking about Mashjar Street until I found it. It was a big side street filled with electrical appliance stores and offices and doctors' offices and various service stores. In it new four-story apartment buildings stood next to old houses belonging to Assyrian families. A fifty-year-old man received me. He was tall and very dark. I knew at once that he was from the south of Egypt, not Aswan but perhaps Sohag. He had a thick head of frizzy hair with gray sideburns extending to his jaw. He looked to me like a black guitar player who'd just come out of the pages of a novel by Faulkner. His general appearance was a mixture of artist chic and the spontaneity of day laborers. When he spoke, welcoming me, I discovered that his Akhenaten-like lips, his black eyes, and his thin-ness made him a model Sa'idi, standing under a big white sail of one of those clay-pot vessels that sailed down the Nile all year long.

He said, "The chairman of the board of directors has approved your appointment in the bureau, which as of now is made up of the two of us until, God willing, we expand in the future. The bureau offers press material on Iraq in return for ads to be published from time to time on our pages. We work under the auspices of the foreign correspondents section in the Iraqi Ministry of Information which gives us freedom of movement throughout Iraq."

I smiled happily and said, "Finally I'll have a regular job. What are the hours?"

He said, "You come in from 8:00 a.m. until 4:00 p.m., and if we have evening assignments, we'll work them out together. I need a photograph of you and tomorrow we'll go to the Ministry of Infor-mation to get you an Egyptian correspondent ID."

He went to get some tea. I noticed that the office was pleas-antly cool despite the very high temperature outside. I realized there was a small cooling machine next to the desk. I had not seen such a small size before. Baghdad's dry atmosphere makes it pos-sible to cool the air by circulating water in front of an air current that brings the temperature down. They call this type of cooler a "desert air conditioner." There was a set of bamboo chairs in front of a simple wooden desk, above which was a seascape painting. I noticed another seascape painting on the side opposite the chairs and several wooden vases colored with abstract patterns. Ustaz Hilmi came in carrying a tray with small glasses. He said, "Pardon me, Abu Ghayib will come to clean the office shortly. He usually takes our orders in the morning then comes a second time in the evening. We rely on ourselves. The office budget is modest, but it will increase after three months. You'll work with me on features on social life, especially women and youth."

I blurted out, "Why is my work confined to these areas? I'd like to write about art and literature."

He laughed, saying, "We'll see as the days pass what you can accomplish. How come I haven't met you in the magazine? Who trained you? How did you join it? Did you study journalism?"

I said, "I had filled the grounds of the Faculty of Arts with 'wall magazines' of cardboard on which the students expressed their opinions about the 'year of decisiveness.' Some journalists came to follow our demonstrations and among them was a group of *al-Zahra* writers. They stood there reading the 'magazines' weighted down to the floor with bricks. They engaged us in a conversation. Abd al-Fattah al-Tawil asked me to work with him. I moved among the various departments. I wrote about sports and various features. Then I wrote for them from here as I traveled between Cairo and Baghdad. I live here with my husband, who works as an engineer in the Amin factory. I have one son whom the doctor asked me to let stay in Cairo under his care for some time. In other words, I am totally available full time."

He got up to the bookcase and grabbed a large, square package. He lost his grip on it. I tried to help him but he refused. I noticed that his hand did not move normally. He handed me the package saying, "This is a gift from the bureau on your first day on the job."

I said, "Thank you. I hope your hand is ok."

Laughing, he said, "This is the price I had to pay for taking part in the people's defense army in 1956. I got a bullet in my left hand, which did not disable it completely, but the elbow lost its range of motion as a result of being cast for a long time. They tried to correct it but even the largest hospital in Moscow couldn't. They decided that the best course of action would be joint surgery, but that kind of surgery was still in its early stages so I decided to leave it as it is. It's not interfering in the least with my work as a journalist or with writing and many people don't notice it at all."

I said, "I am sorry, I didn't mean to pry."

"Come, let me show you around. This is my desk and naturally we'll buy one for you and put it in the foyer. I am using part of the apartment as a residence and I have separated the two spaces using a small door, as you can see. My family lives in Egypt because

Mervat is about to finish college. Rasha is in primary school and I have a young baby daughter, Rana. I travel to visit them and as of now there's no intention to bring them over here to Baghdad and change their lives. In this case, I mean, if we decide that they should come, I'll move my residence to somewhere else."

I descended the stairs full of optimism. I figured that the street parallel to Saadun Street would be Batawain Street. I knew this neighborhood well. The doctors' offices that we frequented last year are in it. Traffic here never stops, day or night. There are many cheap hotels on both sides of the street and in the middle there is a vegetable and fruit market. There are several inexpensive restaurants and coffee shops. Around every corner stands a man grilling small pieces of lamb called tikka on a cart equipped for that purpose. Workers gather around the cart in the early morning. Some peasant women sit on the sidewalk, selling cream next to carts selling turnips and molasses. I remembered the streets of Shubra and Sayyida Zaynab in Cairo. Life of the working classes is the same, only the features here are different. Those casually going through the market have large eyes, huge noses, and varied manners of dress. One can distinguish them from the Assyrians who live in the neighborhood where the Jews used to live. When the Jews left they were replaced by different minorities: mostly Assyrian, some Turkomen, and some Chaldeans and Armenians. Their skinny bodies tended to be short. Their complexion was white or red. There were blond people with blue eyes. I noticed as the days passed the presence of a large number of mentally retarded people in this neighborhood as a result of constant inbreeding among relatives.

I got close to the garden. In that building over there was the office of the pediatrician who looked after Yasir since he was born here in Baghdad. He had bouts of upset stomach whose causes were beyond me. I was by myself and without experience in mothering, waiting for Hatim to come back from work to take us to the doctor who tired of our visiting, so much so that he would shout when he saw me come through the door, "Your son is totally normal, Madam."

I'd say, "But he's crying."

He tells me in the Iraqi dialect something to the effect that he has a 'twist.' Hatim immediately translates, saying, "He means an upset stomach."

The doctor hastens to say, "Give him some gripe water for colic."

Hatim, laughing, said to me, "Our grandma Eve when she gave birth to her first baby knew more than you do."

I would reply, also laughing, "Our father Adam knew how to make babies more than you do."

I took Yasir to Cairo two months after his birth. His health improved but the doctor told me to keep him in Egypt. He said he had a simple herniated navel and placed a bead from a string of prayer beads in it and covered it with a Band-Aid. He told me that Yasir was bothered by the heat and said that I should keep him in Egypt for a year, after which I could take him back to Baghdad. Hatim would not hear of my staying with Yasir in Egypt and told me to come back and leave Yasir with my mother or his mother.

I postponed my departure several times and kept trying to balance my desire to stay with Yasir and going back to Hatim who was threatening to quit his job and return to Egypt. I looked for the Cairo that I knew and it wasn't there. I had left it three weeks after graduating from college. My friends had left for the Gulf or to Europe. I followed up the publication of my articles on Baghdad in *al-Zahra* magazine. I met Latif Girgis and here I was in the bureau where I had dreamed of working when I read one morning the headline: "Baghdad from *al-Zahra* Bureau: 'Writers of the world ask: Do you know a magazine called *Lotus*?'"

I wondered where the bureau was and how to get in touch with it. When I arrive in Cairo I'll find out all the details and I'll join it. My mother-in-law encouraged me to leave Yasir behind, telling me not to worry, that her daughters would take good care of him. Besides, the doctor was nearby and he would follow up on him, and a year was such a short time and then I'd come back and take him to Baghdad, that that was better than needlessly creating a problem with my husband.

I said, "I didn't come to Egypt of my own free will. I came because I couldn't get much help from Yasir's doctor and because Hatim and I stayed up many nights to take care of Yasir. So, why do I have to make that choice?"

She said, "You'll have difficulty in the beginning of course. But when you hear his voice on the phone and know that he is safe near the doctor you trust, you will be able to tolerate the pain of separation. Join the bureau that you were talking about. Think of it as an opportunity to enhance your career." My mother-in-law also said, "What more do you need than encouragement from your mother-in-law and your mother to start working? Don't waste this opportunity."

"But Yasir . . ."

"No buts."

I left Cairo, saying to myself, "A psychologically healthy mother would work and succeed a thousand times better than a depressed mother." I remembered the long nights of boredom, the loneliness, the emptiness inside, and the confusion. I couldn't forget the hours upon hours of small talk with my neighbor. True, Hatim was gentle and affectionate, but where was Hatim? He worked day and night in a factory thirty kilometers away from Baghdad. So why don't I open the door to a new world that would restore me to life? But, will Hatim accept my new life? I was totally devoted to him for a whole year. Now my life will be turned upside down. Why do I let these questions muddy my life?

One week later I became a member of the Iraqi press community and Iraqi society. I spent most of the following five years working closely with Hilmi Amin, traveling all over Iraq. We would begin work together in the morning by identifying the news stories we'd work on and developing them into features. Then we would go to the Ministry of Information to follow up on news and events. We would have an early lunch in the cafeteria and meet friends then go back to the office to continue working according to the weekly schedule.

I gave him one of my poems to read.
He read:

The strings of your guitar from my heart
Cautiously touch my soul.

"This is not your poetry," he said.

I was taken aback and protested strongly, "Of course it's my poetry!"

He said, "I've noticed that prominent poets nowadays are influenced by contemporary French and English poetry. This sounds like that kind of poetry."

I said decisively, "That is not true!"

He shook his head. I did not argue with him. He doesn't know much about me yet. Soon he will find out that this spoiled girl has lived the life of a champion athlete, and cannot find a single reason to attribute to herself something she hasn't done for she is quite convinced that what she does is enough to satisfy her vanity. I smiled, saying with a confidence befitting my twenty-one years, "It is my poetry and I'll bring you my collection of poems tomorrow."

I invited him to my house and introduced him to my husband. My library was how I introduced my real self to Hilmi. I immediately sensed the warmth of his changed attitude toward me. Laughing, I listed the names of the authors of the books that Hatim had bought for me before my coming to Baghdad to entice me with a life resembling mine in Egypt. "Manfaluti, Mazini, Muhammad Farid Abu Hadid, Abbas al-Aqqad, Taha Hussein, and Mahmoud Hasan Ismail."

He said, "Beautiful."

I said, "Boring! Boring! Boring!"

Hatim embraced me, saying, "You don't like my taste?"

I said, "It's too classical. Where's Abu Nawas, Al-Mutanabbi, Adonis, and Rimbaud? Where is *The Waste Land, Bonjour Tristesse?* Where are Sartre, Camus, and Proust?"

Hilmi Amin sided with Hatim, saying, "They are the modernist generation!"

Hatim said, "She bought all she wanted as soon as she arrived."

I said, "These are Iraqi books about art, history, and literature. Leisure enabled me to finish three novels every week. Would you believe it?"

Hilmi accompanied me regularly every Tuesday morning for five years to the bookstores on Saadun and al-Rashid Streets, looking at the new books and buying what we needed. He introduced me to Salama Musa and, of course, Marx and Lenin, in addition to the works of Hemingway and Somerset Maugham. We bought Jack London's *The Iron Heel*. He also introduced me to John Steinbeck and gave me *The Grapes of Wrath* as a gift. But Hemingway's *The Old Man and the Sea* remained a key work that implicitly charted the complex relationship that grew between the two of us, a relationship whose lines got so entangled that unraveling them was not possible any more. Our office in the heart of Baghdad, and under the weight of our exile, came to resemble that little boat on which the old man sailed to try to catch a giant fish, helped by his deep knowledge of the sea and a little boy and how he came back empty-handed after the sharks ate the fish he caught. Hilmi would tell me in an affectionate tone, "You are the catch I am betting on. Please don't ever let me down."

I didn't and Anhar Khayun had not appeared in our lives yet.

Tears filled my eyes. I said to myself, "I am returning to Baghdad without him. Oh my God! And without knowing where Anhar was either! Is she in some other country as some dubious reports would have it, or in a dark dungeon in the hands of the security service? Or did she depart this world altogether? Only God knows! And where is Basyuni and will I be able to convince him to go back to Egypt?"

I got busy working at the *al-Zahra* bureau. As time went by I got to know Iraq, its people, its streets, and its history better and at a deeper level. I laid down a plan at the bureau to visit the Iraqi sacred shrines in Najaf and Karbala, the seats of civilization in Samarra, Babylon, and Ur, the Assyrian and Sumerian monuments, the land of the Kurds and the swamps of Basra, and from Iwan Kisra in Salman Bak to Baba Gargar where Sayyidna Ibrahim's fire was. We wanted to write about this vast, varied, and splendid world that opened its doors wide and allowed us to enter.

I followed up on the problems of Egyptian workers and their increasing numbers in Iraq. I'd pass by a number of them in Tahrir Square in the morning on my way to the office as they waited for contractors' cars to carry them to work sites that were mushrooming all over Iraq. I developed a close working relationship with the Iraqi News Agency and its journalists by working side by side with them on a daily basis. I also had good relations with *Majallat al-Mar'a al-Iraqiya* (The Iraqi Woman) magazine published by the Union of Iraqi Women, *Tariq al-Shaab* (The People's Path), the organ of the Iraqi Communist Party, *al-Thawra* (The Revolution), the organ of the Ba'th Party where many Egyptian journalists worked, and *al-Jumhuriya* (The Republic) newspaper. I also found my way to al-Khalsa village, owned by Egyptian peasants in a precedent of the utmost importance: transferring ownership of Iraqi land to peasants from Egypt with the purpose of reclaiming it.

My colleague Salwa al-Attar, sitting next to me in the VIP lounge, moved while preoccupied in conversation with Mona Abed and her shoulder unintentionally touched my chest. The contact was very painful. She realized what happened and sat up straight on the sofa and apologized to me. During the nursing period a sudden touching of my breast turns my whole chest into a mass of burning pain. The knocks on the door of my memory kept getting louder. I let the memories in.

The foreign correspondent office relayed to us an invitation from the Iraqi Ministry of Information to travel the day after tomorrow to the north of Iraq to meet the Kurdish families returning from Iran after a general amnesty was declared. I couldn't sleep that night.

This three-day trip would be the first work trip for me outside Baghdad. I was worried that Hatim would refuse to let me travel alone to the north. I arranged my arguments in favor of the trip in my mind. I remembered our honeymoon on the mountain of Saffayn in Salah al-Din village and the wildflowers there. The Kurds told me at the time to come in the winter when the north was much prettier with the snow-covered peaks and the quiet after the summer visitors were gone. Hatim agreed to my going on the trip without much fuss. I started to fantasize about my first trip and what it would be like. Hatim asked me while embracing me, "Have you started your trip already?" I came to, and, apologizing, I turned to him.

The merrymaking began as soon as the cars started. I made the acquaintance of a Chinese man and his wife who looked to be about thirty, a Lebanese journalist, two Russians, a Yugoslavian, and a French journalist. There were only two women and that would be typical of all our subsequent trips. We arrived at a military airport where helicopters took us to the city of Erbil in the north. From the helicopters we saw flames coming from the ground. Our escort Hisham told us, "This is the sacred fire."

I said, "Aren't these the oil refineries?"

"Yes," he said.

Hilmi Amin said, "Nebuchadnezzar used to roast his enemies in it."

I said, "Isn't this Sayyidna Ibrahim's fire?"

Hisham said, "Sayyidna Ibrahim's fire is in the city of Ur in Baba Gargar. This is Kirkuk."

I said, "They're right. How can reason accept the eruption of fire from the ground all the time without fearing it? When life on earth was in its infancy, man created gods to stave off fear."

The Russian journalist, Izak, said, "I know Arabic, but please speak slowly, Nefertiti, so that we might all follow you. Sayyidna Ibrahim the Prophet, right?"

I said, "Yes. He is the grandfather of the Prophet Muhammad and the father of all the prophets. The Glorious Qur'an says: *O fire,*

33

be cool and safe for Ibrahim. Can you imagine that the fire would stop and oil would stop erupting from the ground?"

Izak said, "We have our own beautiful myths."

I replied in protest, "This is not a myth."

Laughing, he said, "That's the beauty and your beauty."

I ignored what he said, noticing resentment on Hilmi Amin's face. I said to myself, "I hope this is going to be all right. This Russian seems to be brash. I hope to God he doesn't cause any trouble for me."

The cars took us to a small building. Hisham said, "Let's have some breakfast before going to the camp."

I sat with Chen. She said to me, "I have a daughter your age living with the rest of my children in Peking."

I gasped in astonishment. She was delicate and well dressed in a simple manner and looked very young. She never left my side throughout the trip. I felt her hand patting me on the shoulder kindly from time to time.

She said in her broken Arabic, "My husband Yang and I visited Cairo before and we hope to do so again."

We went back to the cars that took us over rough mountainous terrain to a camp where hundreds of refugee families lived. I tried to understand why they had not returned to their original villages and towns. One of the officials said, "They assemble here first for their papers to be verified and to be revalidated; then arrangements are made to return them to their occupations and previous way of life."

I looked at their faces. They had beautiful Arian features: a strong fair complexion, blue eyes, and blond or red hair, svelte bodies, mostly short. I could sense the secret anxiety that they hid. I came close to one of those who returned, a doctor who spoke with some correspondents in very good English about being happy to return and the wisdom of President Ahmad Hasan al-Bakr and the integrity of the political leadership.

He said, "I regret having left my country and I am sure the Kurds will turn over a new leaf under a unified Iraq."

I felt that his words were somewhat sycophantic, but I wrote them down verbatim, saying to myself, "Why this feeling? He's truly sorry and he also has to flatter them so that he may go back to his country safely. He has taken part in a revolt against the regime in an Arab country, Nora."

I looked for his family and found his wife sitting on some cushions on the floor with the other women. She was a beautiful woman in her thirties with three children, the oldest eight and the youngest still nursing calmly at her breast. She said to me, "I am happy to have returned to Iraq. One's fatherland is home where one grew up among family and friends."

I talked with several women and young men who had returned. I noticed that most of them were educated and they said they were happy to return. We listened to officials as they took us around the camp. They condemned what Mullah Mustafa al-Barzani did and described him as a lackey of the Americans who sought their help to break the unity of Iraq. The officials threatened to deal forcefully with secessionist calls. They explained to us the importance of autonomy and the plans for the future of the region. We had a short meeting with the governor of Erbil in which he explained to us the preparation for the return of Kurdish families to model villages that were constructed hastily to house them temporarily until they were returned to their normal life in their villages, or in other places if their villages had been destroyed during the clashes.

We sat for a break in a rest house. Everyone else ordered alcoholic beverages while I ordered juice. They served us some fancy Kurdish dishes of cooked green wheat and goat meat and some kind of rice and meat pie they called "parda pilaw." The place came alive with our loud conversation and laughter. The waiter asked me, "What would you like to drink?" I heard Izak say, "Get her some anise or goat milk."

I didn't appreciate his comment but before I could answer the waiter, Hilmi Amin said, "Juice, please." I said to myself that Hilmi's intervention meant that he was following the situation and that he was concerned.

The cars carried us to the hotel where we would stay through-out the trip in the town of Shaqlawa, about fifty kilometers from Erbil. The road was rough but of splendid beauty. I followed the towering trees as they receded. I imagined them as mythical beings that moved and extended their arms trying to catch us but were hampered by the dark. Small villages with soft lights glittered in the distance on the mountain. The narrow road began to curve back on itself, each curve about a half kilometer. The bus kept swerving as it ascended with difficulty and our ohs and ahs rose in a cacophony of languages until every turn was completed, whereupon we burst out laughing. Then we began to count: three, four, five, until we reached fourteen as the bus reached the top level. We opened the windows and reached out to touch the fruit trees whose branches extended inside the windows. We put our suitcases in our rooms quickly, put on warm clothes, and ran out to the inviting street that encouraged us to take walks. The air was cool and refreshing. We stopped in front of simple open ovens watching the dough being formed into loaves and baked, emerging with that distinctive smell of freshly baked bread. The stores displayed inexpensive goods with very loud colors. I noticed an abundance of wooden vases like those comple-menting our office decor and realized that Hilmi Amin purchased them here. The village was built in the middle of a plain ringed by mountains. Terrace farming gave the fields a beautiful distinct char-acter as the water gathered from natural springs in the higher eleva-tions trickled down, forming streams that ran down until they hit a certain elevation whereupon they formed a little waterfall. Despite the dark and the long journey I had no desire to sleep. I wanted to stay up and live here the rest of my life.

We returned to the hotel and went into the restaurant where, even though we had been eating all day, we had a great appetite. Izak sat in the opposite chair at the table and got very drunk and began to flirt with me in front of everyone. I didn't know what to do so I didn't say a word. After a short while I asked someone sitting at a distance to exchange places with me. I found refuge with Firas, the Lebanese journalist whom I noticed was following the situation. We started talking about Egypt and his travels there. My mind was not focused as Izak kept calling out loudly for Nefertiti. I said to myself that he was crazy. He had been drinking a lot at every stop when we took our breaks. I saw him coming toward me with a comb in his hand, saying, "May I comb beautiful Nefertiti's hair? Please let me . . . let me."

I said to him, "Go to her in Berlin. She would be happy if you did."

He didn't understand what I meant and said, "No, I want to do it here now."

Firas got up and escorted him to the lounge. I was terribly embarrassed as the eyes of the foreign correspondents and Iraqi officials looked at me. I took my leave to go to my room. I heard some movement outside the door of my room so I opened it quickly in anger. I found a young man on the hotel staff standing guard. The telephone rang. Hilmi Amin asked if I was all right. I said, "Yes. I am very sorry for what happened."

He said, "Have a good night. We'll talk tomorrow."

I sensed an angry tone in his voice. I tossed and turned, unable to sleep. I heard some movement outside the door of my room. What was happening to me on my first trip as a journalist and how would that affect my position in the bureau? I remembered that every time we stopped, Izak would comb his hair. He looked at his reflection every time we passed in front of glass windows or doors and every mirror. He seemed merry and pleasant and pleased with himself. But the day ended on a sour note. I got tired thinking of what happened, my sleep interrupted by anxiety and vexation. I didn't realize that what happened on this trip would leave an imprint on my work and movement in Baghdad for five years.

In the morning we went to the village of Afiya, still bearing traces of the dew of dawn. The peasant women led the cows and goats with the children in tow. We got busy snapping shots of Kurdish homes hidden behind trees. The sheen of the peasant women's attire easily made them stand out in the landscape. We visited some rug and tobacco factories. I wanted to pick some wildflowers as I did with Hatim on our honeymoon but was afraid that that might elicit comments from Izak after last night's scene. We went to the markets of Erbil and I bought Kurdish brocade fabrics. Chen, the Chinese lady, said, "Why buy so much?"

"My friends in Egypt will use the fabric to make evening gowns."

We went up to the fort and Hashim said, "People left it and built houses far away on the foothills after diseases and epidemics spread inside."

I returned to Baghdad, happy, carrying material for a feature, and gifts for the house and my friends. I wrote the feature and submitted it to Ustaz Hilmi in the morning. He added a paragraph about the Kurdish problem and the revolt of Mullah Mustafa al-Barzani and at the end wrote that we would follow up on the application of the autonomy laws and their impact on the Kurds in our future coverage. He asked me to re-read the feature after his additions and try to understand why he made them. Then he called me and said, "You're making good progress in your work as a journalist, but I cannot tolerate any problems in a country as sensitive as Iraq. I received an official letter of apology from the Soviet office as soon as we came back last night."

"So they know that their correspondent misbehaved," I said.

"I don't want to know who misbehaved toward whom."

I found out a few days later that Izak had been reprimanded and forbidden to travel with us for a long time. We avoided the Soviet correspondents after that whenever we met. It seemed that his colleague had informed his bosses about the incident and they dealt with him harshly. I held my peace after that and avoided talking with all men. I turned into a listener unless I was the one asking the questions or gathering material for a feature. Several factors contributed to keep my attitude that way for years.

We received a lot of information and news about the Kurds, some officially in the morning and other items unofficially in the evening. We got some of that informal information from Hilmi Amin's meetings with Iraqi intellectuals and some of it from Hatim and his factory colleagues. Where did Iran fit in all of this?

I asked myself at the time, "What would a country do if it found thousands of refugees crossing its borders from the Saffayn mountains to its land? It had to set up camps for them until the crisis was over. But was the Shah supporting the Iraqi Kurdish secession? And why did he do that when he had his own Kurds who also would want to secede from his rule? Was America behind all the troubles in the region? Why? What is its interest? What exactly do the Kurds want? Who are they? What is their history?"

I started collecting material about the history of the Kurds. Hilmi Amin decided to submit to the Iraqi Ministry of Information a list of books that *al-Zahra* bureau could prepare in collaboration with the ministry, foremost among which would be a book on the Kurds and autonomy. The official in charge of these affairs in the ministry agreed to the project, promising to provide hotel accommodations, to give us freedom of movement, and to allow us to gather as much information about the Kurds' conditions as we cared to and meet whomever we wanted to meet.

Did we meet Anhar at that time? Yes. In various places in Baghdad and elsewhere during celebrations and conferences. But she hadn't started to work with us yet. She joined us a short time later.

I noticed some commotion around me. The official in charge of the VIP lounge came himself to tell us that the bus was waiting for us outside. There was a sudden flurry of activity and we started moving, welcoming the news despite the fact that the plane had been delayed for a whole hour. We knew that the wait at Amman airport was seven hours, so, spending one of those seven hours at the Cairo airport was not such a bad thing. We boarded the plane as if it were our private jet. Salma sat next to me and gave me a piece of chewing gum, saying, "I am very tired. I didn't sleep at all last night. Now I can sleep for an hour and get some rest and energy."

She fell asleep as soon as she shut her eyes. The knocks on the door of my memory wanting to come through got louder. I had been overwhelmed in my work life by the tumultuous events that put me face to face with what was authentic and deep-rooted in the Iraqi experience. I had to start from Kufa when a star in the sky of my memory shone, opening the way for the flood of days to follow.

I felt compelled to visit Kufa because of what I had read and heard about the tragedy of the conflict between the Alids (who supported Ali) and the Umayyads and the story I heard from my Iraqi women neighbors in which they asserted that in the center of town was a spring that erupted under Noah's ark, raising it gradually and causing the flood to begin. The bureau organized a trip to Najaf and Kufa. We went at seven in the morning to the Allawi stop in downtown Baghdad and we rode in one of the Ford intercity cabs. Hilmi Amin and I had each visited both towns previously, but we had not been together. I noticed a large number of tombs covering an expansive stretch of land a few miles before the entrance to Najaf. I said, "Look at all these tombs."

Hilmi Amin said, "The Shia are buried in Najaf to be close to Imam Ali; as for al-Husayn, he is buried in Karbala."

"Isn't al-Husayn buried in Egypt?" I asked.

He said, "Most likely that's a myth. They say that his friends carried his head and escaped, taking it with them. They said that they carried his body and buried it in Cairo or in Syria or in some secret tomb here in Iraq. But whether he was buried here or buried there, he will always be an eternal symbol for martyrdom."

"Do you remember the play *al-Husayn the Martyr* and the problems it created?"

"Of course. Abd al-Rahman al-Sharqawi is my friend. Al-Azhar could not tolerate his vision."

"We need to get these minds working again."

"This is exactly what an intellectual should do. He should look at history impartially except for his thoughts and what he believes to be true, not those things imposed on him. In other words, he should use his reason and put it to work."

We got out of the car. We encountered a small town that looked like all desert towns with its few large houses covered with lead-colored cement paint. We walked downtown on its main commercial street. I saw stores covered with small mirrors cut up in Arabesque geometrical lines. I said, "These are Najafi mirrors."

"Charming. Let's go buy some cigarettes first."

I said, "But these mirrors are used as emblems of what is false or not authentic. When an Iraqi says 'Najaf' he means it is not genuine, an imitation. Because the gleaming lights are reflections on the mirrors and are not captured. That's what I understood."

He said, "No, it is not because of the mirrors but rather because the people of Najaf during World War II were famous for manufacturing car chassis and spare parts and they called that skill 'Najafi craft style.'"

We entered a store. I said, "Can I please have a pack of Sumer cigarettes?"

The store owner said, "Are you from Egypt? Home to Abd al-Wahab, Umm Kulthum, and Shawqi?"

I said, "Yes. Do you like artists?"

He said, "Yes. And I mean Ahmad Shawqi."

I noticed many poems hanging on the wall. I asked, "This is traditional amudi poetry. Who's the poet?"

He said, "This is real authentic poetry. Poetry is amudi poetry. These are my poems. We are all poets here."

We took another car to Kufa. We were struck by the Wadi of Khadd al-Adhraa, thirty-five thousand feddans of rice, a green carpet that the eye cannot encompass. I did not expect the history of the world to be awaiting me here in the country, along with such a special mosque. I saw people circumambulating around twelve shrines and praying a predetermined number of prostrations at each. I began with the Sayyidna Ibrahim shrine where according to tradition he used to pray. On a sheet of parchment it said to perform four prostrations. I stood a short distance from the shrine of Sayy-idna al-Khidr, who enjoys a special status among Egyptians. Here two prostrations were prescribed. Then I got to Ali ibn Abi Talib's court, called Bayt al-Qada'. An elderly lady came up to me and asked why I didn't buy an abaya after she noticed that I had borrowed one from a nearby store that lent out abayas to female visitors. Then I found out that two prostrations were recommended. I did not know beforehand that the Prophet Muhammad had visited Iraq but it was related that when he was taken on his midnight journey to the seven heavens, the angel Gabriel said to him, "Do you know where you are now, Muhammad? You are in front of the Mosque of Kufan." The Prophet, peace be upon him, asked for permission that he may perform two prostrations and he descended and performed prayer there. At the shrine for Adam's atonement, two prostrations were prescribed. Imam Ali's place of prayer was marked by a shrine and so was that of Zayn al-Abidin. There was another shrine, Bayt al-Tasht, then the last one belonged to Imam Jaafar al-Sadiq.

A little girl asked me, "Why don't you pray?"

I explained to her that we were on a working visit and that we would come some other time. The place was quite awe-inspiring. Did the flood actually begin here? Or in one of the other places that compete for the credit? I went out to al-Sahla Mosque, which was the house where the Prophet Idris sewed and prayed, then to the garden of Muslim ibn Aqil, the first Shia martyr. We asked about the house of Sayyidna Ali and they pointed to a very small house no bigger than the house of a poor Egyptian peasant in Egypt. It was built of mud bricks and comprised one room, one hall, and a water well. I saw on the walls three line drawings of Imam Ali in front of Iraq's famous date palm trees. I stood among the people as they sobbed fervently. I found myself catching the mood so I hurried out as my tears flowed profusely. I said, "Sayyidna Ali refused to live in the official amir's residence and preferred this modest house to it."

Hilmi Amin said, "This is a true revered scholar among the companions of the prophet."

I said, "I loved the way he sat in judgment and how he decided his cases. I loved his truthfulness and his sacrifice, even though it is impossible to compare him to Umar ibn al-Khattab because of Umar's charisma and his legend, which has reached us in a more dazzling manner in Egypt, but I don't know why I love Sayyidna Ali better, regardless of the politicized problem that divided the Muslim community because of the fight over the caliphate."

He said, "Politics has deposited all of its poison on this land and the result was the killing of all members of the family of the Prophet, peace be upon him, and the victory of the merchants, Nora."

I said, "This is the Marxist interpretation of the events of Islamic history."

Laughing, he said, "We'll talk about the Marxist interpretation later. For now we have to see the palace, then the mosque."

A short distance from where we were, I read a sign on a small piece of wood that said "The Amir's Palace," and saw an arrow pointing at a big crater with the rubble of the foundation of a building and nothing more. This palace had been built by Saad ibn Abi Waqqas when he built the mosque of Kufa and had it not been for a famous incident, the palace would still be standing. It was related that Abd al-Malik ibn Marwan sat, placing the head of Mus'ab in front of him. Abd al-Malik ibn Umayr said to him, "O Commander of the Faithful, I sat with Ubayd Allah ibn Ziyad in this place and the head of al-Husayn ibn Ali, peace be upon him, was in front of him. Then I sat with al-Mukhtar ibn Ubayda and, lo and behold, the head of Ubayd Allah ibn Ziyad was in front of him. Then I sat with Mus'ab, and lo and behold, Mukhtar's head was in front of him. Then I sat with the Commander of the Faithful and Mus'ab's head was in front of him. I pray to God to guard against placing the Commander of the Faithful in such an evil spot." The Commander of the Faithful said, "May God not show you the fifth (head)," and he right away commanded that the palace be demolished.

I went to Sayyidna Ali's majlis. It was very crowded with people moving about or praying, each carrying a piece of clay that they placed on the floor in such a way that their foreheads ended up touching it when completing their prostration.

I said, "Isn't this a form of idolatry?"

He said, "No. It's a piece of the soil of Karbala blessed by al-Husayn's martyrdom there. It's just a belief."

I said, "Do you see how people touch this sundial? It has dwindled with the passage of time and now has the same stature as a human body. Thank God for the spread of scientific knowledge, otherwise we'd wake up one day and find ourselves worshiping idols again."

We performed a prayer as a greeting to the mosque and toured the place honoring Sayyidna Ali, his majlis, and his life. Then we went downtown where we chose an inexpensive restaurant serving tikka with rice and freshly baked bread. We sat down to eat, pleased with our work so far. Then we started snapping photos and talking with people again until we got tired. Time passed quickly and we didn't have a chance to visit Karbala, site of the famous battle around which much lore has been spun and which ended with the killing of Sayyidna al-Husayn, may God be pleased with him. We decided to visit it at some point in the future. We hired a car to take us back to Baghdad. I remembered Abd al-Wahab al-Bayyati's lines of poetry: "For more than a thousand years people have been weeping for the martyr of Karbala whose shed blood still colors the water and the palm trees in the evening."

I didn't find Hatim at home and when he came home later he told me that he had to go to the bank to transfer money to his brother Imad. I was tired and did not want to go into a discussion that would spoil my day. I went to bed in silence. He followed me, saying, "Why are you angry? I've told you before that I have to share what money I make with my brother."

I said, "You don't have that right any more since we were blessed with Yasir."

He said, "When my father died leaving behind five young children, my brother took the responsibility all by himself because I went to Germany, as you know."

44

I said, "And your father left them enough and then some. And you gave up your inheritance so they could continue their education and so that your mother would feel that she was still in control of things. And I have no objection to that at all."

He said, "My brother could have gone to work in any Arab country and abandoned my siblings, but he has chosen to stay in Egypt for their sake. Therefore he is entitled to share what money I make here."

I said, "But you don't share his profit from the business he set up thanks to your father's properties and you don't have a share in the income of his wife the doctor nor a share in his good health and progeny. Only God can distribute his bounty, not you."

He said, "Nora, you are a reasonable woman and I have never deceived you. Ever since we came to Baghdad I have decided to split our savings and give him his share. So, why are you upset now?"

I said, "You and I and our son are already paying a price by being away from home and family and being separated from each other, while they are taking the fruit of our labor without sharing in the labor. You want to give him a large sum as a gift? That's fine. But to take a share of our livelihood for life? That won't happen."

He said, "Well then you'll have to accept my going back to Egypt to look after my siblings and reverse roles, and he and his wife can go to work abroad."

I said, "I am tired. Let me go to sleep."

He said, "You will not sleep and I won't let you alone."

The stewardess finished explaining and demonstrating safety procedures. I don't think any of the passengers were capable of following the instructions in case of an emergency. The sign to unfasten the seatbelts was lit. I got up to wash my face. On my way back to the seat I asked the stewardess for a glass of water. Nursing makes me thirsty and increases my craving for sweets. I noticed that everyone was busy talking among themselves. The aisles were filled with chatter, reminding me of school bus trips. I picked up

45

the Egypt Air magazine and turned its pages. My eyes caught an ad for camping in al-Wadi al-Jadid, captivating desert with a picture of the sun setting over that great sea of desert sand reflecting an orange color that acquired a deeper red hue at every bend of the dunes surrounding the oasis.

I asked Hilmi Amin as he was describing the drawings of Hasan Fuad, the painter, on the walls of the detention camp cells in al-Kharga Oasis, "Why don't you write your memoirs so that we might know what happened to Egyptian communists?"

He said, "I wrote an autobiographical account of what I experienced in the oases detention camp. Parts of it were published in *al-Zahra* magazine."

I said, "Many men in the Egyptian national movement wrote memoirs about the July 23 Revolution and Egypt's underground political parties before the revolution. We've ended up getting conflicting pictures and the truth is lost."

He said, "The truth is never lost. The only problem is that each of them wanted to be the hero, so he would tell the story with himself as the focal point. But even that is useful because others can respond and correct the narrative. The best of what has been written has been the account given by Ahmad Hamrush, because it is documented and real truthful effort has been expended in telling it, even though I have minor differences with his stand and account."

I said, "How about my recording an interview with you about your life? That would be useful. Then we can transcribe the tapes and one day we will have material for a book that would be helpful for the youth who don't know this history."

"Ok. Let's start tomorrow."

Our morning schedule changed. We started setting aside one hour every day to record Hilmi Amin's life. We started in a very traditional manner about his life in the city of Alexandria and how his family moved there from the south of Egypt looking for work. They settled in the neighborhood of north Ras al-Tin close to the harbor and customs, where his father, and later on his brother, worked. He was the middle son of five boys. His brothers stopped going to school after middle school but he went on. He worked on the waterfront throughout the summer to finance his education. His mother gave him a gold chain (her shabka), which she had held on to against the vagaries and treachery of time, to pay university expenses, but he got a tuition scholarship because of his good grades. In his youth he joined the Muslim Brotherhood, then left them and joined HADITU (The Democratic Movement for National Liberation) as soon as he enrolled in the university. Egypt at the time was seething against British colonialism and he joined the resistance. He fell in love with the girl next door, Ismat, and they planned to get married after graduation. His mother objected since Ismat's father, a distant relative of Hilmi Amin's family, died, leaving the family without a breadwinner. Hilmi's father thought it was his responsibility to support them. So he married Ismat's mother in secret even though his wife suspected the relationship but couldn't be certain. When Hilmi wanted to propose to Ismat formally, his mother angrily told him that Ismat was not suitable for him and that he should propose to an educated woman, a doctor or a teacher. But the engagement took place anyway. Then he was arrested in 1954 with members of the HADITU movement who were split about their position vis-à-vis the 1952 revolution. They took them all to the military prison and a rumor spread among the detainees that they would all be sentenced to death. When his father came to visit him in jail, he told him, "Cash my salary from the customs department and spend it on furnishing Ismat's house and marry her off to the man who proposed to her. I am no good for her. I'll be moved from one prison to another. I love her and I wish her the best." He did not tell him that he was awaiting a death sentence.

The father said, "Ismat will wait for you for years, if you want. She is family."

Ismat tried to object as much as she could but, of course, she ended up marrying another man. His eyes glistened with tears and he stopped talking. I myself cried as I marveled, "How romantic!"

I asked him, "Do you still love her, despite your own marriage and daughters and all the developments in your full life? Do you see her?"

He said, "She is the love of my life. I don't see her often. Only during Eids and family occasions. She married the son of the family next door and I tried to stay away to avoid causing her any family problems, and also out of concern for my wife, who learned the story."

These daily stories about his life brought us closer. I let him tell the story in no particular order, then would ask him about the most intricate details in other sessions to find out intimate details that he deliberately tried to avoid or gloss over. He would laugh when I did that and say, "Are you in the Gestapo? What a tough interrogator you are, Mr. Nour!"

I got bored with sitting there uncomfortably. I could make out some laughter coming from the plane's front seats. The scholar Shahira al-Asi was telling an interesting story as usual. I pushed my seat back and took out a bottle of light cologne from my handbag that was full with the breast pump, the towel, and the creams. I sprayed some cologne over my face and decided to sleep. In my sleep Basyuni with his baby face visited me. God willing, I'll meet with him and convince him to return.

Why am I thinking so much about Anhar? At several points, I imagined the reason for her disappearance was voluntary, after her love story with Hilmi Amin had reached a dead end. Maybe she wanted to stay away for some time to make up her mind for good, but when their separation lasted for a long time she couldn't go back and face him. Or perhaps she liked being away from him and started a new life. She is a good journalist and any news agency would welcome her. I remembered her temporary absence once when she went to Mosul without leaving any information for us. Hilmi Amin almost lost his mind. But then one afternoon she rang the bell at the office and came in. We were about to call it a day. I gave her some files and I left. Love between the two of them was ignited and even

48

though I could see from the anxious and puzzled look in her eyes as she looked at him, wondering what the future held for her, that she was miserable.

During the early days of her disappearance, I imagined for some time that she had gone to Mosul again. I knew that she was very fond of the red anemones that they called the "mother of two springs" which covered its plains and plateaus twice a year, in the spring and in the fall. Then I told myself that she would choose a place he didn't know. My fear for her turned into anger: why was she doing this to us under these difficult circumstances? I was determined to keep all thoughts of danger away from my mind. I was afraid to believe that Anhar would never come back to us. The story of her first disappearance came at a time when Iraq was enjoying a spell of peace: a ruling coalition of five political parties, economic development, international cooperation, and all kinds of cultural festivals. Now things were different: everything was fraught with fear and everyone was worried, waiting for the coming storm, when rivers would be the color of blood, with detentions right and left, when running away to one exile or another was the only way out, a one-way ticket with no hope of return. No, Anhar would not do that to us. She wouldn't make such a decision now. Her disappearance must have another meaning, one that has remained mysterious despite the passing of three years since she left. I must visit her mother, Tante Fatima, and know from her what really happened. Maybe she would tell me what she was afraid to tell others.

I gave in to my memory, letting it savor the days slowly.

Hilmi Amin got ready to travel to Cairo. It seemed like a good opportunity for me to go back to my apartment and do some of the things I have been putting off, especially reading and tidying up the house, to which I haven't been giving much attention. I made a list of books to read and limited them to Iraq. I only left home to get copies of the magazine from the National Company and before leaving the building I'd open the magazine quickly to see if they had published one of my new features. Then I'd go to the newspapers to which we gave free copies. I developed a close relationship with the women who worked at *al-Mar'a* magazine. They would meet me as they gathered around the hearth and invite me to eat with them.

I would say, "Sandwiches, again!"

Laughing, they would say, "You always come at twelve noon, sharp."

"Intentionally, of course."

I would leave them feeling that my relationship with Naglaa and Ilham had grown stronger, while Sajida appeared to be always busy.

Hilmi Amin came back carrying letters from the family and news about Egypt and a new batch of bureau features published in the magazine. I noticed that publication increased when he went to Cairo and after his return tapered off gradually. Our relations with the Foreign Correspondents Office at the Ministry of Information, which they called Directive Relations, grew stronger. Hashim, who has lived in Egypt and who was always jovial, told us about the Dokki neighborhood where he and Saddam Hussein, the vice president, lived and about the coffeehouses where they met in the evening and about the vendors and the teachers and colleagues, and about Orman Park. I noticed how easy it was to deal with Iraqis who have lived in Egypt. For some reason or another we got along well and quickly, maybe because we shared homesickness. There was also Hazim, always quiet, who kept us informed about reaction to our articles and features on the Iraqi side and who got in touch with us to invite us to celebrations and conferences. We became the only press bureau that moved around without need of prior permits to go where we wanted. They encouraged us because they liked our enthusiastic energy. Sometimes we met their boss, Hajj Abbas, an Iraqi Ba'thist with strong nationalist feelings unaffected by the oil craze. He always took pains to remind us of the true generous face of Iraq so that we wouldn't feel bad when we encountered any problem.

I did not feel the heavy hand of security that everybody spoke of secretly until I came face to face with it one day. I had been invited together with Hilmi Amin to a formal party. I asked Hilmi before going home to change clothes, "Does the invitation include Hatim also?"

He said, "If you are invited, as a married woman, it is natural that Hatim should come with you."

I asked him hesitantly, "Are you sure?"

He said, "Invitations always include the wife. So, why not the husband?"

I said, "The situation in Iraq is slightly different."

He said, "No, no. Let Hatim come so you would go back with him at the end of the party."

I presented the invitation at the gate. I noticed the puzzled look on the face of the security officer as he looked at me then at Hatim. Before he could make up his mind, Hazim, who was watching the arrival of the guests from a distance, realized what was happening and came in a hurry to tell us to please come in.

We stood chatting with friends in a beautiful garden as waiters with trays of light finger food made the rounds. I remembered the comic actor Abd al-Salam al-Nabulsi in the Egyptian movie *Hikayit Hubb* (A Tale of Love) when he cornered the waiter saying, "What happened to you? Are you a water buffalo that cannot see? You go round and round while I am going so hungry my tummy is making noises?" I smiled, trying to keep myself from thinking of the security men who were now observing our every move, from a distance. I whispered my observation to Hilmi Amin who said, "Act natural. Vice President Saddam Hussein is here. You have established a precedent today. From now on they know that inviting you means also inviting your husband. They will make inquiries about him and reassure themselves security-wise, then they won't bother you or Hatim ever again."

He added, laughing, "Perhaps they are making those inquiries even as we speak."

"Did you know that ahead of time?" I asked.

"Of course," he replied.

I like to go out early in the morning, to expose myself to the cool drizzle and enjoy the sun which sometimes, coyly, takes her time rising. I follow the thawing of patches of light and rare patches of snow covering the green gardens and sometimes staying on treetops and car roofs. On such days I arrive at the office with my pants wet up to the knee and their bottoms muddy, and my shoes soaked in rainwater. I leave a pair of clean dry shoes in the office that I put on as soon as I arrive. I place my wet shoes in the sun on the balcony railing. The fashionable platform heel style in which the heels rose ten centimeters above the ground did not help protect against the wetness either. I saw that Iraqi journalists were always very well dressed and I didn't understand how they did it, then I realized that they used their work cars in moving about and did not have to walk in rain-covered streets. My appearance after a walk in the rain must cause them to wonder as much as it causes my resentment. Once I said to myself, "I am working and this is a price I have to pay for that and they must also wonder when they read my beautiful feature articles."

I would run on my way upstairs. Our neighbor Karima would hear my footsteps and she and her young daughter Dina would say, "Good morning." I found out from the director that only chance led him to this place when the Iraqi government decided to evict all bachelors from apartments as one way to solve the housing problem in the capital. A number of Egyptians applied to police stations and registered their request for apartments. Most of the apartments in the building went to university professors and *al-Zahra* magazine bureau.

Karima told me, "All the tenants are Christian except for my apartment and *al-Zahra* magazine."

I laughed and told her, "And an Iraqi family and an Indian family."

The dual use of the office as a place of work and residence had created an interesting problem for the bureau director. He used to go to the roof to hang his clothes to dry, because he was too embarrassed to hang them in the balcony. He noticed that his Indian neighbor did not return his greetings if he met him on the street and looked away, knitting his brow. One Friday morning the director went up on the roof and found the clothesline moved away from the apartment of the Indian neighbor. When he met him he moved directly toward him and said, "Please don't be offended if I hang my washing on the roof because I have no choice in the matter."

The neighbor said, "We are an oriental family and we have certain traditions."

The director said, "We are also oriental and we have the same kinds of traditions which I respect."

He never went up on the roof again. The problem was resolved with help from the cleaning and ironing shop.

An increasing number of Iraqi and Egyptian journalists pay the office visits from time to time. Hilmi Amin invited one of them, Muzaffar al-Mosuli, to write critiques of Iraqi art. A few days later the director told me that some of these journalists invited us to a picnic on Friday morning. During a quick visit to the Journalists' Union the following day I ran into some of them and told them that I'd go with them. One of them said, "In the future we will organize an outing somewhere outside Baghdad every Friday and let the beautiful days begin!"

I said, "Great! These outings would be a good opportunity for me and my husband to meet your families."

Some of them said in a soft voice, "Yes."

The bureau director told me on Thursday that the colleagues have expressed their regret for not going on the picnic because they would be busy preparing for a conference. We were not invited by these colleagues to any social events after that.

One day we decided to begin our day by visiting *al-Mar'a al-Iraqiya* magazine where Sajida, Ilham, and Naglaa worked, women journalists about my age, and a veteran managing editor, Amal al-Sharqi. I had gone to them earlier to obtain photos from their archives to use in an article I was writing about Iraqi women, the development in whose lives I was fondly following. They welcomed me and gave me a whole year's worth of back issues. To reciprocate their gift,

Hilmi Amin wrote for them an article on Egyptian women. During our meeting with Amal al-Sharqi, we realized that she and Hilmi had met five years earlier at a conference in Baghdad. They began to reminisce about the conference, wondering about the colleagues that had taken part in it and whatever became of them. A friendship between Hilmi and Amal developed and the director decided to have stronger relations with the magazine.

We asked the receptionist about Amal al-Sharqi but she was not there. We asked to meet with Sajida or Ilham or Naglaa. The receptionist led us to the newsroom. Naglaa welcomed us and ordered tea for us. I took out of my bag two copies of *al-Zahra* magazine and put them on Naglaa's desk saying, "Here is your weekly share."

Naglaa said, "We love Egyptian magazines, and we are trying to develop our own. What do you think of our magazine?"

I said, "I love it."

Sajida came in, with Ilham in tow. We got up to say hello. I noticed that Ilham said nothing while Sajida asked us sharply, "Who are you? What exactly are you doing in Iraq? Do you distribute magazines?"

Her questions came as a surprise to me. I looked at Hilmi Amin to gauge his reaction, since I thought we had already explained to them what we were doing in Iraq and there was no need for such an outburst on Sajida's part. Did she seize upon the absence of the managing editor to confront us so aggressively?

Hilmi Amin smiled calmly and said, "We are a press bureau working in Iraq. We do not distribute *al-Zahra* magazine. That's done by the National Company. But we bring you these copies by way of professional courtesy. A press bureau anywhere in the world depends on relations with national newspapers and magazines."

Ilham and Naglaa joined in the discussion and the three of them began to ask detailed questions in quick succession: "Who pays your salaries? Exactly how many journalists work in the office? Are there Iraqis among them? Do you work for the Zahra organization only? What plans do you have for expanding your work? Are you a branch of the organization? What do your activities include in addition to writing articles and press features? What is your relationship with Iraqi political parties? What is your purpose having dealings with a small magazine like *al-Mar'a*? Do you plan to give other articles as gifts to the magazine? Would such articles be from the two of you only or will you invite other journalists to contribute to the magazine?"

Hilmi answered most of the questions at the same speed that they were asked and I answered some of them. We left feeling that we had absorbed part of the anger that the three young women had toward us. I couldn't get over my surprise at their outburst since, up to that very morning, I thought we were friends. We went out agreeing to meet again the following week. We stood waiting for a cab. Still in a state of shock I asked Hilmi, "I thought Sajida, with her hostile attitude and gruff manner, was behind this confrontation, but the fact that poised Naglaa and jovial Ilham took part made me realize that they all shared the anxiety."

He said, "These questions reflect the three women's insecurity about our presence on the scene: are we going to work in *al-Mar'a* magazine and become their competitors? Especially as it's a new magazine staffed by young journalists, even with the presence of an experienced editor like Amal al-Sharqi, because, as you know, she is only there on a part-time basis. Her primary writing job is with *al-Jumhuriya* newspaper. They are aware of *al-Zahra's* long history in the Arab press. Would *al-Zahra* play a role in their magazine or not? That, briefly, was what they wanted to find out."

We went back the following week and many weeks after that and our relationship with the staff there grew stronger. Amal al-Sharqi invited me to work with them. She said in the presence of Sajida, Ilham, and Naglaa: "Write features for us about each of your trips. Consider yourself a reporter for the magazine."

I looked at the three friends and saw that they were smiling and opening their arms for me and gesturing that I should accept. I said, as I received their kisses, "I accept wholeheartedly."

55

Amal al-Sharqi signed my application for membership in the Iraqi Journalists Union. I was elated, wondering when I would get the Egyptian Journalists Union membership.

I heard some movement. I looked up at the aisle. I saw the stewardess pushing the food carts forward and one steward closing the first-class curtains. Each cart stopped in the front of an aisle and the stewardess began distributing the meals. I leaned my head on the headrest and turned to look through the open window next to Salma. The sky above the clouds was so clear it seemed unreal. Once again I heard the knocks on the door of my memory.

Hamid Marmarji, director of culture in Erbil, invited us to the inauguration of the new cultural season. It was a rather long jaunt this time, eight days. Before we got on the bus, Hilmi Amin warned me, "Last trip we lost all the Russian correspondents in one fell swoop. Let's not lose anyone else this time."

I had promised myself to write many features on the places that we merely went through in the past. I was happy that Hatim had granted me freedom of movement without resenting my being away.

I tried to forget the pangs of being away from my son. The director's words hurt me and put me on notice that I would be under observation, rather than a full participant. I made no comment on his words and throughout the bus trip followed the shepherds in the desert and the herds of camels and sheep. We passed by the sacred fire so I remembered Ur and Sayyidna Ibrahim and also the priestesses of the temple about whom I read with intense interest. Hamid welcomed us very warmly, saying, "The city is teeming with Kurds who feel defeated. Having a dialogue with them is hard, but involving them in a literary gathering is one way the party is trying to reach them and reassure them. The presence of two Egyptian journalists, a male and a female, would be quite attractive for them, especially as Kurdish men and women of letters consider themselves neglected because they are away from the capital. They feel their works are not getting the attention they deserve."

Hilmi Amin said, "Don't worry."

I said, "That is the general feeling of writers from the provinces, even in Egypt, even though being away from the capital gives them greater opportunity to write."

He said, "The problem here is more complicated."

In the evening Hilmi Amin spoke about Egyptian culture before a Kurdish audience that understood Arabic and spoke it fluently. I spoke about the role of women in Egyptian culture. I noticed that the Kurdish intellectuals followed Egyptian culture closely. We got to discussing Arabic magazines and periodicals and how only a few Kurdish authors' works were published in them. Hilmi Amin invited them to publish in *al-Zahra* magazine. Then the discussion got heated and touched upon literature and the struggle for freedom. One member of the audience spoke in response to Hilmi Amin's presentation, "There are only three pillars of literature in Egypt now and you are forty million. In Kurdistan we have thirty literary pillars."

Everyone laughed boisterously and the program came to an end. Their chauvinism and reluctance to acknowledge another, parallel world made them overstep the boundaries of decorum and logic, so they acted in an extremist manner. We met Jamal, the short-story writer, and Sulafa, the poet who assisted Hamid at the directorate of culture. They took us downtown to the old city to meet people in the stores and old-style markets. I noticed extreme poverty and a kindness covering and softening a deep-seated nervousness whose cause I couldn't discern. The houses here in the low-income neighborhoods, as in all Iraqi cities, were one-story structures separated by small gardens. Open sewers ran through all the streets of the city. I had not seen such sewers before. I looked closely at the black matter floating in soapy filth and I was disgusted. I didn't understand how they lived side by side with this filth. When heavy rain fell and I saw the water in the streets rushing toward the lower-lying sewers and disappear, I understood why, but this did not lessen my discomfort.

We talked with people about the question of autonomy, although they were reluctant at the beginning. Then after a gesture from Jamal or Sulafa they relaxed and began to talk to us. The outcome of these conversations was almost always the same: "We want autonomy, but we don't know what the future holds. This is not the first time that governments have talked about autonomy." That was news to us. We thought that autonomy was a new achievement on the part of the Ba'th Party. We went to the wealthy neighborhoods and noticed the obvious differences in the sizes of the houses and the large public parks. We felt as we delved deeper into Kurdish society that we were losing our own footholds. One evening Hamid took us to Jamal's house in a suburb of Erbil. We went into a simply and tastefully furnished house. We found a number of writers there. A fair Kurdish woman, uncharacteristically plump, welcomed us. Jamal said, "My wife, Umm Sargon."

He placed his hand on his heart and added, "Sister of the communist martyr As'ad Khalis who was executed in the events of February 8." Sulafa came in a blue dress, the color of her eyes. She had left her long black hair playfully cascading down her shoulders. She was a picture of vitality and joy. My heart sank as I asked myself, "What does love do to us? How is this lady faring in the midst of all of these swirling currents of which she is not aware? Who said she is not aware?"

Umm Sargon led us to a room in the center of which was a round dining table with dozens of bottles of liquor from all over the world and Iraqi beer and araq.

Jamal said very proudly, "This is Iraqi araq made secretly at home."

I asked Hilmi Amin, "Is making araq at home illegal?"

Hamid said, "It's a crime like possession of hashish in Egypt but it's more a health risk."

We sat around many dishes cooked and baked by Umm Sargon herself: trays of kibbeh, kibbeh with cracked wheat, and Aleppo kibbeh made with rice. We ate and laughed and had a good time.

Jamal asked me suddenly, "Why don't you drink? An Egyptian intellectual who doesn't drink or smoke?"

I said, my heart shaking as I remembered the problem with Izak, "I don't drink."

Hilmi, laughing, said, "Any kind of juice will do."

Sulafa got up to open a bottle of Pepsi for me. During the time I spent with them I got to know the tender love story between Jamal and Sulafa. I had known that Jamal was a married man, but it hadn't bothered me; his presence alone was a cause of great happiness, and that was enough for me. But when I saw the wife, I felt I couldn't deal with the matter easily, even though it was none of my business.

We talked with Jamal about autonomy. I noticed that he was wary of Hamid, which was unusual since Hamid was also a Kurd and it was he who introduced him to us. I asked him about the law and how it was followed on the ground. He said, "In the law of March 11, 1975 an amnesty was declared for all who took part in the revolt which at that time was called 'the lackey pocket.' So everyone came down from the rough mountainous areas where they had barricaded themselves and they surrendered their weapons: students went back to school, employees back to their posts and, for the first time, five Kurds became government ministers and Taha Ma'ruf became vice president."

A voice next to me whispered, "Just a ceremonial post." I turned and found Sulafa laughing and pointing with her eye to Hamid, who had just left the room to answer the telephone.

Jamal went on to say, "Two ministers: One, Idris the son of Mullah Mustafa al-Barzani, is now the minister of labor, and Darwish Adha is now minster of social affairs, a portfolio that has become a Kurdish monopoly, and three state ministers without portfolios."

Hilmi said, "Wasn't Saddam the one in charge of the Kurdish file from the beginning?"

Jamal lowered his tone as he continued, "Since the vice president got the Kurdish file there have been several attempts to assassinate Mullah Mustafa al-Barzani."

Later on we found out that the cultural season was a success and that relations improved. Hamid felt indebted to us for helping to do his work successfully now that the Kurds were actively participating. He started to invite us whenever he organized any activity in a Kurdish town and we accepted whenever we could.

I asked Hamid if I could attend a Kurdish wedding. He invited me to attend the wedding celebrations at the house of the chairman of the executive council of the autonomous zone. The women gleefully explained to me their marriage customs. I took their pictures with their gold jewelry and their unique costumes: long dresses woven with silver threads, vests with hearts of pure gold in their hems, and around their waists they wore belts studded with carnelian and sapphires on top of which were gold chains. They also wore bracelets connected to the ring on the middle finger with netting of gold. They were full of glitter and also showing off their wealth. I wrote about marriage in the Kurdish fashion and submitted the feature to the bureau director, who read it carefully, then gave it back to me, asking me to complete it by writing about the marriage customs in Bedouin and southern communities. I did my research and finished writing after trimming it to be a comprehensive feature. I submitted it. He read it and smiled, "Now it is a beautiful piece. Congratulations."

The bureau flourished and acquired a good reputation among Iraqi journalists and press bureaus. The office became a radiant Egyptian cultural center that welcomed the guests of Baghdad. We collected many reference books about the history of the Kurds and began to study the region in depth, conducting lengthy interviews with Kurdish parties and leading Ba'thist figures, and got to know Kurds, their life, and problems better.

As we prepared for a trip to Mosul the following day to celebrate the spring festival, Hilmi Amin said to me, "Nora, it is time to appoint an Iraqi journalist in the office on a permanent basis to help us with some purely Iraqi matters. I feel that our expansion places a big burden on you."

I replied, "If you wanted to hire an extra journalist for the bureau and if we expand our work, our success will be the greater for it."

He said, "What do you think of Anhar Khayun who works at the Agency?"

I said, "She's fantastic. She's a very appropriate choice. But would she leave the Agency?"

"No, she'd work evenings."

In Mosul we found that Anhar had gone ahead of us to write about the preparations for the celebrations. When we got to the woods she had started a long discussion with Hilmi Amin in the car which they did not stop when we got out of the car at a cafeteria that occupied an elevation in the middle of the woods. They walked together and went farther and farther until they disappeared into the trees.

I noticed how their relationship was getting closer by the day. Anhar was tall and slender. She had smooth black hair, in a fashionable tapered cut. She was in the habit of letting a lock of hair fall over her eyebrows. She had big black eyes and a large nose like most Iraqi women. She was pretty despite having a scar next to the nose, which they called a "Baghdad mark." When Hilmi Amin saw her for the first time he asked me, "Is this Layla who set Qays's imagination on fire?

I looked at her, and said, laughing, "Yes, and he was quite right to go crazy."

"She taunted me about my gray hair, though it's a mark of dignity; she should've taunted me about a shameful thing," he said, laughing as he followed her conversation with another journalist in a garden at the wood, continuing his quotation from the famous song by Nazim al-Ghazali: "The stars are adorned by the moons!"

Anhar used to bring the evening bulletin of the Agency after I'd left the office. She wrote short features for the magazine. They continued to get closer and the scent of the stolen pleasure of love filled the air. I was also complicit in it, as I looked the other way when the two of them found pretexts to work side-by-side, alone. I took pity on her as I saw her rushing in headlong, no longer caring about concealing it from me. And even though the bureau director did not show his feelings readily, perhaps because of experience or because it was his nature, I noticed how he couldn't wait to see her and how happy he was when she was there. What would that poor girl do with a married man, the father of three daughters, one of whom was almost her own age? Did she imagine that he would stay in Baghdad forever? She is of marriageable age and would be squandering an opportunity to marry a young man her own age. Iraqi laws also didn't permit bigamy. And what if he were to return to Egypt tomorrow? What business is it of yours? All these questions crossed my mind when I caught a mutual glance of longing. We were at a formal party and they were sitting apart. Their movements together no longer had that spontaneity that marked them before. She was engaged to her cousin who was a Ba'thist, while she was a communist, and their relationship had its ups and downs. She often expressed unhappiness at the prospect of marrying him and postponed making a decision.

The stewardess smiled at me as she asked me to open the food tray. Salma came to as she took the box, then said, after the stewardess left, "I don't like airline food and yet I eat it. Isn't this another form of Arab repression?"

We both laughed. She went on to say, "I wonder what the Iraqis are doing about food. Do they have problems?"

I said, "As far as I know, they have no shortages. But the tragedy is the squandering of the resources of Iran and Iraq in this absurd way. Also in the number of martyrs."

She said, "May God damn all dictatorships on earth. This man is quite puzzling. We'll go and see."

I said, "Every people deserves its leader. Iraq for some time has played a revolutionary role in the region and that was reflected in Iraqi society itself. No day would go by without new farms and factories, roads being paved and development of new cities and education. A real renaissance! Then came the foolishness of the war.

Didn't we have enough with Gamal Abdel Nasser? Why are we always repeating our mistakes?"

She said, "Every day I hear about delegations going to Baghdad and coming from Baghdad. It seems they have a new conference every day."

I said, "I used to cover at least one international conference every month, not to mention local conferences."

She said, "I'm going to the bathroom."

An Egyptian peasant walking in the aisle reminded me of my first visit to al-Khalsa village.

I didn't imagine when I went there one late afternoon that it would become part of my world or that I would give it that much importance and care about it to this extent. I didn't believe that I would be able to follow up on my belief that our Arab world was really one world that should be integrated. I had arrived at the office early in the morning as usual when I heard voices inside. I found a group of Egyptian peasants whom the director introduced to me saying, "Abd al-Barr, Sabir, Bashandi, and Muftah from al-Khalsa village. We are interested in their experiment, as you know, and publish their news all the time."

I greeted them. Abd al-Barr said, "Why haven't you visited us till now, Sitt Nora?"

I said, "God willing. Ustaz Hilmi has promised to arrange a trip soon."

I noticed that the whole group fit the common stereotype of peasants that I had met before: simple, goodhearted, and wary. Abd al-Barr, however, was slightly different. Was it because he talked easily and took over the conversation most of the time? I don't know. For some reason, I just did not feel that he was a real peasant.

A few days later we were visiting a number of Egyptian intellectuals working at the Academy of Arts. Some of them expressed a desire to visit the village. The director set it up for the following Friday afternoon.

I arrived at the office with Hatim, then the guests started arriving. I was meeting some of them for the first time: the journalist Durriya Awni, the actress Nadia al-Saba', the critic Ahmad Abbas Salih, the Iraqi painter Layla al-Attar, Nasir Fathi, director of the Middle East News Agency in Baghdad, Mahmoud Rashid, the film director, and his wife Samia. On the way I dreamed of the smell of the ovens and the freshly baked fitir mishaltit and homemade crackers, of aged cheese and cream. We arrived at al-Khalsa shortly before sunset. I didn't find any children in the street or shouting soccer players or someone playing hide-and-seek. I didn't see any firewood stacks on the roofs, and no cattle on the road. I found white one-story houses with large gardens in front and a deathly silence. It was a ghost town. I did not feel that I had entered an Egyptian village, but rather a suburb near a city in any country. We went to Abd al-Barr's house where we met his children and his wife Sharbat, who had on a short dress with floral patterns and whose hair cascaded down her shoulders, which made me all the more certain that somehow she was not a peasant.

After we drank tea we went out for a walk in the village streets. I knocked on one of the doors. A peasant woman with a pleasant fresh face and brown complexion opened the door and invited me in, saying, "Welcome, welcome dear. You bring the fragrance of Egypt with you!"

Her husband, Abu Ahmad, came. I sat between the two of them. I felt that it was an authentic household reminiscent of its southern peasant roots. She said to me, her face glowing with happiness, "I got married eight years ago but God did not bless me with any children. My husband has grown-up sons from his wife, God have mercy on her soul. When I came to Iraq, I got pregnant. It was a pregnancy after a long anticipation."

Laughing, I said, "You got pregnant after you crossed the sea!"

She said, "You know that, too? But you are a city lady!"

I said, "But I am Egyptian."

Abu Ahmad said, "It's going to be a boy, God willing, and I'll name him Gamal Abdel Nasser."

I left them to their dreams and went to another house. The group dispersed throughout the village. I knocked on a door. A middle-aged man came out with his wife and children in tow and invited me in. Inside I saw a girl wearing a new satin dress. I asked her, "Are you a bride? How old are you?"

She smiled shyly and said, "Yes, and I am sixteen."

I cried out, "That's impossible! You must be eleven or thirteen at the utmost. Why did you marry her off at such a young age?"

The mother said, "Circumstances, ma'am, I swear by God."

I said in alarm, "What possible circumstances would make you marry off a child at this age? It is unconscionable!"

The mother said, "Sayyidna Muhammad married 'Aisha when she was nine."

The father said, addressing his wife, "The Khalsa project gives ownership of the land to families, not individuals. Among the peasants who came there were some bachelors who had to get married in order to be eligible for the land. There are only a few families here, some of those bachelors had to marry young girls and they wrote down that they were sixteen."

I said, "My God! You brought to your new world your old problems!"

The mother said, "What problems? Everything will be all right, God willing."

I left them, filled with sorrow. I hastened to catch up with the group and found them already on their way back. They said the dark made it difficult for them to see clearly. They also said the fields were far away and we should probably pay another visit. We left the village.

I returned to al-Khalsa many times after that and came to know the inhabitants one by one. When I decided to gather material for a book on the project, Abu Dalaf, head of the farmers' union, provided me with a car. The director of the project also helped me with whatever I needed. My visits there were delightful and friendly as I watched the growth of life in an Egyptian–Iraqi village. But I was also full of trepidation, fearing the vicissitudes of politics. In the meantime I became close friends with some of them. Al-Khalsa was a microcosm of Egypt with its authentic historical roots, the poverty of its people, and the kindness that lay hidden under the weight of their need to make a living. But here they possessed hope for the morrow, together with a wide land that had called to them. They answered the call and sowed and reaped, leaving their destinies to fate and to the hands of careless politicians.

Salma came back and sat down in her seat. She said, "It is such a short distance between Egypt and Jordan, but the problem will be the hours that we will spend in transit in Amman. May God make it go smoothly."

I said, "We are members of an official delegation, Salma. It's ordinary travelers who suffer a lot during that wait. After discontinuing direct flights between Cairo and Baghdad, it became unbearable for them."

She said, "Nora, I wanted to ask you: is it true that Iraqis sleep on their roofs of their houses?"

I said, "Yes. Baghdad in particular is dry and spending the night under the open sky is fantastic, because staying indoors without air conditioning is unbearable. So they adapted their homes by adding higher walls for their roofs and they installed partitions so that everyone would enjoy their privacy. And, believe me: it's sound and enjoyable sleep. I got used to it in Baghdad and tried to enjoy it in Egypt but I couldn't. Not even on the balcony because the dampness at dawn in Cairo has a sting to it and goes straight into your bones."

The captain turned on the seatbelt sign and we heard a voice asking us to return our seats to the upright position in preparation for landing at Amman airport in ten minutes. I opened my handbag and took out two pieces of chewing gum for me and Salma. I fastened my seatbelt and I recalled an unforgettable night, one that delineated the contours of my intimate relationship with Hatim.

I hadn't yet gotten used to sleeping in the open air, a practice I had only heard about in a song by Fayruz: "Did you once sleep on the grass and use the air as your bed cover?" After we returned to Baghdad from our honeymoon, I was surprised, one night, when Hatim took me up to the roof, opened a room, and took out a mattress that he placed on the bed, which was out there in the open air. My surprise was compounded when he asked me to try enjoying the dry air. He lay next to me and embraced me. I closed my eyes in anticipation of the adventure and the pleasure of discovery but sleep refused to visit me at all. It was not that I feared the loss of privacy, but because of the sounds made by a cat running or a car in the street or a plane passing way overhead.

Before that night it had been three months since my arrival in Baghdad. Pregnancy led me to a long sleep, then the perennial morning sickness and ever-present hunger exhausted any ability I might have had to wake up. I welcomed sleep and gave in to it anytime it visited me or whenever a passing breeze carried me to it. Hatim tried hard that evening to get me to pay him some attention but the inner call to sink into slumber was irresistible. He clung to me, took hold of my head and began to play with my hair. My face rose to face him. I opened my eyes and my eyelashes trembled with his hands' rhythm. I saw his nose get so big it swallowed me. His lips roamed all over my skin, which completely detached itself from me behind a distant cloud that I could see but could not reach. The tickles of waking up were feeling their way to my chest but could not prop up my head, which had suddenly fallen under his neck and left me to the seduction of sleep. I felt him clinging to me as he pressed my body. Then I felt his regular breathing. He was fast asleep after he had given up completely on the possibility of having me back. I took shelter in his hands embracing me, leaving wakefulness behind toward colorless circles that glowed in front of me, then fled through a long tunnel that had no beginning and no end. I chased these circles until I almost caught them at the moment that all parts of my body went into hiding.

Suddenly I was stung by a compelling force, trying to wrench me from the well I plunged into with such pleasure. I opened my eyes with difficulty, then I felt them closing again, returning me to my fall into the abyss again. I was aware, even as I sank into the darkness, of the movement of the two hands, three hands, hundreds of hands tearing off the cloaks of sleep, flashing the lights of awakening on my cells by force. I tried to wriggle out from under, feeling choked. I wanted to scream. Where's my voice? Wakefulness knocked on my door rudely. The desire to refuse bubbled in my blood, along with an overwhelming feeling of exasperation. My body whose clothes were being ripped at that moment stiffened and I could feel two hands turning me over lightly, rearranging my body in a position that made it possible to enter me. Before my mind had totally awakened a colossal being was tossing me hither and yon, twisting with every blow it dealt, embracing me then separating from me. I could hear the cracking of my bones as they were crushed under the force of the tornado, then I felt my breasts awakening before me, then getting crushed. The conflict between desire and sleep pulverized me into millions of cells. My moans rallied for the coming flood. I heard the cracking of the collision between the cries of refusal and desire. Neither wakefulness nor sleep was able to reassemble me as a whole. In the midst of my flowing fears I spoke the name of every part of my body again and saw them coming to me meekly, like little chicks hurrying toward their mother. In the morning, looking at my exhausted features as I played the reel of the story for him after his persistent asking, Hatim did not remember, and he learned to pay attention to my desire without anything being said.

Three Other Knocks

1977

Suhayla Bezirgan

Abd al-Rahim Mansur came into the office of *al-Zahra* in Baghdad at nine in the morning in a real state of panic. He cried out, "Thank God I found you here. An order has been issued to deport my wife Suhayla and her family from Iraq."

The news hit us like a bolt of lightning. Hilmi Amin and I said at the same time, "Why?"

He said, "An order was issued yesterday to deport Iraqis of Iranian descent instantly and without giving anyone time to prepare or to dispose of possessions. The order was to take them right away to the border or the airport."

Hilmi Amin said, "Is Suhayla Iraqi or Iranian, Abd al-Rahim?"

Abd al-Rahim said, "In Iraqi IDs there is a space for national origin which is marked by categories with assigned numbers and symbols denoting affiliation based on descent. Only Iraqis who have the Iraqi nationality recorded on their IDs that marks them as Ottoman subjects are Iraqi citizens, for this purpose. Other IDs are marked as Afghan affiliation, Iranian affiliation, Indian, English, or Russian affiliation indicating republics of central Russia. All ethnicities are marked in the ID and so are religions. Suhayla's is marked as 'Iranian' not 'Ottoman' subject."

"So, is she Iranian?"

"No. The only thing that Suhayla knows about her family in Tehran is that she has an old maternal aunt there. Suhayla's family came to Baghdad several generations ago and she doesn't have anybody left in Iran. Borders in the region were open during the Ottoman era for all inhabitants. All members of Suhayla's family work in Iraqi government departments and they own houses in Baghdad. Suhayla's father is deceased and her only brother is a middle-school student. Her mother is a housewife."

I asked, "How about the rest of her family? Did they leave?"

He said, "Her maternal aunt is married to an Iraqi of Arab descent, her paternal uncles are deceased, and her male cousins are studying abroad. She has female cousins who are married to merchants. The police took the men to the airport and the families were ordered to follow them."

I said, "Oh, Abd al-Rahim! Did you need more complications? An Iraqi who turns out to be an Iranian? Are you trying to make it to the Guinness Book of World Records in the category of impossible love? It will all be resolved, God willing. What have you done so far?"

He said, "I went to Security Headquarters and told them she was married to an Egyptian. They asked for papers stamped by the Egyptian embassy. They told me that, so far, there have been no exceptions, and that she had to be deported first. But one of my friends advised me to hurry up and get her an Egyptian passport. Even if we had to send her to Egypt, it would be better. I've come to ask you for help."

I said, "But Egyptians don't need a visa to enter Iraq and getting her an Egyptian passport requires that she get Egyptian nationality."

Hilmi Amin left with Abd al-Rahim to go to the Egyptian embassy. I went to the Ministry of Information to get official information for publication purposes.

Abd al-Rahim had fallen in love with Suhayla the moment he saw her when he went for the first time to start his new job at the Central Authority for Inspection and Quality Control in Baghdad.

He married her right away and now she was five months pregnant. Abd al-Rahim was a gentle, decent man on the up and up and he was an intellectual to boot. I noticed that, during our weekly book run in the bookstores on Saadun and al-Rashid streets, Hilmi Amin bought foundational books on economics and international relations and that these books were a source of joy for Abd al-Rahim and other young members from al-Tagammu' who frequented our office: Sawsan, Atef, Dahlia, Ragya, Maha, and Fathallah. They were all recent graduates who came to Baghdad to work immediately after getting married and they settled in Baghdad and some other Iraqi towns.

From the Ministry of Information, I got a copy of the official statement. It was brief, referring to al-Da'wa Party and its responsibility for the explosions that took place in Baghdad recently, and to the fact that the political leadership had no choice but to deport those Iranians who were playing a double role as spies for Iran. I tried to recall Suhayla's beautiful face, with her big black eyes, thick eyebrows, and dazzling beauty, trying to imagine how she could be a spy. We got some more information and waited for Anhar to get us additional news from the Agency's evening bulletin and to arrange a meeting for us with one of the families being deported so that we might monitor the situation on the ground. Iraqi society was preoccupied with what these people would do, and whether Iraq would witness once again what happened when the Jews emigrated and had to sell their property in a hurry. Would these deportees be able to come back? Or was it final?

Anhar took us to a place where cars carrying deported families gathered. We stood in front of a car loaded with foam rubber mattresses, clothes tied in large sheets, and sacks chock full of everyday household items. Some children stood on these piles and two women, an old one and a middle-aged one, sat next to the driver. Young men and women in their twenties gathered around the car. A man who seemed lost was trying to keep an eye on his possessions, going around the decrepit car, standing in a line with other decrepit cars. I asked Hilmi Amin in shock, "Would those cars make it to Iran? Or even to the next village? Where are the new cars?"

"It's a state of chaos in which everyone gets whatever they can find."

I approached one of the families. I asked the woman, "Do you know anyone in Iran?"

"My husband's grandfather, an old hajji."

"Do you own anything there? Land? Real estate?"

"Where from? That was a different time, the time of the Osmanlis."

The husband said, "We don't own a single fils there: no house, no land, no store."

"What do you do?"

"I own a grocery store in Inner Karada."

"Who did you leave it to?"

"To my neighbors. They are good people. I handed over the store to my neighbor for a bogus sales contract so that when we come back we would find a source of income. I took my things from the house so they wouldn't be looted. If we were spies, good lady, what would they do with our things when we are away? I took all we'll need there, until God provides a way out and until my family finds a way to make a living. What little money I have will barely last until I find a job. In the meantime we can use our things."

A boy standing on top of the car waved a cassette tape at me as he followed the conversation between me and his father. I asked him, "What's on the cassette?"

Laughing, he said, "Adel Imam in the play *A Witness Who Witnessed Nothing*," and he started to mimic Adel Imam: "Why did you bring me here? Okay, shall I go home now?"

The grandmother cried in anguish, praying to God to deliver them and to turn the evil directed against them back at those who had done them wrong, and went on to say, "What is this Da'wa and where did they come from? What have we got to do with them? They are not human. Who'd agree with those explosions? By God, child, we know nothing except our home and livelihood and our children. Those Iranians, what've we got do to do with them? We just mind our own business, just that."

The man said, "God is generous, Umm Ali. He'll resolve it."

I moved on to talk with another family, some of whose younger members were standing next to the car. I asked one of the young men about the reasons for their instant deportation. He said, "I don't know. I was coming back after visiting my father in the factory and I was surprised that my cousins were arrested and there was this order of instant deportation, as you can see. What saved me was that I was at school in Jordan and have just come back by chance to visit my family. I swear to God we've done nothing. They have released one of my cousins. As for the rest, we don't know if they are still here or were forcibly deported. And the girls: one is married to an Ottoman Iraqi and the other to an Iranian Iraqi. We've been dispersed. Whoever asked about marriage and who was subject of what? We are all human, we are all from Iraq."

"What are you going to do?"

"I'll go with them to look for this family about which we know nothing, except for tales from our grandfathers. I know the name of the village they say we came from in the Ottoman era. Maybe I'll find relatives of the old lady there. And after the family settles down I'll go back to school in Jordan."

"Do you expect help from the Iranians?"

"Please! Who'd accept us? If the Iraqi government considers us—Iraqis born here going back several generations—spies of Iran, what would the Iranian government consider us?"

A group of policemen arrived on the scene and ordered that everything loaded on the cars had to be brought down. Women screamed loudly and children began to jump out of the cars and the policemen began to search the cars and throw everything they found on the ground until the search was completed and orders were given to proceed. The noise made by the decrepit cars was drowned out by the sound of weeping.

75

Afterward I found nothing in the newspapers and magazines coming out of Egypt except for a short news item saying, "A number of Iraqi families of Iranian descent were deported on suspicion of their involvement in recent explosions, along with al-Da'wa Party." I remembered the boy carrying the Adel Imam cassette and Suhayla who was miraculously spared deportation through the personal intervention of the minister of the interior, as a single exceptional case of an Iraqi-Egyptian woman.

I asked Hilmi Amin why my investigative reports that I had sent to *al-Zahra* were not published. He said, "This is a very sensitive situation, Nora. There must be other considerations. Let's wait for what the coming days will reveal."

March 1977

Love

We gathered a lot of information on the Kurds. The office filled up with reference books in Arabic and English about their history, their revolts, their heroes, and their customs and traditions. We traveled to Erbil to complete our on-site research and Anhar promised to catch up with us in Erbil. She didn't. I noticed that Hilmi Amin was worried when he talked to her in the morning. She did not say absolutely that she would not come. He said he would call her the following day, adding that her boss had given her an assignment that she hadn't finished yet. Her boss had made it clear that she couldn't go to Erbil before she had.

I said, "We still have three days. I want to take some aspirin. I think I have a fever."

He said, "Yes, please do us all a favor and stay. We have a lot of work to do."

We finished our work at the rug factory and the car took us back to the hotel. We passed by the old city. Hilmi Amin stopped the car in front of a man who sat on the ground with a pile of fresh shelled walnuts spread on a cloth in front of him. We bought some and Hilmi Amin pushed them toward me and said, "Eat these right now, right in front of me, to get rid of that cold."

The restaurant prepared some hot soup and the waiter said as he served me, "I'll put the pot on a special table for you so it will be ready for you at any time."

The hotel had not been officially opened yet. They were still finishing work on it and there was no telephone service. There were only three workers on the staff. Anhar arrived in the evening and we were very happy that she had come. I took my leave to go to my room after I felt a fever coming on again. I fell soundly asleep right away.

I awoke in the middle of the night not knowing what time it was. I rang the bell but no one responded. I found myself sweating profusely. I decided to take a hot shower, then change and go out looking for a waiter to get me something to drink. I left the room and headed for the front desk. The whole hotel was pitch dark, except for a faint light at the end of the corridor. I looked for anyone from the reception staff and didn't find anyone. I turned around to go back to my room, irritated. I caught a glimpse of someone moving at a distance. I was startled, but my eyes got used to the dark as I walked further in the corridor. I saw a person moving on tiptoe with his back to me. I realized that it was Hilmi Amin. I moved quickly to wish him goodnight without waking those asleep. I saw him turning to look behind as he knocked on the door. I stood still and saw Anhar opening the door and saw him go in quickly. I went into my room and began to ring the bell in anger, knowing that nobody would respond. I asked myself why I was angry: was it jealousy? God forbid. I was afraid he might be abusing his authority or exploiting her. After all, he was a married man and she was a young girl. That's their business. I picked up *al-Jumhuriya* and began to read but I couldn't understand a thing. The headline was "The American Recipe, and the Artificial Severance of Diplomatic Relations." I gave up on reading. I felt my fever getting worse. I took some aspirin as I heard the sound of a door being closed carefully, then the sound of another door closing more carefully. I didn't know how much time passed. I felt the sun's rays stinging my eyes. I had forgotten to close the curtains and Iraqi windows don't have wooden shutters like ours.

I got off my bed. According to the clock it was five in the morning. I remembered Hatim saying, "If I wake up at three o'clock in the morning I'd find it (the sun) right in the middle of the sky." I smiled when I remembered that. I'll call him from the nearest public telephone in the evening when he comes back to our house. I left my room and sat in the lobby. The waiter brought me a glass of hot milk and said, "Drink it right away. It will make you sweat and get well, God willing."

I said, "You speak Arabic fluently."

He said, "Yes. Most people in my generation speak Arabic. We've learned it in school. Some mothers still don't know Arabic but they follow Egyptian movies and speak some sentences."

Laughing, I said, "Thank you, Kaka Abu Sami."

Smiling, he said in Kurdish, "You are a beautiful lady."

I went out for a walk in the city. The sun was sending its soft rays to tickle the dew, which I saw trembling as the rays touched it, revealing very dense green foliage of walnuts and wispy pines. I looked up at the top branches and swayed as they swayed in the light wind. I walked until I got tired and I felt the fever coming back. I went back to the hotel and found that Ustaz Hilmi Amin and Anhar were waiting for me to have breakfast together.

The waiter served me some hot orzo soup, saying, "Drink it and take something to reduce the fever."

I said, "Okay, Doctor Kaka Abu Sami. I needed it at night and not now."

He said, "I am at your service."

I said, "I am going to work. I am tired of being asleep."

Hilmi said, "Let's go and on our way stop at the hospital so the doctor can see you."

I saw that Anhar was somewhat distraught, not showing the happiness that was expected during the first few days of a love story. Was it fear of the future or a sense of guilt? I looked at him as he moved with great confidence. I saw that he was calm, his face displaying a relaxed joy or maybe it was an arrogant sense of victory.

We met Jamal and Sulafa at the Culture Palace. Jamal talked to me about the difficulty faced by Kurdish writers especially publishing literary works. I asked him in jest, "Are you not one of them?"

He said, "No, I am Syriac. And I also have difficulty publishing my work." Then he added, "When will you publish your first collection of stories?"

I said, "I'll finish my first novel first, then a story collection."

He asked me, "Who is your favorite author?"

I said, "I don't know precisely. At every phase I have a different favorite author."

Hilmi Amin was surprised and said, "Fahmi Kamil is her favorite author as far as I know."

I said, "At some stage, yes. But I wish I could write like Erskine Caldwell or Albert Camus who uncovered hidden traits in the human psyche. But now my writer is incontestably Steinbeck."

I couldn't, as I talked, separate the author from the human being. I let my feelings lead me. I had met Fahmi Kamil in Baghdad and accompanied him to visit the shrine of Imam Musa al-Kazim, but the way he acted that day shocked me so much I couldn't forget it. And when I saw him in Cairo later, I didn't get near him. A curtain of mystery and arrogant impatience stood between him and me. When he visited Baghdad a second time, I couldn't care less.

When I returned to Baghdad, I didn't tell Hatim anything about what happened.

April 1977

Troubles Looming

The bureau director got ready to go to Cairo for the second time since I worked with him. Today he asked Muzaffar al-Mosuli to bring requested articles to take with him to Cairo. Muzaffar asked him, "Will Mrs. Nora be in the office while you are away?"

"No. She'll be off and so will Anhar," he said curtly as he looked at me angrily. In the evening he gave me strict instructions not to open the office and to deliver the complimentary issues of *al-Zahra* that we got from the National Company directly to the newspapers. Then he said, "It's likely that I'll be detained in Cairo."

He noticed my crestfallen look and the panic on my face and went on, "Nora, you know I am a Marxist and that my name is on the top of the list for arrest at any time. In case of emergency, and of course if I am barred from leaving Egypt, you have fifteen days after my scheduled return. If I haven't come to Baghdad, take over affairs in the office: get in touch with our colleague, the Egyptian journalist Galal al-Sayyid. He is a respectable man who'll help you liquidate the affairs of the bureau and dispose of its possessions."

His words made me sad, but I soon overcame my sadness. It occurred to me to ask him: if he was arrested in Cairo, why should he close the bureau? Couldn't the magazine send another journalist?

But I thought better of it and said instead, "There's no reason for Egypt to have a disagreement with the communists now, especially when you live and work in Baghdad."

He said, "When the time comes, they will not ask where I live or work. Just do what I told you to do."

I went home in disbelief. Things couldn't be turned upside down so simply, the world I'd fallen in love with couldn't end just like that when I was just taking my first steps toward success. As usual he was exaggerating and if I pointed that out, he would say that my youth led me to a false reading of the situation.

Reading took up all my time throughout the vacation. My neighbor Sabah would come and ask me, "Why don't you go to the office any more? Is Ustaz Hilmi Amin not coming back from Egypt?" Panicked, I would tell her, "No, he'll come back, God willing."

I was afraid she would go back to her old ways and take up my whole day. Going to work for *al-Zahra* put a stop to most of the problems she had created for me. She would say, "What are all these books for? You're wasting your money and your husband's money on this nonsense. Ever since you started working, you have been reading even after he comes back from the factory. He and Shukry, poor things, are busting their backs. You are neglecting him and he doesn't complain."

I said, "Hatim married me knowing I am a journalist. My work does not interfere with my taking care of him. As for reading, what bothers you so much? Hatim loves it and he reads with me. Don't worry."

I got fed up with Sabah's morning litany. I was afraid she might be right and told Hatim what was happening and asked him if I were really neglecting him. He said, "She looks at your work as simply a means to making money and does not understand why you are living abroad if you were going to spend the money before you go back to Egypt. I love you and I love your work."

I didn't realize the days were so long. I would begin my morning by dragging a foam rubber mattress chasing the sun all over the house, lying on my stomach and placing a book in front of me. If I stopped reading for one moment and if Sabah and her children were not around me, I would see Yasir crying and asking about me, and Ustaz Hilmi behind bars. I saw myself running around trying to liquidate the bureau in Baghdad. I tried to banish those thoughts and get busy baking a cake to surprise Hatim and ask him to take me to the central post office on al-Rashid Street to call my mother and ask her about Yasir.

I said to him, "How is it there's no telephone at the magazine office in Baghdad, and no telephone in your house in Maghagha in the seventies of the twentieth century?"

Hatim embraced me and said, laughing, "When will you come back, Ustaz Hilmi?"

Hilmi Amin came back from Cairo in a strange mood: happy somehow, but distracted and not quite at peace with himself. He said to me with a sorrowful face, "I submitted an official memorandum to appoint you to the magazine, but the request was rejected by Fahmi Kamil, the editor in chief."

"What exactly did he say?"

"Postpone this request for the time being."

I recalled the unpleasant trip on which Fahmi Kamil accompanied me to the shrine of al-Kazim and I had a hard time understanding the whole thing. I asked Hilmi Amin for an explanation. He said, "I don't know precisely what goes on in his head, Nora. Just focus on your work. That is your strongest point and that's what will enable you to respond to him in the future."

I tried to find out from Hilmi Amin what happened in Cairo and whatever happened to his expectations that communists would be rounded up and the bureau closed. But it was no use. Talking to him only made things more unclear. Sometimes he would say, "It's a critical situation," and at other times he would say, "Nobody knows anything."

I would say, "But we are still at work. What determines whether we continue to work or not?"

His answer sometimes would be, "Yes, we are. For the time being. Nobody knows the circumstances of the two countries."

I got a little depressed, then I got rid of the sad feelings, saying to myself, "Nothing stupid will keep me from my work. I will work more and more and gain experience." I agreed to write for any newspaper or magazine that asked me for a feature or an article. The newspaper *Hokari* translated my features into Kurdish and published them in a regular column with the title: "The Kurdish Woman." I impatiently looked forward to being published. It hurt when I remembered Fahmi Kamil's unfriendly position, but I carried on, determined to succeed.

I noticed a few days later that Hilmi Amin was in a very jovial mood: he was no longer frowning all the time and he looked much younger. I asked him, laughing, "You're hiding something from me. What happened in Egypt? Is it a new love story? Your face is all lit up and your eyes have an unusual gleam."

He laughed and admitted it, saying, "Stop it, you naughty girl!" Then he sat on the armchair in front of the desk saying, "Okay, what do you want to know, Sitt Nora? I was surprised to receive a telephone call from Ismat. You know her, don't you?"

I said, "Of course, your first but not your last choice." Anhar's picture appeared at once in my mind's eye.

He said, laughing, "Anyway. She wanted to meet. My time was very limited, as you know, so I invited her to lunch at home. She took a car from Alexandria that waited for her outside. She said, 'As you know, your friend Farid bought our old house for his son, but his son is not keeping up with the payments and I don't know what this whole deal will come to and I don't know what to do. My daughter is getting ready to be married and I need the money.'

"I asked her about the details of the contract and promised to send for Farid and compel him either to honor it or we would revoke it. I asked her, 'How is Gamal? I know that you've raised him well.' She said, 'He's fine. He's doing very well.'

"Then she looked at me a long time and before she got up to go back home, she said to me, as her face turned red as if she were still

84

sixteen, 'Life has passed us by.' I patted her on the shoulder and said, 'God knows what's in the heart, Ismat. May God bless your children.' I saw her tears flowing and my heart almost shattered. If I could I would have embraced and held her but neither time nor place allowed any of that. I said goodbye to her while Fayza and the girls stood there.

"I did not believe it when we were granted a general amnesty. Ismat had gotten married. I came out of jail to find that I had been fired from the customs department. I worked at *Rose al-Yusuf*. We, Ahmad Bahaeddin, Salah Hafez, Hasan Fuad, Abd al-Ghani Abu al-Aynayn, Salah Jahin, Heba Enayat, Higazi, the painter and cartoonist, and a large number of young men and women wanted to change the world. But most of us were arrested and sent to the oases detention camps for five consecutive years. I had gotten married and my wife worked in an attorney's office and raised Mervat, which was very hard on her. She waited for me all those prison years tirelessly until I got out and went back to work as a journalist but this time for *al-Zahra* magazine."

I saw some tears. I stopped recording, saying, "We'll get to the details tomorrow."

I wonder what happened to those memoirs that I transcribed myself? Has Tante Fayza taken them or did Hilmi send them to a publisher? I remembered us singing together Wadie al-Safi's mawwal:

> I don't know who to cry to,
> Or who to complain to,
> Where can I get patience and fortitude?
> To bear this sleepless, tear-filled night
> Like a sailor lost between coasts.

I wiped away the tears flowing from my eyes and began to recall our days, so crowded with events.

Second Text

Three knocks on the door of my memory restored life to days that were lingering as they turned toward disappearing forever. I tugged at the end of the thread of time that used to tame mountains and humans. The days broke loose and came tumbling down on my heart. I tried to stop their ruthless flow and pay attention to what was happening around me, but I couldn't. Inside of me there was a rush seeking to recapture the flow of the days and once again feel the pleasure of the pain that didn't contain the moment. I was carrying my suitcase to the airport on my way to Baghdad, to take part in a conference about educating Iraqi women after teaching them to read and write, not believing that I had indeed left my six-month-old son with my mother-in-law in Maghagha, two and half hours away from Cairo. I was hoping to find out why and how my Iraqi friend and colleague at *al-Zahra* had disappeared. I also wanted to visit my house in Dora, hit by Iranian bombers, and see if my neighbors there were all right. I also hoped to meet Basyuni Abd al-Mu'in who joined the Iraqi army and became part of the war with Iran with no prior knowledge of the horrors of war, and to give him a letter from his family urging him to go back to Egypt.

They took us from the cramped arrival lounge to passport control. Members of the delegation objected. Kamilia Sabri said, "We are an official delegation to Iraq. This is unacceptable."

The passport officer said, "This is our system. Wait outside until the plane that will carry you to Baghdad arrives. This is a small airport; we cannot handle all the passengers."

Shahira al-Asi said, "We want the manager of the airport."

The officer said, "He's unavailable for the time being."

Salma turned to us and said, "Would you ladies accept to wait in the street for seven hours or longer?"

We all said in unison, "No, absolutely not."

Kamilia said to the officer, "There you have it. You've listened to what they think. They will not go out. We were told that the organizers of the conference had an agreement with the management of the Amman airport that it would be our host until we get on the plane."

Another officer came and after consulting with his colleague he told us, "This procedure is not meant to be against you in particular. This is the system that applies to all. I do not have any special instructions regarding you."

We said, "Where is the Iraqi official in charge? Please open the VIP lounge so we can sit there."

He said, "There is no Iraqi official in charge. I don't have any instructions. Please, make room for other passengers to go out or stand in line."

We all moved away from the exits. A small group of other passengers stood watching us without saying anything. We saw them later going past the baggage area, going out of the gate, grumbling. An officer came and told us in a commanding tone, "Stand in line to get your passports stamped. Another plane has landed and there is not enough room for all the passengers."

Kamilia said, "Please, speak in a more suitable tone."

He said, "I don't know any other tone. Please obey the instructions. Wait outside."

Mona Abed said, "Aren't you used to dealing with delegations going to Iraq?"

He said, "Yes."

She said, "Why don't you deal with us the same way then?"

He said, "Their representative arrives early, pays the fees, and acts as your host."

I said in disbelief, recalling the Iraqi strict discipline, "Where are the Iraqis now?"

He said, "I don't know, Ustaza."

Tahani said, "It doesn't make sense that the manager of the airport would not be available. This is still the workday."

I did not believe that the Iraqi representatives could be absent. Has Iraq changed that much? I had been away from Iraq for only two years. Maybe the war has caused everything to come unglued.

One of the officers came back and said, "You'll get your passports stamped and I'll personally accompany you to the departure lounge where you'll sit until it's time for your plane to take off, then you'll go to passport control and pay the fees."

There were several protests and objections, "This is not logical. We will not go out."

The officer said, "When the Iraqi representative comes, he will reimburse you for what you've paid and you'll wait in the VIP lounge."

We discussed the matter among ourselves. There was no other way but to accept this compromise.

I said, "There's nothing outside except rain, strong winds, and great crowds at the doors. If the plane is late—and this happens a lot—we'll find ourselves in the street for days and they will not take us to the airport hotel. They use water hoses to disperse the passengers who jam the entrance when they announce an airplane's imminent departure."

Mona Abed said, "Oh my God! I didn't know that."

I said, "Guests usually are not subjected to such treatment. Something very serious must have happened. These Iraqi officials will be disciplined harshly. Anyway, the most important thing is for them to arrange for us to get on our plane. We have to make this a condition before entering Jordan."

Kamilia said to the officer, "We agree on condition that you give us a piece of paper giving us the right to get on the first plane to Baghdad."

He said, "Getting into the departure lounge means that you've already finished passport procedures before the outer door is opened for other passengers. That's the best I can do."

We agreed reluctantly. They stamped our passports for entering Jordan. We asked about our bags and he said, "You don't need to get them now. You'll get them in Baghdad."

Salma said, "I want my suitcase. In the midst of this chaos, I won't be sure of anything."

There was a lot of arguing back and forth and she ended up getting her suitcase amid shouts of anger and frustration. We went out to the street. We were shocked to see huge numbers of Egyptians waiting in the open air, some sleeping while holding on to their bags. Some huddled against the gusts of wind that slapped us across the face, catching us by surprise. Two policemen made a clear path for us in the midst of people by using clubs that gave off red flashes. One of the Egyptian workers waiting for their planes said, "Three days, you godless people!" Another said, "They seized the opportunity because we are a people whose government would not stand up to them. So they can get away with anything!" People realized we were on our way to the departure lounge so they followed us.

The officer said, shooing off the people, "Move out of the way. There are no planes now." Security men saw to it that we got in. The other passengers stood there watching what was happening and trying to rush through the narrow passage at the same time. We got through, one by one. The other passengers' shouts grew louder, "Three days in the rain! Do you have no fear of God? You Godforsaken country!"

The officer went to one of the other officers guarding a controlled entrance and told him, "This is a delegation. Let them go through for the 10:30 a.m. plane before the main gate opens. Understood?"

Then he turned to us and said, "Sorry. This is how things are these days."

We sat in a line like obedient schoolgirls, watching from a distance those standing behind the glass wall. We got to talking about the conditions of workers who left Egypt looking to make a living and the injustice and oppression they suffered, from their native sponsors right through to their low wages. My tears flowed as I murmured the words of the song written by Salah Jahin:

A marble statue at the irrigation canal,
An opera house in every Arab village:

These are not just dreams or words of songs,
These point the way to a new era.

I went to the bathroom to empty the milk from my breasts. Why didn't I feel this rush in Cairo, even though I often left Haytham with my mother for many hours? Have you forgotten the day Salim Ahmad, the executive editor, asked you to leave the meeting right away? At the door he told you, "Go home." When you didn't understand he said, "Nora, you're soaked!" I looked at my chest and found the blouse dripping wet and the fabric clinging to my chest as it I were naked, looking like those women that went into the water while wearing their galabiyas, revealing the contours of their bodies. I thanked him and got out of there. But it was a rare occurrence.

I stood in front of the sink and took out of my handbag the pump and a small towel that I moistened with water. An attendant came in. She had a very red wrinkled complexion with her hair, which was also red, coiled in a braid and wrapped around her head covered with a scarf. She looked at me and asked me if I was a mother and where did I leave my baby, with my mother or my mother-in-law? Then she told me to leave everything just as it was because things were safe there.

I took the things I needed to the toilet, fighting off tears of longing for Haytham. I asked myself, "Has he gotten used to Fattum's breasts? Did he get to sleep or is he crying because I left?" The tears came. I wiped them quickly. I haven't even made it to Baghdad yet. I kept squeezing my breasts dry until I felt exhausted. I wiped them with the wet towel, then applied lotion and waited for that to dry, getting very tired. I went out of the stall spraying cologne on my body. Sarah Badr came in. She asked me, "What are you doing, Nora?"

I fell silent then said, "My son is still nursing."

She said, "You nursing mothers bring all this heartache on yourselves. You carry a bag, a towel, a pump, eau de cologne, and lotion: a whole pharmacy. I didn't get married or have babies and I don't plan to."

I said, "Good for you, you're tough!"

I left the ladies room after returning the "pharmacy," as Sarah put it, to my handbag. I noticed that my colleagues had gathered around large tables. Kamilia waved and I went to the empty seat next to her. She said to me, "Nora, we were talking about Baghdad's stand vis-à-vis the Iranian revolution. Naturally we disagreed. You were there during that period. We would like you to tell us in detail what the Iraqis thought of the revolution and why they turned against it, especially since they are Shia."

I said, "The ruling clique is Sunni even though the majority of Iraqis are Shia. And the story of the Sunnis and the Shia is quite different from what we, as Egyptians, think it is."

Mona Abed interrupted, mimicking the Egyptian comic actor, Fuad al-Muhandis, "Keep us apprised of the situation, step-by-step, I beseech you."

We all laughed. I said, "I was sitting in my garden at night. I think it was February 1979. Hayam's coquettish voice came on the radio saying, 'This is radio Monte Carlo.'"

Mona said, "Yes, that is quite coquettish. Please trill your 'r' as she does and step-by-step, I beseech you."

We laughed. "It was martial music and Qur'an!" I said mimicking the Egyptian actor Ahmad Zaki, then added, "No, no, seriously. The news was announced on all radio stations as follows: 'Riots continued in the capital, Tehran, and all Iranian cities, for the second week in a row. Informed sources have said that the shah of Iran has today left the country with his family heading for Paris. Radio Tehran has announced that Prince Huwayda, the prime minister, has ordered the army to be deployed in the streets to quell the riots. The Associated Press has reported that all Iranian political parties have declared an open rebellion and civil disobedience.'

"I turned on the television. The Iraqi announcer on the official channel mentioned the news in passing, just a neutral, matter-of-fact report about riots in Tehran in which all Iranian political parties had taken part. The early morning Iraqi News Agency bulletin did not add much. My Iraqi colleagues made no comments, waiting for an official Iraqi position. Hilmi Amin, director of *al-Zahra* bureau, was happy when I saw him. He gave me some additional information about an Islamic revolution that aimed at bringing justice to the Iranian people, who lived in abject poverty, and at returning their looted resources to them. The news kept coming, fresh news almost every hour. Tehran recognized the Palestine Liberation Organization and the Palestinian people's right to Jerusalem as the capital of Palestine. We requested a meeting with Abu Abbas, the official in charge of external information. We noticed that the news from Tehran was received cautiously.

"I said to Abu Abbas, 'Congratulations, finally Iran is joining the Arabs against Israel.'

"He said, 'That's okay.'

"Hilmi Amin said, 'Baghdad's position has been a little late in coming, don't you think?'

"Abu Abbas said, 'We are waiting for a statement from the party. The situation with Iran is very complex as you know, and we have to wait until things clear up.'

"We went to the cafeteria on the first floor of the ministry building. That's where we used to meet our journalist friends and media personalities. We gathered around a light meal, exchanging bits of news from international news agencies, sensing the caution all around us.

"Abu Ziyad said, 'Khomeini has lived in exile here even after Iraq signed the Algiers Treaty with the shah. And he continued to live among us until the government asked him to leave.'

"I said, 'The Shia in Najaf await a nod from the religious authorities in Tehran to begin fasting the month of Ramadan or settling on the first day of Eid al-Fitr.'

"Jassim said, 'We have strong organic relations. It's one contiguous region as you know.'

"I said, 'I've seen Iranian pilgrims praying in Najaf before going to Mecca.' When I asked them the reason, they wondered at my question and said, 'Is hajj accepted without prayer first for blessing on Sayyidna Ali and al-Hasan and al-Husayn?'

"We returned to the office with one impression: caution.

"Hilmi Amin said, 'In the Algiers Treaty, also known as the Algiers Accord, there were some political articles and others that were topographical in nature. Iraq's main concern was to stop Iranian support for the Kurdish rebellion and that was why it accepted the treaty, even though Saddam gave up half of the Shatt al-Arab and that part became part of Iranian territorial waters. And, indeed, the shah of Iran stopped supporting the Kurds, and Iraq, in turn, stopped supporting Khomeini and the Iranian revolution. Khomeini was living in Najaf and his speeches were recorded on cassette tapes and smuggled into Iran.'

"I said to Hilmi Amin, 'I don't understand why Iraq is taking its time to declare its position.'

"He said, 'With intricate relations and long borders between the two countries, positions have to be cautious. This is similar to what happened in Egypt with the Libyan revolution in 1969 which toppled King Idris al-Senussi and his dynasty. Libya had diplomatic relations and an embassy in Egypt. Egypt could not support the revolution on the first day unless it had common interest with the revolutionaries. Iraq now has a well-respected treaty with Iran. And Iraq is now carrying out development plans that it can afford with the rise in oil prices after 1973. They certainly don't want to embark on an adventure as Egypt did with Iran's Mossadeq after 1951, then the Americans staged a coup soon after that. The situation in Iran is still unclear.'

"I said to him, 'But the shah has actually left Iran, and the opposition parties, be they the communist Tudeh or the various Islamist factions, have all taken to the streets.'

"He said, 'Don't keep a closed mind and don't just look at the picture from outside. These are relations among countries and not Nora's relationships with her friends. Also don't forget the sensitivities of the Iranian religious authorities and Khomeini who was forced out of Iraq. All of these are factors that do not allow for quick congratulations on the part of Iraq. The Iraqi government must first understand what is happening in Iran, then declare its position.'

"I said, 'That means we'll have to wait and only report the ambiguous situation.'

"He said, 'Leave all of that to me. We too have to take cautious steps, and be very precise in the way we write it. Luckily we have several days before they go to the press.'

"In the morning I learned that Khomeini had announced the fall of the shah while still en route from Paris to Tehran. We at the office expected Iraq to issue a statement in support of the revolution, but it took two whole days, then the government sent an official cable congratulating the people of Iran and hoping for neighborly relations.

"It was a surprise when a cable signed by Khomeini himself was received. It started with greetings to those who followed the right path, and then came the rest of the message. The cable, and its structure and content, left me only with the feeling that it was dry and reserved."

Kamilia said, "No, it's a cable with a very obvious meaning, but you missed it."

Sarah Badr said, "I also didn't understand."

I said, "It was only much later that I found out that that formula was used only with a country in a state of war or about to pick a fight. It became obvious that Iran's new regime was harboring ill will toward its neighbors. It seems people in the media among whom I moved were all aware of this without discussing it overtly."

Salma said, "And Hilmi Amin, was he not aware of that? I can't believe it."

I said, "The whole situation was one of wait and see. We attributed the general mood to sensitivity between the Shia and the Sunnis, for the government was in the hands of the Sunnis and there was fear that the Iranian revolution would be exported to Iraq."

Angel Rushti said, "Then what happened?"

I said, "I was happy with the revolution and I cried with tears of joy when Radio Tehran announced the expulsion of the Israeli embassy and gave the PLO its offices in the capital, Tehran. I followed the news with great interest since I was not sure how the Iranian Islamist parties would deal with the leftist parties that took to the streets, making it possible for the revolution to take hold. Would they get along? Or would there be waves of violence after that? Then Abu al-Hasan Bani Sadr became president, and he was not a man of religion, and the engineer Mahdi Bazirgan, who also was not a man of religion, even though he was an adherent of political Islam, became prime minister. Given these developments, I followed what was happening with bated breath.

"The streets of Iran were still in a general state of chaos, then the revolutionary trials began and we were full of apprehension about the direction of events, then you know the rest. Iraq demanded that it get back the territory it had previously ceded and the war began."

Angel Rushti said, "We heard of explosions carried out by Iranian groups in Baghdad itself before you left Iraq. Tell us how you managed under those conditions."

Mona Abed, again mimicking the Egyptian comedian, said, "Yes, keep us apprised of the situation, step-by-step, I beseech you. I mean, where were you? And how did you react?"

I said, "I was getting ready to return to Egypt for good. My personal circumstances were very difficult. I think it was July or August, which are so hot that Iraqis have proverbs based on them. I was doing my job and also taking care of shipping stuff, all by myself. I was also buying gifts for family and friends, then going home to look after Nagat, Hatim's sister, who was staying with us together with her husband. She had had several miscarriages and the doctor ordered bedrest for her throughout the pregnancy, and also because Hatim could not leave the factory during working hours for any reason. That day I went to Mustansiriya University to cover the Arab Economic Conference."

Mona cried out, "Really? You were at Mustansiriya University itself?"

I said, "Yes. I had followed the conference in previous years because I felt that I was very close to its guiding principles by championing the al-Khalsa experiment, which applied the desired model of Arab integration.

"I left before the end of the morning session to go home before rush hour. The car covered the distance at a speed I did not expect. I was surprised to see Nagat standing by the gate of the villa, waiting for me, with Yasir next to her, playing. Her face was very pale and I didn't understand why she left her bed in spite of the doctor's orders. I asked her, 'Has Yasir been bothering you that much?'

"She said, 'Where have you come from? Television has just announced an explosion at Mustansiriya University.'

"I ran toward the TV. I found the announcer rebroadcasting the news, saying, 'A few minutes saved participants in the Arab Agricultural Economic Conference from certain disaster. But the real casualty was damage to the architecturally unique Mustansiriya University building.'

"Pictures of the university with its beautiful blue mosaic, both before and after the explosion, took up the screen. That segment directed most of its anger at the Organization of Islamic Action and al-Da'wa Party for plotting explosions in Baghdad, Harun al-Rashid's capital, and accused them of being lackeys. It threatened them, saying that the hand of the state would catch up with them wherever they were."

Salma said, "There's a lot of talk that those incidents were bogus."

Mona said, "Tell us more, Nora."

I said, "Hatim, Yasir, and I were once in al-Rashid Street buying gifts. We had walked for a long time and drunk a lot of juice. I had a sudden attack of diarrhea. Hatim showed me the way to public restrooms under the viaduct of Tahrir Square. We headed for them while I suffered excruciating pain, but found that they were closed. I couldn't stand it any more, so we went to a nearby office of a tourist agency. I said to the clerk, 'I need to go to the toilet, please.' The woman's face turned white when she saw how desperate I was. She looked at her colleagues as she accompanied me to the bathroom. Hatim and Yasir stood waiting for me inside the tourist agency office. When I came out after a few minutes, I found that everyone in the office was outside. I saw a man hesitantly standing inside the office entrance and young frightened women standing outside. I didn't understand what was happening, then I noticed that Hatim was putting back some papers in his pocket. I asked him what was happening and he told me, 'Come, let's go out first. They panicked so I showed them my ID and told them that I was an engineer and that my wife was a journalist. And even though some of them were somewhat reassured, some were still reluctant and fearful, as you can see.'

"He placed his hand on my shoulder and held Yasir's hand with the other hand and started climbing the stairs to the street level.

"I turned around and looked behind me and I saw one of the young women go into the bathroom, then gesturing to her colleagues that it was safe. The workers went back inside and I saw their very pale faces give off mysterious smiles. Two months after the Mustansiriya University explosions the war started. No one knows how long it will go on or where it will lead, whether the Iraqi organizations or the Iranian government were behind the incidents leading up to it, or whether the Iraqi government fabricated them. The result is that there is a war between the two countries now."

I took my leave to go to the bathroom to empty my breasts, fighting off my longing for Haytham whenever I saw the drops of milk disappear in the sink. I noticed that the hot water helped me finish my task quickly. I went back to my colleagues and sat in their midst. Siham Fathi said, "What kind of a trip is this? I want a cup of coffee."

Kamilia Sabri said, "Coffee is not important. What is important is to find out when we are leaving this airport."

Tahani Yusuf said, "I'll go to the manager of the airport. We're not asking for them to treat us, just to provide some coffee and light snacks and we'll pay for them."

Shahira al-Asi said, "Yeah, women's power at work!"

We heard one of the employees saying, "Oh, what a beautiful bird you are!" We turned around when he repeated his exclamation. We realized he was talking to us. We laughed. He was a Jordanian young man, about thirty years old, trying to mimic the Egyptian dialect and to flirt with the actress Mahasin Tawfiq who was sitting with her friends complaining about directors. I looked up through the glass door separating us from the street. I saw some Egyptian peasants wearing gray and brown galabiyas and woolen skullcaps, covering themselves with colored shawls against the cold, standing like lifeless but sad ancient Egyptian statues. I remembered the peasants from al-Khalsa.

I had published a number of articles about al-Khalsa, whose inhabitants I loved and for whose experiment I was very enthusiastic. Hilmi Amin asked me after I had become a source of information for anyone who wanted to write about it, "Why don't you turn these articles into a book? We could submit it as part of our project to the Ministry of Information."

I said happily, "Yes. If I ask the peasants to tell me their life stories that would be good human-interest material. It could be a literary and a socioeconomic book also."

The February sun helped me move around. It was beautiful sunshine, sometimes interrupted by short periods of rainfall that would soon give way to the light again. It was the most beautiful month of the year after November. Al-Khalsa was thirty-five kilometers from Baghdad. I went into the homes of the peasants, recording stories of their life in Egypt and how they ended up in Iraq and why. They were a diverse group of people representing life with all its contradictions. Some of them were able to withstand the shock of being away from home and stuck it out, cooperating with Iraqi engineers and thriving. Others could not cope and returned to Egypt in the first few months. As people gradually acclimatized, the numbers leaving the project dwindled until those who had stuck it out settled down and sent for their relatives to join them and strengthen their family support. In time, the village reached its target number of one hundred families.

Abd al-Barr stuck close to me whenever I went to al-Khalsa. He chose which houses I should go to and sat with me until I was done, then he would take me to his house to eat. I got tired of his persistent company, but Hilmi Amin told me, "Don't be alarmed. In the midst of peasants and workers, you will always find someone who dreams of being a writer or a journalist. He brings us news in the hope that I'll help him be a writer. He has given me some writings that he composed about his life and about the village."

I said, "Why didn't you tell me before? I feel that he doesn't let me enter certain homes and he embarrasses me in front of the other peasants as if he's afraid I'll speak with them without him being there."

He said "I chose not to tell you so there'd be no clashing. In the end you are a professional writer and he's an amateur."

I visited Amm Wadie at home. I felt I was indeed in an authentic Egyptian village house. He was not an accidental peasant like some of those who had come to avail themselves of the benefits of the project. I kept working on the book and acquired more profound knowledge of the peasants. They began to tell me things that had been difficult for them to tell me in the early recording sessions. Abd al-Barr's problems were endless. Every week he complained about the manager of the project for a different reason each time, and expected us to support his point of view. Or he would quarrel with his wife, Sharbat, or one of the other peasants. Abd al-Barr himself was quite a character with a strange story. He had narrow eyes that radiated cunning and slyness. He had a laugh permanently pasted on his face, but it was a suspicious laugh. He had big broken teeth that protruded from his lips and whenever he was about to say something he would hold on to the hem of his galabiya as though he was getting ready to run. He was obstinate and persuasive. One day I asked him about his story. He smiled as he shook his head conceitedly, saying, "Ustaz Hilmi knows my story and that's what brought me closer to him, because he appreciates it and understands everything I had to go through. I am the son of a poor village who failed in his studies and fell in love with a girl from his village. She finished her education and moved on to a different kind of life while he stumbled and couldn't catch up with her."

He added in sorrow, now shaking his head more slowly, "I had many jobs: I worked as a cook and a guard and as a farmer. Then I married Sharbat and tried to bring her up to my level."

Then he bowed his head and said, "Please, don't misunderstand me. I've tried to teach her how to read and write by all means. I'd tell her to study with her children their simple lessons, but she resisted."

When Sharbat heard him mention her name she came over and said, "He beats me, Mrs. Nora, very hard and rough. Where can I go after leaving everyone and following him? He beats the children and doesn't buy them clothes. Please help me."

Abd al-Barr looked at her from head to toe for a long time as he sat cross-legged. He waited until she finished while suppressing his exasperation and said, "She leaves the house anytime she wants to. Would you believe it, Ma'am, that she left the house while my daughter Amal was still nursing? I had to feed her myself using a bottle. Sharbat did not feel she had a sacred duty called motherhood."

Then he went on to say, "Would you believe that she reported me to the Iraqi police saying I was pushing her to engage in immorality? They detained me for several days on her account until I proved myself by witnesses to my good character, neighbors who testified that I was above suspicion, and she couldn't prove what she alleged."

I said, "Please, folks, we are your guests, so let bygones be bygones. Thank God you're both all right."

She said, "He beats me until I vomit blood."

He said, "My lot is not a good piece of land and it doesn't get enough water, and yet my rate of production is high to the amazement of the whole village. I am an excellent farmer. Today, early in the morning I gathered okra and cucumbers. I sorted the produce according to quality, separating the better from the lesser quality so

I could sell it for a higher price. When I came home I found that she had mixed the two piles together again, wasting my hard work all morning long."

We talked to them about cooperating to cope with being away from home and to bear life's hardships, and how they needed to work side-by-side in order to succeed and to keep the family strong. Then we left after sensing that things were returning to normal.

Tahani came back with the airport manager and a waiter carrying in one hand a large brass coffee pot and dozens of round demitasses stacked together in a column in the other hand. He began to pour us bitter coffee fragrant with cardamom. The women cheered joyfully and Tahani passed around pieces of chocolate and cookies, saying, "Just a snack to tide us over."

The coffee and the sweets dispelled our boredom and a merry mood prevailed. Umm Kulthum's voice came over the airwaves after a long time that we spent listening to Fayrouz. Farida Sabri swayed with the music, mouthed the words in admiration and said in a loud voice, "Ya salam ya sitt!"

Sleepless and alone, rapt in ecstasy,
I talk to your ever-present likeness,
Tears flowing down my cheeks,
Not dreaming you'd be pleased with me,
Despairing of attention,
I am even deprived of your displeasure.

The airport manager engaged in a conversation with Angel Rushti about his school days in Egypt. There was a commotion at the outside gate and passengers arriving.

Widad Iskandar said as she pointed at the passengers standing outside the airport, "What have these people done to deserve this?"

The manager said, "For the time being, there's nothing we can do for them. There's a plan to upgrade the airport but it is still being studied."

Tahani al-Gammal said, "If you built just a tent or even a tin roof, it would provide some protection and their suffering would be alleviated a little bit until God provides a better solution."

Sarah Badr said, "It's a lot worse during pilgrimage season in the port of Aqaba."

The airport manager said, "I am at your service. I'll be in my office if you need anything."

Memories came back, playing games with me. They didn't want me to enjoy any relaxation or companionship with the group I was sitting with, even though we didn't get to meet much in Cairo. Abd al-Halim Hafez was now singing about love, eyes calling out and longing and hearts.

After I came back from Baghdad I was busy house-hunting in Cairo, being pregnant, giving birth, and caring for a young son. I didn't have enough time to connect again with professional colleagues and friends. My life in Egypt was quite different from the life I made for myself in Baghdad. But it was a temporary phase that would soon come to an end, especially with my mother and mother-in-law nearby. I tried to convince myself to overcome my fear of not knowing where I was heading, as the voice of Abd al-Halim Hafez sang his pleas to his heart not to run away but to give in to love and its commands.

This present trip would not bring *al-Zahra* Baghdad bureau back to life and would not bring its scattered personalities back from all corners of the world. It was a phase that had come to an end, the good with the bad. If only I could find out where Anhar was now, that would be the best news of all and I could correspond with her from Cairo without any fear on her part. Early on, during the first days of her disappearing without a trace, I had concluded that she most likely had run away from Hilmi Amin and that he alone held the secret and could answer the question whether or not this is what had happened. He was the only one who knew whether their story together was behind the disappearance or there were other reasons for it. I couldn't ask him even though I imagined that our relationship allowed me to broach the subject; I decided to leave it up to him to find the appropriate time to tell me himself. I soon changed my mind as I heard the pained voice of Tante Fatma, Anhar's mother, as she received me in tears asking, "Did you find anything about Anhar, dear daughter?"

Many months had passed and so many things had changed before I could turn the story of her disappearance into a game of riddles, using clues from Papa Sharo's famous children's programs on the Egyptian radio, by asking for instance, "I wonder where you are, Marzuq?" Then in a surprised tone of voice, "The island's crown?" Then in a tone of despair, "The bowl?" When I pull this away, Hilmi Amin would smile calmly and change the subject.

I shrugged my shoulders. I wanted to shake off the memories but, instead of falling off, they climbed onto and into my head.

I had noticed that Hilmi Amin was growing more tense. He put off going to Cairo until several issues had been resolved. At one of the conferences we met Samir Latif, a former high-ranking media official. He was very reserved with Hilmi but I didn't want to draw the bureau director's attention to that. I did not express any objections when Hilmi asked him to take a letter to Tante Fayza, saying, "Please call her and tell her that the shawl she wanted me to send to her will be a little late."

Samir said, "What shawl?"

Hilmi said, "An Iraqi shawl for the winter, I won't be able to go to Egypt in the near future. I'll find a way to send it with one of my colleagues."

Two days later I was surprised when Tante Fayza called me at home. She sounded very worried. She asked me about Hilmi's news, the story about the shawl and whether he was sick.

I told her no, that he was not sick but that the colleague he had asked to carry the shawl said that he was carrying extra baggage and couldn't bring the shawl to her, and that Hilmi wanted her to know that he would send it to her at the earliest opportunity.

She said, "He frightened me and the girls very much. I was surprised when he called at midnight, then he hung up without telling me who he was. I gathered from the sounds of car horns around him that he was calling from the street as if he were afraid of something or another. Please, Nora, tell me the truth."

I said, trying to calm her down, "Please don't be upset, Tante, and I'll have him call you tomorrow evening because telephone service in the morning is really lousy. If there's no service at all he will send you a telegram."

I told him what happened. He got very upset and promised to call her in the evening. I told him, "Anhar can help you if you can't get through. She can use the telephone at the Iraqi News Agency. We don't usually ask them for anything, but this is an exceptional circumstance."

He said, "Keep Anhar out of Fayza's business."

I said to Hilmi Amin as we were on our way to al-Khalsa that I noticed that I liked the homes that I entered by chance better and that I found in them all the information and human-interest stories that I needed for my work. Then Abd al-Barr would come quickly if he found out that I had entered a house other than the one he had recommended, and he would just sit there like a monkey on my back. And of course I would not be able to shake him off, especially at meal times. I asked Hilmi not to accept his invitations. I said to him, "Last week I reluctantly accepted all invitations from peasants while at their homes and insisted it just be some aged cheese and Egyptian bread, all just to keep Abd al-Barr at arm's length."

At the entrance of the village a young boy told us that Engineer Mahdi wanted to have some tea with us.

When we finished the tea, the peasants who had gathered in the engineer's office exploded, all asking, "Why do you know this man? Why do you support him? He is bad. He steals his neighbors' crops and beats his wife and doesn't give her any food. He is quarrelsome for no reason and he even doesn't know how to farm." One of them said it and they all burst out laughing.

Mahdi the engineer listed many details about the problems that Abd al-Barr created. He concluded by saying, "I want to keep Abd al-Barr away from the village so that the project can proceed the right way."

Hilmi Amin said, "I'll vouch for him one last time and I promise you that his attitude and actions will improve."

He went to him in his house and came back. I didn't find out what took place in that meeting, but I noticed, as the days passed, a change in the way Abd al-Barr treated me and that he behaved more calmly. The village realized that Abd al-Barr's personality was changing.

The book began to take shape and whenever I finished transcribing one cassette tape, I went back to record another, as Hilmi Amin encouraged me to get it done before the bureau's circumstances, the country we were living in, and the situation in Egypt changed. I did not have the same worries nor did I feel any impending changes on the horizon. I wondered what would make Iraq close the bureau and what conditions would make the magazine close it. We didn't cost the magazine anything. They could change the bureau director or terminate my job, but our success made that impossible now. Surely Hilmi Amin was just exaggerating everything.

The 18th and 19th of January demonstrations in Egypt provided a rude awakening from my dreams. Hilmi Amin's words about the necessity of finishing certain tasks quickly before conditions changed now appeared logical and the idea of freezing the activities of the bureau or changing its management and workers seemed likely despite all the success that we had attained. *Al-Zahra* magazine's newest issue came out with the sensational title on the cover: Days of Fire.

On the cover was the picture of an old woman wearing an ordinary black galabiya that women of the poorer classes usually wore, carrying a bottle of whiskey. Behind her were broken shop windows and smoke. The headlines inside read: "The government opens juvenile houses of correction, letting out inmates to turn the people's uprising into an uprising of thieves," written and reported by Fahmi Kamil, Sabri Hanafi, and Mahmoud Othman. Other headlines read: "Another Cairo Fire"; "The Hungry, Deprived People's Uprising." Among the reports was one that read: "The vice president's house in Alexandria was looted and sixteen television sets were found in the house. Central Security forces used tear gas to disperse the masses that came out to demand a life of dignity."

I felt as if I were on a small boat tossed by giant waves in a tumultuous sea. The sense of confidence that I had acquired working in an Egyptian press bureau disappeared. I was in a sea without end, facing an unknown destiny. The problems that concerned me were not just Iraqi problems, now they were joined by Egyptian problems. Iraqi journalists gathered around us asking us about the news. We answered their queries and we accused the Egyptian government of collusion in the incidents. They expressed admiration for the Egyptian press, especially *al-Ahali* (The Population) newspaper and the magazines *Rose al-Yusuf* and *al-Zahra*.

Muhammad al-Jaz'iri said, "We learn from the Egyptian press everything against the government."

Hilmi Amin said, "There has been a liberal tradition for a long time in Egypt. If opinions of the opposition did not find an outlet in the press, they would find their way in some other manner. But generally we go through phases: sometimes the government is forced to allow some freedom of expression, then suddenly attacks the press and once again shows its vicious fist."

Mahmoud Bulhaj whispered in my ear, "Our press used to be more free before."

The Egyptian government accused the left of inciting the masses and we heard of widespread detentions among journalists and accusations that leftists were lackeys and agents of foreign powers and that they took part in plots to overturn the regime. New waves of Egyptian leftist youth, most of whom were members of al-Tagammu', began to arrive in Baghdad. They came to our office, most of them with letters of recommendation from Khalid Muhyiddin or Rifaat al-Said or some veteran leftists who were colleagues of Hilmi Amin, to help them find jobs. Some had been arrested and detained previously in the student uprising of 1972 or during the latest uprising. Some of them were still pursued by the police. They would pay a visit, or, for some, several visits, to the office before I'd hear of them settling down in or around Baghdad. Among them was Basyuni. There was also a woman who puzzled me for a long time and of whom I changed my opinion several times. Hilmi Amin had introduced her to me one morning in the office, saying, "Dr. Ragya, M.D."

After she left he told me, "She and her husband are members of a new communist party. Her husband was arrested by chance as the police were raiding an apartment in Heliopolis. They thought they were the intended targets, so they quickly burned their papers and the rising blowing smoke gave them away. Her husband helped her escape from a door in the back of the apartment. She stayed in hiding until she was able to travel. A member of al-Tagammu' brought her to me yesterday and I took her to Mahmoud Rashid's house to spend the night. We'll find a job for her in a nearby hospital, God willing."

I said, "Did Mahmoud Rashid agree to put her up so simply?"

He smiled and said, "Isn't it enough that I introduced her to him?"

I said, "I didn't like her. Does she have anything proving what she is saying is true? How was her husband arrested without her? How did she make it out of the airport if the group she belonged to was ordered to be arrested? Besides, what's with the dark glasses and the leather jacket?"

He said, "Wait a minute! Hold your horses, are you a police officer?"

I said, "You had no right to take her to Mahmoud Rashid's home because he's a low-key guy who minds his own business, his being a leftist notwithstanding. I don't think it is implausible that she is under surveillance from the Iraqi security. So why get the man involved?"

He said, "Putting her up for a week will not attract attention and I will personally monitor her movements."

I said, "I have a special sense that sniffs out informers. Perhaps because during my college days many students were recruited by state security to monitor our activities. I became so good at it I could feel their presence behind my back."

He said, "Look at you!"

She provoked me every time she came to the office. I asked myself, "Why am I so repulsed by her? Is it because of those theoretical discussions that she initiates and insists on her point of view in them without regard for the feelings of others? Is it because she has a complex, mysterious personality? How can she not be mysterious when she belongs to an underground party and has had all this experience at twenty-five or younger?" Dr. Ragya was appointed rather quickly to a general hospital on the outskirts of Baghdad. She moved out of Mahmoud Rashid's house to a place closer to her job. She became a regular visitor at the office where she met Atef, Sawsan, Abd al-Rahim, and Suhayla and joined this group of young friends.

On one of her visits to the office she told me the story of her departure from Egypt. As she started talking my aversion to her began to dissipate gradually and I cautiously got closer to her. She said, "I fell in love with a colleague in college, but he didn't finish school because of his constant running away from the police and being arrested several times. I finished school and we got married and I worked in a hospital during the day and in a private clinic in the evening and that was how I provided support for the family. We lived by ourselves sometimes in furnished apartments we rented and sometimes with the comrades. I terminated my pregnancy by abortion on the eve of my departure to Baghdad and Hashim divorced me so I'd be free if my situation changed in Baghdad or Beirut where a number of Egyptian leftists work in Lebanese newspapers or with the PLO. We debated where to go and I chose Baghdad."

Ragya presented me with an incredible model of a young woman leading a communal life, moving among furnished apartments and marrying a student pursued by the police. I asked her in disbelief, "Where's your family?"

She said, "My brother is a member of the same organization. You have no idea what a wonderful revolutionary my husband is and how much he loves Egypt."

Ragya was quite specific in the way she presented the story of her life: an underground party, detention, escape, abortion, and divorce. I was shocked. I didn't quite absorb the whole experience. I was quite touched by her abortion, so much so that I didn't take my eye off her belly. But I still had some uneasiness about her. It was no longer suspicion of her being an informer, but it was uneasiness nonetheless. I was measuring her behavior by my own customary yardstick and not according to other criteria that might have been there but about which I knew nothing. I noticed the difference between Hilmi Amin's assessment of her, and mine. He believed her the whole time and I believed her sometimes, until she did something that confused me. I noticed that she was developing a strong relationship with Anhar and I thought that was quite natural since they both were communists, and lonely, and came to the office in the evening.

I asked Hilmi Amin one day, "You've always said that there were attempts by Egyptian security to penetrate the bureau. Why couldn't Ragya be the one that Egyptian security has sent to report the whole scene in Baghdad back to them. Especially now that she has gained easy access to everyone's houses and knows the details of everybody's lives."

He said, "There's nothing to fear and she is not a dangerous person. It is natural that Ragya does not feel comfortable with you and treats you in a gruff manner, because she looks upon you as a bourgeois young lady without any concern for public life, one who feels happy about her and her class's achievements, especially as you are a champion athlete. She does not see in you the struggle for social justice. Young communists in Egypt have a long and hard story. They accuse us of dissolving the party for Gamal Abdel Nasser's sake and they reject our cooperation with him. They place the responsibility for what happened these last few years on our shoulders.

She comes from a different world and does not see you for what you really are because she and her cohorts are too busy holding previous generations accountable. These young communists want to make a way for themselves in which the past is quite distinct from the present. They do not understand what you are doing in the public arena. So she considers you just a bourgeois woman."

I said, "A rotten bourgeois woman, please."

He laughed long and heartily.

I lost contact with most of my Baghdad friends. I didn't meet them in Cairo or anywhere else and I don't know where most of them have gone. Are they still in Baghdad or have they left? Maybe a question to the Central Bureau of Inspections and Quality Control would tell me where Abd al-Rahim Mansur and the rest of the group have gone. The atmosphere in Cairo is still uncomfortable for people like them. I know that some wives have taken their children back to Egypt. Sawsan called me and told me that Samia and her children had come back to Cairo and we met one time. Tomorrow I'll call and find out. Maybe they have returned to Baghdad just as Titi did now that things are more quiet. None of them got involved in the war except Basyuni Abd al-Mu'in.

I looked around. Some friends were busy talking among themselves. Others were busy reading. They all looked tired and some succumbed to intermittent, uncomfortable sleep, leaning on their suitcases. Boredom and weariness took over the departure lounge at the Amman airport, which was now full of passengers on their way to London. There were young English women and men with large backpacks. There were some Palestinians who looked well-off, and Jordanian Bedouin. I wanted to sleep. A beautiful little blonde girl was jumping around, leaving her father's side, going to her brother sitting with his mother, then going back to her father, then her brother again. The boy was Yasir's age when he came back with me to Baghdad after his health was restored.

I am an Arab soldier with my rifle in my hand
Defending my homeland against the evil aggressor
Bang, bang, bang
Boom, boom, boom.

We burst out laughing to see Yasir with Madu and Amani, son and daughter of Titi, holding short sticks as they ran around shouting "bang!" and "boom!"

Why worry at such an early age about soldiers or homeland? But it seemed they adapted the patriotic song to their purposes and found their own fun with it.

Yasir completely changed my life. Sometimes he would ask if he could come in from the back to my study while I was busy writing.

"Mama, I want to tell you that I love you."

"Come in."

I opened my arms and kissed him. "Why don't you play a little bit with your gazelle Zuzu until I am done, then we'll play together."

"I want to sit with you here without speaking."

"Take these papers and draw on them."

"Mama!"

"Yasirrrr!"

I could feel his glances trying to follow my every movement while he, without raising his head, pretended to be engrossed in the paper in front of him. I smiled at his innocent little act of deception. I went back to writing my article, then raised my head after a short while. I found a wonderful smile all over his face, happy that our eyes had met.

"I drew a soldier, a rifle, and a dog."

"Draw your beloved Zuzu, or draw a ship or a forest."

When I felt him kicking in my tummy, I was the happiest woman in the world. I hoped the baby would be a girl. I picked the most beautiful features from our two families for her: my father's eyes, Hatim's nose, and my mother's complexion.

Hatim, laughing, said, "She'll have a potato on her face which she'll get from Susu, and Imad's crooked ear."

I laughed. It would be a catastrophe if she took the smallest eyes in the family and the biggest nose. I'd call her Inji.

The early months were very hard. An ever-present sickness made it impossible for any food to stay in my stomach. This would last for three days in a row and then maybe relief would come with a piece of fruit which I'd eat and fall asleep. I kept losing weight and I turned into a frail ghost that loved to sleep. My Iraqi women neighbors kept trying to entice me with all sorts of food and dishes, but it was no use. They said it was happening because it was my first baby. My condition changed completely when we moved to the house in Dora. We had been visiting the family of one of Hatim's colleagues at work, another engineer. He invited us to move to the upstairs apartment in the house where he lived. Hatim agreed after a long discussion, as he was averse to getting too cozy with acquaintances or neighbors. I pushed the idea because I wanted companionship.

On the first day Sabah noticed my constant vomiting and commented on my emaciation. The following day I was surprised when she knocked on my door as soon as the company car picked up Hatim and Shukri. She held in her hand a plate of fried hot green peppers covered with pieces of tomato. I asked her what it was and she said, "This is our breakfast: oven-hot bread, and food enough for a whale. Take an antiemetic."

Behind her came her son Wa'il and her daughter Hanaa, and Fathiya, her husband's niece, a fourteen-year-old girl. They opened the fridge, taking out different kinds of cheese and pickles, and began to wash lettuce and put oranges in front of us. We sat eating with a hearty appetite while laughing.

The morning sickness stopped. I had hot peppers in the morning with Sabah and the children. After breakfast we went to the market together to buy fresh food for the day, then came back to prepare it together. I stole a few minutes here and there to read before Hatim returned. I loved Sabah's goodness and also her gruffness. But I was sometimes shocked by her habits, which were different from mine. Before coming to Baghdad, she used to work in Egypt at the main office of the Sharqiya governorate in the city of Zaqaziq. She had married Shukri, her neighbor, and had a child. She had not yet gone back to work when her husband got a work contract in Baghdad. They decided to take Fathiya, who was taking care of the baby, with them to Baghdad. They were hoping that Sabah would find work in Baghdad, but she couldn't even though she applied to all government departments and despite a promise from the company where her husband worked to get her a job. When they gave up on getting a job, they decided to have two more babies so that when they returned to Egypt, the child-rearing phases would be over.

Both Sabah and Shukri came from poor families that sent some, not all, of their children to school. The work opportunity in Baghdad fulfilled their lifelong dream: to make money. They had furnished a house and bought a Kelvinator refrigerator on the installment plan, thus outdoing their colleagues who had bought the more modest Ideal eight-foot fridges. From their first day in Baghdad they decided to save enough money to buy a plot of land on which to set up a fruit and vegetable refrigerated warehouse. They were actually able, within the first year, to save half the price. They bought the land, paying a down payment and taking a mortgage for the rest of the price. Thus their main concern in Iraq was to save money. They talked about nothing else and they cut down their cost of living to the minimum. I didn't realize that Hatim and I, leading a normal life, were provoking them beyond words. Shukri usually deposited the bulk of his salary in the bank, keeping only their estimated expenses according to a very strict plan and budget that they never deviated from. Sabah brought eggplant and pepper for breakfast, replacing eggplant with potatoes when their price was lower. She also gave each of her two children an egg. On Fridays each member of the family also ate an egg, an event that Shukri celebrated, shouting as he came in from the garden, saying, "Eat eggs, a protein that you, sons-of-guns, or your forefathers, never dreamed of."

Every Thursday she cooked one kilogram of mutton that she divided over two days. Sometimes she bought a chicken in the middle of the week. And when she and I discovered frozen fish in the Assyrian market nearby, she bought fish instead of the chicken. Such a celebration of food and what they bought or didn't buy would have been dismissed as the pride felt and demonstrated by a poor family feeling that it had gone up in the world. But they did not keep it in the family, so to speak, but began to observe me closely. It started as a simple story, but then it quickly escalated. We would come back together from the market carrying bags of groceries. The children would come noisily through the garden gate and then take from my bags the fruit, cheese, and chocolate which I, laughing, gave to them. I noticed, however, angry glances in Sabah's eyes. With time I discovered that those angry glances prevented them from touching her own bags. It became more pronounced and noticeable day after day. This was also accompanied by another phenomenon that was also growing: Sabah began to ask for things that she had seen me buying at the market. It started with meat and then extended to medications and personal care items that she would send Fathiya to borrow but never returned. Then I discovered that she was calculating our equal income from the factory and our unequal spending, as far as she could tell. After all, there were only two of us and five of them. This petty behavior began to bore me. Our stories about our life before we came to Baghdad showed her a kind of life she had not before heard existed. And even though I had completely accepted the fact that her life was different from mine, she did not accept that difference. Her reactions became more intrusive: a word here and a word there, seemingly unintended, and a ready refutation of any new piece of information I cared to give. Then she began to ask questions about my relationship with Hatim, brought about by our sitting close to each other in front of her. She would come up to my apartment at five in the morning, touching my wet hair and asking me with a smile, "Did you have a bath today?"

I would say, "Yes," hoping that she would explain to me why she asked, but instead she would smile even more broadly and say nothing.

I asked Hatim one day why Sabah was asking about my bathing. "Isn't it natural for people to bathe?"

He laughed and patted me on the cheek, "This is women's stuff. She's snooping around about our intimate relationship."

I would write to my mother about the details Sabah asked me about and which sometimes brought me to tears, but which I was too embarrassed to tell Hatim. I expected her to just barge into my apartment as soon as Hatim left. The delicious breakfast filled with laughter turned into a big chore. She got angry if I picked up a book to read or if I did anything but cook. I began to make up excuses, that I was going on errands, or that my husband had asked me to run to downtown Baghdad. She would ask me sharply, "Where do you go three, four times a week? Are you keeping secrets from me?"

I would smile and not answer her. I just took my books to the Zawra Park and sat there and read. When I came back she would be angry. "You haven't cooked for your poor husband who will soon come back, hungry."

I asked her calmly, "How do you know I haven't prepared dinner?"

"I know everything you have in your fridge."

"I'll grill some meat."

"And you call that a proper dinner? Your husband is a young man who needs a lot of feeding. Give me two pieces of liver because Shukri craves it."

I got to the seventh month. I booked a plane ticket to give birth in Egypt. Sabah tried to persuade me against it, saying, "I gave birth to Hanaa at home last year with help from the nurse who lives in front of the bridge. I'll also give birth to a new baby before you, here also. There's no need for all these travel expenses. Fathiya and I will take very good care of you."

I felt the truth in her words and that she genuinely wanted me to stay. She went on, "There's no need to burden your husband with additional expenses. You should keep your money for yourselves instead of throwing it away. Save it for a project in Egypt that brings income for the two of you."

"I haven't witnessed any births in my life and have never gotten close to a baby. I need my mother's advice and help."

"We are here."

I discussed the subject with Hatim. He refused to consider Sabah's suggestion, saying, "Why the risk, without the family's help? Come back safely with the baby and don't worry. We have enough money, thank God."

I went shopping every day, buying gifts for the two families and for our friends. I felt light in spite of the pregnancy, wearing my usual clothes. Then I bought a maternity dress and put it on. I waited for Hatim.

"What's that?"

I got close to his chest, "I want a picture in this maternity sack. I want to feel that I am really pregnant."

"You still have two months during which your belly will get larger and you'll feel you're pregnant."

He began to take pictures of me in various parts of the house, saying, "Stand there, Umm Atris, there, Umm Sharbat," calling my baby other funny names. We went out on the balcony. He placed the camera on a table and ran toward me and embraced me hard. We heard Sabah's voice before the lens shut and before the flash lit, saying, "What's with all the pictures?"

She was standing in the garden directly under the balcony. Hatim said, "She wants to send the pictures to her girlfriends."

"Who likes being fat and flabby?"

"Look what a graceful gazelle she is."

A very tall and statuesque African woman carrying a baby girl on her back in a brightly colored wrap tied around her belly entered the departure lounge at Amman airport. The baby's legs dangled from the sides of the wrap as she slept in spite of the crowds and the movement all around her. I was unaware that three hours had passed, then this baby with her peaceful face and her fresh, glistening black face came into my view and aroused my longing for Haytham and Yasir. I was drinking my coffee and enjoying thinking of nothing in particular when milk poured out of my breast all at once, a sudden rain without any clouds or lightning or thunder. I had not counted on this surprise, thinking that being at the airport would make it possible for me to go to the bathroom without any problem. I stood up, stung, trying to avoid being inundated, but it was too late. I remembered that I had not put an extra blouse in my carry-on bag. I thanked God that I didn't let my suitcase go to the storage area at the airport. I opened it, extremely embarrassed, even though all of my traveling companions were women since the men in the delegation had gone ahead of us to Baghdad. I took out of the suitcase a clean blouse, a bra, and a slip and put them in my handbag.

Abla Widad Iskandar asked me, "Do you need anything, Nora?"

I turned toward her. Milk had covered a considerable area of my blouse. She laughed and said, "Go quickly to the bathroom, or else you'll catch cold."

Sarah Badr said, "I swear women are such poor creatures, even the intellectuals."

The restroom attendant said, "I'll go out and not let anyone in until you've changed."

I told her, "There's no need to cause anyone any trouble. The airport is filling up. I'll go into the stall and when I need to wash up I'll call you to hold them off a few minutes."

I undid the blouse buttons unable to control the milk gushing out of my breast at top speed. I pressed the rubber ball of the pump and let the air out as I placed the horn of the pump. Milk flowed until it filled the cavity and I heard the sound of it sliding off. I emptied it, then pressed it against my breast again, feeling as if my muscles were coming apart. Some tears escaped my eyes brought on by feelings of longing for Haytham and fear for him. I remembered my grandmother's words, "Do not nurse while crying. Tears poison the milk." Does the makeup of the milk and its taste really change when one is crying? Yasir was very sensitive to my feelings and would shun my breast if I was sad. Haytham did more than that: he would burst out crying if I gave him my breast without giving him my undivided attention. He would take it while whimpering, then would stop, opening his tearful eyes, letting me hear the sound of his anger without letting it out of his mouth, then would go back to sucking it. The intervals between the pauses would get longer until he got busy sucking again, then falling asleep, his message of rebuke having been delivered: "Don't take me when you are not totally devoted to me, otherwise, I also don't want you." I let my tears flow all over my face, asking myself if there was anything in life worth leaving my nursing baby for. I moved the pump to the other breast, just in case. I called the attendant, saying to her, "Give me five minutes."

I heard distant footsteps and her voice telling me it was okay to come out. I washed the upper half of my body then put on my fresh clothes. I asked the attendant if she had a plastic bag for my wet clothes and she said she did. I gathered my things and left, remembering airports and other places I passed through in various parts of the world that had breastfeeding rooms with cribs and facilities for babies. I said to myself, "A breastfeeding room when passengers spend days in the street to catch their planes? You are really weird, Nora!"

One of the airport officers came and asked us to stand in lines in front of passport control and asked us to pay the fee for leaving Jordan. A buzz of refusal by the conference participant women rose. I knew these details and that it was useless to object. Jordan had decided to levy those taxes. In the end the women gave in. Then we were surprised to see two men running toward us, in handsome official suits, black hair, and rugged features. One of them said, "Please excuse us. We are from the Iraqi Embassy. Our colleagues responsible for your trip were involved in a traffic accident on the way and have been taken to the hospital. We only knew about it half an hour ago. Give us your passports."

We heard voices of protest from passengers who had arrived before us. Some, as we came to know, had been waiting at the doors of the airport for three days. The voices got louder and we heard people knocking on the glass barriers. Then we heard a loud commotion and saw, as we went through, a fire hose turned on, drenching the passengers waiting at the door. Tears rushed to my eyes as snow fell and the young came to blows, trying to force their way through the door. The picture grew fuzzy and they appeared like ghosts dancing, falling, then standing up again in one colossus as if it were a giant snake divided into hundreds of parts, slithering but not leaving their places despite the water hoses and the insults. Oh my God! We were united by sorrow, so we proceeded to the plane in silence.

We sat in the jumbo plane. Some Egyptians came in. Most of them were educated youth and some were peasants with deep and dry furrowed faces. Behind them came a group of Kurds in their traditional attire: the billowing pants, broad fabric belt, the vest, and the large turban. Noha asked me, "Are these Iraqi costumes?"

I said, "Yes, Kurdish."

She asked, "Do they really worship Satan?"

I laughed and said, "No, they worship God. Salah al-Din al-Ayyubi was a Kurd. They have Indo-European origins. They are Sunnis even though they have long borders with Iran. As for those who worship Satan, they are a very small sect called Yazidis. They believe that Satan, in all of creation, has the strongest faith in God Almighty because he refused to prostrate himself to any other."

She said in surprised innocence, "Can any creature disobey God?"

I laughed and said, "He acted like a child. What can we do? He refused to obey but accepted God's will so that the earth would be populated. This is what makes his personality appear charming and captivating in some people's eyes. Interestingly, they never pronounce the Arabic letter 'shin' so as not to summon him up, ever."

She asked, "Where did the word 'Yazidi' come from?"

I said, "Perhaps from the name Yazid, son of Mu'awiya, who killed al-Husayn ibn Ali, may God be pleased with him."

Kamilia said, "Have you been able, Nora, to understand the different sects in Iraq: Kurds, Arabs, Shi'a, Sunna, Alawis, Turkomen, and Armenians?"

Noha asked before I could answer Kamilia, "Is it true that the Shi'a believe that Sayyidna Muhammad took the mission that was originally intended for Sayyidna Ali?"

I said, "The region of Iraq and Greater Syria had witnessed bloody conflicts during the early phases of the formation of the Islamic state. The divisions resulted from political rather than religious conflicts, the way we all agree on the meaning of the word 'religious.' The Shi'a believe that Ali and his offspring from his wife, Fatima, daughter of the Prophet, are the main authority for Muslims after the death of the Prophet, peace be upon him, and that they are more up to the responsibility and more worthy of being followed than others. They also believe that Ali was more worthy of succeeding the Prophet than all others, and that's the root cause of the conflict."

Salma said, "But there is a group that believes that Sayyidna Ali is God."

I said, "Yes, they are called the Alihiya and they can be found in Iraq and Kurdistan. Imam Ali fought them and ordered their bodies burned in Kurdistan. They are still under the influence of Indian and other eastern philosophies. They believe that the message was coming to Sayyidna Ali. When he ordered them burned they said, 'This is the greatest proof that Ali is God, because God punishes by the use of his fire.' They are very small groups, and there are others such as al-Birgwan al-Sawliya, and they have been disowned by all Islamic sects, because they don't read the Qur'an and are no longer considered Muslim."

Kamilia said, "Isn't it really strange that everything that has to do with religion in human history is the most fanatical and violent and dangerous part of it? People forget secularism and all the logic they have learned in life whenever the clarion call of religion is sounded and they let the genie, the mindless genie, out of the bottle. Religion of whatever kind is humanity's real pain, and reaction to it is not governed by any logic."

I said, "You are right. Science disciplines reactions but does not eliminate them. We still don't know much about the human psyche. Perhaps because religion touches upon those areas of fear that were handed down from the first humans when they were alone in the wilderness and they looked for a god and worshiped whatever they feared: fire, the wind, or ferocious animals."

Silence prevailed in the plane for some time. Some passengers busied themselves reading and others in hushed conversations and some went to sleep. The Kurds came knocking on the door of my memory.

The Iraqi Ministry of Information informed us that peace had prevailed in Kurdish villages and on this occasion invited us to visit the village of Harir in the middle of the mountains and to accompany a caravan of health and social workers and artists, including singers, a musical band, and a theatrical troupe. We knew through the grapevine that there were pockets of resistance still holding out, but faced with insistence from our friends at the ministry, we agreed to go on the trip and took with us Mervat and Rasha, Hilmi Amin's older daughters, who happened to be in Baghdad at the time. Tante Fayza refused to come along out of fear for Rana's safety. Anhar was not invited. The caravan took us to the city of Erbil at noon and we found our friends from the culture directorate waiting for us. They were very happy to see us and told me that my articles in the newspaper *Hokari* have made me very popular among the Kurds. I noticed the impression those articles made whenever I met a group of people and mentioned my name. Mervat said, "You're quite a celebrity!"

I said, embarrassed by the attention, "I didn't imagine this kind of reaction, and in a different language? I think it's because it's a small society."

In the evening we rode with Hamid, the director of the cultural center, in a new four-wheel-drive car that made it easier to negotiate the rough terrain to Harir Valley. We moved as part of a motorcade, preceded by police cars with specially armed officers and protected in the back by armed vehicles.

I said to Hamid, "Are we in for a battle or a concert?"

Hamid said, "We're concerned for your safety."

Hilmi Amin said, "A single incident in this motorcade could result in an international scandal. And the Iraqis are determined to extend services to the Kurds in every part of this inaccessible mountain."

I had walked these mountain paths before. Once with Hatim early in my stay in Iraq and later during my visits to compile information. But most roads then connected the major cities. This road was different as it got to the faraway villages. I was happy whenever I heard or read about paving new roads in the middle of these rough mountainous areas and thought it contributed to the development of the region and extending services to all Iraqis, especially medical services, schools, and factories. But some Kurds have told me that the goal of building new roads was security, not development. I thought this view was not fair: the state had a right to protect itself and keep the peace. I had to admit that I never supported the view that the Kurds had the right to secede because I believed in unity, even though I also believed in their right to a life of freedom and dignity within their own country, Iraq. I was also a firm believer in their right to fight for social justice and developing their country. My views on the Kurdish revolt became clearer as time passed and as I read a lot about Kurdish history, about their failure to establish a Kurdish republic in recent history at least. I was quite surprised and pleased to learn that, for a few days, they did have a state: the Mahmoud or Mahabad Republic. The day I found that out I went to Hilmi Amin with my discovery after spending a whole night summarizing the history of the region in a neat timeline.

I told Hilmi, "Finally, I found a twin to the Zifta Republic."

"Where?" he asked.

"Here in beautiful Kurdistan. I read this somewhere:

In the 1920s, the leader of Kurdistan was Sheikh Mahmoud al-Hafid (the Grandson) who was called 'the King of Kurdistan,' who tried to wrench recognition of the Kurdish kingdom at the San Remo conference where Ottoman possessions were divvied up, but the British preferred to unite Iraq within Iraq's borders. The rebellion of Sheikh Mahmoud al-Hafid was put down. In the 1930s Sheikh Ahmad Barzani, the older brother of Mullah Mustafa Barzani, led a large Kurdish rebellion throughout Kurdistan with the blessing of the Soviet Union. That rebellion was quelled by the king of Iraq with the help of the British in the forties. In 1952, Mullah Mustafa Barzani declared the Mahabad Republic in north-eastern Iraq on the Iraqi–Iranian borders but that rebellion was quelled by the shah and the British together. When the Republic fell, Mullah Mustafa Barzani fled on foot, walking with his followers on mules, seven thousand kilometers, then he sought asylum in the Soviet Union. The Soviet army gave him the rank of general and called him the 'Red General.' He stayed in the Soviet Union until the coup d'état that ended the monarchy in Iraq, and Barzani was welcomed as a patriotic hero. Quiet prevailed until 1962 when the Kurds staged another rebellion that continued to simmer, and Kurds kept fighting for independence until the second Ba'th coup of 1968. Then came the March 1970 declaration that gave the Kurds autonomy, with free elections to follow, but the Iraqi government did not live up the terms of the declaration and another rebellion started."

Hilmi Amin said, "You didn't find this last part in books."
I replied, "Yes. This is what the Kurds told me, in explaining the reasons for the renewed rebellion."
I went on to say, "The rebellion continued on and off, then was back on in 1973 during the Kilometer 101 negotiations in Egypt until Iraq signed the Algiers Treaty in 1975 and the shah stopped

supporting the Kurds. The law of March 1975 was declared and implemented, giving Kurds autonomy, and a general amnesty was declared. An agreement was concluded whereby it was stipulated that the government of Iraq would include five Kurdish ministers and a vice president."

Hilmi said, "Bravo, Nora! Great work. The Republic of Zifta declared its independence from the Kingdom of Egypt after accusing the king and the political parties of corruption. But their most beautiful achievement was building a music kiosk in the middle of the only public park in the republic."

I said, "How romantic! I found information about it in the book *Days in History* by Ahmad Bahaa al-Din."

He said, "All revolutions are romantic, despite the sacrifice and martyrdom. Writing about history needs people like us, non-historians, to make it a little more human and less formal."

I looked at him closely. He did fit the description of a romantic dreamer. Dreams pushed one in the direction of revolution and change, and being a romantic made one face the brutality of regimes with words and art while unarmed.

I read a sign saying "To Hajj Imran." I asked, "Is it a village or a town?"

Hamid said, "It is the last post on the Iraq–Iran border. The last small village."

I contemplated the towering mountains. How like those solid rocks the Kurds were! They say that Kurds are obstinate. Why not? Isn't a person the product of his environment? I observed a herd of black goats. I was surprised how small and short they were the first time I saw them. That day I asked myself as I followed a herd of cows: how do such short and thin legs support fat cows? It seems they get that way from moving around the mountains.

I noticed terraced gardens on the mountains, pear, plum, and walnut trees. Where, I wondered, did they plant wheat, clover, and rice? They had to have wheat at least since most of their food was green wheat kernels.

The elaborate preparations for the motorcade and the heightened security measures told me that the Kurdish question was more complex than I had thought. The narrow path around the mountain swerved, presenting a scene among the most splendid I had ever seen. The mountains receded quickly and gave the land room to stretch and then the mountains stood sentinel at a distance, making it possible for the sky to let the golden rays of the sun bathe the whole scene. I was enthralled. The flow of the motorcade going down toward the plain continued. I asked the driver to stop for a little while to take some pictures. He said, "The road is narrow. If we stop the whole column will have to stop also."

I said, "I won't have another opportunity to take pictures on our way back because it will soon be dark."

He looked at Hamid and began to talk to him in Kurdish. Hamid said, "By all means, please."

The driver swerved at the bend and hugged the rocks of the mountain, stopping the car to let the other cars pass just barely, and said, "You can get off here, please."

I took two or three pictures of the Harir plain and dashed back to the car, which had kept moving so that the last car in the column would not pass us even though the whole convoy had slowed down involuntarily. I noticed that Hamid and the driver were uneasy. I looked up at the mountains searching for ghosts. Thank God there were none.

We arrived at the small village that had a few houses with big gardens and traditional crops: wheat and corn and some fruit trees. The village was famous for its birds being the tastiest. We went into a huge pavilion. A red-haired petite Kurdish singer got on the stage. She was obviously very popular. The audience repeated the words of the songs after her and girls stood in front of her with their bright gilded costumes dancing dabka shoulder to shoulder with young men. The singing summoned everyone who had stayed behind in their houses and the pavilion got very crowded. I learned from Hamid that inhabitants of the surrounding villages had been there since noon, awaiting the caravan. Old women sat on mats away from spectators' seats. Everyone got busy singing and dancing. The people of the village called out to one of the young men and forcibly brought him to the stage. He shared the microphone with the singer and began singing with her. The whole place lit up when a group of horsemen with beautiful costumes came onto the stage riding thoroughbred horses. The scene was unreal, as if everyone had just come out of the pages of a book I hadn't read before. It was much better than any scene in the movies and more real than actual reality. I looked for the security men and the police cars that escorted us to the Harir plain but couldn't see any of them. No one could guess or predict Iraqi security measures. They come suddenly onto the scene in an orderly manner and they disappear just as suddenly, always shrouded in mystery. As a matter of fact, all aspects of Iraqi life were shrouded in mystery, perhaps because it was a different way of life, unfamiliar to me. Or perhaps because I had not dealt with the state in Egypt or elsewhere. I had lived the life of an Arab student away from formalities. What would I know about authorities or regimes? But in Iraq it was different. Definitely different.

I heard quick rolling drums and beats on the long tabla that I loved, then the voice of Anwar Abd al-Wahab rang out in tones reminiscent of Indian songs. The singing was in Arabic and was received with wild, loud applause. I couldn't believe that they appreciated Arabic singing with such enthusiasm. But then this was Iraq. I saw from a distance a beautiful young woman coming toward me. I recognized her at once. It was the poet Nariman. We had met on one of my previous visits and she had given me a copy of her first collection of poetry written in Kurdish. When I asked her how I could read it, she said, "Learn the title of your weekly article in the Kurdish magazine."

I opened the book and read the presentation above her autograph in the corner of the page: "To a beautiful Egyptian poet in whose eyes we saw love, so we all loved her."

I was overjoyed and kissed her. She took out of her handbag a necklace of dry clove buds strung together with red corals, and placed it around my neck. It had a strong fragrant smell. I held the coarse necklace laughing and said, "Isn't the poetry collection enough?"

She said, "This is part of our culture. Kurdish women whom you've loved and written about wear it."

The clove reminded me of the dentist. Iraqis used it a lot in cooking. I was very happy with it and began to imagine fingers piercing the thin, coarse buds and stringing them in magnificent clusters studded with coral. I said to myself that perhaps they pierced the cloves while they were green and soft. Nariman also invited me to a poetry festival they planned to have in Erbil so that I could meet Kurdish poets. I told her I'd be delighted to go.

I knew that she worked as a doctor at the Erbil hospital during the day, then volunteered in the evening shifts in nearby villages, and yet took the time to attend all cultural events. I asked her how she got there. She said, "By the cars on the road."

I said, "But, is that safe?"

She shrugged and said, "What can a citizen do? One must live and move around. This is my country."

We got engrossed following a man singing Nazim al-Ghazali songs. I discovered that most of those attending spoke Arabic and we shared in the joyous celebrations. We were then invited to supper at long tables in the open air. They served us their famous dish of cooked green wheat and mutton and rashta, which is a kind of pasta, with cracked wheat.

Jamal said, "The artistic caravan will continue for three days and in the morning the medical and agricultural caravans will also begin their work. But you will go back with the police cars to Erbil to sleep at the hotel."

Time passed in conversation with friends, then the groups that were to spend the night in the Harir plain left and officials from the culture directorate stayed with us.

I asked Hilmi Amin, "Why don't we go back with Hamid's car rather than wait for the police cars?"

Laughing, he whispered to me, "Hamid is a Kurdish Ba'thist with a price on his head from the Kurdish rebels because he works with the authorities and they consider him a traitor."

Hamid sent one of his assistants to the police station to ask why the cars were late and the man came back and said they were on their way. At 2:30 a.m. one of the men came in and whispered a few words to Hamid. Hamid said, "Let's take the car. The police will follow."

We headed for the mountain guided only by the car's headlights in the middle of the pitch-black night. I liked this adventure of moving on the mountain, when every rock lit by the car lights appeared like a mythical animal. The quiet was so beautiful. I looked behind and I couldn't see the police car. It hadn't followed us yet. As time went by I sensed an unspoken tension coming from Hamid's direction. I attributed this to its being late and everybody being tired and, in Hamid's case, to the serious responsibilities he had. Then I remembered what Hilmi Amin had said and wondered why they considered him a traitor. Didn't everyone have a right to believe in an idea and defend it? I thought that Hamid was faithful to his country and believed its future to be in unity, not in secession. Iraq was a special country after all. But what did a Turkish Kurd, a Russian Kurd, and an Iraqi Kurd have in common and what tied them together? Peoples live together as neighbors and they unite. They invent reasons for uniting, to gain strength in numbers. These people, however, are looking for ways to be divided. Once again I looked behind me and I didn't see anyone. I didn't like the silence that enveloped the car. I asked Hamid, "Won't the police car follow us?"

"Yes," he said.

Rasha, who woke up frightened, said, "Are the armed rebels going to attack and kill us?"

I said, "Look behind that rock there: there's a whole armed battalion of lions and tigers."

"Really?" she said. Then she figured out I was joking and burst out laughing. Our laughter grew louder whenever we saw a big boulder and imagined it to be a tank or an armored vehicle. We kept shouting, "The barrel of a gun! A soldier on the move. Dust of their feet! Sounds of explosives!" I mimicked the Egyptian comedian Sayyid Zayyan in the Egyptian version of *My Fair Lady* shouting, "Remove the house! Remove the house!" We continued mimicking comic lines we had heard on the radio, moving from play to play and from one program to another, and had a lot of fun. We laughed so hard that we shed tears. I felt that Hamid was shocked to see this rare Egyptian talent of turning any situation into a laughing matter. I saw Hilmi Amin smile in a dignified manner as he saw us in the rearview mirror and as he undoubtedly heard us. His smile gave way to uproarious laughter and Hamid was also drawn into our laughter, which seemed to wipe the frown off his face. But his clenched hands clutching the steering wheel told me he was not relaxed despite our loud laughter, which I suspected reached foxes in their holes and wolves in their hiding places on the top of the mountain.

Hilmi Amin told a joke: "Haridi came back to his village in southern Egypt, having obtained a doctorate in logic. The village had a celebration for him and his cousin Hasanayn asked him, 'What's that logic you keep talking about?' Haridi said, 'Are you married?' Hasanayn said, 'Yes.' Haridi said, 'From a big family?' He said, 'Yes.' Haridi said, 'And of course your wife is a virtuous lady?' Hasanayn said, 'Yes.' Haridi said, 'And you have a dog that your wife takes care of?' Hasanayn said, 'Yes.' Haridi said, 'That is logic.' Hasanayn left and on his way met his friend Awadayn. So he asked him, 'Did you, Hasanayn, understand this logic that Haridi is talking about?' Hasanayn said, 'Are you married?' Awadayn said, 'Yes.' Hasanayn said, 'Do you have a dog?' Awadayn said, 'No.' Hasanayn said, 'Then your wife is a whore!'"

Hamid said, "Aman passed by a kaka (a Kurdish man) sitting in front of a river and asked him, 'Can I cross the river on foot because I don't know how to swim?' The kaka said, 'Yes, cross it.' The man went into the river and after a few steps, his foot slipped and he struggled with difficulty to avoid drowning. He came back to the riverbank and asked the kaka, 'Haven't I asked you if the water was deep?' The kaka rolled his fingers into a ball and said, 'A duckling no bigger than this has just crossed here.'"

Hilmi said, "There was a man who, whenever he passed the corner near his house, saw a fat, black woman praying 'May God bless you my son, Khaisha, and may you become president of the republic.' Some time passed, then once he saw her at the same spot watching the president's motorcade in silence. He asked her, 'Why have you stopped praying for your son?' She laughed and said, 'Here's my son, right in front of you. May your turn be next.'"

We all laughed and Mervat, Rasha, and I went back to mimicking comic situations and punch lines from popular radio shows. The car proceeded, running away from unknown ghosts that might materialize before us at any moment, until we arrived at Erbil and went noisily into the hotel, paying no attention to the silence that enveloped the sleeping city. As I was getting out of the car I noticed a machine gun under the front seat. I couldn't believe that we had been sitting on top of our only means of protection the whole time without being aware of it. Of course it would have been impossible to use that machine gun had we been actually attacked. One bullet to the driver would have toppled the car deep down into the wadis at the bottom of the mountains.

We slept soundly and had a long rest the following day. Hamid came in the evening to accompany us, together with Jamal and Sulafa, to the village of Ayn Gawa, a suburb of Erbil. We walked in its clean streets, then went inside the house of one of the local musicians to drink tea. I found out that there was not a single illiterate person in the village. I took some pictures and wrote an article that I sent to *al-Zahra* magazine with the title "Little Paris in Northern Iraq." These were the happiest days in my life. I felt I was growing up and developing as a journalist.

I never forgot that trip, nor the tension I felt there. And here I was, coming back to Iraq, which was in a real state of war this time. A war with armies, tanks, planes, and rockets blowing up towns along the twelve-hundred-kilometer borders. Between that war and the ethnic conflicts with the Kurds and the religious conflicts between Sunnis and Shia, Iraq has had its share of problems. As for us and our simple capabilities, we keep looking for our relatives and friends, wondering about their disappearances: Where are you, Anhar, Basyuni, Tariq, Suhayla, Fathallah, and Ragya?

The Iraqi stewardess rolled the food cart as Muhammad Abd al-Wahab sang:

"This is one Arab people / United on one tumultuous path toward renaissance."

Noha said, "Why am I so hungry? Didn't we eat cookies and chocolates at the Amman airport?"

Kamilia said, "What else have you eaten all day long? That doesn't count."

I said, "Bon appetit! What kind of trip is this, without singing?" I began to draw on my memory of school trip songs and started singing. Mona, sitting behind me, belted out a folkloric song that all the passengers listened to, laughing boisterously.

Then there was silence in which the only sound heard was that of eating implements. I raised my head and turned it to the right and the left languorously. The stewardess came back saying, "Tea"; another came saying, "Coffee." I took some tea and asked for a little glass, the way they served tea in Iraq.

I remembered the samovar that we bought for the *al-Zahra* office and placed in the reception area as if it were a piece of art. We seldom used it to make tea: only during parties. We used an Aladdin heater in the winter and we placed a large kettle on it to boil water for the tea and to add some humidity. I extended my foot lazily as Noha got into a conversation with Kamilia.

I felt sleepy and my body began to succumb, but my memory took me back to my early days in Iraq, during the years of success and prosperity, before the change in direction.

*

I couldn't keep up with the festivals and cultural events in Baghdad. As soon as I was done covering one conference, I'd begin on another. Hilmi Amin decided to distribute the material that we had generated, written, and produced to Iraqi newspapers and magazines. We signed a contract with the cultural supplement of the *al-Jumhuriya* newspaper, *Alif Baa* and *Funun* magazines.

At the opening of the Palestinian Cinema Festival the scope went beyond Arab cinema to covering political art that celebrated the struggles of peoples of the world. Artists from all over the world were invited. Among them was the world-famous actress Vanessa Redgrave, who believed in the right of the Palestinian people to return to their homeland.

I went to interview her at the Dar al-Salam hotel. She had on a simple and light muslin dress, and a pair of sensible shoes. She had no makeup on. I looked closely at the color of her eyes, which were a pale hue between green and gray. Her gaze was piercing, steady, and very focused. She sat answering my questions in a simple manner and did not ask me any questions, as other celebrities usually did after I finished my questions and after the formal interview was over. She thanked me and got up to go to another appointment. I ran to the office carrying the first international interview of my life. My life? I had just begun.

When I submitted the written-up interview to Hilmi Amin, he wrote the introduction himself, discarding my introduction. In it he said that the value of an artist is not in his art or his artistic choices only, but in the cause he believes in and fights for. I liked his introduction better. Several years have passed since that interview, during which I have met many famous artists, men and women of letters and thinkers, but I have never forgotten this impressive woman who had respect for her ideals and art and who stood by another people's cause.

We got busy once again working on the book we were writing on the Kurds. We finished our fieldwork, listening to the views of representatives of all Kurdish political parties about the current autonomy and what they wanted to accomplish. We also gathered the historical material and settled on the information we would use. We decided to review our conclusions after we got it all organized. Based on all the information we had, we inferred that the experiment, as presently constituted and implemented, was impossible to sustain. Hilmi Amin asked for an appointment with the information official in charge of the joint book project with the bureau. He went alone, without me, to the appointment. When he came back he said, "They hid from me the fact that Mustafa Tiba had written a book on the Kurdish question and autonomy and that the ministry had rejected our book. This saddened me greatly: we reached the same conclusions that Mustafa had reached. I am certain of it without having to go and ask him. I discussed with them much of the information that the book would contain and analyze and presented my view of it. They got very upset and tried to convince me to drop certain data, but I refused and decided to abort the project. We will begin with your book about the peasants as the first fruit of the collaboration between *al-Zahra* bureau and the Iraqi Ministry of Information."

I said, my eyes filling with tears, "All this effort for nothing?"

He swallowed hard and lit a cigarette, then said, "Nothing was lost. In culture and in politics there's no such thing as a wasted effort. We've learned from the material that we've compiled; we got to know the Kurdish region better and learned much about the inner workings of the Iraqi government as it faced the Kurdish problem. We've also gained contacts and friendships with the Kurds. These are experiences and information we could never have gotten without our work on the book. Right?"

My eyelids got heavy. The plane turned into a spaceship. The passengers rolled around in the air while I sat in my seat. I was seeing my body parts separating from me. My forearm was at the ceiling, my leg by the door. My head spun around and came back to me upside down.

My eyes were focusing on my face. I was astonished. I couldn't find my fingers to close my eyes. My head smiled at me. Anxiety was gone. I asked my head about Anhar Khayun. Aunt Fatma, her mother, was coming toward me wearing a blue dress the color of the sky and the sea. She was dancing like a ballerina atop a marsh boat at an equal distance between the ceiling and the floor. Hilmi Amin came to dance with her. I asked him, "Who said there's no land for tomorrow?" Hatim appeared and carried me off the plane seat and twirled me around. He changed the music to a tango. I was full of lust. Many eyes got loose and ran away in the middle of the aisle. Eyes. Eyes. I looked for Yasir. Hatim said he was in the forest with his gazelle, Zuzu. Rajaa, Ilham, and Sajida stood up, crying. Amal al-Sharqi ran away. Suhayla Bezirgan got onto a horse that went up the mountain, then flew away. Abu Lu'ay, Anhar's boss, opened his mouth guffawing. He extended his hand to me and I shied away. My neighbor, Abu Samira, patted me on the hand and Abu Dalaf gave me a car going to Cairo. Ragya wound a lot of gauze around her head. Haytham held an automatic rifle and stood on the roof of our house in the Shurta district with Jasir, his friend from next door, and Subayha was shouting in the air in celebration of the Iraqi soccer team winning the Young Men of Asia Cup. Umm Ali, Bayyati's wife, sang, "Keep your weapon awake / If the whole world fell asleep, I'll stay awake with my weapon."

Saadi Yusuf gave me a red anemone and said, "Goodbye." The theatre director Jawad al-Assadi took it from me, saying, "The Elephant, O King of Time." Basyuni Abd al-Mu'in came in at the age of five wearing a pair of shorts, holding a basket of toys and a slate board and chalk. He gave them to me and said, "I am grown up now." Muhammad Abd al-Wahab took the microphone and sang:

This is one Arab people
United on one tumultuous path
Toward renaissance
Who better than us knows the right path, righteousness, dignity of
soul, and well-kept pledges?

I smelled fermented dates, cardamom, and cracked wheat boiling on stoves in huge stock pots outside the homes in Ayn Gawa. An anguished woman appeared, standing on the wooden radio shelf in our house in Zamalek in Cairo, asking, "I wonder where you are, Manzuq?" I told her, "At the Farabi Bar." A storm started from the cockpit, sweeping away everyone on the plane. Tied red sacks got up from the plane seats and moved with difficulty toward the aisles. My head got away from the tip of the sack and looked at me in panic. In place of the eyes were black cavities where bees buzzed. Another sack struggled to stand on its feet. It removed the cover. It opened its mouth for the bees to get out. All the heads were getting away and turning into dark mouths and eyes which filled the flying sacks and the bees covered the sky. My head hanging upside down in front of my face said, "You're dreaming, Nora." I said, "I know." It said, "How are you?" in the Iraqi dialect. "Wake up. We are landing, landing, landing." I said in the Iraqi dialect, "Good. Good." Kamilia said, "Welcome back. You caught some sleep."

The Iraqi stewardess announced that we'd arrived in Baghdad safely. It was midnight. The temperature outside was four degrees Celsius and it was raining heavily. She asked us to be quiet and not to move. I looked out the window: a total blackout. I remembered Cairo in 1967, with the glass windows all covered in blue. The plane landed using faint lights as markers on the runway. The wheels stopped and total silence enveloped the plane inside and out. The stewardess was still gesturing to us to be quiet. We were filled with cautious anticipation, realizing that we were really in a state of war. For one reason or another, the passengers stopped talking. I recalled the image of the airport that I knew: a constant buzzing sound and everybody coming and going noisily, with optimistic faces. I felt tired. I let my head fall back and gave in.

Three Other Knocks

November 1976

Explosion

> There was an explosion today at Baghdad airport that caused a great number of casualties in the terminal. The shattered glass was responsible for the bulk of the injuries among passengers and their families. The casualties included over two hundred Egyptians wounded as the explosion took place at the time of the arrival of an Egypt Air flight from Cairo. The wounded were taken to the airport hospital. The number of those killed was seventy persons and ten of the wounded were in critical condition.

I stood motionless in front of the television screen until the news was finished. It was 9:00 p.m., Hatim was getting ready to go to bed. Our day was coming to an end. "What are you going to do?"

I said, "I'll go right away, of course."

"I'll come with you."

I said, "Of course not. You have work tomorrow and I don't know whether I'll work all night or not. I'll call the Iraqi News Agency first to know which hospital they've taken the wounded to, then I'll leave a message for Hilmi Amin."

He said, "Nora, I'll go with you to the hospital where the picture will be clearer. Then I'll leave you."

I said, "No problem."

We went to the emergency room. We found dozens of wounded suffering from severe burns. All the beds in surgery and internal medicine were taken. The other wounded were scattered on seats in the corridors where visitors were not allowed because of overcrowding. I sat in the midst of the wounded asking them what happened. They all told the same story: a few minutes after the arrival of the Egyptian plane, while everyone was waiting at the baggage claim area, a bomb exploded right where the bags were, instantly killing all those nearby, mainly airport workers. And because of the new airport's modern design, with lots of glass and metal pipes, the explosion carried a lot of flying glass that injured people inside as well as dozens of meters outside. This was what considerably raised the number of casualties.

I asked a hospital official about the total casualty number, as people usually greatly exaggerated the numbers. He said, "Why don't you speak to the hospital director?" The director was not there, according to officials. I thought that didn't make any sense in such an emergency. Other officials were afraid to give me any figures. By coincidence I saw the journalist Imad al-Bazzaz in front of me and I asked him. He said, "The news has been published by the Agency and this is what you'll get, Nora. So don't try anything."

I said, "It's my right to verify the data, not just take the Agency's figures without support."

He said, "You're obstinate. The director of the hospital won't take responsibility for telling you before clearing it up with security."

I looked again for the director until I found him in his office, which I had visited several times before. I asked him. He looked at the paper in front of him and said, "I can give you a list of the names of the Egyptian casualties. The number of the Iraqi casualties are exactly as announced."

I went to the injured to ask them if there was anything I could do for them. Some gave me telephone numbers to inform their next of kin where they were. I met by chance our neighbors Dr. Michael and Tante Violette, from whom I found out that most of the Egyptian Copts in Iraq had been there en masse, waiting for an Egyptian priest they had asked the Coptic Church to send because they had difficulties with priests from other denominations. I found the priest, Father Hydra Abadir, with massive burns on his face as if his skin had been completely stripped off. He lay in his bed surrounded by people, but he seemed to be holding his own. I said to him, "Praise God for your safety, Abuna. Welcome to Baghdad."

He said, "May it be God's will."

Dr. Michael stood up to introduce me and my husband to him. I asked if there was something I could do.

Father Hydra said, "Thanks, my daughter. The doctors are all around us and God is the Healer."

Tante Violette said, "Are you going to the office now?"

I said, "Yes. I have to send the news to Egypt right away."

She said, addressing Hatim, "You'll let her go just like that? You're a man with a strong heart!"

Hatim said, "People in Egypt are very worried now. Publishing the names of the casualties will calm their anxiety. This is her job and her mission."

We left quickly. Hatim went home and I went to the office accompanied by Dr. Michael and his wife. I found Hilmi Amin waiting. I asked him, "Should I tell the Egyptian News Agency the news as I have verified it or send it to *al-Zahra* and have the scoop?"

He said, "Humanitarian considerations are more important than a scoop, Nora. I contacted the ambassador a short while ago and told him you'd get the information. He has a representative from the embassy who's on his way to the hospital right now. Come, let's dictate the story to the embassy and the Egyptian News Agency, then send our detailed report to the magazine by ticker, and afterward I'll take you home."

In the morning I found him sitting with Dr. Michael and his family and some youth next to the bed of Father Hydra, who was cutting up a round bread roll and distributing the pieces to those around him. I sat on a chair in front of him. He gave each of those present a piece of bread until only the heart of it was left. He gave it to me smiling in joy, saying, "Here, daughter, you deserve the heart. We found out that you've sent the names to Egypt and reassured them about us."

I took it from his hand, then returned it to him saying, "Thank you very much, but I am fasting today."

He said, "Take it and keep it until iftar."

I said, "Where would I keep it? Here, Amani."

I was surprised when Tante Violette jumped up in front of her nine-year-old daughter, saying, "You got the heart, Amani! You got the heart!"

The girl smiled and put the piece of bread in her mouth and moved her feet happily as if she were savoring a piece of chocolate. I didn't understand what was happening. Dr. Michael said, "You've won it, Amani. You've won it."

I asked myself, "What exactly have I given up?" I looked at Abuna, whose face grew redder despite all the layers of shining ointments, and said, "Thank you very much."

"You're a good Egyptian girl."

"When will you be discharged, God willing?"

"When the doctors decide. I'd like to get out soon to meet the congregation."

I said them, "Did you have difficulty worshiping before?"

One of those present said, "The presence of a Coptic priest is important. And it's happening for the first time here. It is true that the incident has spoiled our joy, but Abuna is now with us here in Baghdad to shepherd his flock and take care of the church, get to know the problems of his parishioners and help them."

I said, "Here they have Chaldeans, Syriacs, and Assyrians. I think they are somewhat different denominations."

Abuna said, "The Lord looks after all of us. When the Holy Pope found out the desire of the flock for a priest to come and shepherd them, he welcomed the idea greatly and his request was granted by the Iraqis."

I didn't like what happened and realized that the large crowd that welcomed him at the airport would attract the attention of security and that it wouldn't end well. The Christian Egyptian situation was different from the Christian Iraqi one, as I understood from their discussions that sometimes took on a mysterious character when I mentioned the relationship between Christians and Muslims in Egypt. I wondered why that was so, because all my life I never felt there was religion-based discrimination in Egypt. We were once sitting at Dr. Michael's house with a group of friends, most of whom were Christian university professors. The invitation was on the occasion of Tante Fayza's visit to Baghdad, and for one reason or another someone brought up an incident of a Christian being persecuted in Baghdad. I said, "Thank God we don't have Muslim persecution of Christians in Egypt. And, as my Iraqi friends tell me, religion is not a big issue here. Perhaps there are more problems between Sunnis and Shia than between Muslims and Christians."

Amani replied sharply, "And the killing of the Christians in the era of the martyrs, wasn't that killing by Muslims?"

We all burst out laughing but when the laughter stopped, a gloomy silence took over. The anecdote, joke really, that the girl said, attributed to the Muslims what the Romans did to the Egyptian Christians, several centuries before Islam came on the scene. But it revealed the amount of misinformation that the girl was absorbing, creating a sense of persecution by Muslims of Christians before Islam.

Hilmi Amin said, laughing, "What's this, Professor? Correct your daughter's history."

Dr. Michael said, "Yes. She's just a child and things got mixed up."

I left the hospital with Hilmi Amin. I told him about my apprehensions concerning the Christian Egyptians gathering in this manner and what Iraqi security might make of it. He said, "So long as it is a normal religious celebration of an Egyptian priest coming to Baghdad on religious business, it would be acceptable. But that doesn't mean that security will be indifferent to it. This is a security state that is extremely sensitive. The important thing for the community is to tread carefully and not get into any trouble."

I asked, "What kind of trouble?"

"If they just keep to themselves, things will pass. But if they move one step toward Iraqi Christians, security will not let them advance one centimeter."

I said, "Even in the religious realm?"

He said, "They'll need to move extremely carefully, with balance and wisdom."

I said, "What are all these secret spider webs in different societies?"

"In all societies there are different sets of secret webs. One of them is religion. Learn how to observe and analyze what you see so that your journalistic assessments will be correct."

I said to him, "Sometimes I feel they are hiding something."

He said, "This is the nature of minorities. They need to stick together to acquire and strengthen group solidarity."

I said, "But in Egypt they are in the millions. How can they be a minority?"

He said, "Relative to the total population they are."

I met Father Hydra several times after that, sometimes at Dr. Michael's house and at other times in our office. We gave him donations of clothes we no longer needed to distribute to the needy in the church. He accepted them happily and told us whenever someone in the congregation needed money or to solve their problems with different branches of the Iraqi state. He was a wise, cultured, and meek man who recognized the humanitarianism of the atheist Hilmi Amin and respected that in him and always prayed for him. He recognized my understanding that all religions were equal. I liked his flexibility. This was my idea of a man of religion.

Iraq announced that the perpetrator of the Baghdad airport explosion was Muhammad Hasan Sheltagh, a man of Syrian origin, and that he had placed an explosive device in a suitcase.

The perpetrator appeared on Iraqi television exhibiting signs of fear and confusion and confessed to all details of the operation. He said that he was put up to it by the Syrian regime and that they had planned it to coincide with the hajj season to guarantee the highest number of casualties. Both television and radio kept broadcasting the confession, and interrupted different programs and movies to rebroadcast it.

April 1977

A Visit

We received news of mass roundups of leftists in Egypt. Hilmi Amin was afraid of being prevented from leaving Egypt on his return or that he would be arrested if he took the bureau press material to Cairo as usual. Large clouds of uncertainty hung over the office, dispelling its usual optimistic atmosphere. I was suffering from being separated from Yasir, but tried to hide my pain so that Hatim would not remember that he forced me to leave my son behind or remind Hilmi Amin of his inability to go to Cairo. I woke up filled with anxiety and preferred not to speak. Hatim asked me what the matter was and I said, "Nothing." I went to work, moving around in silence. And even though it's been months since I came back from Egypt, I still had not adjusted to my separation from my son. I was surprised to see Hilmi Amin standing before me while my tears were running freely down my cheeks and I held a picture of Yasir. He said, "Go to Cairo."

"It's been only a few months since I returned. I cannot ask Hatim to pay for a ticket so soon."

"Go on a business trip for the bureau. I usually carried our features, reports, and ads to submit to the bosses at the magazine. The bureau will pay your fare to do that for me."

He fell silent as I impatiently awaited his next sentence. He said, "Ask Mahmoud Muwafi about the circumstances of arrest of journalists or leftists. At least we would understand the news we've been getting."

I said anxiously, "Is this true? Do you really agree to my going to Cairo?"

He said, "Of course it is true. When have I ever told you something that wasn't true?"

I said, "You are the sweetest Hilmi Amin in the whole the world. When do I leave?"

He said, "Tomorrow, if you like."

I went home in a totally different mood, jumping for joy and singing songs of happy return and warm and affectionate reunions. I told Hatim and he said that I was lucky, going back to Yasir and leaving poor Hatim behind, all alone. I said, "I'd only be gone for one week. I'll book a ticket tomorrow on the first flight."

As soon as I arrived in Cairo I traveled to Yasir in Maghagha. On the way I was assailed by apprehensions: What if he didn't recognize me? I had left him several months ago, still a baby. He would have gotten used to his grandmother and his aunts. That would be too much to bear.

I saw in front of me a small child, with a brown complexion, smiling. He looked closely at me with mischievous eyes as I embraced his grandmother, eager to hold him tightly close to my heart. I was afraid to scare him away. I kissed him. He laughed. I carried him. He looked at me with inquisitive but unafraid eyes. I sat, still carrying him, and took out of my bag a toy space ship. I placed it on the floor and moved it. Its top was lit and projected a picture of moons and stars making crackling sounds. I let him get off my lap and stop in front of the toy until it stopped moving completely. He turned it on again as he moved the rug away from its path. He had figured out that it would turn quicker on the tiles. He called out to his aunt to watch his new toy.

I took a fire truck from the bag and placed it in front of the spaceship. I extended the moving ladder and took down the water hoses and asked his aunt to fill the reservoir with water.

He stood, puzzled and asked me, "I tate it?"

"Yes."

"I tate one."

His aunt asked him, "What's your name? What does your father do?"

He said, "Yasil Hatim. Daddy chanic gineer."

She said, "What does mama do?"

He said, "Ja nist, ha ha ha."

He bowed his head as he played with the fire truck hose and looked at me slyly.

His aunt said, "Where are they?"

"Badad," he said.

I carried him and took him back to Cairo. We took with us his young nanny, Nadia, with whom he played at his grandparents' house. He didn't object. He got into the car with me, telling me about his friends, and then slept in my arms the whole way to Cairo. When we arrived, he ran toward his grandmother, into her open arms. He played in the house, which he seemed to know quite well. My mother told me that she brought him to Cairo every so often to see the doctor. He ate while playing until nightfall. Suddenly he seemed to remember something and began looking for his aunt. I told him that she would come after two days. He went back to playing, then he looked at me with an unspoken question in his eyes and shouted in a soft voice that hit me right in the stomach: "Natia, Naaatia."

I carried him. He began taking turns looking at me and at Nadia. Then he kept moving from my arms to her arms then mine again saying, "Mama," then "Natia," his tears flowing down his face until he fell asleep.

In the morning I went to the magazine offices. I turned in the material to Sabri Hanafi and told him about Hilmi Amin's suspicions and apprehensions. He said, "These are very strange ideas. Where does Hilmi always get these suspicions from?"

I met Fahmi Kamil on my way out. I extended my hand to shake his. He extended his with unmistakable coldness. Sabri Hanafi said, "This is Nora. Don't you recognize her?"

He said, "Yes."

I went home and called Mahmoud Muwafi and asked to meet him since I didn't find him at the magazine in the morning. He invited me to his house. I called Tante Fayza and told her that I was carrying gifts for them sent by Ustaz Hilmi Amin and I conveyed to her Hilmi's apprehensions and my coming visit to Mahmoud Muwafi. She told me that she'd go with me. I found her in front of the apartment building, getting out of a cab. I noticed a deceptive, classy beauty that made her look in her late thirties rather than in her mid-forties. She looked very Egyptian with her big, honey-colored eyes and her light brown hair that cascaded smoothly onto her shoulders. She was well dressed in a simple manner that was pronouncedly different from Hilmi's appearance. Her style told me she had been keeping up with fashions for a long time. I compared her attire with that of Hilmi and asked myself, "Why hadn't her taste rubbed off on him?"

A young maid ushered us into the salon and after a short while Mahmoud Muwafi, very tall and jovial, came in. He greeted Tante Fayza warmly, an indication that the two of them had known each other for a long time. Then he said, "We did not expect all this success so fast. It seems you have spread very widely in Iraqi newspapers and that is why we are investigating the possibility of expanding our bureau outside Egypt and opening new ones."

He added, "I told Hilmi Amin when he asked me about you that all those you've worked with encouraged your joining the bureau and that you're a good journalist."

I said, "Ustaz Hilmi Amin has mentored several generations and he is taking good care of me. He is working around the clock. I leave him in the afternoon and the following morning I find that he's finished other tasks, which means that the bureau is open twenty-four hours a day, as if it were a news agency and not a press bureau."

He said, "That's the Hilmi Amin I know. He wants to transform the bureau into a central bureau for the whole Middle East, and he is right, the region needs and can support such an expansion and the Iraqi experience deserves close coverage. What you are doing is indeed extremely important."

I asked him directly, "Can Hilmi Amin come to Cairo without risk of being arrested or banned from traveling?"

He was astonished. "Why would he be arrested?"

I said, "In Baghdad there is a rumor about interrogating communists on trumped-up charges."

Mahmoud's wife, Buthayna Amer, came in carrying glasses of juice. Before serving us she called out to her son angrily and asked him, "Where did this briefcase come from?"

The boy said, "It belongs to our neighbor."

"Take it to them," she said. I saw it there. It was the same black leather Samsonite briefcase. I didn't understand why Buthayna was asking about it.

She went on to say, "I am sorry. A state security officer is living next door and I am always suspicious of their things."

Mahmoud said, "Reassure Hilmi that there are no problems with his coming to visit Cairo."

Tante Fayza said, "His coming here is a lot easier than our going to him in Baghdad. The tickets are costly and the girls are in school and the trip is hard. At least when he comes to Cairo, he can get some fresh air and get out of Baghdad's stifling atmosphere and get some rest. Besides, as a journalist he gets fifty percent discount on his airfare."

Mahmoud said, "He should come to Cairo so we can see him."

I thanked him and we left. When we got into the taxi, Tante Fayza said to me, "I was uncomfortable about that briefcase."

I said, "What briefcase?"

"The one that belongs to the neighbors," she said.

I said, "I don't believe it. Mahmoud Muwafi is one of the most important patriotic journalists."

"He may have been forced to do it. Tell Hilmi to wait a little. Tell him everything that took place. He'll understand. He must get his information some other way."

I tried to make sense of the whole situation but got lost. I said to Tante Fayza, "I don't understand anything. What has Hilmi Amin done against the Egyptian government while he is working abroad to get him arrested?"

She said, "When the roundup begins, they won't care whether he is in Egypt or India. They have a list which they go through indiscriminately. They call them protective campaigns. And sometimes they make up charges of belonging to organizations working to topple the regime. But, on the whole, Sadat has not opened the door to detentions."

I said, "God preserve us!"

She said, "Take care of yourself, Nora. Stick to your journalistic work only."

I said, "I defend my opinion any way I can and working in journalism gives me an opportunity."

She said, "He never settled down in his life, always under threat, no matter which government. Baghdad came as a respite, where he can get some peace of mind and a little increase in his income to help in Mervat's marriage expenses."

I got out of the taxi in Tahrir Square to buy a few things from downtown and left Tante Fayza to continue on to her house after she promised me a visit with the girls. I said to myself as I crossed the road in front of Issaivitch Café, where the intellectuals sat, that Tante Fayza had learned caution from Ustaz Hilmi. They are both a little crazy, right? Why all this fear? What is this strange world I find myself in? But, as the Egyptians say, "One who is burned by the soup blows on his yogurt." The specter of prison was still too vivid before their eyes, and raising children in the absence of the bread-winner was an experience they would never forget.

I spent my time between the magazine and home. I tried to spend most of the time with my son, cursing the world and the circumstances that made me leave him. I took him to the doctor. He was suffering a severe skin allergy. He changed his medication but refused to let him go back with me to Baghdad.

151

I went out of the doctor's office crying. I booked a return ticket, asking myself about the losses we were both incurring because of my work in Baghdad and my inability to take him there or stay with him. On the eve of my return, I took him back to his grandmother in Maghagha. I said to him, "Papa Hatim and I love you very much."

He said, "I know."

I ran outside, into the street. I spent a sleepless night as my mother tried to ask me in jest about my neighbor in Dora in Baghdad, Sabah, saying, "You've finally found someone to teach you to be careful and cautious."

I went back to Baghdad, to the city that I loved and knew perhaps better than Cairo where I was born. I returned with a wound in my heart that I knew only work would keep my mind from dwelling on: being away from my son, Yasir. I found that Hatim had hidden little, tender gifts for me everywhere: in flower vases, with the toothbrush, and in the sugar container. In the morning I took the food that Tante Fayza and the girls had sent with me to the office. I found that in my absence Hilmi Amin had been very active, that he had put together an exhibition for three Iraqi painters in al-Khalsa village in collaboration with *Sawt al-Fallah* (Voice of the Peasant). Now we had a home in Iraq to which we could invite Iraqis.

Hilmi Amin was surprised at Sabri Hanafi's opinion, saying, "Sabri has always been wrong in his assessments. How did you leave things with the chairman of the board?"

I said, "I asked his secretary to set up an appointment with him. A week later she asked me to call him at home because he was sick. When I explained to him my circumstance and the way I've been appointed in the magazine, which was not yet official, he said, 'Go back to Baghdad and the matter will be brought up before the editorial board next week.'"

Hilmi Amin said, "And why didn't you wait until next week?"

I said, "My leave was finished and I didn't want to appear irresponsible to you. My presence or absence would not influence their decision, anyway. Besides, the material on the al-Khalsa book is almost complete and I want to go to the village tomorrow to meet the movie crew members."

He said, "What's the latest news from Cairo?"

I put a cassette tape of Ahmad Adawiya in the recorder, letting him judge for himself. The recording was a song everyone agreed was vulgar and in poor taste but which was playing everywhere.

December 1977

Ustaz Gamal

I sat down writing a piece after Ustaz Hilmi went out with Anhar and Abu Ghayib finished cleaning the place. I heard the bell ring. I didn't expect them back so soon. I found an extremely tall young Egyptian man. He said, "Is Ustaz Gamal there?"

I thought I had seen him before but I didn't know where. I said, "Who's Gamal? We don't have anyone by that name."

He said, "Hilmi. Hilmi Amin?"

I said, "No, he's not here. Who's this Gamal you were asking about?"

He said, "Nobody. When does he come back?"

I said, "In the afternoon, after five. And who are you, sir?"

He said, "I am Fawzi al-Meligi. He knows me."

I said, "Would you like to leave a telephone number?"

He said, "No. I'll pass by."

When Hilmi Amin came back, I told him about Fawzi al-Meligi's visit and asked him, "Who was this Gamal?"

He fell silent and started lighting a cigarette and said, "This was my code name in HADITU, before July 1952. Give me a detailed description."

I said, "He had black hair, and a fair complexion. I didn't feel comfortable looking at his face and he was extremely tall."

Hilmi Amin's voice suddenly got louder and spoke very fast and angrily, "I don't know anyone fitting that description. Did you let him into the office? I told you before: it is forbidden for anyone to enter the offices in my absence. Where was Abu Ghayib? Did he see him?"

I said, "I told you I did not let him in. Abu Ghayib was running errands for the tenants. I also said that I didn't feel comfortable with his being there. I don't understand why you are angry, even though I haven't given you cause."

I went back to my desk and sat to write my feature without saying anything more. Anhar sat, silent, her face pallid, pretending to read a magazine.

Hilmi Amin left the room. I heard some noise in the kitchen. He came back a little later holding a glass of coffee. I noticed a change in his tone when he said, "I am sorry, Nora. You know that Sadat has decided to finish us off. Wherever we are, we are targeted for assassination."

I said, "I don't know. I don't understand why Sadat would assassinate the Egyptian left. He might put them in jail. Yes. But, assassinate them? Why? Does the left represent such a threat to the Egyptian government that he would send an agent to assassinate a journalist, admittedly a communist journalist, working in another country? Or is there something I don't know that would make this action seem natural?"

He said, "You know everything about me. These rulers are power crazy. They don't understand the meaning of patriotic opposition. They have become so vain and arrogant that they don't accept the existence of a single opposition figure objecting to what they do. And, as you know, the man has gone crazy."

I said, "He is not Idi Amin and Egypt is not Uganda. Up till now he has been applying the law. There are no more political detainees or detention centers in Egypt. There are people charged with political crimes. He is just a weak ruler who cannot compete with Abdel Nasser's charisma or people's love of him, and he cannot fill the vacuum after him. So, he has had to take a different path, perhaps the opposite path to get people's attention, because he cannot play the same role. He figured it out his own way and came to the conclusion that the United States was the winning horse; so, why not ally himself with it and carry out its plans in the region? As for assassinations, I don't think so, because he can change the region with his cunning underhanded methods without appearing before the world as someone who kills the opposition, but as a man of peace instead."

He said, "Your experience with this secret world and with relations with third-world dictatorships is very weak. I hope I am wrong and that you are right."

I said, "Maybe you should rest a little and we can discuss this tomorrow."

Anhar said suddenly, "I don't trust rulers. All Arab rulers. They can liquidate anyone with a dead heart, drag him to death if they want to, or dissolve him in acid to make him vanish forever."

I said, "Egypt is not Iraq."

Hilmi said, "True. Egypt is not Iraq, but times are different now and conflict has become unavoidable."

I said, "That's not necessary in your case, because you don't represent a real or great threat. I'm not going to repeat it; when things calm down we can talk matters over together."

Anhar said, "If the bureau stopped working, as you tell us from time to time, and you end up in exile and pursued even here in Baghdad, would you think of leaving for Europe? And which would be safer for you?"

Hilmi said, "If the circumstances here are good, I'll open a press agency and get an unpaid leave from the magazine. In that case we can expand, because we would be a private agency and Iraq would welcome such a set-up. And here the situation will be more secure because it is close to Beirut and Yemen and is part of the homeland. My life here is not a real exile." Then he went on to say, "To be perfectly honest, I would not be able to bear being in a country which speaks a different language and has different customs and traditions. Europe, for me, would be another prison."

I said, "And if you ascertain that here is not safe?"

He said, "I'll take my chances. I might go to Yemen, but not to Europe, because if Sadat decides to assassinate the opposition, he'll get us no matter what."

Anhar said coquettishly, "I'd prefer to go to Paris. More freedom there."

I said, "Paris or Brazil?"

She said, "Brazil has to do with work. I have a friend who works at a news agency there and he tells me that jobs are available. It is also far away from the whole Arab world, but Paris, that's where intellectuals go."

Anhar stopped speaking suddenly and gave Hilmi Amin a long look full of questions and hope. I felt I was out of place, so I said, "Time to go. See you tomorrow."

They both said, "Goodbye."

Third Text

Three knocks on the door of memory restored life to days that were lingering as they turned toward disappearing forever. I tugged at the end of the thread of time that used to tame mountains and humans. The days broke loose and came tumbling down on my heart. I tried to stop their ruthless flow and pay attention to what was happening around me, but I couldn't. Inside of me there was a rush seeking to recapture the flow of the days and once again feel the pleasure of the pain that didn't contain the moment. I was carrying my suitcase to the airport on my way to Baghdad, not believing that I have indeed arranged to leave my six-month-old son with my mother-in-law in Maghagha, two and a half hours away from Cairo. I was hoping to find out why and how Anhar Khayun, my Iraqi friend and colleague at *al-Zahra*, had disappeared. I also wanted to visit my house in Dora, hit by Iranian bombers, and see if my neighbors there were all right. I wanted to meet with Basyuni Abd al-Mu'in who joined the Iraqi army and to give him a letter from his family urging him to go back to Egypt. Among the tasks I set for myself was visiting *al-Zahra*'s office to complete liquidating its affairs and to look for Hilmi Amin's articles. I planned to do all that while attending and giving a paper at a conference for educating women after teaching them how to read and write.

I asked myself as I set foot on land at the airport, "Did you want to bring Haytham to a country in a state of war? Just to breastfeed him?"

The officials welcomed us, apologizing repeatedly for what happened in Amman. We exchanged glances, surprised at how fast the news traveled. They asked us to go to the line of cars waiting outside and to take the cars, saying that we'd find our suitcases at the hotel.

"The capital is calm. No one knows when the rockets will hit the city. There are skirmishes on the borders. Whenever a building is blown up we rebuild it quickly. There's only one building that we've left as is, in ruins, downtown on al-Rashid Street as a reminder of what Iran is doing to us. You'll see that tomorrow," the escort who took the car with us summed up the situation, and then fell silent. The convoy proceeded in a joyless manner, quickly and without any interruption, along the rain-battered roads. I was familiar with Iraqi officials' silence. They showed the guest great respect, but also placed a distance and an impenetrable wall between themselves and that guest. They would politely inquire about one's health and work, then fall totally silent. I learned to observe the driver as he looked at the rear-view mirror with a sweeping glance without anyone realizing it: a quick neutral glance that didn't overlook a detail. The instructions usually flowed from one official to another with a small gesture. Everyone was so polite and stiff. That was the Baghdad in which I lived my most beautiful years. There were now bridges I had never crossed before and towering gates of a new neighborhood in the heart of the old city. I had seen that neighborhood totally surrounded by shantytowns that were blown up and rebuilt. I had left Baghdad before it was completed. There was a new Baghdad erupting. Huge apartment buildings were replacing small homes in the ancient and venerable Salhiya neighborhood. There was a gigantic picture of Sadam Hussein, five stories high. I had never heard of such a colossal size except for those of Mao Zedong. The car turned right from Gamal Abdel Nasser Square, crossing the Tigris and passing by the Radio and Television Building and proceeding parallel to Abu Nuwas Street. I remembered the masgouf fish grilled there over an open wood fire and the famous restaurants along the river and summer nights and the Baghdad Hotel, the only deluxe hotel in the capital until I left it in 1980. The al-Mansour Hotel loomed high in the distance. The cars suddenly turned toward a building I had not entered before: al-Rashid Hotel, carefully proportioned, white marble magnificence, thermal doors, "the world's most technologically advanced hotel, fully automatic, Baghdad's pride," according to our escort as he opened the car door.

We could see a faint light at the entrance. The garden was totally dark. We slipped into the hotel noiselessly. Rooms were assigned quickly, then we found ourselves having dinner in a cafeteria that was open twenty-four hours a day.

I heard the clock ring two o'clock in the morning as I opened the door to my room. I ran to the bathroom and opened my blouse, and before I could take out the pump from my bag, milk had flowed out of my breasts. I was soaked in a pool of warm liquid. I let it flow and wet my clothes, no longer in a hurry to take them off. I turned the water on and got into the shower and began to watch the milk drops as they dissipated in the water, changed color, and disappeared down the drain. The strong gushing stopped. I held the pump and pressed it hard against my breast. I felt my veins relaxing and the quick pulse slowing down gradually until the heat cooled off. I wondered at the pain caused by my fingers as they pressed against my body. I remembered Haytham's mouth, which I felt at the beginning but which I forgot as the sucking slowed down and settled into a rhythm. I never thought of my breasts as vessels. And despite my knowledge of women's physique and their makeup, the mental image was quite different from what we felt. I never felt that my son was sucking milk from a container outside my body, but rather from my whole body, as if the milk came from all my innermost veins, from a spring spread all over the cells responding to what my son needed. But here I was, becoming aware of the vessel.

I decided to begin the day early in the morning by pumping the milk and collecting it in a glass so that I would know the amount I had to keep producing every day. The sound of Haytham's crying at the time of his first nursing awakened me. My breast was softly stinging, not yet at a crisis level, just a little tickle allowing me to move around in the room to fully unpack. During the night I had just taken out my woolen suit and left it out so that the wrinkles might disappear before the opening of the conference. I found the music channel and let the music fill the room. Now the room was mine. I placed my papers and books on the desk, my perfumes and makeup on the dresser, an empty glass on the nightstand, my toothbrush and body creams, towel and slippers in the bathroom. I created my small world and would soon get acclimated to it, even though in hotels I am usually woken up by every whisper outside my door, or every movement in the corridors.

I asked myself as I was going to breakfast, "Why wasn't I afraid of bombs or being in a city under bombardment? Was it because I had known and lived in peaceful Baghdad for such a long time? Did I summon that city to mind as one of its daughters deserving to share in its collective destiny? Or did I know that the real war was out there, not in the capital?"

I shook off those thoughts and got busy thinking of setting up my own program, parallel to that of the conference. I would do that by the evening at the latest. I would meet my women friends from the women's union and *al-Mar'a* magazine and also some politicians and journalists. I had to arrange other times to meet authors and visit the office, al-Khalsa village, and my friends. When? One of the hotel workers approached me and said, "Good morning, Ustaza. I am Said al-Sheikh from Sharqiya province in Egypt. I have been working here in this hotel ever since it was opened. Are you, Ma'am, a journalist from Egypt?"

"Yes. Can I be of service?"

He said, "I and any of the Egyptian workers in this hotel are at your service. If you want to change dollars, I am at your disposal. The dollar in the black market is much higher than at the bank. May I ask you for a favor: would you take some money to my family in Sharqiya? I'll give you my family's telephone number in Zaqaziq and my brother would come and get the money from you. Please, I have children in school and you know the rest."

I said, "But you, Said, don't know anything about me."

He said, "Pardon, Ma'am. The Egyptian pound here has a very high value because customs officers at departure time don't ask any questions about Egyptian pounds and they prevent us from taking dollars and Iraqi dinars out. Therefore we sell them at any price. Why have we left home if we can't send money to our families?"

I said, "They have every right to protect their economy and you have every right to send your savings to your country. But you knew what the law here was before you came. Anyway, prepare the sum you want to send."

I remembered a conversation with the Iraqi minister of labor at the end of 1976, almost six years ago. Baghdad then had opened its doors to Egyptian workers without a visa. Millions of young Egyptians came. It was estimated that before the end of the eighties they had reached five million Egyptians.

I asked the minister, "Why aren't Egyptian workers permitted to transfer their money except for a small percentage of their wages?" (Twenty-five percent for those hired and contracted inside Iraq and fifty percent for those signing their contracts outside Iraq.)

He said, "They should bring their families here and spend the rest of their savings buying land or investing in commerce or real estate like all Iraqis."

I said, "Not every expatriate can bring his family. And even if that were possible, he cannot bring all those he's responsible for.

This creates a black market for the Iraqi dinar and the dollar which leads to smuggling, not because they are criminals, but because they are in need."

He said with utter and amazing simplicity, "We are one nation with an eternal message. The laws give contractors the right to transfer half their salaries. This is enough to support their families in Egypt."

He was a young man, about forty. He had on a white suit and striped shirt of the latest fashion back then. A model Iraqi official par excellence: a rare smile, calm nerves, total self-confidence, and an unseen barrier between himself and anyone he talked with. Only the deputy prime minister Tariq Aziz had any popularity among intellectuals and journalists.

The situation remained the same. Egyptian workers were still smuggling their money to Egypt.

The cars took us to the Monument to the Unknown Soldier. I climbed the stairs to find a large, expansive plaza, with Iraqi army soldiers and officers standing on both sides. Behind them were lines of non-army officers wearing the dark khaki army uniforms. I was struck by the great number of women wearing black. I rushed to my friends among them to shake their hands as my tongue could not form, let alone articulate, questions to them. I saw friends who appeared strong in their everyday lives, not easily revealing their true feelings but rather telegraphing them in a way that often shocked me. For the first time I saw them gushing with emotions and as we hugged I heard many stories of martyrdom. There was not a single Iraqi home that had not lost one or more of its men. They were now overcome with tears as they led us forward to recite the fatiha for the souls of the martyrs. Some of them went to the front of the lines after regaining their self-control and took upon themselves the task of organizing the delegations. I knew that they organized this type of visit almost weekly to present the point of view of the state and advocate its cause. Ilham stepped closer to me and told me in whispers that she had heard a message from her brother whom they had officially declared to be a martyr a year and a half earlier on the Red Cross program on the radio. His wife and children had been in mourning since the announcement. Now she didn't know anything additional, but she hoped he would return safely soon with the prisoners-of-war exchange. The ceremony ended. I tried to ride with her in a large car carrying Iraqi journalists but I heard a calm, commanding voice, "Please, come to this car." I obeyed to spare my friend any kind of rebuke. Here she was just a public employee doing her job. Our own arrangement placed me in a special car with three other guests. We arrived at the conference site. The hall looked like a beehive. One sign indicated that the conference was being held under the auspices of the prime minister. The ministers entered the hall quietly. I noticed that they were all wearing military uniforms and solid shoes, that they were all thin and had frowning faces. The speeches touched upon Iraq's struggle against imperialism, Iranian occupation, and the people's ability to stand fast. Then we were invited to lunch, compliments of the minister of defense.

The Egyptian scholar, Shahira al-Asi, said as she laughed, "Why are these ministers so skinny?"

Manal al-Alousy, chairwoman of the Union, laughed as she said, "It's the slenderizing law."

Shahira said, "There's nothing wrong with slenderizing, but still they look too skinny."

A few words were said, about how just the cause was and how defending the homeland took precedence over all else, even though Iraq did not want the war. I was amazed but I said nothing. I looked at the Iraqi women sitting at the tables around me: Arab women, Kurdish Ba'thist women, and nationalist women. After the collapse of the coalition of five parties, including the Communist Party, that used to rule, Iraqi communist women totally disappeared from Iraqi conferences. The Iraqi censorship office objected to their being mentioned in my book on Iraqi women and crossed out the names of pioneers. Even actresses and piano players, all of a sudden, have become enemies.

I heard from my friends that President Saddam had been a neighbor of Shahira and Naima al-Asi in their house in Dokki during his studies in Cairo and that they had remained in touch. Shahira's laugh resounded throughout the dining hall. She was a strong, vivacious lady whose way of thinking and learning I admired. She dealt with the place confidently, but how well did she really know people here?

We went back directly to the sessions, and papers were given one after the other. I was happy because, among non-Iraqis, I was the most knowledgeable about the Iraqi experiment in combating illiteracy. I was there from the very beginning and wrote several articles about it. The plan for the project was to eradicate the illiteracy of men and women under forty-five within three years. A presidential decree was issued stipulating that all men and women were to attend classes in the evening and punishing those who failed to attend. Thus a man would be summoned to the police station in his neighborhood if his wife missed one class. Everyone attended regularly and the project was a success. The irony, both sad and funny, was that the project was modeled on a previous Iranian experiment, but the Iraqi success rate was higher because they were more strict.

Several times during the sessions I sneaked off to the bathroom, carrying an empty cup, which I had added to my handbag, anticipating the constricting stall where I would have to pump the milk out. I followed a regular regimen of emptying my breasts every three hours. I felt awkward leaving the sessions so regularly, especially since my name was placed in front of my seat with the Egyptian delegation.

I hadn't gone to the *al-Zahra* office yet. Talking to myself I said, "Nora, this is only the first day." Tante Fayza had told me that she had sold the apartment with its contents to a young Egyptian man to use as a residence. When I asked her about our papers and books and whether she had shipped everything, she said, "I shipped most personal effects and some papers. I didn't ship most of the books.

I left them for him with the furniture, telling him that I'd send a colleague to check the papers and books again, for maybe some of what I left behind was important."

I decided to ask the driver of the car on our way back from any activity outside the hotel to pass by the Sheikhaly apartment building and to leave a note to Abu Ghayib with my name and telephone number at the hotel so that the new owner of the apartment might call me and arrange for a time for me to visit.

They took us immediately after lunch to al-Rashid Street to look at a stately apartment building that had been blown up during a bombardment raid. They fixed everything around it and left it in ruins as a testimonial of the destruction perpetrated by Iran. On the road we could see the white Toyota taxis, the latest car models and luxury passenger cars, mostly Volvos which the Iraqis loved, and a few Mercedes Benzes, whose numbers increased when President al-Bakr allowed them to enter the country duty-free with their owners if they held advanced degrees as an encouragement for Ph.D. holders to return to their homeland. The small and old model cars that had been present in great numbers before had now disappeared from Baghdad streets. The red buses with upper decks reminded me of how Hatim and I used to run to the upper deck when we first arrived in Baghdad, early in the morning on a Friday before the burning sun of July began to do its worst.

I awoke from my reverie when I heard the voice of my escort, Layla, as she explained the raid that destroyed part of the bridge and some buildings. I got depressed and quite angry as I recited that Arabic proverb to myself: "He beat me up and cried and ran ahead of me to complain." I couldn't hold Iraq innocent in this stupid war. Maybe I was wrong, but how do I reconcile the present with all of Iraq's attempts to pick a fight with Iran in the past? The car stopped and they set a time for us to return to it, leaving us to wander freely in the area. Siham and behind her several friends came up to me and she said, "We won't leave you. You know every nook and cranny in Baghdad. What should we buy?"

I said, "The lower value of the Iraqi dinar vis-à-vis the dollar and even the Egyptian pound makes anything here cheaper. Buy Iraqi kilims, pure wool blankets, and hand-knotted Persian rugs if you can carry them. But I, of course, will buy books published by al-Ma'mun publishing house. You can't beat the price: one Egyptian pound and sometimes half a pound a book."

She said, "You hit it on the head: books."

We started to move. I pointed to al-Sahah Building, saying, "Saddam, his wife Sajida, and their infant son Uday were living here in November 1963. The forces of Abd al-Salam Arif stormed the place to arrest him but luckily he had fled the building a few minutes earlier. Then he was arrested a long time after that."

Sarah Badr said, "He escaped to Egypt. Didn't he?"

I said, "He escaped more than once. What you're talking about was in October 1959 after taking part in the attempt to assassinate Abd al-Karim Qasim. Then half an hour before the raid on his house he escaped from the house of his uncle, Khayrallah Telfah, whose daughter he had married. They didn't find him, but arrested his cousin Adnan. He moved from place to place until he crossed the Syrian borders, and from there he made his way to Egypt."

Salma said, "They told me there was an inexpensive duty-free shop."

I said, "There it is, the duty-free shop, then a store for small appliances, then the largest store in Baghdad, Orosdi Bak, and on the opposite sidewalk the Murabba' Café."

Kamilia said, "They say the Egyptians have turned it into an Egyptian haven."

I said, "There's everything here. A contractor can come here to hire men of all crafts. The alleys opening to the street have turned into an Egyptian quarter. Here you'll find prostitutes and dancers, some of them Lebanese who claim to be Egyptian, since Egyptian dancers are better known. There are unbelievably underage prostitutes. As for the 'official' red light district which gained fame in the thirties, it is in al-Bab al-Mu'azzam neighborhood. It was known as the Alley of Rogina Murad, named after a courtesan who became famous during the British Occupation. She is the sister of the most famous female singer in Iraq, Salima Murad, wife of Nazim al-Ghazali. An interesting story is told of another Iraqi courtesan whose name is Hasana Malas. The story's incidents take place during al-Shawwaf's coup attempt against Abd al-Karim Qasim in 1959, which was supported by the United Arab Republic (Egypt and Syria). The Egyptian embassy was inundated with leaflets denouncing the government of Qasim and saluting the struggle of Hasana Malas and Abbas Bizo. The fiery announcer Ahmad Said read the report on *Sawt al-Arab* (Voice of the Arabs) radio, describing the pair's fantastic heroism. It was a big scandal throughout Iraq because she was the most famous courtesan and he was the biggest pimp in the city. That was a big blow to the media of Abdel Nasser, who was in a propaganda war with Abd al-Karim Qasim. This main street extends until al-Shurja, an Arabian bazaar where spices abound. You can buy cardamom, which they call 'hail' here. From this street is al-Nahr Street, parallel to the River Tigris, where they sell fashionable clothes, and it extends to the gold market."

Then I laughed and said, "You can buy a gold lion."

Mona said, "An official picture of the lion eating a man."

I said, "Yes, in a sense, eating him." We all laughed. Then I continued, "The surrounding streets have numerous markets: Safafir Market, where they sell copperware and woolen kilims. It resembles Cairo's Khan al-Khalili. Then there are other markets in side streets: the Sabonjiya for soap and related products, the Aba Khanah which is a market for upholsterers, al-Bazzazin where they sell cages for pigeons, although the Iraqis don't eat them, and pet birds and rabbits, which they also don't eat because they menstruate. The Shia don't eat catfish, which they call 'gray.'"

Kamilia said, "Why?"

I said, "One day a Shi'i worker from the Marshes asked my husband whether the Egyptians ate gray. And Hatim said yes and the man said, 'Even dogs won't eat it.' We asked our Shi'i friends about the reason and they said it had muddied the water while Sayyidna Ali performed his ablutions. I said, 'Bravo, it saved its whole kind from being fished in Iraq and other places where the Shia are.'"

I pointed to a large building and said, "This is the central post office. You can call Cairo if you wish. I'll go in to see if I have any letters in my mailbox."

We went in together. I found Abu Wisam in his usual place behind the glass window.

He said, "How are you, Sitt Nora? Long time no see."

I said, "I've been away. These are my friends from Egypt and they want to call home."

"With great pleasure."

I said, "I also want to open my mailbox to see if I've received any letters."

He said, "Please, go ahead. Abu Mervat has paid the rent for two years in advance. Where's he? Is he out of town?"

His questions revived a painful memory but I got a grip on myself and went to the mailbox while nodding. I found various papers mostly in Hilmi Amin's handwriting which I knew quite well, some letters with a tape saying "Opened by the censorship," a small brown notebook belonging to Anhar Khayun. I put everything quickly in my bag so as not to draw the attention of the man who was now speaking with a colleague of his while pointing in my direction. I saw the man's hand raised in greeting. I called my house. No one answered. I called my neighbor Salwa Mandur and I told her that the situation in Baghdad was reassuring and that I hadn't contacted her brother Tariq yet and that I would try calling my family the following day.

Siham asked me as we left the building, "Did you find anything in the mailbox?"

I said, "Old invitations, too late of course, and some promotional material."

I began to describe to my friends the different places and what they had to offer, but I was thinking about the papers I had found.

We visited some bookstores and bought many valuable books at very inexpensive prices, and we tied them with twine and wondered how we were going to carry them back to Cairo.

So, the letters had been opened by the censors. That made some sense, but what about Hilmi's and Anhar's papers? Had they also been opened? And why did Hilmi Amin put them in my mailbox? Did he want to keep them out of the office or did he intend for them to come to me? And why? Did he want me to read them or just preserve them? Did he want to save them when he felt that he was dying and did not want Tante Fayza to see them and dispose of them? Did he want to spare her the hurt? And why did he place this responsibility on my shoulders? My God. Could these be the memoirs he was recording with me? I remembered what he said when he talked about Hemingway's *The Old Man and the Sea*: "You are the boy in that novel. You are the crutch on which I lean. Don't let me down."

Do the papers have any indication where Anhar might be, whether she is alive or detained somewhere? Did he put these papers in a place so obvious, within the sights of the censors, so that they would miss them, thinking they had already censored them? Nora, stop all of that until you've found out what they were first.

I came to as Mona was asking me, "What do you think of this leather?"

I said, "It is typical Iraqi design and you can hang it on the wall. Buy it."

We bought some inexpensive gifts. I let them take the bus but I walked to our old office, passing the Ministry of Information, Tahrir Square, and Batawain Market up to Mashjar Street. Baghdad had witnessed speedy development, riding the winning rocket of oil wealth. What happened to it? Why are we Arabs unlucky? Could petroleum be our curse? I didn't find Abu Ghayib downstairs. I climbed the stairs which I knew quite well. The third stair after the landing on the first floor was still broken. My eyes welled up with tears. I rang the bell. No one opened. I wrote a note of my schedule and telephone numbers at the hotel and pushed it under the door. I looked at the closed wooden doors of the apartments of Karima and Engineer Ali and Tante Violette and Dr. Michael. I couldn't bring myself to knock on any door and I ran away from the whole scene. I don't know why I remembered the Egyptian humorist Mahmoud al-Saadani's first visit to us in the office. Maybe I needed a smile.

I heard the noise and recognized his voice. Hilmi Amin had told me they had met the night before at the Baghdad Hotel and that he had promised to visit us. He had left *al-Khalij* (The Gulf) newspaper after having a disagreement with them. They couldn't tolerate his acerbic humor. He stood in the middle of the office, scrutinizing it as Hilmi Amin was saying to him as he pointed at me, "My colleague, Nora."

He said, "Bravo, bravo, old chap. A real office, heh? How did you manage to do it so fast? Heh?" Then he turned toward me and said, "Is working for an Egyptian magazine better than working for your Iraqi magazines?"

I realized that he didn't recognize me. We had met at *al-Zahra* offices in Cairo once a long time ago. I loved his articles and his humor. I decided to play a game on him by using the Iraqi dialect, so I said, "Ustaz Hilmi is a good man. You have free press, not like these wooden newspapers."

He said, guffawing, "Wooden newspapers? Good man. What kind of wooden dialect is this? Hilmi has been harassing you, of course. I know him well. Quite a playboy on the sly."

I said, taking on a very dignified tone, "No, I swear. He treats me exactly as if he were my father."

"How disappointing! Listen, Hilmi, I want one like her, you hear me? Just like her!" he said.

"If you like, I can get you my friend to work with you. She is a good girl."

Hilmi Amin couldn't continue to play along and we both burst out laughing as he looked at us in amazement. Then Hilmi said, "Don't you remember Nora, Mahmoud? Our colleague from *al-Zahra*? The athlete?"

I said, "Hello, Ustaz Mahmoud. We miss your words and your laughter around here. We are all so pleased you're in Baghdad and we hope your presence will change the city completely. Maybe you'll teach them to laugh."

I came into the conference hall as the delegates began to be seated. I went to my seat and placed my bag next to me, feeling as if it radiated with an invisible energy. I gathered my strength to concentrate on what was going on.

We changed our clothes quickly at the hotel after a quick dinner to go to the theater to attend a prestigious fashion show presented by the Iraqi House of Fashion. In that show women graduates of the ballet institute presented a review of the history of Iraqi fashions accompanied by dance music. The designer Feryal al-Kilidar used the latest colors and muslin, georgette, and silk to demonstrate the succession of civilizations in the land of Ishtar. I loved the show since I saw it for the first time in the mid-seventies and wrote about it fondly. The designer transformed the models into butterflies moving lightly from the Sumerian to the Akkadian and the Assyrian civilizations, going across different eras clad in soft delicate fabrics or hand-woven ones and embroidered with motifs from each civilization. I go gaga whenever I see her embroidery of al-Wasiti's illustrations of the maqamat of al-Hariri on muslin fabric using the latest fashion colors; every year I've seen the show. Her fashions would say that the region had a Roman influence, so we see fabric skipping one shoulder, leaving it bare, and that the Persians were here leaving their imprint on the turquoise colors and the form of stylized simple flowers. From bedouin clothes with their loose fitting Arabian abayas to the black garments of peasant women on tall, slim figures, the models looked like goddesses alighting gracefully from heaven to soft, rhythmic Iraqi music and the verses of Abd al-Razzaq Abd al-Wahid captivating every spectator. The show's message announced to the world that the civilizations that came one after the other on this land were fighting to survive.

The idea of war has always seemed stupid to me, an idea whose price was not paid by soldiers alone but also those around them. Defending one's land was one thing and getting into a useless fight for reasons of vanity and the like was something else. Judging from a lot of information that I had gathered during my work here before and from my personal experience, I was never convinced that war was inevitable. I say this despite knowing the fanatical attitudes on both sides of the Iraq–Iran divide. I have studied the history and witnessed the intermarriage among the various parties in the region, which only recently saw the creation of the state of Iraq. I've known about the antipathies between Persians and Arabs, Shia and Sunnis, the tangled elements of the history of Zoroastrian, Babylonian, Akkadian, and Assyrian civilizations and cultures. My travels all over Iraq, north and south, gave me the right to interpret events according to an intuitive sense that went beyond reason and data alone, and to see and analyze what was being said on a different scale. My journalist friends wanted to sum it all up, dismiss it really, in short and easy press reports: they wanted to advocate for their cause, ending the war, or whatever. I didn't comment. I returned to my room filled with thoughts and feelings, my body weary and my spirit confused. I wanted to leave myself open to enjoying the show whose butterflies transported me to Ishtar's heaven, but a persistent current of curiosity and desire was eating at my heart, pushing me to unravel the secret trove of Hilmi Amin and to know. I turned on the music, then emptied my bag on the bed. My hands trembled as I went through the papers. As I had expected, there were invitations to attend artists' exhibitions. How I loved their posters. I called it the poster revolution, back then. There were invitations to plays; a panel discussion on Iran's role in the region; a flier for a Syrian kebab restaurant; one for a store selling potato chips and various seeds and munchies; a letter from Tariq Mandur telling me he had settled in Suleimaniya, written on August 1st, 1980, a whole month before I returned to Egypt; a letter from the postal and telephone authority saying in reference to your previous letter, we regret that we are unable to provide your office with a telephone at this time in view of the difficulty of extending lines in your area; a letter from Tante Fayza sent from Egypt a few days before her arrival in Baghdad. Hilmi did not receive that letter and she did not look for it. Perhaps Hilmi Amin deliberately did not give her the key.

Anhar's Papers

I saw Anhar's notebook in the middle of the papers. I examined it as I turned it over. Ustaz Hilmi Amin had given it to her as a gift and had given me one just like it that he had brought from Paris at my request. It was a notebook of natural-colored coarse paper, and its pages were fastened together by a twine thread knotted daintily at the bottom of the notebook. My daily work with paper made me fall in love with it in all its forms and shapes. I loved its primitiveness and the ancient scent that wafted from it because it was manually cut, forgoing the precision that has come to dominate our lives now. I opened the cardboard cover on which Anhar had affixed her first color photograph. It would have been better if she had placed a black and white picture of her to be more in line with the ancient feel of it. She wrote on the first page:

These are my days; if you disavow them, you disavow knowing me forever. I am doing this for the sake of my mother.

Anhar Khayun

These are private papers as I expected. I couldn't have left them in the post office and I didn't know if I had the right to read them. When did they arrive at the post office? Did Anhar leave them for Hilmi to read or did she keep them in her own drawer and he discovered them when she left? Has Tante Fayza laid hands on them after his passing? Did she read them? And why has she left them behind in the mailbox? Could Anhar have mailed them to him after she left? But Hilmi didn't mention in his letters that he knew where Anhar was. I opened the first page and read:

My story begins many years before my birth in a dreamlike place, enveloped in a fog that hides houses, humans, and plants and makes events seem as if they've never happened. Water covers the whole area endlessly and mornings appear on the horizon veiled in dusk until the sun rises fully, wiping away the morning's mystery and dew, giving the entities of that world a chance to reveal their features. Our houses appear in the midst of the water as if they were the nests of large birds made of bamboo sticks, tree branches, and palm tree fronds. Grass grows in our pathways in the water and it rises like tips of sturdy spears drawing the map of our world. We have constantly to control the growth of the grass and also feed our cattle and to make room for shallow-draft balam and mashuf vessels, as well as other kinds of boats and canoes, which are our only means of transportation. Our houses are little islands at the mercy of the waters, which, if they rise, could submerge the houses. But it seems that there is a covenant between us and the waters that makes it possible for both of us to live side by side: the water would not rise without giving us advance notice. We have learned to read the water's ciphers from early childhood by using platforms or kibashas made from reeds and rushes to raise the houses above the water level.

My story resembles the place: mysterious and magical, treacherous and kind, simple and harsh and fatal. Yes, it can kill. Don't wonder at that, for whoever does not respect the will of the marshes ends up losing everything, including their life. My story, which started before I was born, is the story of love and hate, ecstasy and blood and peace. I'll go back a few years so that you'll come to know all the contradictions that have shaped my life and which made me realize, when I saw you, that your coming into my life was not a coincidence as you imagined, because fate, which spun the black and white threads of my life like a spider's web, would not have brought you into this world of mine for no reason. When we first met I thought of you as a savior and this was why I always came back to you whenever the circle pushed me out, since I had already been caught in that mad part of the web of life.

I was born to a mother from a large clan living in the midst of the marshes in one of the villages of Amara Province. Her family were peasants who owned several buffaloes and cows and did some hunting and fishing in addition to cultivating rice and some other crops on the bits of land scattered among the islands in the marshes. It is largely a poor society governed by strictly observed ageless customs and traditions but it is also a homogeneous, closely knit society. One morning the village woke up to news of the killing of Mahdi al-Khayun, a young man said to be one of the most handsome and manly youth of the clan, at the hands of his friend Abbas Khatir. The two had been rivals for the attention of a splendidly beautiful young lady, by the name of Khulud. And because Mahdi was the son of the chief of the Banu Asad clan, and a sayyid descended from the Prophet and his daughter Fatima, he thought he was more worthy of her and decided to marry her. He started writing poetry extolling her beauty and declaring his love for her and followed her everywhere she went. But he knew that he had to obtain the approval of his friend Abbas because he was her cousin and as such had a right to her hand. Mahdi also knew that Abbas loved Khulud and would not give up that right. Abbas had warned him more than once to stay away from her but it was no use. One day Abbas saw his friend and Khulud together so they fought and Mahdi, who was not yet twenty years old, was killed. His friend went to jail since it was deemed to have been a quarrel. But the story did not end there. The clans met and decided to marry off the brother of the slain man to the killer's sister, as was the custom, so that she might give birth to a son who would take the slain man's place. It was a custom that came about originally from a lofty idea and not out of a desire for revenge as it became with the passage of time, because it brought closer the two fighting families in a marriage producing a child who would then belong to the two families. Thus life would return to normal. According to custom, the head of the clan had the right to choose the killer's sister. If the killer did not have a sister who was a virgin, he would then choose his cousin, and the process would continue until it got to the youngest daughter in the whole clan. Neither the girl nor her family would have the right to refuse the arrangement.

Thus my mother, at the age of nine, was taken, crying and wailing, to the slain man's family. She lived in their midst until she grew old enough and she married my father, Mahdi's younger brother. According to custom, the marriage had to continue until the woman gave birth to a son, whereupon she would have the right to go back to her own family or to stay with her son. But if she gave birth to girls then she had to stay with the family until she had a boy. We call such a woman a fasliya, and the word is used as an example of the utmost humiliation and disgrace. Thus a woman who is oppressed or mistreated by her husband or his family might say, "Why are you doing this to me? You think I am a fasliya?"

My grandmother tormented my mother in every conceivable manner. She assigned to her all the hard work at home and outside. My mother suffered all the insults and she had no rights whatsoever to complain or return to her family. But all the hardships she endured made her the most skilled girl in the village in cooking, baking, cultivation, weaving, animal husbandry, and making dairy products. The days also revealed a splendidly beautiful young lady despite the hatred heaped upon her every day from the early morning by my grandmother, who spent the whole day bewailing her slain son, singing heart-rending elegies of her son, declaring a grief that would never end and a state of mourning with the color black covering everything.

And despite my grandmother's attempts to strengthen the roots of hatred toward the little girl in her young son's heart, my mother's care of him as the only one close to her in the whole family won him over. So, when it was time for the two to get married, my mother's femininity sprang into full bloom and she became a beautiful wildflower that all the young men of the village desired. Unfortunately, she looked like Khulud, her cousin who was the cause of Mahdi's killing; all the more reason for my grandmother to hate her more than before. My grandmother would shove her roughly whenever she passed by her and she would fall and get bruised and wounded all over. Some of those wounds left deep scars that stayed with her all her life.

My mother's complexion was the color of red plums because of her work outdoors under the relentless rays of the sun. They made her wear a long black dress and covered her long hair under a large black turban with thin tassels, the usual garb for peasant women in that area. As children we would see her emerging out of the thick reeds and the morning fog on the mashuf as if she was the beautiful sunrise or one of the houris of paradise with her captivating beauty and her gentle spirit. As I remember those days I almost choke on my tears and I realize my father's secret affection for her since he was afraid to show the slightest interest in her or feeling toward her in front of his family, who lived in the same house with us. What aggravated the situation even more was the fact that my mother had given birth to four girls and not a single boy that would have given her the right to go back to her family. She got pregnant every two years upon weaning her daughter. My grandmother kept pestering my father to take a new wife who could give him a son and to have my mother serve the new wife until my mother would also bear him a son and leave. But my father decided to apply for a job in Baghdad and take his little family away from the climate of hate in which he was living. When he got the job, my grandmother went to the family living next door and got him engaged to their daughter and got him married quickly. Then she pressured him to take his new wife with him to Baghdad, keeping us in her house. You can imagine what happened to us until my mother had our only brother. Two years afterward, my grandmother took the baby and kicked my mother out. I would see her in the morning and the evening furtively checking on us through the reeds, without us daring to speak to her. Then my grandmother fell sick as a result of long months of hard work that my mother used to perform. Then she became bedridden, unable to care for us. My mother appeared one day in our courtyard in a scene that I'll never forget, saying to my grandmother, "I don't know any other mother besides you. You are my mother. Why are you shunning me?"

"What brought you here?"

"You. My children are cared for by their family. They are your children, I know, and I don't fear for them but I cannot stay away from you. I want to serve you in your old age."

"I will never forgive your brother."

"Yes, you will. One day. For he too lost his youth."

My grandmother screamed and kicked her out mercilessly, saying, "I will never forgive him no matter how long I live. And you will be deprived of your baby just as your brother deprived me of my son, the apple of my eye, Mahdi."

My mother left in tears but she came back the following morning. She took the cattle to pasture, she cleaned the house and cooked, then left without talking to anyone. I remember that day very well as if it were yesterday. It was winter and the water had been rising as usual since January. My grandmother and my cousins were building kibashas under our house using reeds and papyrus. But in February when the water rose to unusually high levels, people of our village began to remove the reed crossings and the palm tree trunks that they used as bridges connecting the various islands. By the middle of the following month, the waters had risen even further, submerging many of the low-lying islands. Neighbors began deserting their homes. I'd look at my grandmother's eyes and see fear but also pride. I wanted to tell her, "Why don't we call my mother?" Then I'd refrain when I heard her crying in the night, weeping over Mahdi as if he had died only yesterday. My mother kept coming and going and I could hear her footsteps outside reinforcing the foundations, and when the next morning came we would know that we had been saved one more day. Did my grandmother know that my mother was doing that? The question perplexed me. If she did know, why didn't she invite her to come in? And then we'd all help her. Many of our clan were unable to continue living on their islands after the water kept rising all the time. They abandoned their houses and were taken in by other families until the water would recede. They all remembered the big flood in which the stores in the market, government offices, the school, and the brick homes built on the riverbanks all went underwater.

The family built narrow pathways of reeds and papyrus. I would see my mother riding the mashuf, using a pole to push it forward, bringing more reeds to us. I would ignore her so that my grandmother would not chide me. We would exchange furtive glances as tears flowed down her cheeks. She kept coming and she kept working. Then the water rose suddenly on March 20 and the flood reached its highest point. We rejoiced, knowing that God would soon send us relief, since the highest flood levels occurred between the rising of the Pleiades and its setting over a twenty-five-day period. Once that star set, there would be no increase in the headwaters of the river. My grandmother used to say that the water of the Euphrates needed twelve days to travel from the source of the river to the marshes and that there would be no rising in the level of the water once those twelve days from the setting of the Pleiades had passed. But the star disappeared and the excess water kept coming on the twenty-seventh and the twenty-eighth days.

My grandmother said as she cried, "This is not water. This is a disaster. Oh my son, Oh Mahdi! Woe is me! If only you were here!"

I raised my head. My mother was standing there in her black clothes and big turban, emerging from the dusk of dawn as if she were an invincible being inspiring awe. She said in a commanding voice, "Anhar, gather your sisters and brother and carry everything you can to the balam standing outside. Come on, girl, hold on to my arm." Then I saw her carrying my grandmother in a lightning quick movement, taking her out to the balam. In a few minutes we looked like an army detachment pulling up its camp quickly for fear of an enemy attack. She had gathered a lot of reeds and papyrus, and my sisters and I kept reinforcing the platforms of our island and my mother moved with energy the likes of which I have never seen in my life. My mother came back on the forty-second and forty-fourth days until my grandmother gave in and let her take care of the house. Our life went back to normal. My father came with his new wife and learned of what happened, but there was nothing he could do. He spent two days with us and one day after he left, my grandmother died. He came back and took us all to Baghdad. And for the first time I saw my mother smile even though she looked after his new wife as if she were her own daughter and cared for her children as if they were her very own. She continued leading the same kind of life she was used to in the marshes: working all the time, wearing her black clothes and eating her usual simple, coarse food even though my father's financial conditions had improved considerably. He went into business with my cousins in a commercial enterprise that brought him a handsome profit, which led to a better life and education for us. I was lucky that my father insisted that we get an education despite my grandmother's objection. I was also lucky or unlucky, I don't know, to have taken in and clearly understood everything that had befallen my mother, and I took an oath that my life would not be owned by anyone and that I would never place myself at the mercy of customs or traditions. For that reason, when my cousin proposed to me and I had no objection to him, I told him that I would try the engagement and if we were successful, that would be good and fine, but if it were not successful, then the marriage would not proceed. My uncle got very angry, but my father reassured him, saying that it was a good idea and that it would benefit his son more than it would benefit me, and that he, my father, ultimately had the last say in the matter. Thus I found myself once again at the mercy of tradition, repeating what happened to my mother without power to bring about any real change, in spite of my education and the death of my grandmother. My mother stood by my cousin, urging me to go through with the marriage, saying that what God had decreed must come to pass. I asked to finish my university education first and to get a job before marriage. My cousin agreed reluctantly, but my mother got angry and said I was "overdoing it." And even though the Regional Command of the Ba'th Party had issued an edict against a girl's marriage to her cousin against her will, and although the government had instructed girls to go to a police station to report such a compulsory marriage, declaring any contract of this kind null and void on the spot, only one girl in Baghdad went to a police station and reported her father, her uncles, and her brothers. It was a big scandal which no other Iraqi girl was able to go through.

I tried seriously to get close to my cousin Muhannad, whom I had known since I was a child: he had a good moral character, was successful in his studies and his job. But as time went by I felt that invisible barrier that was always there since my mother was constantly crushed by words that called her the ugliest of names. I couldn't escape that hatred that my father's family held and which at times came out of nowhere. I couldn't have that equanimity that made it possible for love to take root and grow. I couldn't find a strong enough reason to convince my father and mother to break off the engagement. Therefore I decided to face the problem head on, myself. At the beginning I couldn't understand the reason for the great effort my mother was exerting to make me agree to the marriage, urging me to get closer to Muhannad, whom she loved and looked after and invited to dinner, when he could enter our house at any time. I had suspicions about her reasons for accepting him so readily: did she think that a fasliya's daughter would not find a husband unless her cousin married her? But two of my sisters had married outside the family in a very short time. Did she still feel guilty about my uncle who was killed by her brother?

I joined the Communist Party. I read widely and got a job as a journalist, to get a closer understanding of society. It was then that a concept that I had completely missed dawned on me: the concept of women being living embodiments of their dispossession, that they not only perpetuated but reinforced that which repressed them. My self-awareness made me realize the true extent of the tragedy that my mother was living: she was now preserving the very traditions that had so thoroughly destroyed her life, without any rancor. She even wanted me to be a carbon copy of her, to beget "men." I said to myself, "I'll belong to the man I love because he will also belong to me." That was what I felt when I saw the piercing glances of your eyes that told me that love was your number one goal in life. Do you know when I fell in love with you? And why? Not when we met at the party's party, and not because of something to gain, as you might think and as you sometimes spell out when you're drunk, but when you told me one morning that sacrificing for the sake of the homeland was no good if you were not first and foremost responsible for your family. At that time I did not know the status of Aunt Fayza. I thought she was your wife and I loved you even more when I realized your responsibility toward her. But I found myself in a trap bigger than the one in which my mother was caught: torn between her duty to her clan, which sacrificed her, and her duty to us, her children.

You know something? My mother once confessed to me that she dreamed of freedom despite falling in love with my father and was counting the days to get pregnant again and give birth; perhaps it would be a boy, in which case she would go back to her family. She didn't think for one moment that being free meant abandoning us, her daughters, and my father. She told me, "I kept the nine-year-old girl inside me, thinking, all alone, of her childhood that had been snatched away from her, of her youth which had been wasted, of her family home where she chased little chickens and gathered the eggs from the coop. When the boy came she was happy and couldn't wait to wean him and for the two years of nursing to be over." When the moment of freedom came, suddenly there was revealed to me the connection between the child I had been and the woman I have become. When my mother-in-law kicked me out, I understood the lesson and discovered that I had been the victim in all cases. I also realized that your grandmother did not hate me as she imagined, that there had grown between us an affection, an interdependence."

I told her, "This thread, mother, is the kind of love that ties the victim to the executioner. Because an executioner cannot be an executioner without a victim."

My mother said, "But your grandmother was also a victim. She was not just the victim of my brother who had killed her son, but the victim of her own son himself, the victim of coveting a woman he knew full well was not his."

I said, "How do you know that Khulud was not in love with Uncle Mahdi? Can you be certain the two were not in love with each other?"

My mother looked very confused. It seemed she hadn't thought of this obvious possibility before or that she had deemed it improbable because it would have meant that her life had been wasted for the rash act of a man defending something that did not belong to him, and that he deprived his cousin of her beloved and did her another injustice when he came out of jail and married her, for no one in the clan dared approach her, since she was his fiancé or because she was the source of bad luck.

My mother said, "The two families had read the fatiha of Imam al-Abbas and pledged to marry Khulud to Abbas when they came of age. Great harm would come to the parents of the boy and the girl if they did not fulfill their pledge and go through with the engagement. Anyways, let's leave the past in the past. I have loved your grandmother and pitied her when I understood what it meant to have a son whom I raised with my tears, my hard work, in joy and strength, then have him snatched away in the prime of youth before wedding his bride. I understood her pain, so I had sympathy for her and that was why I returned when she kicked me out."

I said, "I love you, mother, but I will never be like you. I will be what I want for myself first and foremost."

She said, "When I left the house, I stood confused outside the door, not knowing where the balam would take me. The reeds that stood in my way for the first time cut me and the wounds gave me back the feeling of being alive. Finally, I cried from the pain as any human would. I couldn't find my way to my father's house even though I knew where it was even in the dark. My mother had died a long time earlier, after my brother went to jail and after my marriage. My father married my aunt to raise his children. I realized at that time that I knew nothing in my life except the prison where I grew up. I couldn't recognize the features of that child that I had been in my father's house. I confronted myself. I brought it out and sat her on the edge of the balam which was making its way with difficulty through the sharp tips of the bulrush and told her, 'Finally you've come back to life.' The girl looked at me for a long time and then asked me, 'Who are you?'

"I cried. You know why? I missed my present life at the time. I arrived at my father's house a total wreck. I kissed his hands that were shaking from the insult and told him, 'Don't get angry; I'll return to my children in the morning.' The following morning saw me going around the house from the outside, seeing you on your way to school and back, gathering firewood and piling it up by the door, cutting grass for the cattle, picking up your clothes from the clothes lines, folding them and leaving them neatly bundled on the wooden barrel. At night I went back to my father's house to listen to my stepmother's constant wailing and complaints. One day I pushed my way into my mother-in-law's house when I heard of her falling ill and the rising water. I knew that she missed me and tried to believe that I had already fulfilled my reason for existence, giving her a little boy to replace her son. But believe me, daughter, no one replaces anyone else. The boy that she had waited for for a long time was my son, not hers. Your grandmother aged suddenly the moment she saw the baby, because she realized the truth. She couldn't confront me or the family with that realization. Hence her decision to kick me out was the only practical solution so that her failure would not be there in front of her day and night. The blinders were taken away from her eyes and she knew that she loved me as I loved her for we had shared a life together, even though on the surface it was characterized by hate. This was because neither of us had a self-image in our memories without the other since her son was killed. I was her shadow and she mine."

I said, "This is the most painful kind of dispossession no matter what noble sentiments were associated with it. I will seek a man who will give me my share and your share of lost love. And I will find him and he might give me as much as was denied you."

She said, "My beauty has won your father over. He loved me. Between us we have this shared intimate life and several children. So, don't feel sad for me. I've lived a happy life."

I fell in love with you, Hilmi, when I realized how much you loved your family and homeland. And I am telling you it was I who chose you. It was I who decided that you belonged to me even before you met me and fell in love with me. I am Ishtar's daughter.

I closed Anhar's notebook. I did not know how it found its way to the mailbox, but I knew that I'd do my best to get it to her. How will you find out where she is in a few days, when Hilmi Amin, with all his contacts, could not find out? Maybe he did and maybe she can explain to me what he wants of me. I became aware of the sound of the water that I had turned on to fill the bathtub before I opened Anhar's papers. I slid into the water whose warmth relaxed my nerves and banished exhaustion from my muscles as I tried to coax the last drop of milk from my breasts in a semiconscious, mechanical manner. When I was done I came out of the water, refreshed. Now I didn't want to sleep at all or waste even one minute of my time in Baghdad. I wanted to breathe its air and bring back to life all that I'd experienced in it. Faces, smiles, places, and music came back to me in a long reel of Iraqi writers of whom I have been fond: al-Jawahiri Abu Furat, Bayyati, Saadi Yusuf, Gha'ib Tu'ma Farman, Fuad al-Tekarli, Jalil Haydar, Hasab al-Sheikh Jaafar, Aid Khasbak, Yasin al-Nusayyir, Muhammad al-Jaza'iri, Kamil al-Sharqi, Hamid Said, Muzaffar al-Nawwab; Jawad Salim's monument in al-Nasr Square, Dia al-Azzawi, Dia Hasan, Layla and Suad al-Attar, Lut-fiya al-Dulaymi, the shrine of Mawlana al-Kazim, Najaf, Karbala,

Kufa, the Malwiya Minaret of Samarra, the fire of Baba Gargar, the marshes near Basra, Anhar Khayun, the mountains of Saffayn; Jamal and Sulafa, Hamid, Nariman, Nafi'a and Layla and Juwan, my neighbors in the Shurta neighborhood, Umm Safaa and Umm Sami, and my neighbors in Dora neighborhood, Abu Dalaf, Umm Jamal, and Umm Samira.

I got up to call Anhar Khayun's house in Kazimiya. I dialed the number and heard it ringing for a long time. I asked myself whether it was that late. Maybe the young members of the family were out and Aunt Fatma was an old lady who wouldn't answer this late. I shouldn't be disturbing people like this. Tomorrow I'll try again after breakfast. I changed the world music station on the radio and heard Nazim al-Ghazali singing an Iraqi mawwal:

Boast your superiority to wearers of crowns of ivory, roses, and light
Boast your wine superiority to the best of vineyards.
Play hard-to-get, for that inspires poetry
And melodies are sought after by those in captivity.

I called Fathallah in Mosul, "How are you and how's Maha? I am here in Baghdad for a week and I'd like to see you both."

"Hello, Nora. We miss you very much. We are fine and Maha is swamped in her graduation project which gives me patience to stick it out under these circumstances until she is done with school."

"Are circumstances so hard?"

"Here in Mosul, it is safe. But things have changed considerably, what with the pressure of work because of the war and conscripting all young men into the army. All of that has added to stress in our lives. Besides, we, Maha and I, hardly see each other and Maha is always in the middle of an emergency. Leaving now means looking for a new university and having equivalency procedures that we don't need and endless paperwork."

"In socialist countries there are many universities that accept transfer students."

"Socialist countries are chock full of Iraqi communists after the party crisis. Unfortunately, Maha is still at school. I'll let her call you as soon as she comes back."

"Do you know where Basyuni is? I have a letter from his family."

"He is in an area near Basra, working in a shop that's part of the roads department."

"Great. We have a trip to Basra in three days as part of the conference schedule. Would you please tell him that I'll be at the Sheraton? He can confirm the appointment with me by telephone at al-Rashid Hotel. I can be reached after midnight or before 9:00 a.m."

He said, "I've tried many times to convince him to go back to Egypt, but he is reluctant. Sometimes he is persuaded when the war situation gets bad or when he receives a letter from his mother or his fiancée. But usually the temptation of the money is too strong, especially since his salary increased threefold in one fell swoop. Maybe you can convince him to go back."

"Is there a chance to see you and Maha before I go back to Egypt?"

"I'll do my best to get some time off. Maha will be very pleased."

I remembered Maha, her very kind heart and spontaneous spirit. I wished that I could see her and that their circumstances would permit them to come to Baghdad.

I called Tariq Mandur for whom I also had a letter from his sister. He was now working in Suleimaniya after a long story of failure in Baghdad that ended when he settled down in the beautiful north. The owner of the tea and beer garden where he works told me, "In the morning I'll let him know you called."

I postponed calling Abd al-Rahim and Suhayla until the morning when I could reach Abd al-Rahim at work and find out news of the rest of the group. I opened the door to the balcony and looked into the dark, trying to see the sleeping birds. I remembered the way I sat in the balcony of my apartment in the Dora neighborhood looking at the sky over Baghdad and wrote:

I love you, winter night,
Looking from the window
At the trees and the empty streets,
Waiting for the moon to rise,
And the wind to calm down.
Looking for the sleeping birds,
Seeing the flowers trembling in the dark,
But standing their ground.
The universe does not feel me spying on it.
I love it in its silence
And when it erupts in revolt.
I love the universe the way it is.

I wanted to re-live my days in Baghdad. I pulled a woolen kilim
that was spread on the floor and placed a pillow behind my back and
began to contemplate the emptiness in front of me. I was trying to
penetrate the rubber wall of the dark. My mind lit up with days that
have not been erased from my memory and have given me as much
feeling of success and happiness as they have caused worries in my
life. I remembered my visit to al-Khalsa after returning from my
first visit to Cairo.

I was almost done collecting my material when I learned that an
Egyptian documentary film crew was shooting there. Hilmi Amin
told me that Abd al-Barr had offered his memoirs to the director
Hadi al-Nahhal but that the latter did not accept them. And he said
that Hadi would not give in to Abd al-Barr's sneaky ways of course.

The cameras were shooting throughout the village and all of a
sudden Abd al-Barr was accused of stealing some chairs that the
moviemakers had been using. The missing items were actually
found in Abd al-Barr's house but the director went to the police
and got Abd al-Barr released by claiming that he had asked him to
guard the equipment while the team was away. Hilmi Amin spent
many hours talking to Abd al-Barr about the new beginning and the

dream that he was living now and which was being jeopardized by petty things. Abd al-Barr denied everything, but his wife added her voice to the recriminations, "Yes, he does all that people are accusing him of. That's all I've got to say."

Abd al-Barr said, "What does a woman who worked as a servant in other people's houses understand? She's still living with the mentality of slaves and cannot run the affairs of her own house as its mistress."

I was done collecting my material and organized it in the form of charts of agricultural output as the time drew near for al-Khalsa to celebrate its first anniversary. Then I thought, while writing the history of the one hundred families I should write a history of Egyptian peasants. I asked myself whether I could present that history in a short chapter or not. I began to look for reference works and Hilmi Amin gave me some and helped me find some other works in the bookstores. Then I brought back the rest of what I needed from Cairo and began to write.

Hatim let me devote my time fully to writing after coming home from the office. He started a small project: to change the landscaping in the garden. He got totally engrossed in it and when I went to him while working, he would tell me, with the hoe still in his hand, "The results will surprise you."

The garden did indeed look bigger, simpler, and more delightful to look at. Hatim had removed the unused chicken coop and planted flowers of one color in one of the garden beds. I finished writing my book and gave it to Hilmi Amin. The following day he signed his approval of it and we submitted it to the Ministry of Information and it was accepted for publication.

I found myself thinking about the village as it entered its second year. The peasants had gotten the better breeds of cows that the project provided, and the addition of these cows introduced improvements into every family's house and added something that had been missing: fresh cheese, milk, cream, and butter. The output of the crops was rising and the land was responding and

189

becoming more pliant under the peasants' hoes. There was a ready market for grains and produce. Debts were forgiven and monthly salaries kept coming thanks to a resolution from the farmers' union. Access from the village to the capital was made easier when a new bus line started operating. Public health improved and you could see results on the faces and bodies of al-Khalsa villagers, whose higher income was also reflected in the furniture and the courtyards of their houses. The fields acquired new vitality thanks to the work sheds that the peasants built and the cattle and other animals that lived there. The family reunification plan was proceeding smoothly. Peasant and land became friends after it drank up his sweat.

Out of the blue the Egyptian newspapers reported that Abd al-Samad al-Bahrawy (Chairman of the Board) had stepped down from his job. I told Hatim, "So, his illness was political. He knew he would be forced out of his post."

Press circles awaited new orders, changing the editors in chief of some Egyptian newspapers and magazines. With uncertainty in the air and Hilmi Amin's apprehension about being arrested if he went back to Cairo, especially now that his reading of the situation proved to be correct and Sabri Hanafi's and Mahmoud Muwafi's assessments had missed the mark, I decided to go to Egypt as soon as possible to find out what my status in the magazine would be and how the bureau would fare.

When my father saw that I was in a great hurry to go to Magh-agha to see my son, Yasir, before nightfall he said, laughing, "He is just a little piggy."

I decided to deliberately greet Yasir as I did the rest of the family and to sit down normally without grabbing him and showering him with my kisses while my heart was being torn apart. I made a gesture to his grandmother and his aunts not to tell him anything, but it didn't take him long to come to my bosom. I had sat down, putting all the new toys that I had brought for him on the floor. I wound the spring of the bumblebee and it began to buzz and rise a little from the floor, then land after a little while. I played by myself without inviting him to participate and watched his eyes as he watched me. He came and leaned on my shoulder and reached out to touch the bumblebee. Before long he was rewinding the spring without saying anything. Then he smiled and played some more and then he brought his mouth close to my cheek and kissed me. Tears ran down my cheeks and I did my best to hide them. We spent an enjoyable time together and I was happy that he hadn't forgotten me, as my last vacation had brought us a little closer to a normal relationship. I stayed for two days in my mother-in-law's house. I noticed that the southern Egyptian accent I had detected in my previous visit was getting thicker and thicker. It wasn't the influence of the family as such but rather that of peasants working in the fields. I thought it was more likely the influence of his nanny, Nadia, and the neighbor's children. I caught him as he was chasing the old dog with a stick while the dog panted. I said to him, "Have pity, Yasir."

"I am playing with him," he said, not fully pronouncing the letters.

He skipped away from my hands and ran after the dog, which slowed down as it wagged its tail.

"Come here," he said in his not fully formed words.

I smiled. I took out a packet of sweet crackers and called out to him to come and get it. He took the cracker out of my hand and ran with it to the dog that was lying down in the sun. He placed the cracker in the dog's mouth, which it opened wide, revealing an absence of teeth. I saw my son's forearm disappear and I was paralyzed by fear. The dog gave in, wagging its tail happily while my son threw himself down on it. How can I convince him? And convince him of what? He was living his life and availing himself of its pleasures. I remembered Hilmi Amin telling me that the Arabs used to send their children away to other communities in the desert with their wet nurses to open up to the world and run and play with sheep and camels and that, according to him, was more healthy. He also told me about the English sending their sons to boarding schools. "So, you are not the first person to leave their son in a different place." The tears well up in my eyes. I asked the doctor, "When, doctor, when?"

"Not much longer," he said.

I picked up the tape recorder and began a conversation with him which I recorded, noticing how, in the new dialect he was acquiring, he pronounced the "q" as a "g" and the "g" as a "d" sometimes, and I sang with him a children's nonsense song.

I took Yasir and the recording to Cairo. There I met Sabri Hanafi. He was calm as usual and told me he would do his utmost to help me. I went to the office of Ahmad Harfush, who welcomed me warmly. Then Fahmi Kamil came and he also gave me a warm welcome with a broad smile and asked me, "How's Hilmi Amin and the bureau?"

I said coldly, feeling that his smile did not mean anything, "Fine."

The telephone rang and Ahmad Harfush picked it up. His face changed color as he said, "Yes. Is that so? Any reason? Thank you." He put down the receiver and looked at us in silence, then said:

"They have decided to stop publishing the series I am writing on the July 23 Revolution, without any comments."

I said, "So, they are changing the magazine's publishing policy?"

No one said anything. I took my leave, totally disheartened. I met the chairman of the board of directors several days later. He told me that they would discuss the whole situation concerning the bureau in Baghdad in a special session and that my own position would be discussed as part of that overall picture. I went back to Sabri Hanafi who told me, "The real threat to the bureau now comes from the Iraqi government itself. With the changes that took place in *al-Zahra* magazine, Iraq might have it shut down."

I didn't know where he got this idea from, and whether it had any Iraqi sources. I made no comment. Things were moving faster than I could catch up with.

When I told Hilmi Amin he said, "Sabri is an eternal optimist even when he is beaten down."

My Days

I stretched my arms as far as I could. I need flexing exercises to realign my bones. I yawned as I closed the balcony door. When I went into the room, I was pleasantly surprised by the warmth. I saw Hilmi Amin's file on the desk. I took it to bed and leafed through it. It seemed he transcribed the tapes that he had recorded with me and filled in the gaps. I read:

When I was dictating these memoirs at Nora's suggestion, I knew that of course there was much that I would not record, that I needed to write myself, directly. Our daily recording sessions helped refresh my memory. Her question to me today, which she asked me deviously while laughing, about women, has whetted my appetite for writing about the subject. Nora has avoided talking about Anhar and I appreciate that, even though I know full well that she notices things. I had told her about Ismat but I didn't tell her anything about the joy of my first discovering a woman's body. Now the time has come for these memories to be a true autobiography.

I was visiting Cairo on our first school trip. My next-door neighbor gave me a cardboard box in which she had placed a roasted duck, noodles, some loaves of bread, and a few oranges and bananas to deliver to her married daughter who was living in Cairo. And even though it was December, and there was no way the food would go bad, she made me swear that I would deliver the food to her as soon as I arrived in Cairo. I was too embarrassed to refuse even though I wanted to stick to the trip's program with my classmates. After sunset I looked for the address she had given me in Shubra Gardens until I found it. It was a two-story house where the bride was living in a small apartment on the first floor. I rang the bell and heard a gentle voice and the little window in the door opened: "Who is it?"

I said, "I am Hilmi. Hilmi Amin from Kom al-Shuqafa."

She opened the door, Saniya said, "Welcome, welcome, Hilmi. Look at you, you're a grown man."

I gave her the box and thanked her and tried to take my leave to catch up with my colleagues, but she swore by all that's sacred and insisted that I had to come in. She said that her husband Abd al-Fattah was away on some official business for three days and that God had sent me to her from heaven. She left me in the living room and I heard pots and pans clanking. Then she came in with a large tray on which was the food that I had brought her from Alexandria. When I declined her invitation to eat she said, "In the morning we'll have to throw all of it to the cats."

I sat and joined her, still very embarrassed. Then I tried to take my leave again. She said that transportation would be difficult at that time. She would not let me go and accompanied me to her bedroom.

I said, "I'll sleep on the couch in the living room."

She took down a mattress and put it on the floor in the guest room and gave me a blanket and said, "Have a good night."

I was not quite fast asleep yet when I felt violet perfume tickling my nose and realized that she had slipped under the cover. I was dumbfounded by the surprise as she placed her hand on my organ, which came to instant erection under her palm. She started removing my underwear in which I had gone to sleep. I didn't know what to do. I started listening in my mind for footsteps behind the apartment door. I looked in her eyes begging for help. She turned on her back and pulled me over her as if I were a cover. She said, "Let it be. It will know its way." Of course it didn't know anything. All I had were memories of my friends' conquests in the world of women and the sound of a bed making rhythmic cracking noises in the room of my brother who got married and continued to live with us with his wife. She took my organ by her hand and placed it inside a very moist, wet hole that clamped it. I felt I was riding a wave of fire that kept going up and down with me on top, clinging to it and swimming smoothly. I fell down a seething chasm and a new world opening up for me that I didn't want closed ever. I was visited by an overwhelming din that wanted to get out, then strong and quick convulsions that put me on top of a bolting horse that took me for a frenzied ride. I heard a sound like a bleating of a goat that felled me to the ground, washed by the water of life and sweat. I fell back and started gazing at the ceiling unable to say anything. She rose on her elbows and kissed me on the lips, then she lay down on her back, naked, her hand on my chest.

She said, "Hello, novice!"

I could hear her regular breathing for a few minutes. Then she got up and lit a cigarette and gave it to me to smoke it together. When we finished the cigarette, I slipped under the cover to sleep. She said, "It's early."

Then she got on top of me, holding my head with both her hands. When I penetrated her unassisted she laughed loudly, saying, "Now you're talking, you devil, you!"

She sat up rocking, massaging my body with her hands and kissing my face as if she were a different woman. She aroused me slowly as desire coursed through my veins, filled with the insatiable hunger for a vagina that I'd just met for the first time in my life, squeezing me slowly, then letting go. I succumbed to her soft fingers moving on my chest. I held the palm of her hand and kept kissing it as I recalled a scene between Vivien Leigh and Clark Gable. She said, "Go easy."

She placed one of her breasts in my hand and shoved the other one in my mouth. She wriggled as she smothered me with long, deep kisses. The rhythm of her going up and down quickened until I exploded and felt her clamping me more forcefully. Then I heard the sound of a thin, shrill bleating as her eyes looked absently at nothing. Then she withdrew and fell down to the mattress calmly, with tears covering her face. I asked her in my semi-conscious state, "What's wrong? Did I hurt you?"

She patted my body and took me into her bosom, saying before falling asleep, "May God protect you."

In the morning she came in carrying a breakfast try, saying, "Sorry, I woke you up early so you can catch up with your friends before they go to the Pyramids."

195

I have never forgotten Saniya. She remained a secret flame with permanent residence in my memory whom I summoned whenever I felt emotionally cold or lonesome. She has always been the spark lighting the fire of my lust.

Do I have the right to go on reading? How would I know what he wanted me to do with these papers if I didn't know what they contained? I turned off the light.

I got up at five in the morning as usual. I pumped the milk out of my breasts, took my bath, and sat down to look over the paper that I would present in the first morning panel. I had prepared an educational program listing simplified books in literature and other disciplines, as well as the various branches of science that had a direct bearing on the target group of women who had just barely learned how to read and write. I went to the restaurant for an early breakfast, setting aside time afterward for making telephone calls. Before going to the session I called Anhar's house again and let it ring until it automatically stopped. I called the exchange operation and asked her if I could ascertain that the number and line were working properly. In a few minutes she called back and said that the number and line were okay but that there was nobody home. I asked her to please call them and tell them that I was in Baghdad and that I wanted to visit them. I called Abd al-Rahim Mansour at the Central Authority for Quality Control and left him a message to call me.

The hours passed quickly. One of the women speakers dwelled on the phenomenon of citing non-Iraqi thinkers. I raised my hand and said, "When you ask experts from other countries, they will not give you the answers that you already have, otherwise why invite us to take part in the discussion?"

I ran to the bathroom before my breasts overflowed with milk to avoid public embarrassment. When I went back to the hall my wonderful escort, Layla, came to me carrying a glass of tea with milk. Mona Abed smiled, then laughed out loud. Layla asked why Mona was laughing and why they were all smiling so slyly.

Mona said, "I remembered a naughty joke that says that a customer in a coffee house ordered tea with milk. The waiter took the glass of tea to the woman manager of the coffee house to add milk to his tea from her breast. The customer protested loudly and the waiter told him, 'We've run out of milk. You should thank God that the man who owns the coffee house is not here!'"

Layla looked at me for a long time then at Mona Abed, not understanding the joke, then when she did she burst out laughing so hard she almost spilled the tea.

The second panel was devoted to combating illiteracy among peasant women. During the question and answer period, Widad Iskandar asked me about the experiment in al-Khalsa and I told her that the Egyptian peasant women did well.

We sat around a big table to have lunch at the invitation of the minister of planning. My friend from the Iraqi News Agency came and sat by my side. I said to him, "What a nice surprise! I was going to call you today."

He said, "It's been a long time, Umm Yasir."

We got into a long conversation about Egypt and Iraq and all kinds of topics. Then I asked him about Anhar.

He said, "I don't know whether she got a long unpaid leave or resigned. I've heard she's in Brazil. Abu Lu'ay, her boss at the Agency, said that he had met her in what-do-you-call-it, Detroit, in America."

I said, "Is she alive?"

He seemed to be taken aback but he said, "Why shouldn't she be alive? Yes. She's just gone abroad. You know how communists move."

I said, "Did her mother join her?"

He said, "I don't know. She's your friend. No? I remember that I saw you together often."

I said, "She used to work with us in *al-Zahra* bureau. Then she suddenly disappeared."

He said, "Let me ask around. Many people went to Europe and America. And even to Yemen and Beirut."

I said, "I just want to find out how she's doing. Unfortunately I don't have the telephone numbers of her relatives."

Layla came to say, "We are going to the mosque of Mawlana al-Kazim. Are you coming?"

I said, "Yes. I'll come right away. Do I have five minutes?"

"Sure, sweetie."

I ran to the bathroom to empty as much as I could of my breast so I could catch up with the buses. Ten minutes later, I was getting on the bus, out of breath. I sat in the back watching the streets that I loved as we crossed the suspension bridge. The streets were still crowded with cars. The rain stopped and the sun's rays began to dry the water that gathered just below the sidewalks. I leaned my head on the glass of the window and remembered an incident that took place at the final resting place of Imam Musa al-Kazim and which had remained with me for a long time.

Baghdad had caused quite a stir when it held a conference on Zionism in the fall of 1976. That was the first conference that I covered as a correspondent for *al-Zahra*. A high-caliber Egyptian delegation came to the conference, some of whose members I had met and some I had only seen on television. Among them were Mahmoud Amin al-Alim, Abu Sayf Yusuf, Ahmad Hamrush, and Fathi Ghanim.

I asked Hilmi Amin, "Who is Abu Sayf Yusuf?"

He smiled and said, "He was the head of the Egyptian Communist Party at one point. When they arrested him, Alexandria had a blackout and he was escorted under heavy guard."

I met these illustrious men in the lounge of Baghdad hotel. I looked at Abu Sayf Yusuf's face, looking for things that made him so frightening and dangerous that it required them to blackout the streets of Alexandria to get him out of the city, but I found nothing of the kind. I was happy comparing the image I had for each of them in my mind and their reality.

From my younger days I summoned the image of Mahmoud Amin al-Alim as I saw him providing a weekly political analysis of the news, with his halo of gray hair. Now I saw a simple jovial man, although time had left some of its heavy traces on his face. He told us about Paris and his exile there. The big surprise, though, was with Ahmad Hamrush whose articles I have been reading regularly but whom I had not met before. I found him to be very spontaneous and gentle in his demeanor, reminding me of my paternal uncles and their openness and love of life, qualities that made me fall in love with those that resembled them the most. Mr. Hamrush told me to wait for his wife to whom he wanted to introduce me. When she arrived everyone got up to greet her, showing great affection for her. They asked me to take her on a walking tour in the city because she loved the sun. She was tender and kind and I saw why everybody loved her.

When we returned to the hotel I found Fahmi Kamil sitting in the midst of the delegation. I had met him while I worked in the sports section in Cairo. The head of the section had introduced me to him, saying, "She wants to be a literary writer." He said, "Great! Good for you!" When I heard he was coming to Baghdad I decided to interview him and to sit with him for a long time. Hilmi Amin agreed that we would conduct the interview for *al-Jumhuriya*.

Hilmi had taken him to the office the night before and showed him the physical aspect of the bureau since he was the editor in chief. He introduced me to him, saying, "Nora says you're her favorite writer."

I smiled as he asked me, "Have you read *Zizi and the Crown?*"

I said I didn't like reading novels published serially but that I'd buy the book as soon as it came out.

He said, "I advise you to read it."

He seemed happy to have made my acquaintance and said, "Do you know that your father and I were classmates?"

I said, "Yes, and Father told me about your meeting this week."

He said with a surprised look on his face, "Really? Does the news travel so fast to Baghdad?"

I said, "I was on the telephone with my father yesterday."

Hilmi said, "The driver is here. Let's go to al-Kazim."

On our way I told Fahmi Kamil that al-Kazim was a low-income neighborhood that was crowded because Iraqis loved Mawlana Musa al-Kazim and thought his shrine a blessed place. The mosque was built in a unique Islamic style of architecture decorated with faience and colored mosaic and that its dome was pure gold and that its walls on the inside were lined with mirrors and had silver and gold doors.

The car stopped and I took my leave to get an abaya from one of the stores in front of the mosque. When I returned a few minutes later I heard Fahmi Kamil's angry voice—his back was to me— saying to Hilmi Amin, "Why did she come with us? I don't have time to waste."

I was annoyed and I tried to get over my annoyance before talking to them. "Please, let's go to the mosque first."

I noticed how pallid his face had become and it was obvious that he couldn't contain his anger, which showed on his face more clearly as we crossed the street. Indistinct words came from his mouth at great speed as he gritted his teeth in vexation. I didn't understand what he was saying and he seemed about to explode. I asked myself whether the reason for his rage were the few minutes that it took me to get the abaya, or was it something that had to do with Hilmi Amin and the bureau? He stood inside the mosque for a few minutes, then went out to the courtyard, saying: "I suggest we go to the bazaar. The bazaar is the real place. As for shrines, they were built to be in the service of the marketplace, to attract customers."

Then he added in an annoyed but very confident tone of voice, "The merchants understand that, which makes me respect them because they are realistic."

Hilmi Amin said, "Materialism and the scientific approach to life would not exactly put it like that. We start by loving the poor and try to understand why they are like that: is it because they are sick or prisoners of ignorance? Those merchants that you respect are the reason behind the poverty of the poor. The poor look upon those shrines as the abode of leaders for justice. This also calls upon us to respect their dreams, because they strive to assert certain values. And even though those heroes died more than fourteen centuries ago, the poor are still loyal to their principles."

I said, "The market is this way."

We walked in a street that resembled Muski Street in Cairo, chock full of people and goods, tiny stores selling clothes and soda pop and cakes and milk and Iraqi-style grilled meats: liver, heart, and other meats which they call mi'laj. Fahmi Kamil's voice rose as we were avoiding bumping against people, "This is the dirtiest place on earth. It's ignorance and backwardness. It's filthy!"

We didn't comment on what he was saying. I followed him in silence. He was moving as if he were whirling around, semi-dazed, and it seemed his head was in a different world. He looked around, taking in the details of the scene, seeing the stagnant pools of water on the ground and looked more annoyed. He kept shifting his gaze from face to face and showing extreme disgust, then slowing his steps as if to capture the full picture in his mind. I followed him in shock. I wanted to defend the place I loved, not because of the mosque's unique architectural style or the artistry displayed in its decorations, but because of its simple people who reminded me of the inhabitants of Sayyida Zaynab, al-Husayn, and all the poor neighborhoods in Cairo. I kept asking myself: Where did the unjustified hate come from?

I followed them from street to street without saying anything until we got back to the hotel. I took my leave to go home and told the bureau director that I'd be going to the session of the conference on my own. I began to think of the act of deception of which I was a victim when I imagined that I could get a clue about his personality. The mental image I had of him was quite different from what I saw up close. I was not enthusiastic about accompanying him anywhere in Baghdad. I told Hilmi Amin how much I resented the opinions of our guest. He said, "A novelist likes to check the details of places as well as people because he needs those details later when he writes."

I said, "Be that as it may, the image I had of him was the product of my imagination alone."

I got busy with the guests of the conference and the participants. I wrote short features that I submitted to *al-Mar'a* magazine. I asked myself whether I also would go out to that vast expansive world. There was a Mexican woman editor in chief who had not married and a German woman, happily married with children. All of these women were focused on their goals, successful and self-assured. I wondered when I could bring Yasir over from Egypt and live like normal mothers. My tears welled up.

And here I was coming back to Imam Musa al-Kazim's final abode, visiting it with the guests as if I were a stranger to the place. That meeting resulted in my not being appointed to *al-Zahra* magazine. When circumstances changed and Fahmi Kamil was forced out of his post as editor in chief, Musa Shafi', the new editor in chief, demanded that I leave Baghdad and come back to Egypt to prove my allegiances, as he put it. When I asked him, "Allegiance to whom?" He said, "To Sadat." I said, "My allegiance is to Egypt and not to Sadat and my husband's contract in Iraq is not over. I will not divide my family. When he goes back, I'll go with him."

I turned to Layla, our escort, who was asking me, "Why are you hiding in the back? Are you tired?"

I said, "No, I wouldn't miss a visit to al-Kazim."

We went into the large open space in front of the mosque. We split into several groups to put on the abayas that we borrowed from neighboring stores. I stood with scholars from the Soviet Union and India. Anisa in her Pakistani-style dress came and stood with me. She wrapped her arm around my waist and said, "This style is unique!"

We entered the mosque together. I saw Iraqi women crying as they held on to the gilded bars around the mausoleum. A policeman came and chastised them. One woman fell to the floor, crying for her martyred son. The policeman said, "What are you doing, woman? Go. Go home."

A girl held the hand of the grieving mother, saying, "Come on home, grandma. Please, let us go." The mother sat on the floor, oblivious to all that was happening around her, wailing for her son, the apple of her eye.

My tears poured out. Anisa asked me what the woman was saying. I said, "The policeman wants to move her away from the mausoleum. She is crying for her son, the martyr, and complaining to Imam al-Kazim."

We all cried copious tears. Layla said, "The president does not approve of anyone crying over a martyr or receiving condolences for him. Martyrs belong to the homeland."

In my heart I cursed all the dictatorships of the world and I went out sobbing, wishing I could disappear. I heard a voice saying, "Nora, aren't you coming with us?" It was Siham Fathi calling me. Rajaa hugged me, saying, "I didn't know you were that fragile."

I remembered Hilmi Amin saying, "The poor look upon these shrines as the abode of leaders for justice." Where are you, Hilmi? Why did you leave us so soon?

We strolled about and Anisa looked around. Jon came and held her hand. Mona Abed laughed and said, "Look at the love birds!"

Anisa did not understand the Arabic expression but she figured out what it meant and her face lit up with a big smile. We all stopped crying. Jon, the cameraman who came with a television crew from Norway, and who fell in love with Anisa the moment he saw her at the conference, accompanied us to a jewelry store. There he bought a piece of jewelry called chaff al-Abbas, which was a palm of a hand sculpted in the shape of a plant called afs or gall apples with a bead in the middle. He put it on a chain and placed it around her neck as we applauded. A beautiful feeling enveloped all of us even though none of us asked where that relationship would take them. I don't think they worried about that. They both let their feelings carry them far. I chose a piece of cloth wrapped in gold threads. I wanted to ask the salesman if it were a Shi'i symbol, but I didn't ask and wore it around my neck. The night had fallen quickly but it didn't stop us from continuing our strolling in that neighborhood overcrowded with people and life. We went back to the buses that took us to the hotel.

I pressed the voicemail button and found a message from Basyuni in which he said he would come and meet me at the Sheraton in Basra. I felt relieved. I also found a message from Maha telling me when she would be at home. I called her right away before getting ready to go to dinner at the home of Fuad al-Tekarli, my friend, the famous Iraqi writer.

Maha said, "Congratulations, Nora. I heard you had a new baby: what did you name him?"

I said, "Haytham. May it be your turn next, or is there a crown prince I didn't know about?"

She said, "No. It's on hold. We are postponing having babies until I finish school. Fathallah set our goals a long time ago, as you know. And we are here all by ourselves and no one from my family or his family can come to Iraq to help us. Maybe after the war is over we'd reconsider. Unfortunately I tried to arrange for some time off during the graduation project but I couldn't. But Fathallah will come and see you, God willing. Did you see what happened to Hilmi Amin?"

"Yes. Where are Abd al-Rahim and Suhayla and Atef? Do you still visit with them?"

"Of course, but circumstances have changed since you left and then there is the war. Sawsan went back to Egypt but Dahlia is still here. I don't see her much. And Ragya, you know what happened. I'll call you every day."

I called my house in Cairo. It rang and rang and no one answered. Where could they have gone? I called again and I got the busy signal. I called the operator and she said, "The line to Cairo is not working for the second day in a row."

I emptied my breasts and took a bath. Then the telephone rang and a woman with a sweet voice said I had guests, Engineer Atef.

I said, "Please say hello to them for me and tell them I am on my way."

I found Atef together with Suhayla and Abd al-Rahim with their two sons, Ali and Omar. I said, laughing, "There is not one family in Iraq that would name their sons 'Ali' and 'Omar.' It is only because the father is an Egyptian Sunni and the mother is an Iraqi Shi'ite."

Sunhayla said, "Many of my Shi'ite women friends are married to Sunni men. There's also intermarriage involving Kurdish women and Arab men, even though that is more rare, but the phenomenon is on the rise, especially after the education of girls."

I asked them how things were and Atef said, "Sawsan is thinking of coming back to Baghdad after the end of the school year so she can transfer the two girls to an Iraqi school."

Abd al-Rahim said, "Iraq has changed a lot, Nora. The pride is gone. They now feel that they have gotten embroiled in a messy situation. And even though development programs are all up and running, the joy of achievement has faded and people are going through a very sad period."

I said, "This is exactly what I've noticed."

We talked a long time about everyday details and avoided forbidden subjects. We didn't even mention his name. None of us dared. I saw Fuad al-Tekarli and waved to him. I introduced him to them. They took their leave so I could go with him and promised me another visit. Abd al-Rahim asked me in a soft voice, "Do you know what happened?"

I said, "Yes. Were you with him?"

Atef said, "Until the last minute, the night before he left for France."

I said, "Do you have any news about Anhar?"

Abd al-Rahim said, "Absolutely nothing."

I saw them off with the hope that we'd get together one more time before I went back to Cairo. I gave them my schedule as far as I knew it at the time and went with Fuad al-Tekarli.

His wife, the Tunisian translator Rashida, apologized for the tightness of the apartment, saying, "We left the big house to Fuad's sons from his first wife, God have mercy on her soul."

It was the first time for me to visit an Iraqi in an apartment. Iraqis were used to living in houses surrounded by gardens so that they would be able to sleep on the roof during the summer. Rashida had translated his famous novel *The Long Way Back* into French; then she married him. It is one of the best Iraqi novels and the one I loved the most. He had told me before that he had written it in eighteen years. But I was puzzled by a question which occurred to me every time I met him: Why was he not arrested even though he made the protagonist of his novel a Ba'thist who was the embodiment of corruption in the whole work? The novel was a resounding success all over the Arab world and we all feared that he would be detained or at least fired from his post as a distinguished judge. He came and sat by my side. He was gentle and polite as usual. I asked him if he had an explanation.

He said, "I don't know. All the writers and intellectuals throughout Iraq asked the same question. After the novel came out I realized they were sending a young man to me every day to make sure I was still functioning as a judge. I noticed them without anyone saying anything, of course. I think they preferred silence to publicity, otherwise the novel would be more widely circulated if they arrested me. I don't know. I really don't know."

Rashida happily hovered around us. She was beautiful, younger, and very much in love with him. A few friends joined the dinner party. After we ate, Jad Ibrahim Jad, the Palestinian author, told me, "Nora, I used your two books about the Egyptian peasants in al-Khalsa in my documentary about the village."

I asked him, "Did you mention in the credits that the material relied on my books?"

He said, "To tell you the truth: no."

Then he turned and spoke to the Palestinian artist Latifa Yusuf about something else, as if there was nothing to it. I was so shocked by what he had done to me and my work that I lost that warm feeling of affection that I had felt throughout the evening.

Latifa, laughing said, "Congratulations, Nora, Ustaz Jad admires your work very much."

I smiled but couldn't reply. I had told him when I first met him at the Dar al-Salam Hotel that I loved his novel *In Search of Wa'il Mursi*. He asked me, "Are you not the one who writes about Egyptian peasants?"

I said, "Yes. And my book about them will come out soon."

I presented him with a copy when it came out, then gave him my second book, which chronicled their experiment over four years. I met him in Cairo and in other capitals and I presented him with my stories and novels, and I never thought he could do that to me.

I went into my room on my third night in Baghdad extremely exhausted and feeling very bitter about what Jad Ibrahim Jad, whom I loved and respected, had done to me. I just didn't understand it. I turned on the television. The president, in uniform as commander in chief, appeared, meeting a Bedouin clan in the desert and thanking their sons for volunteering in the war before their conscription age. He said, "They should finish school and God will provide."

I changed the channel. I head a singer singing a silly song. I looked for lively Iraqi music with strong brass instruments but could not find any. The news came on, including segments on the conference. I changed the channel looking for Iraqi dabka dance music. I remembered a Kurdish folklore troupe and how I danced with them in the mountains several years ago. Tears came to my eyes. Oh, Baghdad!

Then there was a song listing the ninety-nine good names of the president. I turned the television off and turned on the music channel. A plaintive Iraqi mawwal tugged at my heart:

Woe is me! Woe is me! Woe is me!
I say as a dove was cooing near me,
I beseech you in the name of love
To spare me the calamity of separation!
You're unjust even when fate wants to be fair.
Please, come!

I don't like this hotel. There's something not quite right with it, something uncomfortable. Maybe it is too sharply defined, with obvious lines, with nothing to interrupt the symmetry, lacking a touch, a smudge of art. It represents itself as a luxury waiting for a missing human touch. I don't find enjoyment in cold beauty. I've become quite adept at the quick rhythm of conferences in Baghdad and the care shown the guests. In the evening, friends, male and female, come. Time is never enough to reminisce about our shared memories. But the women did not waste a lot of time. They spilled their guts about loss in a painful session of confessions.

I noticed that many of my friends were pregnant. It was a phenomenon that might have passed unnoticed because Iraqi women, on the whole, loved to have many children and large families regardless of education or work. Iraqi women amazed me by their physical strength and multiple pregnancies and the way they took care of large families and large homes. They, for the most part, lived with the husbands' families until the husbands built homes of their own. Some of my friends had stopped having children after a certain number and some of them had already married off sons or daughters. What happened? I gathered bits and pieces of information as we were having lunch. Manal al-Alusi began to ask the participants about their pregnancies and about news from the front. Layla, my escort, said, "The party has called upon Iraqis to have children after a large number of young men were martyred. The Women's Union has adopted the call. Did you know that Manal had a new baby girl after you left?"

I said, "Is it possible? With all her responsibilities?"

The population of Iraq when I left it was about twelve million, most of whom were young. Those of conscription age were drafted and the others volunteered to serve and were placed in the reserves, men and women. That is why they are all wearing military uniforms. The war had created among women a new kind of relationship that I hadn't perceived before in the circles in which I moved. They were united by fear of the unknown that was awaiting them all. They made concessions to the sovereign decrees that struck at the heart of their earlier gains. There was a decree to give any man marrying the widow of a martyr ten thousand dinars, a car, and a lot to build a house on. It permitted a man to have a second wife after it had been outlawed except with a court's permission after proving that his wife was barren or had an incurable disease or was totally incapable of fulfilling his conjugal rights. They told people that these were emergency laws to fight the extermination of the Iraqi people. Some workers at the hotel told me that dozens of Egyptian young men married widows of martyrs all over Iraq and that many enticements were offered to Egyptian youth to join the Iraqi army for extremely high salaries, especially since most of those young men had received prior training in the Egyptian armed forces. They told me that the Murabba' Café on Rashid Street was witnessing these kinds of deals between brokers and young men daily, in addition to direct recruitment by Ba'thists of Egyptian workers in factories and companies.

I asked Imad al-Bazzaz, an Iraqi Ba'thist journalist friend whose knowledge and integrity were unimpeachable about these issues, and he told me, "There are marriages between Egyptian men and martyrs' widows, but not as extensive as you've been told. Iraqi families are wary of strangers in general. Besides, Egyptians are not permitted to join the Iraqi army. What you heard had to do with an auxiliary logistics corps that undertakes paving roads and repairing them to help the movement of the troops."

I asked another Iraqi journalist and he said, "There are no Arab volunteers in the army, but there are volunteers in the militia called 'special task forces' who undergo commando training."

I said to myself, "Oh my God, whom should I believe?"

I remembered that the chef Said al-Sheikh had promised to arrange a meeting for me tomorrow with an Egyptian hotel employee who had married the widow of an Iraqi martyr, so he could tell me about his experience.

I looked at the glass I had placed on the nightstand and noticed that it wasn't totally full even though my breasts had stopped producing milk. I was quite alarmed. I jumped into the water in the bathtub and my muscles were so relaxed I almost fell asleep. The steam got thick and gathered on the ceramic tiles, then it formed clear crystal droplets that glistened on the wall, looking like a magic lantern displaying the varied colors of the spectrum that carried me to a different world.

Hilmi Amin got ready for the arrival of his family by buying different kinds of cheese. Baghdad had witnessed some relaxation in the regulations limiting the import of food products. They distributed dairy products in small quantities, not more than two tins at a time. Hilmi Amin began to hoard them and ask his friends to tell him where to get some other kinds, which he would then go and buy from far away. I never saw him so energetic before. He asked Abu Ghayib to clean more thoroughly and made sure to buy different kinds of apples, bananas, and chocolates. I went with Hatim to the airport to welcome the family. He had three beautiful daughters, one of whom was about my age. We followed their arrival from behind the glass barrier. They didn't see us because they were busy trying to get his youngest daughter to stay in her baby carriage, but to no avail. She insisted on walking and holding her mother's hand. Hilmi Amin waved to them and the two older daughters ran and embraced their father. The young one tried to escape from her mother's grip but the mother would not let go. The little girl cried out, "Mimi, Shasha, come."

The wife came in slow steps carrying the little girl and pushing the baby carriage. She stopped in front of us in a dignified manner. Hilmi Amin shook her hand and gave her a formal kiss on the cheek. I couldn't help noticing how reserved he was. He snatched the child from her hands and she cried, "Mama! Mimi! Shasha!"

He kissed her as he hugged her fondly. The mother extended her hands and took the child, laughing and said, "In a short while, like every time, she won't leave you alone."

He introduced them to Hatim. "Fayza, Mervat, Rasha, and Rana. Of course you know Nora." The girls rushed to embrace me. "And this is Hatim, her husband about whom I told you a lot."

We crossed Baghdad until Bab Sharqi and we left them at the door of the building, agreeing to meet for dinner at our house in two days and then start work the morning of the third day.

They arrived at our house in the evening, a beautiful and happy family. I had never seen him so happy. I wondered if he was in love with Anhar. I remembered his formal kiss with Fayza at the airport. Was he acting dignified in front of us? Had the news of his relationship with Anhar reached her? How did he manage that balancing act with the two women? And what would Anhar do? Would she go on working at the office while the family was there or would she stay away until they were gone? Wouldn't the wife discover that thread tying Anhar to Hilmi? Women have radar focused on the area surrounding husbands and Fayza's radar must be working overtime because Hilmi was living by himself away from her. Mervat came into the kitchen to help me get the dinner ready. We hit it off right away, and before inviting them to come and sit for dinner I had found out that I was two years older than her, that she was in love with a classmate in college, and that he would propose to her next summer. We found Rasha standing behind us, then suddenly she said in a harsh tone, "What are all these secrets?"

They all burst out laughing. Rana threw her body on Rasha's leg while laughing. Mervat carried her and sat down for dinner. Hatim started telling Tante Fayza anecdotes about Baghdad, while she remained silent for the most part. I attributed her reserve to the difference in age between Hatim and me and her. I invited them to a tour of the house. Hilmi Amin said, "You go ahead. I'll smoke a cigarette." We went around the garden and the first floor. Then we went up on the roof. I told them that the Iraqis slept on the roof during the summer.

Tante Fayza asked in alarm, "And you? Do you sleep on the roof? Aren't you afraid that the neighbors would see you?"

I said as I smiled, "We don't hear or see anything. Just the sky."

Rasha said, "See or hear what?"

I said, "Cars and people in the street and the neighbors."

Mervat said to Rasha, "Hush. You don't understand anything!"

Tante Fayza's smile disappeared. We went down to the second floor and found that Hatim had made the tea. I held Rana from her armpits and whirled her around the living room as she screamed, and her eyes opened wider with splendid slyness. I let her go and she ran toward her father, then came back looking for me. I went to her making a fake growling sound and I snatched her up. I opened Yasir's room and gave her many toys. She clapped her hands in glee. Mervat and Rasha came and I told them, "Finally we've signed a love contract."

I begged Ustaz Hilmi to let the girls stay with me, at least Mervat and Rasha. He thanked me, saying that Fayza needed them both to look after Rana. He promised to send them to me some other time.

In the morning they opened the door for me and made a big noise. I said, "Please lower your voices, otherwise the director will fire me."

I went into the office in which I smelled uncharacteristically strong coffee. I apologized to Tante Fayza that we would work for a short while and not keep Ustaz Hilmi long.

Hilmi, noticing the girls' excitement, said, "They know that I am not on vacation."

I presented him with the bulletin and the news, saying, "This is from the listening department's brief from Monte Carlo and London broadcasts."

Mervat said, "When did you get it done? We only left you at midnight."

We took Mervat and Rasha to the ministry. Colleagues gathered to greet the two girls, inviting the family to their homes. We reviewed the dates for upcoming conferences and trips and the latest news, then we went out to al-Rashid Street. We bought some gifts, then I left them to go home after I promised to take them to al-Khalsa the following day.

I bought some candy for the peasants from Batawain market. I knocked on the door. Hilmi Amin smiled when he saw me. He told his family how I had spent the whole winter wearing wet clothes and he described how he told my father in Cairo how I looked when I came into the office every morning with the legs of my pants wet with mud. He coughed and he laughed without taking the cigarette out of his lips, until tears came to his eyes.

I said, "You are my witness. Al-Khalsa is a village to which I go every day and it wets my clothes with water and mud."

Tante Fayza said, almost in disgust, "I will not go to some place where it would be difficult to keep Rana clean."

Hilmi Amin said, "Get ready. We are in the summer now and there is no rain."

Abd al-Barr met us at the entrance of the village. He wanted to take us to his house. I said to him, "The fields first. We'd like to see the donkeys."

He sent his son to Amm Wadie's house and brought a big mule. Rana screamed and we helped Rasha get on top of the mule's back. She stayed up there all day long and refused to eat with us and took sandwiches from Mimi while she kept a little stick with which she beat the mule's leg as she screamed.

Tante Fayza said, "If you're afraid, why don't you get off?"

Rasha said, "No."

Rana went reluctantly to the mule and asked Rasha to take her up. Mervat put her in front of Rasha, but before she returned to where she was, Rana cried, "Mama! Mama!" Mervat went to her and put her on the ground.

My tears flowed. The memories were too much even though they were beautiful. I wrapped my body in a large towel and came out to the room. I heard Nazim al-Ghazali continuing his traditional Iraqi mawwal.

I picked up a piece of paper and tried to arrange my own schedule to coincide with breaks in the conference program. I was used to their surprise announcements of unscheduled activities due to security precautions. I must go to *al-Zahra*'s office as soon as I can first, but I have to make sure the new owner would be at home. I still had the key. Oh my God! How I miss Hilmi Amin. I opened the balcony. It was the first time for me to see the city from such a height. I remembered Hilmi's words: "Baghdad is changing, Nora." I sat staring at the space in front of me, imagining the houses. I was surrounded on all sides by the calm of a capital expecting an air raid.

I recalled all the Egyptian friends with whom I lived in Baghdad: young leftists, colleagues, and neighbors of the office. I wondered where Anhar was now and whether I could reach her. Could Imad al-Bazzaz get me concrete and certain news about where she was? He seemed certain that she was still alive. I remembered my neighbors in al-Shurta neighborhood and at Dora and my fellow journalists. Could I wear the clove necklace and find Nariman who had given it to me as a gift before the big fallout which resulted in betraying the Iraqi Communist Party? Could I call Erbil? Would I be able to see my Arab and non-Arab friends whom I had left behind before my departure? Or Baghdad's own denizens who had left? I wish I could recover those days and return all of Baghdad, with all its people, to my bosom in a fond embrace.

The rain stopped. I wrapped the wool robe tightly around my body and imagined the houses of Baghdad hidden in the dark, shining as they always were and as I had known them. I remembered my visit to Syria and the material I gathered about the joy of both the Syrian and Iraqi peoples about the restoration of relations. I tried to understand the history of the relationship between the two governments. But I found it to be very complicated and whenever I was able to obtain information about that relationship between the two branches of the party, I was surprised by other pieces of information that would complicate matters even further. I tried to make use of Hatim's anecdotal knowledge, but it turned out that he knew only those parts of the story that were known publicly. I couldn't find a book in the bookstores that would give me a detailed history. I consulted the "Encyclopedia of Iraqi Civilizations," but I found that the banned volume eleven covered that period. I began gathering information from Ba'thists and Iraqi communists and from some of the party's own publications. I also consulted the revolutionary leaflets about the Syrian Ba'th Party that I had brought with me from Damascus.

Hilmi Amin insisted that I do all of that without help from Anhar. When I asked him, "Why doesn't Anhar give us a detailed report?" he said, "It is the effort you yourself exert that will teach you, and you will never forget a piece of information that you worked hard to get."

I thought about it but I came to the conclusion that what he was saying was not the whole truth. I had been noticing some troubles in the love story. But what did work have to do with personal relations? I spent many nights trying to gather all the threads. I found that the Ba'th Party had been established first in Syria in 1947 and was led by al-Bitar. Then it merged with the Syrian Arab Party led by Akram al-Hurani and Michel Aflaq and was named the Arab Socialist Ba'th Party.

I asked my friend Hashim, an employee in the Guidance Department at the Ministry of Information who had lived in Egypt and attended school there with Saddam Hussein, how the Ba'th Party came to Iraq for the first time. He explained, "The party came into Iraq via students in the early fifties. Its founder was Fuad al-Rikabi. They based its foundations on an old nationalist liberal party named al-Istiqlal (Independence), which was led by Muhammad Mahdi Kubba, which worked with the leftist National Democratic Party that was led by Rifaat al-Jadirji. As for the Iraqi Communist Party, it was at the time an underground party. In 1946 it became attractive to the youth as a revolutionary party that did not believe in working through legal channels, nor in liberal elections, but promoted instead revolutionary realism, which aimed at bringing about change by revolution or coups."

He added, "Then suddenly after the coup of Shishikli in Syria, Michel Aflaq's decision to run for election created confusion among the cadres of the party. Then there was another coup and Michel

215

Aflaq was detained, so he engaged in self-criticism and declared that running for election was wrong and that he shouldn't have done it."

I tried to understand something about the period between Michel Aflaq's detention and the Party's return to political life in Syria and Iraq almost simultaneously in 1968. I found that one of the important events of that time was the assassination of Abd al-Karim Qasim carried out by Ba'thist young men in 1959. The union between Egypt and Syria had been established and the government of the United Arab Republic had surreptitiously set up a broadcasting service that operated on the Syrian–Iraqi borders and broadcast revolutionary communiqués. A revolt started as a military insurrection led by Abd al-Wahab al-Shawwaf in Mosul. Fierce battles took place and Shawwaf was killed. The rest of the officers were arrested and executed. I remembered Shawwaf Square and finally understood how it got that name.

I started reading the novel *The Long Days* written by the poet Abd al-Amir Muaalla, in which he told the life story of Saddam Hussein and the attempt to assassinate Abd al-Karim Qasim. When Abu Khalid, a communist university professor who specialized in modern history and politics and who was a friend of Hilmi Amin, visited the office, I seized the opportunity and asked him, "Why didn't the Iraqi left, at the height of the communist surge in Iraq, accept a union with Egypt and Syria? And what were Abd al-Karim Qasim's reasons for not accepting the union when he, as far as I understood, was a popular hero?"

Abu Khalid said, "Abd al-Karim Qasim's revolution comprised several political orientations. They called themselves 'The Free Officers' just like those who launched the July 1952 revolution in Egypt. Abd al-Salam Arif was closer to both the nationalists and the Islamists. Abd al-Karim Qasim was somehow closer to the left. Arif supported the Arab nationalist tendency. People demanded a total union with Egypt and Syria. But the left was against that for several reasons. The most important one was the repression of the Egyptian Communist Party by the government;

most Egyptian communists were in detention camps. I think they were in the Oases."

Hilmi Amin said, "We were in all Egyptian jails."

Abu Khalid said, "The Communist Party in Syria was dissolved and in Lebanon, Farajallah al-Helou, the head of the Lebanese Communist Party, was arrested. It was said that Abd al-Hamid al-Sarraj, Abdel Nasser's man in Syria, had ordered him to be tortured to death, then placed his body into acid until it dissolved."

I said, "Oh my God! Nasser didn't do anything of the kind."

Abu Khalid said, "Abd al-Karim Qasim's conditions were somewhat rational. He wanted a federation with Egypt, Iraq, and Syria, in which they would keep their autonomous structures. The slogans in the Iraqi street reflected the contradiction in opinions." Then he laughed and said, "The nationalists shouted: 'Full union' and the communists replied: 'Federation we choose! Union under our shoes!'"

I said, "Goodness gracious! To that extent?"

Hilmi Amin shook his head without saying anything. Abu Khalid went on, "The situation escalated so much that a group of young Ba'thists decided to assassinate Abd al-Karim Qasim. They had no intention of seizing power, as they later testified. They knew that Qasim moved around by himself without a motorcade, just himself and the driver. They waited for him in al-Rashid Street and shot him. The bullet hit his hand. Qasim drew his revolver and shot back at his assailants. A traffic cop also returned fire and a bullet hit Samir al-Najm in the chest. There was pandemonium in the street. Saddam Hussein escaped to Syria. The conspirators were sent to the famous Mahdawi court. They were young men who believed in individual solutions and they gained great popularity among the people during the trial, emerging as heroes. Then Abd al-Karim Qasim pardoned them, saying, 'Let bygones be bygones.'"

Abu Khalid continued, "In 1963 the party had become stronger and staged two simultaneous coups, seizing power in both Syria and Iraq. And because they were unionists, they formed a joint delegation and a joint command. Michel Aflaq visited Baghdad and blessed the revolution. The joint delegation visited Abdel Nasser and demanded a full tripartite union."

Hilmi Amin said, "But Abdel Nasser was preoccupied with Yemen. He had been stung from his experience of union with Syria, from which he emerged very bitter. So he didn't take the matter seriously, especially since he noticed that each side was engaged in grandstanding."

I asked, "In what way?"

Abu Khalid said, "The power in Syria was in the hands of the military Ba'thists, but in Iraq it was in the hands of both military and civilian leaders. Then the military faction, or what is known as the Ba'thist right, staged a coup against the Ba'thist left. Ahmad Hasan al-Bakr in 1963 was prime minister and Abd al-Salam Arif was president. When the nationalists staged a coup against the Ba'thists, the nationalist officers allied themselves with the Ba'thist officers against the civilians in power at the time. The civilians had a militia that they called 'The National Guard.' The air force used its planes to strike that militia in what was later referred to as 'The Massacre of the Left.' Michel Aflaq was there at the time. Then the leadership of the Syrian regional command was arrested and exiled to Madrid and in Iraq the Ba'thists were arrested and imprisoned."

I held my head in my hands and said, "Please stop for a minute. I've totally lost track. Who staged a coup against whom? Was it a daily occurrence?"

He said, "It was called the 'age of coups': eight coups in twelve years."

I said, "What I don't understand is that the differences were minor and most of them worked together: nationalists with Ba'thists and Ba'thists with Ba'thists. Let's pause here for some time because things are now jumbled in my head."

Abu Khalid said, "I'll tell you an interesting story. You know Nizar Qabbani, of course. You may have memorized some of his poetry."

I said, "'I've given you the choice, so choose death in my arms or within the pages of my poems.' Of course I know him and I love his poetry. He is the poet of our early youth."

Hilmi Amin laughed, "And where are you now? In old age? Nizar was Syria's ambassador at the time in Madrid."

Abu Khalid said, "Yes, Nizar Qabbani arranged a way to go back to Beirut for members of the regional command who had been exiled in Madrid. During that time the Syrian Ba'th Party took a stand that was different from that of the Iraqi Ba'th Party. In 1966 military officers led by Hafez al-Assad, who was minister of defense at the time, staged a coup against the civilian wing of the party and Asad became prime minister. Then in 1970 al-Assad staged a coup against the coup which in Syria they called the 'Correction Revolution' and later became president. He sentenced to death those members of the national command against whom he had staged the coup. Among them were Michel Aflaq, the secretary general of the party, and his three deputies: Shibl al-Aysami, Munif al-Razzaz, a Jordanian, and Elias Farah, a Syrian, in addition to several other Syrian party officials. They all escaped to Beirut."

I said, "I think this was a major turning point in the history of the party here and in Syria."

He said, "Yes. Some of those who escaped continued in politics and others left it. Michel Aflaq gave up and said, 'I've given up on politics' and he immigrated to Brazil."

I said, "What happened in Iraq between the arrest of the Ba'thists in 1963 and the year of the revolution?"

He said, "They regrouped until the Ba'th military staged their famous coup in July 1968 which was led by two non-Ba'thists. One was the commander of the Republican Guard and the other the chief of military intelligence."

I said, "Thank God we've finally arrived at something I recognize. You deserve to drink Egyptian tea in large glasses and not Iraqi tea in little glasses."

Abu Khalid, laughing, said, "Not so fast. The story hasn't ended. There must be Iraqi surprises for that to happen."

I said, "What now? It's enough, Abu Khalid, I cannot keep up with all the details."

He said, "Thirteen days later, Saddam Hussein held a luncheon banquet at the Presidential Palace to which he invited the two lead participants in the coup, who were not Ba'thists. But Abd al-Razzaq Nayif, chief of military intelligence, by coincidence, was in London on official business. The Republican Guard commander accepted the invitation. After lunch, and while . . .

I interrupted him, "Don't tell me it was the citadel massacre all over again!"

He laughed and said, "Almost. He washed his hands and when he turned around, he saw soldiers aiming their machine guns at him. He said to them, 'We've just eaten bread and salt together!' They said, 'Your turn is over. An order has been issued that you be exiled to Turkey.' Then Iraqi intelligence killed Abd al-Razzaq Nayif in London."

I said, "And thus the story ended. Not a happy ending at all."

Hilmi said, "From that moment, from 1968, the Ba'th Party in Iraq has been in power and so has the Ba'th Party in Syria. Each party accuses the other of being disloyal, a lackey, and a traitor, and that it, each one, is the true Ba'th Party, and the antagonism has continued."

I said, "Take five. Tea is better. Please don't start on other topics before I come back and tell you a real joke, one that has actually happened."

I heard the bell ring. Anhar came in and welcomed Abu Khalid warmly.

Abu Khalid said as he bit into the cake, "This is homemade! Don't tell me you baked it, Umm Yasir?"

I said, "Please enjoy. The story is as follows: while I was a child the radio was on and they were announcing about a coup d'état in Syria and listing the names of the participants: Staff Colonel so and so, Staff Colonel so and so, Staff Major so and so, Staff General so and so. My father came in and asked, 'What happened?' Amm Hasan, the cook, said, 'It seems the Staff family in Syria had a coup.'"

We laughed and Hilmi said, "He's right. Yes, the Staffs. What's your question?"

I said, "I want to know the difference between the two factions of the party in Syria and Iraq, briefly."

He said, "The Syrian Ba'th is described as the Ba'thist left whereas the Iraqi one is thought of as the Ba'thist right."

Anhar said, "This is an apt description."

I said, "Why did Michel Aflaq return to Iraq and to politics after he had washed his hands completely of it?"

He said, "The Iraqis wanted something to support the legitimacy of the Iraqi Ba'th Party, so they sent Omar Alali, the minister of information, as a member of the regional Iraqi command of the Ba'th Party to Brazil with a message to Michel Aflaq saying that it was Iraq that would build the Ba'thist state. Michel Aflaq returned first to Beirut and in 1971 came to Iraq. They also invited those members of the National Command who had been sentenced to death by the Syrian Ba'th Party and reappointed them in the National Command. They issued a resolution making Michel Aflaq the secretary general of the party and Ahmad Hasan al-Bakr the assistant secretary. This way the conflict over influence between the Syrian and Iraqi parties continued."

I said, "During all that time hasn't there been any relaxation in the conflict? As far as I know the Iraqi Ba'th Party fought side by side with the Syrian army in the 1973 war. Why hasn't this been reflected positively in the relationship between the two factions of the party?"

Anhar said, "When the war started, Iraq sent several armored brigades to Syria despite the political differences. Damascus was in imminent danger of falling because the distance between it and Qunaytra was only sixty kilometers. And, indeed, Israeli tanks were on their way to Damascus and got within thirty kilometers of it, but the Iraqi Tenth Armored Brigade repelled the attack and a large number of Iraqi youths were martyred and were buried in a cemetery that bears their name."

I said, "That, then, was a good gesture from Iraq. Why haven't they reconciled?"

Anhar said, "The long antagonism has caused a deep wound between the two sides. The Iraqi attitude healed the wound somewhat but it didn't heal completely. Syria built a dam on the Euphrates river and when the low water season came, all the gates were closed, so water dried up in the Iraqi part of the river, which led to a major political crisis."

I said, "But it was resolved ultimately and the river is flowing in the two countries."

Abu Khalid said, "Yes and the atmosphere now is conducive to conciliation, because now the Iraqi Ba'th Party has a leftist orientation and is opening up to the Soviet Union. There are currently two communist ministers and that is why Michel Aflaq and Ahmad Hasan al-Bakr were able to open channels for talks about unifying the two branches of the party. There is thinking among some in the party that it must learn from Abdel Nasser's experiment of unity with Syria, because it was based on Abdel Nasser's charisma. That is why they want it to be based on sound ideological foundations and that it should start first among the Ba'th Party cadres and units, then the different ministries, then ultimately on the level of the people as a whole. They agreed that Ahmad Hasan al-Bakr be the number one man in the new system of the national command since his military rank is higher than that of Hafez al-Assad, who will be his assistant."

I said, "Where is Saddam Hussein in this arrangement?"

Abu Khalid smiled and said nothing. I turned toward Anhar but she also did not say anything, nor did Hilmi Amin. I said, "I imagine that al-Bakr is grooming Saddam to succeed him and that this is about to take place, since Saddam is his nephew and al-Bakr's health is not at its best, and that is why Saddam does almost everything, which means that all the actual strings of power are in his hands."

Abu Khalid and Anhar both laughed and Anhar said, "Saddam Hussein is not al-Bakr's nephew, but rather he is the nephew of Khayrallah Telfah, father of his wife, Sajida. But Saddam and al-Bakr are from the same al-Bejat clan."

Abu Khalid said, "The question of preparing to transfer authority to Saddam is a matter that nobody knows anything about. Besides, I would like to suggest, Sitt Nora, Umm Yasir, that you slow down a little and keep your opinions and your guesses to yourself, for such an opinion can send you at any time to Abu Ghraib."

Anhar heaved a long and sad sigh and said, "That is quite true."

I said, "I am an Egyptian journalist and analyzing the news that I get is very important."

Hilmi Amin said, "Nora's work in the bureau is to cover the arts and write features on social matters. I thank you. We understand what you want to tell us and I am sure that Nora now has a clearer picture. My aim behind this conversation was to help her because she has exerted a great effort in writing a report, which was quite sufficient until the talks about unity started and it became necessary to know the rest of the details, because we would like, as a news organization, to cover the region and we did not want to make any mistakes, even by chance."

I said, "I am optimistic. Iraq is making progress and there is a surplus in the balance of payments. A coalition front is in power and citizens have begun to feel the flow of oil revenue affecting their lives positively. My first observation in the Iraqi street is the disappearance of long lines in Orosdi Bak to buy china or tea glasses. Now I can buy a lot of vegetables and fruits from the market instead of just okra and eggplant in the summer and spinach and cabbage in the winter. I have even found grapes in the market in the dead of winter."

Abu Khalid said, "This is true and, God willing, all good will come to all of Iraq and also Syria."

Anhar said, "Yes, if God wills it."

I said, "If this union works out, the whole region will lift off like a rocket."

Abu Khalid got up to take his leave on the promise of a meeting soon, after Hilmi Amin comes back from Damascus bringing with him a bottle of Syrian araq. Hilmi Amin closed the door after him and came back directly to me, saying angrily, "Are you crazy? How could you ask the man such a question?"

I said in alarm, "What question?"

He said, "Anhar, wait in my office until I call you and please close the door." Then he turned to me, "About Saddam Hussein's position in the unified party."

I said, "It occurred to me that this new arrangement would not appeal to Saddam Hussein because it would set him back and place Hafez al-Assad ahead of him."

He said, "This is obvious to all of us, Sitt Nora, but he cannot say something like that here. It might cost him his life. He is an Iraqi communist, and even though Iraq is ruled by a front of which the Communist Party is a part, this does not mean that communists are safe at all, in a country where a coup and killing can take place in no time at all. And even though Saddam Hussein seems to bless the unity, we don't know exactly what al-Bakr has promised him and how the party would be restructured. We don't know anything about the relationship among the Iraq regional command or the relationship between them and members of the national command, nor what the coming days will reveal about those vying for power or about rapprochements that nobody anticipated. Abu Khalid, like any Iraqi, would never talk about such matters even if he trusted us. He would not trust a place in which he is sure Iraqi intelligence has planted bugs whose recordings would be used against him later. Nora, please, I want you to come out of this meeting much more cautious than before and not to ask any Iraqi about power struggles or relationships, ever, ever, so that you would not jeopardize this bureau. Do you understand? This is an order. Understood?"

I hadn't expected this kind of anger at all. It seems that, unbeknownst to me, I had entered a danger zone. I said, "Yes, understood. I'll go now. I wish you a happy trip and don't forget Rana's jacket and Yasir's jacket. I would like a red one."

I told Anhar that I'd see her the following day at the Agency to review our work. I went out to the street. I stopped at the market. I couldn't believe my eyes: fruits and vegetables of summer and winter side by side. I went into a narrow street crowded with horse- and mule-drawn carriages. I saw tubers that looked like potatoes but they were thin and not straight. I turned some over with my hands. An Assyrian woman said, "Take it. It's more tasty than meat."

I said, "Thank you. We don't know it in Egypt, but I'll try it."

I heard a noise behind me. I saw a car trying to go through the narrow street and another one standing in front of it, not allowing it to pass. The two drivers exchanged insults and one of them got out of his car and grabbed the door of the other one, trying to open it by force.

"What do you want, sister-fucker?"

"Me? Me a sister-fucker, you filthy lowlife? I swear by my family I'll kill you!"

The exchanged insults grew louder and passersby, men and women, tried to stop the fighting. A man shouted, "The police, the police!" Each of the drivers jumped back in his car. One car backed off quickly and the other car followed as the vegetable carts made way for them and both cars were able to get through. Before the policeman arrived on the scene, men and women had resumed selling and buying. I felt a need for some cold water. A vendor said, "Egyptian oranges, Egyptian lady."

I said, "Really? Give me five kilos."

I carried the oranges happily but I was still shaken by Hilmi Amin's panic. I went home and on my way through the market I was hoping to hear Cairo vendors hawking their merchandise: "Sweet oranges! Baladi oranges! Blood oranges for juice!"

I will never understand the Iraqis, even if I stayed here for years. Even Arabic words had different psychological connotations for them from what they had for someone like me. Words that had something to do with violence were not used for the same meaning in our Egyptian dialect. Several situations came to mind bringing home that difference. I was once sitting with my neighbor Umm Safaa in the garden of my house in al-Shurta neighborhood soon after my arrival in Iraq. Her daughter was playing nearby. The girl, Safaa, said, "I want to slaughter the apple." Umm Safaa picked up the knife and cut up the apple. I asked her, "Why does she say 'slaughter?'"

She said as she pointed to the slices, "She wanted to slaughter it."

I figured out that that was the common meaning of the word and that she had not invented it. I said, "We say 'slaughter' for living things."

I remembered another scene that took place near the door of my house in Dora. I was opening the garden gate, having come back from the market. Umm Tayih passed by and we stood talking. And while I was playing with her son Mahmoud, she said, "My son was crushed by a car."

I held on to the gate because of my shock and I asked her, not believing her calm and the matter-of-fact tone of her voice as she told me the news, "How? Where is he now? At home or in the hospital?"

She pointed to the child standing next to her with dirty clothes on and said, "I am not talking about Tayih but Mahmoud, a few minutes ago as I was returning from the bakery. Don't you see his clothes?"

I looked at the child, who looked safe and sound, playing. I understood from her that a car was passing by and it touched the boy, who then fell to the ground and messed up his clothes. I realized that the meaning of the words was different. I wonder how their daily life acquired these usages. Was it because of the enormity of events in their history? Or was it the other way around?

I went to bed. As I reached for the light switch to turn off the light, I saw Hilmi Amin's notebook. I looked closely at it, wondering whether I had any right to read it and why it was in my mailbox. Tomorrow I'd decide whether I should go on reading or keep it closed until God decides the matter. Perhaps after visiting the office I will be able to decide one way or another.

Three New Knocks

August, 1977

Rasha Hilmi Amin

As we took a walk through Abu Nuwas Street, Hatim said, commenting on my merry mood, "I didn't imagine that Hilmi Amin's daughters' visit would cheer you up like that."

I said, "They are girls: one my own age and another as young as Yasir."

He said, "This is our favorite restaurant. Let's go."

I smiled. I knew that he liked it because of its romantic ambience: soft lights, quiet, and situated on the bank of the Tigris. It reminded us both of Gabalaya Street, close to our house in Zamalek; it was a street for lovers, with its restaurants and several dance halls, and we would spend time there during our engagement. Anhar was sitting with a young Iraqi man in what appeared to be an intimate conversation. He was holding her hand. Hatim started to move in her direction. I told him, "She hasn't seen us. Let's go in without disturbing her." We headed for a table inside. Anhar raised her head and saw us. She moved her hand away and looked confused. We greeted her and went to our table. After a few minutes she left, waving to us.

In the morning I told Hilmi Amin, when he asked me casually about Anhar, that I had seen her yesterday at the Umm al-Jarra

Restaurant. He said, "How? She said she couldn't come to work yesterday because her mother was not feeling well."

I realized I had made a mistake. I said to him, "Please don't tell her anything. She knows you're busy with your family."

He asked me, "Who was she with?"

I said, "I don't know. A group of Iraqi friends."

I began to blame myself for being so hasty. But I was happy she was falling in love and happy that my suspicions about their relationship proved groundless. I remembered that night in Erbil. Thank God it was a passing affair. Tante Fayza did not need to have a younger rival. Hilmi Amin's family vacation was coming to an end in a few days and they would be off to Egypt. Hilmi Amin arranged a dinner party at the Ramsis Hotel close to the office and invited all those friends who had invited the family on several occasions during their stay. Rasha sat next to her father. Whenever he ordered a bottle of beer, he poured a little in her glass. Mervat and I noticed that her laughter was getting louder. We tried to have her join us but to no avail.

Mervat said, "Rasha is very attached to father. She acquired many of his cranky traits and nothing from my late mother."

I said, "Late mother? Then who is Fayza then? Is she your stepmother and Rana's mother?"

She said, "No. Fayza is my aunt. She came to live with us after mama's death, especially since mother left Rana before she was one month old."

I said, "You all call her 'mama?'"

She said, "My aunt refused to marry after her husband was martyred in 1967. She didn't have any children of her own, therefore we called her 'mama,' and also because she is my mother's only sister and her only close relative."

I said, "I don't know anything about that of course, but I imagined Tante Fayza being so formally dressed all the time was because she was living in the office. It never crossed my mind that she was not his wife. But why has he never told me that his wife had died?

He told me a lot about his life, but never mentioned that. May God make it up to you! Now I understand why he always says 'sorrow is my mate' for no reason. I always attributed it to his unsafe life and to jail."

Mervat said, "Please don't tell him I told you."

We heard Rasha laughing as she asked her father, "You love *me*, don't you?"

He said, "Of course, sweetie."

I noticed Fayza's anxious gaze. She placed her hand on Rasha's shoulder and pressed it hard. Rasha withdrew her shoulder and poured some more beer in her glass.

Mervat came close to my ear and said in a whisper, "Nora, I sense there's something mysterious between my father and Anhar."

I was taken aback by the remark, but I said, "No, you shouldn't think that. She is a good journalist and she helps us understand the complexities of Iraqi society. She is also engaged to her cousin."

Mervat said, "I know. It's just a feeling. We want him to marry Tante Fayza."

I said, "Quit feeling and behave."

Mervat said in a loud voice, which was heard by Anhar, mimicking a famous scene in a classic Egyptian movie, "Ay, my tooth is hurting!"

I said, carrying on the dialogue from the movie, "You should stop eating ice cream and wearing out men's hearts!"

Anhar said, still playing the game but with an Iraqi accent, "Are you a spiritual doctor, sir?"

I commented on her confusion of accents and Mervat said, "The best thing I can do is extract all my teeth like father and put on dentures. That's much better than daily pain at the dentist's office," mimicking an old man's pronunciation.

I looked at the bureau director and found him engrossed in a conversation with Tante Violette. I looked closely at Mervat and found a sly, smiling look in her eyes. I said to Anhar, having noticed that her face had acquired a pallid look which I believe Mervat also noticed: "Thank God, my teeth are good even though my wisdom tooth is reluctant to come out and is giving me a hard time."

Tante Fayza said, "The wisdom should come first."

I was surprised when Hatim said, "It is there, in abundance."

I said in a soft voice to myself, "He should've ignored it."

Mervat said, "Papa, watch out. Rasha is drunk."

Hilmi said, "Have no fear. The fresh air outside will do her wonders and she'll be all right. A little mirth does no harm."

I told him, "You promised to let the girls come with me."

"Okay, but it is difficult for Rana to leave Fayza."

Rasha shouted as she jumped up and held her father's neck, "Thank you. You are the best daddy in the world."

It was midnight when we left the hotel heading home. We started singing as the car took us through the dark streets. It was a famous Egyptian song in which a young woman was saying to a young man:

Who told you to live in our alley
Capturing my heart and disturbing my peace of mind?
You either find a resolution to our situation
Or move out and leave our alley.
"What do you think, Mimi: should he move out?"
"No, by no means."

Then we began to sing another funny song, about a woman as she came out of the bath, with cheeks as delicious as peaches, except now someone was saying "oranges" and "watermelons" in addition to peaches.

As the car turned onto our street, Hatim said, "Lower your voices."

Rasha raised her voice saying, "Peaches, peaches, peaches."

Mervat said, "We are causing quite a racket."

We placed our palms on our mouths as we finished the song and sneaked quietly into the house so as not to awaken the neighbors. We helped Rasha climb the stairs since she looked exhausted. Hatim opened the door and turned on the light. Rasha slipped out of our hands and ran to the balcony door, stretched her braids as far as she could, and screamed, "Aieeee."

We were dumbfounded, then we came to and ran after her. I held her in my arms, saying, "What's wrong, darling?"

She stood as if in a daze looking at me with anxious eyes, "Nothing. I am very good. I am better than you all."

Hatim said, "Take her to change and give her a cup of hot milk."

She walked between me and Mervat without resistance. Then she placed her hand on my face and stroked it, saying, "I love you, Nora."

I said, "Of course, darling, and I love you too."

Then once again she dashed off to the balcony, holding her braids and screaming, "Aieee."

Mervat cried and said, "What's wrong, darling? Do you have pain anywhere?"

Rasha looked at her in amazement and asked her sister, "Why are you crying, darling? Are you tired?"

We went to the bedroom and changed her clothes. I went to get the milk. Hatim said, "She drank a lot of beer. He should've paid attention to how much he was giving her."

"I thought she was used to it with him. I think she was taking more from his bottle when he was busy with his guests."

"The Iraqi beer is much stronger than Egyptian beer. She'll sleep right away."

"My God, her voice travels far in the quiet night and the neighbors can hear it even though our house is surrounded with gardens on all sides."

"Don't worry. They'll think you are having labor pains."

"What labor! They see me every day and know I'm not pregnant."

"They're used to it. Iraqi women give birth every day."

"Don't be unfair to them. Your own mother has kept giving birth until the day before yesterday."

"Because my father was quite a man! Don't you want a baby in nine months?"

"No. In seven months. Let's hope the morning comes in peace."

I carried the milk to Rasha. I heard her telling Mervat, "Tomorrow we buy the red blouse from the store near the office."

Mervat said, "What red blouse?"

Rasha said, "The red blouse. I told you."

I offered her the milk. She said, "I don't like it."

"Drink it for our sake."

She took a sip, then jumped out of the bed, shouting, "May God ruin you, government." She jumped in the air. The glass of milk flew out of her hand. She shouted, "Ruin you, government!" She kept jumping and shouting the same thing with every jump. We jumped after her trying to catch up with her. Hatim came. He held her close to his chest and patted her. Mervat cried hard, saying, "Shasha, sober up. Sober up, please, in God's name."

She left Hatim's hand and ran, then came back to Mervat and embraced her, looking at me, then asked me, "Do you know Aunt Fayza?"

I said, "Yes, of course, Rasha."

She said, "No. You don't know what she really is. She is a drug dealer. She evades the police and hides the drugs in our house. Shall I tell you a secret?"

I said as I patted her on the back, "Yes, go ahead. Tell me."

She said, "She used to do that with mama, mama Fawqiya. Haven't you noticed that she is a carbon copy of her? But the real boss is Fayza. She's the ringleader."

I said, "Calm down, Rasha. Let's go drink the milk and take a hot shower so you can go to sleep and in the morning you'll tell me everything."

She screamed, "The government! The government is behind the door. Fayza has brought the government here. Shut the doors. They came for me instead of Fayza. Fayza is the ringleader!"

Mervat started sobbing and saying, "I can't see her in this condition. I just can't, Uncle Hatim, please call a doctor or let's call my father."

Hatim said, "No. She'll sleep it off and nothing will happen to her. She's just a little excited. She'll be okay."

Mervat said, "Rasha, darling."

Rasha said, "Who's this Rasha? Rasha is ugly and a bitch. Don't speak to her. Keep your arms away from me. Go away. Aieee."

I hugged her hard and pulled her to the couch I was sitting on. She went to sleep meekly on the spot, as if nothing had happened. I sat motionless, afraid to take her to bed lest she should wake up again. I was also afraid to get up and leave the couch lest she should wake up and fly into a rage again. I felt her whole body shaking and from time to time she would say, while still asleep, "The government, the government, daddy. The gang." Then she would fall totally silent. Hatim came after about an hour and helped me get up without disturbing her. He also placed a pillow in place of my thigh where she was leaning her head. I straightened her legs and took off the slippers from her feet and covered her with a blanket. I noticed that Mervat had assumed a fetal position. I helped her straighten up and covered her. Hatim and I left on tiptoe. Hatim took me to bed and wiped my tears, saying, "May God be with you." I cried.

At five in the morning Hatim made breakfast and came in sounding his usual reveille. He kept doing it, but to no avail. I opened my eyes and said, "Have a heart, it's our day off. We'll go in the afternoon, after lunch. Have mercy."

He kissed me, laughing and saying, "You'll get used to laziness, Umm Yasir, and you'll grow fat. I have made a royal breakfast for us and our guests. I hope you appreciate it. The weather is wonderful. Get up."

I said, "Please, let us sleep some more."

He said, "If you can help me go back to sleep, I'll leave them alone."

Our limbs scattered in space, then joined, then scattered again. I lost track of everything until I heard the mu'ezzin calling the Friday prayer at noon. Then I heard Hatim's singsong voice chanting in the living room, "Lunch, lazy bones!"

The three of us came out to the living room in our nightgowns. We discovered that the mu'ezzin was calling the sunset prayer and that it was five-thirty.

Rasha said in all innocence, "How could we have slept for so long?"

Mervat said, "May God ruin your house, government!"

Rasha said, "Which government? The Egyptian or the Iraqi?"

Mervat said, "The gang government. Don't you know the gang?"

Rasha said, "I don't understand what you're talking about. Please tell me."

Hatim said, "The meat is almost done on the grill. Please make the salad, Mervat, and please wash your pretty faces."

We laughed and stood in line in front of the bathroom door. I went up to the bathroom on the roof. Hatim came after me and said, "Don't press the poor girl. She doesn't remember anything."

I said, "No, we are just playing with her."

He said, "How about me? Don't you want to play with me?"

I said, "The girls are downstairs."

He said, "Today is a holiday." Then, quoting Gibran via Fairouz, "Have you slept on the grass one day and used the sky as your comforter?"

Mervat called out, "The meat is done, Uncle Hatim."

We sat to eat in the balcony. Mervat said, "A gang? How unfair of you! And mama Fayza is the ringleader? I'll tell her what you said."

Rasha laughed and begged us to tell her the whole story, now that she had heard bits and pieces about it. Mervat kept teasing her. I noticed that Rasha's laughter was not carefree, that her smiles were beginning to dissipate as we continued our mocking comments until her face turned into a rubbery mask, not that of an innocent, eleven-year-old child. Sadness started to find its way to my mood and I became quite dejected: I wondered, daughter, why you are in pain and what's going on in your little head, leading you to this state? Are you afraid that Tante Fayza will take your mother's place? But Fayza was doing them a great service: raising an orphan girl and looking after the girls in Cairo after refusing to get married after her husband was martyred. So, why does Rasha refer to her as the ringleader and why is she confusing her with the police, the government, and her mother? And why does she call herself ugly?

Mervat said, "Where've you gone, Nora? Uncle Hatim is speaking to you."

I said, "It seems I didn't get enough sleep." We all laughed and Hatim said, "Again? Don't be so greedy."

Hilmi Amin called after a little while. We asked him to give us another day. He said he would pass by us tomorrow afternoon to pick up the girls. We were overjoyed.

We started making plans for the next day. We decided to go to the Assyrian quarter and to the market to buy what we needed for a picnic on the banks of the Tigris, not far from the house, then go back home to make dinner.

I let them sleep in after Hatim left for work. I sat down to write my article until they woke up and came to my study. Mervat leafed through my papers and Rasha stood in front of the bookcases looking for a book of adventure. Mervat said, "Have pity on your eyes and your complexion! God help Uncle Hatim! I will not be like my father. For me it is marriage and the comfortable luxuries of life."

Rasha said, "I want to be exactly like my father."

We prepared a quick breakfast. I said, "Life here begins at dawn, lazy girls. I wanted to feed you some headcheese, some pacheh, as they call it here."

They both screamed in dismay, "Oh God, no way."

"This is a great Iraqi breakfast dish. Or turnips in molasses, which they call shalgham."

Mervat said, "You want to kill us?"

"No, feed you, you skinny girls. There's no market now. We'll go in mid-afternoon because they take an hour for rest at noon, an English system."

I went down to the garden to water the plants. I pulled up the hose to the second floor to wash the vines and the trees from above.

Rasha came into the balcony. She wanted to water the plants with me. I began to sing some popular tunes, placing the hose in front of my mouth as if it were a microphone. The water got into my mouth. Mervat took the hose and sang as the water gushed all over her face. When I said, "Encore!" Rasha made fun of her sisters singing and said, "Give me the hose."

They started fighting over the hose and both got wet. I extracted the hose from their hands and in the process they sprayed me. I took it by force and sprayed them until they fell to the floor and made quite a racket in the balcony. My next-door neighbor Sabah came to the garden under the balcony and asked, "Is everything all right?"

"Yes, we're just playing. Come up and play with us."

"You seem to be in a good mood. Did you have company last night? Did you have a dog?"

We laughed and Mervat said, "Yes, a dog. No. A cat."

I said, "A snake."

July 1979

Treason

Baghdad felt different these days. There was something unusual about it. There were indications and manifestations of joy without any reason that was known to us. The media were broadcasting songs to the accompaniment of brass bands. They frequently played a song glorifying the Ba'th Party that went something like: "Hooray for the rising Ba'th, hooray!" as if an important event was going to be announced soon. The female television announcers wore the latest fashions and they looked more cheerful than usual. Vice President Saddam Hussein's movements during the last few months gave rise to many questions among the people, who expected to see him suddenly at their places of work in the factories, schools, and government departments. When he appeared he would either reward them, causing trills of joy to ring out, or he would fire them or transfer their boss. Sometimes he would demote someone from his position as the head of an organization to an ordinary worker's job without uttering a single word, all as the television cameras rolled. Saddam became a legend throughout the entire country, from Baghdad to Basra to Suleimaniya to Amara, as if he stood atop the entire map of Iraq. People talked of nothing except what he did, either in fear or joyfully.

When I conveyed to Hilmi Amin the impression that Saddam resembled Abu Khatwa he said to me, "Haven't you figured out what's behind all of this?"

I said, "I feel they want to tell us something. Is he really about to assume power? I've noticed how elated Manal al-Alousy, head of the Women's Union, looks these days. I know that she and the members of the Union are staunch supporters of his and I know that she is very close to him. But I cannot ask her," then I laughed, "after the famous incident with Abu Khalid."

He said, "Ask me about anything you want to know, but do not ask a single Iraqi before I know what you want to ask them about, especially in politics. Yes, I expect him to assume power sometime soon. And why not? All the circumstances are ripe for that now, and they are actually objective circumstances. The old man's health is failing and he no longer appears on most occasions. The Shi'i Iranian threat now has clear, specific names, from al-Da'wa Party to the Organization of Islamic Action which, as far as I understand, has a strong military wing, at least strong enough to cause anxiety to Iraq.

"The Iranian revolution considers Iraq, Saudi Arabia, and the Gulf region to be fertile soil that is ready for Iran to export the revolution. Saddam has also begun to open up toward France, from which he is buying the nuclear reactor and which is helping him develop rockets, and weapons agreements, some of which we've heard about. There is also some movement toward Japan, which means curbing reliance on the Soviet Union and the Eastern Bloc."

I said, "Wouldn't members of the national and regional commands oppose this accession to power after the union with Syria? I've heard some rumors about there being two currents and two schools of thought in the party about Syria, and Saddam specifically."

He said, "All the more reason to expedite announcing his accession to power."

I said, "I noticed that the decorations in the streets in preparation for celebrating the 17th of July are unusual this year. I even asked Hatim about celebrations of previous years and he said they seemed much more elaborate this year. He said the workers expect an announcement of something big, maybe al-Bakr's stepping down and Saddam replacing him. When Hatim says that, it means that the rumor has reached the street or that it's a trial balloon."

Hilmi said, "Wow! We are now analyzing trial balloons!"

I said, "I learned about trial balloons in a practical way and paid attention to it since the movie *Ascending to the Abyss*. Do you remember it?"

He said, "Of course. Tomorrow will come soon enough and I remember how people created a surprise for the government, which suddenly realized that they and the people were not on the same page at the moment Abla, who collaborated with the Jews, was arrested. The people applauded her arrest wildly, thus expressing their opinion frankly about normalization and Sadat's going to Jerusalem."

Saddam took over. Machine guns expressed joy by shooting the sky over Baghdad. I've never in my life seen more mass hysteria. I began asking myself, "Could it be that the party orchestrated all of it?" But, no. I believe it is Saddam's charisma that makes people throw themselves under the wheels of his car and welcome him with all these fervid chants all over Iraq. Don't you remember, Nora, what you heard after the 1967 setback in Egypt that the crowds that were awaiting Abdel Nasser's motorcades were arranged in return for five pounds and a bottle of milk per person? This is the talk of biased people. Egyptians adored Gamal Abdel Nasser, despite all the people on the right, and his massive funeral is the best proof of that. I wonder what the left thinks. What does the Iraqi Communist Party think of what is happening? But where is the party? Doesn't it have to be there to have opinions? Most of the members have been put on trial or executed or emigrated. Nothing can stand against Saddam Hussein's power. That was already a fact when he was vice president. Now that he is president what will happen? I remembered that Anhar was a member of the Iraqi Communist Party and I thanked God that she had not been arrested and that she had not fled Iraq. I love her and I love working with her. We understand each other easily, but understanding Hilmi Amin is hampered by the barrier between a boss and an underling, no matter how great the friendship. How about the age difference, Nora?

We received news that the celebrations that have disturbed the seven heavens over Baghdad did not end well and that a great catastrophe was about to be announced. We were told that that announcement would be made on July 18 and 19, one day after Saddam took power.

All Iraqi newspapers had one banner headline:

The Conspiracy: A Failed Attempt at Toppling the Regime

The news gave details about uncovering treason inside the Iraqi Ba'th Party and a secret organization composed of some members of the regional command in Iraq in collaboration with some members of the command council of the party in Syria, with the aim of toppling the regime in Iraq and seizing power. The state, we were told, has come into possession of the names of the traitors who had taken part in the organization at all levels. Some names were revealed. At the top of the list was Adnan Hamdani, minister of planning, a member of the national and regional commands, the closest person to President Ahmad Hasan al-Bakr, and one of those most enthusiastic supporters of union with Syria. Also named were Ghanim Abd al-Jalil, a member of the regional front, Muhammad Ayish, president of the Federation of Labor Unions and secretary general of the Labor Bureau of the party, Muhammad Mahjub, minister of education, and a long list of other high-ranking leaders.

Baghdad was dumbfounded. I didn't find anyone in the street who had a comment on what happened. Ordinary Iraqis were terribly afraid but silent, while Ba'thists parroted what Baghdad Radio was saying, namely that the details would follow shortly when the trials began.

Saddam Hussein, president of the Iraqi Republic, announced that the trial would be public and that retribution would be meted out by the peers of the accused at every party level.

We moved quickly, following up on events between the Ministry of Information and the Iraqi News Agency. Our work had usually been confined to features with a certain amount of political analysis from time to time, usually written by Hilmi Amin and with great sensitivity. I watched Ustaz Amin's dilemma, now that the bureau had become a private press bureau. I would hear his real daily analysis of what was happening around us and of the domestic and international conflicts, and what he, as a member of an Egyptian political group, thought about the "internal Iraqi affairs" as he put it. I also watched Anhar, sad and afraid, and her loss of appetite and weight. I attributed that to the wave of arrests of communists but also to her relationship with Hilmi Amin. I tried to comfort her and tell her to take care of herself. Her eyes would well up with tears and she would say, "God is generous."

Tomorrow would be an official holiday because of the anticipated high temperature. We got secret details from some of the families of those accused of treason: Ghanim Abd al-Jalil's wife had a severe nervous breakdown and hysteria and was taken to the Medical City Hospital and the accused leaders' families were deported and their properties confiscated. Hatim alerted me to read clan relationships behind the names and how the present crisis would result in a big problem in the future because the clans of those leaders were among Iraq's largest and most influential. I asked him, "Is a clan stronger than the state with a new ruler at the helm?"

"Yes," he said.

"I don't think so. Iraq is changing," I said.

The weather forecast said the temperature would reach a high of fifty-two degrees Celsius and warned against staying out in the sun. I said, "Oh God! Do we need this?"

Hatim said, "The air cooler is on."

Machine guns kept firing live ammunition at the sky and the television kept broadcasting songs celebrating victory against enemies of the country with refrains like "Hooray for the steadfast Ba'th, hooray." People stayed confined to their homes because of the heat, turning on air conditioners and coolers at the same time, which resulted in power cuts, starting early in the morning. The effect was a cheerless atmosphere, in spite of all the songs they broadcast. We were transfixed in front of the television, following events.

Hatim said, "What's this? How?"

The streets of the capital were filled with crowds carrying banners. Ba'th Party members stood on both sides of the street. Armored cars of the army and police appeared together moving in a large procession, followed by flatbed trucks on which red sacks were stacked. I asked Hatim, "Are these stones? Where are the accused?"

The trucks kept coming, followed by tanks and heavily armored cars and they all entered a structure that resembled a stadium. They stood in one line in their dark khaki color with brown spots. Then the engine roars stopped all at once as a large crowd wearing identical uniforms shouted various slogans. They did not announce the name of the building so we tried to guess what it was and we ended up assuming that it was the Baghdad Stadium. A truck left the line and moved forward, then came to a stop. The driver got off to open the tailgate of the truck and a number of soldiers lining the two sides of the road climbed into the truck and pushed the red sacks, whose upper ends were tied, with clubs. The sacks moved, fell back, then tried to stand up straight. We both screamed, "The detainees are in the sacks!"

The soldiers pushed them forward and they moved without seeing the edge of the tailgate and they fell down in a pile on the ground. They tried to stand up but fell down again. The soldiers fell upon them with their clubs. The detainees in the sacks kept jumping as the clubs rained down on them. One of them collapsed; a soldier hit him. He got up staggering and bumped into one of his fellow detainees. They both fell to the ground.

The announcer shouted, "Traitors of the homeland: enemies of the country! Retribution, Baghdad: treachery of the Syrian Ba'th! You have eaten and drunk in this country, from its bounty, so why the vileness and the treason?"

244

The sacks were made to stand up. One of the soldiers undid the ropes that tied them together. Some of the accused managed to free their heads from the sacks somehow. Then the soldiers opened the sacks one after another and tied the tops again under the neck to reveal the head clearly. The cameras focused on the frowning faces, the disheveled black hair and bloodshot eyes and the contusions and the bruises that covered the faces. One man stepped forward to read out the names of the accused, members of the National Committee, and then asked the other members of the committee to step forward and execute their colleagues. They tied the accused to poles. Some of them were kept blindfolded, their faces covered by big bags. (We found out the following day that those whose eyes had been gouged wore special bags on their heads to conceal their eyes.) We heard shots and the blood-soaked sacks fell to the ground amid the crowd's shouts for revenge. There was a power outage. Sweat poured out of our bodies and the heat frayed our nerves. The horrific scene had dealt us a heavy blow. We put towels on our thighs to dry the sweat that was flowing like rain. We turned on the battery-operated radio.

"Shouldn't I have been on the scene?"

"Everybody is on the screen right now in front of your eyes. What more do you want?"

"At least I should have been in the midst of the people to hear what they have to say directly."

"No one will be able to tell you anything other than what you're hearing here. The ones who will tell you the truth are your own friends and you've heard enough from them the last few days."

His arm reached out to hold me and he said, "I cannot do without you, Umm Yasir. I have every right to protect my beloved. Thank God you did not go out. The center of Baghdad will be hell on earth."

The power came back and with it television transmission. The scene did not change much. Another party level was on trial. This time it was members of the regional command. The positions of the accused were recited, as were the roles they had played in the conspiracy to overthrow the government. They carried the sacks to the poles and members of the same level in the party acted as the firing squads. Executions followed one another in quick succession. The party ranks kept getting lower and the names that filled Baghdad with pride and arrogance fell and their glow dried out in blotches of disgrace. Hatim drew my attention to the complex network connecting the party and the state. He said, "Notice that each party official is also responsible for one of the major institutions, especially in the more sensitive departments: security, planning, industry, and information."

I looked at Hatim as if with new eyes. His knowledge of Iraqi society was increasing every day, perhaps more than mine even though I was the journalist. It was all thanks to his daily contact with the workers and his getting close to their personal and family life. Iraqi engineers and workers did not hide their standing in the party or the name of their clans. He was able to see clearly the secret network of relations in the factory. And because he was an outsider, he understood the linkages but insisted on applying a set of rules and administrative orders equally to everybody, in order to avoid certain clashes. Therefore his colleagues loved and trusted him. They invited him several times to join the Ba'th Party, dangling before his eyes a high post in the party, one of whose goals was Arab unity. He told them simply, "I am Egyptian, performing a specific job, and I will not join the party." They finally accepted his point of view and did not pressure him. But at least they had given him the opportunity to see the reality of their world.

It was now two o'clock in the afternoon. The heat was at its peak: fifty-two degrees Celsius in the shade but it felt as if it were rising. Electrical power followed its own erratic system: we assumed that they cut it off from certain areas and restored it to other areas on a rotational basis to reduce pressure on the grid. That was the only logic in this mad scene that flew in the face of logic. Radio and television were still listing the names of the accused and broadcasting military marches and shouts. Cameras and microphones kept moving from street shots among the people and the trial in the stadium. Hatim sneaked to the kitchen to place skewers on the grill. He came back, carrying a bottle of juice for me. I said, "Do you think I can swallow anything?"

He said, "It is four o'clock now and soon you'll be very hungry."

I had been moving since the early morning between the couch and the floor whose rug I had removed to feel cool, but it was no use. I gathered every vessel I could and filled it with water and placed the filled containers throughout the room. I turned on the ceiling fans, so that when the power came back on it created other forms of cooling to help the air cooler that was overworked. Every hour or so we moved between the shower and the living room. We had on light cotton clothes. And even as we moved we kept our ears and eyes whenever possible glued to the sources of the news. The scene of our coming out wet from the bathroom turned into a comic scene as we noticed the disappearance of the drops of water as soon as they made it to the very hot floor. We looked like sea creatures from the North Pole panting on a rocky island below the equator.

At five o'clock I brought the food in front of the television. I could only chew a few small bites. We were content to eat some yogurt. I took the rest of the food back to the kitchen. I wanted to take a short nap. The charges were now being leveled at lower-level party youths. They were lined up in their sacks and young members of the party stepped forward and opened fire with their automatic machine guns, then the sacks fell down in their pools of blood. I said in the Iraqi dialect, "What is that? What's that?"

Trying to get me out of that mood, Hatim said, "Now you're speaking Iraqi? What else are you hiding up your sleeve?"

My crying got louder. He got up to help me come back up on the couch. I told him, "Get me out of here! Get me out! I don't want to live in this cruel city that kills its sons this way. Can you imagine the lives of these young men who executed their colleagues? How will they live after this experience? The dead are dead, but those who will live have been totally destroyed."

247

He held me tight, wrapping his arm around my body while I tried to get away. I said, "Why this way? Political coups happen everywhere in the world. Trials, fair or unfair, are held and prisons all over the world are packed with political prisoners, but why this brutality? I don't want to stay here. I don't want to be a journalist, or have anything to do with public affairs. I don't want literature or art. I want to be a little donkey, a cow, or a bird. I don't want to be involved to this extent in all human grief."

"Nora, please snap out of it. Please, my darling."

"Where are the mothers? Where are the wives? The children, Hatim, where?"

"They bear the consequences of their actions. What are you protesting, Nora?"

"Not in this savage way. These are one-third of the command. This means that there was considerable support for this view."

"Imagine what would have happened if that coup were successful: they would have traded places, the killer and the killed."

"Why is it done in the street, Hatim? I will never understand Iraq. I will never understand it even though I love Iraq very much. I will not understand."

"What has this to do with Iraq? The people have nothing to do with it. It's a struggle for power."

"Every people deserves its leader. Isn't that what we've believed all our lives?"

"So, it's an attempt to give the people a chance to choose their leader. Revolutions have victims."

He hugged me hard. I understood his logic and the way he thinks. He can reach conclusions easily and once he does, the case is closed, while I dwell on all the details. When he finds me trapped in perplexity, he hugs me or leaves me by myself for hours to calm down while I contemplate the sky over Baghdad, then he closes the door and leaves. Then he invites me for a stroll in Zawra Park, where we walk hand in hand and then dine out and come back home after I get over my bad mood and dark thoughts.

Actually, he could never get me out of my bad moods unless I myself had reached some degree of equanimity. And that could come from an unexpected source: meeting somebody unknown to me who would remind me of Egypt, or an old girlfriend of mine, or even a neighbor coming by. Hatim would be surprised that I had come out to the world again and turned the page. But today I wanted to close my eyes forever and erase from my memory all that I had seen by any means possible so that I could live in this country and adjust to the place and go back to work.

I went in the morning to the office, since staying at home alone after Hatim had gone to work would have driven me crazy. When Hilmi Amin opened the door my tears came down like a torrential rain. I turned into a little, inconsolable girl. He gave me a big hug.

I said, "Did you see what happened?"

He said, "Yes. The tape was played in all the party branches, in addition to television. In other words: viewing was mandatory."

I said, "You say 'tape.' Was it recorded?"

He said, "Of course. Do you imagine they would leave an event like that to chance? It had already been done and recorded and released only after control over all Iraq had been achieved."

I said, "Do you think Saddam's rise to power was engineered to happen at this time in particular or was it a matter of who is faster, who would get there first to beat the other one?"

He said, "Nothing is known for sure so far, but what is certain is that the side that accused the other of selling Iraq out to Syria has triumphed. As we concluded in our previous analysis, Saddam would not accept to be the third man in the Iraqi–Syrian Ba'th Party hierarchy."

I said, "Why weren't Syrian–Iraqi relations discussed openly, so everyone could come to a final agreement, instead of the coup attempt and accusations of treason?"

He said, "All the reasons that the accused gave during the trial for having a different point of view from that of the party were unacceptable, since the party, as far as I've learned, allows every issue, no matter how minor, to be discussed within the party committees. Therefore the reason it was considered treasonous was because it was not discussed within the committees of the party, but was secretly arranged with the Syrian side."

I said, "Who knows? These are countries of many coups, whether here or in Syria."

He said, "You are right. Who knows where anyone in power today will be tomorrow?"

He went on to say, "I don't think, Nora, that we will see any Syrian–Iraqi cooperation, at least in our present job."

The Iraqi–Syrian Ba'th Party file was closed. The borders were closed on both sides. Once again our activity was confined to Iraq alone.

August 1977

Jerusalem

Hatim called out in alarm, "Nora! Nora! Where are you?"

"On the roof. What's wrong?"

"What are you doing on the roof now? Come down, quick."

I said as I came down, somewhat worried, "I was returning the bedding to the storeroom. It's getting cooler, thank God. Why are you so tense?"

"Sadat announced in the People's Assembly that he was ready to go to Jerusalem."

"Oh my God! What a catastrophe! Did Hilmi Amin call?"

"It came in the news. They called the visit 'treason.'"

I picked up the phone and kept trying to call Ramsis Hotel, angrily. I never heard of a press bureau without a telephone.

Hatim said, "Wait till the morning."

I said, "Who knows what the consequences will be in the morning?"

We heard knocks on the door. Shukry and Sabah came in asking, in alarm, about the repercussions of this bizarre announcement for Egyptians in Iraq.

Hatim said, "Nobody knows. We know exactly the same as you so far."

The telephone didn't stop ringing. All the Egyptians we knew called. They were worried that the visit would lead to their expulsion from Iraq. Within hours the Iraqi street reached a boiling point after the media roused people with zealous rhetoric. I kept moving among Iraqis and Egyptians and went to several police stations. We ran all over following the reaction to the events and the news. The Egyptian embassy was not closed. We wrote reports describing reactions on the popular as well as the governmental level. On our way back from the Ministry of Information, we heard a group of young Iraqis commenting on a pregnant Egyptian woman as she crossed the street, saying, "A she-donkey which wants to have a donkey!"

Hilmi Amin said to them, "Shame on you! Men don't attack a woman for any reason!"

One of them said, "Go back to your country, you lackeys of Israel."

Hilmi Amin said, "This kind of talk is pointless. The Egyptian people have paid the price with thousands of young men to defend Palestine. Why don't you go to school, instead of standing idly on street corners."

I took him by the hand and we crossed the street, saying, "Don't get mad at them. They are just being enthusiastic. I've never seen you so irritated. When I passed these young men, they would repeat refrains from Egyptian songs."

He laughed, saying, "They were flirting with you?"

I said, "Yes and they'd say 'Your love has set me on fire,' and many other expressions like that. This is what will last. As for talk of treason and the like, this is the enthusiastic reaction to what they hear and see on radio and television all day long."

Two days later we went to al-Khalsa village to see how the Egyptian peasants were doing. I was quite afraid that the experiment would collapse. People received us with their usual warm welcome. A few minutes into our visit, Engineer Mahdi, director of the project, got out of his car. Before shaking his hand I asked him, "Any news?"

252

He said calmly, "Everything is under control. A petty-minded announcer came to the village and enthusiastically asked the peasants to condemn the visit and to badmouth Sadat. I kicked him out at once. He said, 'This is party work.' I said, 'I am responsible.' He said, 'I'll tell the higher-ups.' I said, 'Go ahead, tell them.' And of course he couldn't do anything and left angrily and no one else will come. My responsibility is to protect the village against passing whims. This is not a propaganda project; it's an experiment that requires care and stability, not politics and its fickle turns."

Hilmi said, "You are right," and he continued, "What do the peasants have to do with Sadat's visit to Jerusalem?"

Hilmi said, "No one asked their opinion whether he should go or not!"

I said, "And nobody has asked them before making any decision."

I looked at Engineer Mahdi for a long time. This man did not know how much I loved him at that moment and how I considered him a sincere friend, even though I knew nothing about him as a person. I just followed his work and I saw that he loved the peasants and knew every inch of this reclaimed land. He gauged the abilities of every peasant and gave to each from his rich experience to help them achieve the highest productivity of their land. He kept track of their needs and adjusted his planning accordingly, and persuaded upper management levels to give the peasants additional support. He studied why certain families succeeded in staying and settling down and why others failed, so he helped them adjust with the help of an excellent team in the Agricultural Unit. It was through his efforts that, after getting cows and chickens, they also got apiaries. And when they began to reap the fruits of their labor, he and the Unit showed them how to get loans to buy trucks to move their crops to the market and to serve neighboring villages also. The village grew and began to take root in the new land and to have its own entity and distinct character.

I realized as Engineer Mahdi was talking to us about Sadat's problem that only wise, thinking people were capable of changing society. A revolutionary comes first with his courage and rush, then he needs support from calmer people. I wanted to ask him whether he was a Ba'thist or not, but I wasn't sure I should: What did it matter whether he was within the party or outside? What mattered was that he was making it possible for the project to succeed.

The Iraqi government issued a decree making it punishable by a six-month jail sentence for anyone to insult any Egyptian because of Sadat's visit to Jerusalem. The resolution came about to calm Egyptians' anxiety about staying in the country and silenced those tongues that had treated Egyptian workers, in particular, insolently. For the first time in many days, Baghdad went to bed quietly, but the repercussions of the events were far from simple or over. There was a growing desire among Ba'thist intellectuals to repudiate Egypt. Iraqi unions called for relocating Arab unions from Egypt to Iraq.

We anxiously followed what was happening in Egypt. Egyptian journalists outside Egypt decided to hold a meeting in Paris to discuss the situation. Hilmi Amin made his preparations to travel. We went without prior arrangement to the Journalists' Union to renew our memberships. We met some colleagues who started talking to us about the treasonous act and its impact on the region. They said we had to move the Union of Arab Journalists from Cairo to Baghdad.

Hilmi Amin said, "The Egyptian Journalists' Union is now engaged in a struggle against Sadat, and instead of supporting it, you want to kill it? Isn't that strange?"

Angry shouts rose, "Yes, we have to move the Union!"

Hilmi Amin said, "The presence of the Union of Arab Journalists in Egypt would strengthen the position of the Egyptian Union which is expecting to be targeted and its members and journalists to be arrested, because of their opinions."

One of those present said, "We shouldn't let Arab unions stay in a country that betrays the cause."

Hilmi said, "The Doctors' Union is struggling against Sadat and the same goes for the Lawyers' Union. They are independent unions whose members are subjected to brutal repression by the head of the state, and you know these matters in detail, just as I do."

Someone said, "How can the Arab Union issue statements from Cairo condemning Sadat's treason? It must be moved to Baghdad."

Hilmi said, "Please don't just pay lip service to patriotism. Let's admit the real motivation here, which is opportunism, pure and simple. You want to grab what the Egyptians have achieved in their long struggle and their pioneering work."

"This is not true. We must teach Sadat a lesson he cannot forget. We must boycott Egypt and impoverish it so it would revolt against him and against his treason."

Hilmi Amin choked as he said, "The idea of impoverishing Egypt and so on is so naive. It won't happen."

I said, "A revolution cannot be manufactured outside the country."

"We should expel Egyptian workers from all Arab countries, so they'll rise up and kill him."

Another said, "Kill whom? The Egyptians didn't do anything. We are the ones who will pay the price for the treason."

Hilmi said, "This is just empty talk. You won't pay anything until Israeli soldiers arrive on the banks of the Tigris."

Two journalists said, "Excuse me, the chairman is waiting for you."

The chairman met us at the door of his office and ordered tea for us. Then he asked us about who would attend the Paris meeting.

Hilmi Amin said, "Only those members of the Journalists' Union in exile."

The chairman said, "Some Egyptian journalists here in Iraq, like Nora Suleiman, Ahmad Ezzedin, Hala El Badry, and others want to attend and they are members of the Union of Arab Journalists and they are practicing the profession, so why shouldn't they attend?"

Hilmi Amin said, "If we open this door we will face many problems. This is a professional meeting to be attended by professionals who are members of a specific union. It should be conducted in accordance with rules that would preserve its legitimacy so that their decisions might be binding on their union."

The chairman said, "If you need any help, we are here. Sitt Nora, please understand the enthusiasm of our colleagues. There was some crossing of the boundaries of course. Egypt's role cannot be denied by anyone and no one, be they Arab or foreign, can cast aspersions on it. A decision to boycott will have adverse results in the long run. God is generous. Don't be angry: blame it on us, or as the Egyptians say, rub it off on us."

We thanked him and left, full of sorrow for the lack of understanding. We felt that we were dealing with political amateurs. The position of the Ba'thists was so unbelievably different from that of the communists. Was it power? Or was it the makeup of the party itself? Was the fact that the party was in power the reason for this arrogance? I looked at the signs hanging over the walls of tall buildings in the streets of Baghdad as the taxi was taking us. I told Hilmi Amin, "I can't stand superlative adjectives and the way they are being used: the biggest, the greatest, the most perfect! My God, is it an Iraqi trait? Or is it the insanity of wealth and power and megalomania?"

Hilmi said in exasperation, "They're a little happy with themselves. They want to dominate every Arab union and put it in their pockets. But I am not going to let them get away with it. We are at a critical juncture and it doesn't make sense that the Egyptian national movement should receive blows from all sides."

I said, "And how will you do that?"

He said, "Don't worry about it and have no fear."

Fourth Text

Three knocks on the door of memory restored life to days that were lingering as they turned toward disappearing forever. I tugged at the end of the thread of time that used to tame mountains and humans. The days broke loose and came tumbling down on my heart. I tried to stop their ruthless flow and pay attention to what was happening around me, but I couldn't. Inside of me there was a rush seeking to recapture the flow of the days and once again feel the pleasure of the pain that didn't contain the moment. I was carrying my suitcase on my way to Baghdad to take part in a conference about educating women after teaching them how to read and write. I could not believe that I have indeed arranged to leave my six-month-old son with my mother-in-law in Maghagha, two and half hours away from Cairo. I was hoping to know why and how Anhar Khayun, my Iraqi friend and colleague at *al-Zahra*, the Egyptian magazine in Baghdad, had disappeared. I also wanted to visit my house in Dora hit by Iranian bombers and see if my neighbors there were all right. I wanted to meet with Basyuni Abd al-Mu'in who joined the Iraqi army and its war with Iran and to give him a letter from his family urging him to go back to Egypt. Among the tasks I set for myself was visiting *al-Zahra's* office to complete liquidating its affairs and to look for Hilmi Amin's articles.

On the first day of the conference I was surprised to find note-books of memoirs of both Hilmi Amin and Anhar Khayun in my mailbox. I left my card and my address for the new occupant of the apartment and immersed myself in the work of the conference, as memories continued to catch up with me. And then there I was, starting a new day in Baghdad.

Haytham's crying awakened me at five o'clock in the morning. I reached with my hand, looking for him so I could pull him toward me, give him my breast, and go back to sleep. My hand hit the cold empty area of my bed. I sat up halfway and placed a small pillow behind my back, turning on the light and placing the pump on my breast. I wished I could sleep for a bit more; one hour of additional sleep would push me to the peak of my energy. I closed my eyes. Haytham wouldn't let me sleep. A slap from his little hand on my cheek woke me up again. I turned on the radio and soft music filled the room. I began to carry on with my waking-up routine. I saw Hilmi Amin's notebook that I had left on the nightstand after reading a few pages the night before last. I opened it after a short hesitation.

He wrote:

Ismat

I released Ismat to the sky. I liberated her because I was madly in love with her. I was in utter, deadly despair. I was being subjected to daily torture—being whipped—as well as the torture of hearing the other prisoners being tortured. I was expecting a death sentence and my father readily accepted her engagement to another man who had been asking for her hand. She lived in my fantasies even though I was married to another woman and had fathered a beautiful daughter I had named Mervat. I hadn't tried at all to see Ismat before I was arrested again and detained in the Oases camp. I arranged in my imagination a daily tryst with her to make a dent in the wall of time, of distance, and of separation. I set for her an hour for which I had prepared myself since waking up in the morning and going out on the farm detail which we requested. When the camp administration agreed to the garden, we turned that patch of desert into a real garden. I waited for her every day as I followed the journey of the sun as it inclined. When everybody around me withdrew and when they closed our cells, I called out to her, "Ismat," and she would come like a soft specter. She would tell the story of our days together, our love, and would ask, "Don't you get bored with our talking?" I would tell her, "It's all I have in these days of dearth." I hear her bouncing laughter. I recall the two of us running on the sand of the beach and being embraced by the waves as I sneaked out at dawn to see her with her sisters and girlfriends as they flung themselves into the water, turning into mermaids. She would sense my presence and leave them to their mirth and laughter as they threw handfuls of wet sand at her. We would take off chasing the horizon until we got out of their sight. It was a daily date we had kept ever since we were kids.

My wife comes to the detention camp once a month. She takes the train to the city of Asyut then an intercity taxi to Kharga Oasis, then the prison. She tells me about my daughter, Mervat, who is wearing her hair in braids now, and she tells me what is happening in Egypt and the world. I miss my house but Ismat has a radiant pendulum that shimmers and moves in front of my eyes, reminding me of those fleeting days and how much I miss her. I didn't ask myself how much I miss her. I didn't ask myself how I would see her after I got out. I knew that we had a date, even though she had never written to me. I only received an oral message from her through my wife. She just said, "May God bring your ordeal to an end."

A few days after my release I was standing in front of my mother with open arms. She cried for a long time before holding me in her embrace. Her voice got louder as she called to people in our alley one by one: "Muhammad, Alaa, Hilmi is here. Yusuf, Fatma, Abu Mahmoud, Salwa, Fathiya, Zeinhom, Hilmi is here."

Ismat came in the midst of the family and the neighbors. I didn't look at her eyes. I didn't exchange a single word with her, but we knew what we were going to do. When the hubbub died down, we sneaked to our favorite spot behind the house where the fields were still under cultivation. We disappeared into the darkness and the rustling cornstalks. I had gotten tired of just speaking with her for years. I let my hands roam freely on her face and my lips, looking for each of her cells to kiss it. My hands reached to squeeze her breasts and feel every part of her body to make sure she was actually there. I sat on an old stone leaning against the wall of our house and sat her on my thigh as I passed my hands over the contours of her body, discovering the feminine changes that marriage brought to it.

I said, "I missed a lot."

She said, "I am all yours."

I kissed her hard and my lips squeezed her lips. My nose caught the scent of her lust and that heightened my mad desire to disappear totally and forever into her body. My own body began to writhe as I felt her coiling on my thigh. Neither of us could control our desires. My hands reached out, stripped the lower half of her body, and held on to it. She turned around, opening her legs, to face me and descend upon it before I could free it totally and plunge into her. She screamed as she buried her face in my chest, cupping her mouth to prevent her screams from alerting others to where we were. I clung to her as I saw her traveling further inward. Now she was not seeing me, but looking deep inside herself and giving herself up with her whole being to it.

I continued my thrusts and hurried the pace to reach the farthest horizon of our passion that was killing us. I aimed my thrusts at a target that I knew quite well despite the strong tremors of her body. She opened herself fully to me and I saw stars shimmering. I reached my fingers to her soft hips as they kept coming back to my thighs. I felt totally intoxicated when I found myself caught in a semicircle sucking me in with a regular rhythm into her mouth and her vagina. I lost myself completely in her as time stopped and her body oozed with honey and milk invading my nose. I discovered that I knew the scent of her coming even though this was the first time she gave herself to me. It was the smell of passion; of waves breaking on moss-covered rocks; the smell of wood soaking and decaying in the water; the smell of a winter morning or a moist summer breeze; the smell of hot black pepper; the smell of the bitter cactus flower which I had bitten one afternoon with her a long time ago; the smell of her laugh; the smoothness and softness of her skin and my deprivation.

We did not need to learn how to control our own rhythm. We've been dreaming of it for so many years. The smooth harmony came from nights of longing and desire. I wished each of my fingers were a penis and that I wouldn't ever stop my thrusts. She came down on me, squeezing me, and easing our simultaneous explosion. She rested in my embrace and even though I still had a great thirst for her, she slipped away to her mother's house and left me unable to close my eyes, looking at the green fields stretching in front of me until dawn came and, still in disbelief that I was free, I entered the house to sleep many hours until my mother awakened me, saying as she laughed, "You really were hungry for sleep."

I went back to Cairo, and when I saw Ismat after a short time on a family occasion carrying a little boy and rocking him, I knew without a moment's hesitation that he was my son.

Did that really happen? Or was it one of those dreams brought on by loneliness, senility, or hallucinations conjuring up the impossible in this closed apartment in Baghdad's stifling heat?

She named him Gamal, my code name.

I closed the notebook, saying to myself, "God forgive you, Hilmi. I didn't need this kind of sexual provocation so early in the morning!" I took my bath, quickly estimating the time in Cairo so I could call our house; maybe I'd have better luck in the morning.

I heard my mother's voice in Cairo reassuring me about Haytham, Yasir, and Hatim. She said, "Everyone is fine. Please focus on your work and I hope it was worth the trouble. What's the news about the war? Are you safe?"

"It is sad here. I wish I could stay to gather as much information as I can. I don't sleep much, day or night, so I can convey how things are. It turned out that the idea of taking Haytham with me to Baghdad was a crazy and impossible one, but not the big scandal I was afraid it might be. The city is safe: people have gotten used to working and living their lives and waiting for the news. It's very much like Cairo during the War of Attrition in the late sixties. The front is relatively far unless Baghdad receives a direct hit, which is rare now."

"Are you going to extend your stay? How's your milk?

"Most likely, I won't stay longer. For Haytham's sake I have been pumping the milk exactly on time. But I have noticed that the yield decreases in the evening."

"It won't stop coming, God willing. But make sure to keep doing it regularly. Don't give up."

"I'd like to hear Yasir's voice."

His voice choked as he placed the telephone in front of his mouth. He said, "Mom, come, come."

I said, "I'll be with you in a few days and I'll bring you a very big toy."

He burst out crying. I heard my mother's voice saying, "Take care of yourself. Goodbye."

Layla, my escort, who accompanied me throughout, told me that after the conference sessions in the evening, we would get ready to travel to Basra to visit the front and the local branch of the women's union there and that I should pack because the train would leave at five in the morning.

I said, "The trip usually takes eighteen hours. Isn't traveling by train dangerous and closely monitored by the air force because they carry weapons and soldiers?"

She said, "No. The raids have targeted military trains and no civilian train has been hit."

From the balcony of my house, which overlooked the Baghdad railroad line in Dora, I used to watch trains as they moved back and forth. I knew the schedule during my long stay in the house and I could distinguish the various kinds of trains from the whistle which the trains blew as they came through at specific times from Basra harbors, carrying factory equipment and raw materials to the capital, which was building huge industrial compounds at a dizzying speed. When Hatim and I stood in the balcony, we could feel the vibrations under our own feet before hearing the train's movement on the tracks. Hatim would tell me in admiration, "Watch the development! These are new factories. Iraq is building. It has the money, the desire, and the perseverance. We will be here so long as this train carries new equipment."

Iraq's balance of payments surplus was considerable and the oil revenue was converted into investments in factories, roads, and agricultural projects. There was a sense of pride in Baghdad. Where was that now from what I've been hearing? Even though construction has not been halted, this was not the Baghdad I knew.

I remembered the day I heard of the bombing of my neighborhood in Dora. It was only nine days after I had left Baghdad, and the war with Iran started. Today I would go to my neighborhood during the break between the morning and evening sessions.

Chef Said came to me after I finished breakfast and said, "I have with me my colleague Mahmoud Abu Wafiya, whom I told you about, Ustaza Nora."

262

I said, "Why don't you go ahead to the lounge and I'll catch up with you."

Siham asked, "Problems?"

I said, "No. I like to speak to Egyptians here."

I said, "Hello, Mahmoud. It doesn't look like this is your first marriage."

He said calmly, "Yes. I am married in Egypt and I have children. One of them is in college."

I said, "Why did you marry an Iraqi woman? Is she a martyr's widow?"

He said, "Ustaza, there are whole streets without a single man. They're all women. An Egyptian young man now lives in lower-income neighborhoods and mixes with people in a way that used to be unusual. I've been living here for five years, and I know Iraqis well."

I said, "But you haven't told me why you got married again."

He said, "She's a neighbor's daughter, and here, I am a bachelor. Her mother-in-law is sick and she has children. Her grownup sons are in the army and one of them is the martyr. I used to help taking the mother-in-law to the hospital. I thought I should marry the daughter rather than have people talking."

I said, "And you took the ten thousand dinars?"

He said, "Yes. I took the money and put it in the bank. I haven't spent a single millieme on my children in Egypt. My new wife's children have their martyred father's pension. Her mother-in-law has accepted me because she knew I took care of them from the beginning and before the marriage."

I said, "Frankly, don't you intend to run off to Egypt after getting the money?"

Said smiled and said, "I tell you this is not possible. Mahmoud used to support the family before marrying the widow, and as I told you, he's a good and generous man. But other men have taken the money and run. God will repay them."

Mahmoud said, "Rest assured, Ma'am, my wife is pregnant and all the money in the world would not persuade me to abandon her."

I said, "How about your wife and children in Egypt?"

He said, "Thank God, I have been providing for them. I send them money regularly, and I'll visit them next summer, God willing. Going back and forth has become quite a burden after relations were cut."

I said, "Yes." I realized that Layla was signaling me to move to the conference hall. I took my leave and walked with the other delegates as I recalled the bitter moment when relations were cut.

Baghdad radio announced that relations between Iraq and Egypt had been severed. The embassy closed its doors the moment the announcement was made. I had the home telephone number of the ambassador's wife Layla, and I called her before going to the office. I asked her what was happening. She said that the ambassador was in Egypt and that they would be evacuated according to the usual protocols.

I said, "You are used to this. Right?"

She said, "This has never happened to me. The minister plenipotentiary and the consul and other members of the embassy staff are with me and they know the procedures. I will leave as soon as we arrange a flight. I've actually started packing."

I said, "I'll come right after I go to the office first, since Ustaz Hilmi Amin might want to come with me."

She said, "You're both welcome."

Egypt Air had cancelled all its flights from Baghdad to Cairo and the bookings were diverted either to Damascus on Syrian Airlines or Amman on Royal Jordanian Airlines or to Cyprus. Airlines immediately increased their scheduled flights to carry Egyptian workers from and to Baghdad, and fares doubled at the same time. Egyptian workers in Baghdad were apprehensive about a total breakdown in relations, which were getting worse every day, and there was an escalating war of words. Then Baghdad announced that Egyptian workers would stay in their positions as long as they wanted and that their currency transfers would continue according to the system in place.

During one of my usual book-buying outings with Hilmi Amin, I saw lines of Egyptians in front of the central post office, waiting to call their families in Egypt by telephone. We entered Orosdi Bak to buy some supplies for the office. I saw a porcelain tea set exquisitely painted. I loved it and paid for it, and when I went to the customer pick-up station to get it, the clerk told me, "Sorry. Please come in the evening. We've run out of the sets on hand, but we'll get some more from the warehouse in a short while." I also noticed some fine Czech crystal, and since Hatim and I had not gone shopping together recently, I called him at the factory and asked him to pick me up to spend the evening downtown. I went back to the office where Dalida, the Egyptian-born French singer's, record about Egypt was playing. Anhar, whom I hadn't seen in a while, came. I noticed that she was worried; it seemed that she caught Hilmi Amin's anxiety about the uncertain future of the bureau, like a boat without a rudder in the midst of waves. She asked me as if she were a frightened child, "Will the bureau close down like the airlines?"

I said in the Iraqi dialect, trying to allay her anxiety, "What's wrong with you? Your face is as yellow as a lemon!"

She smiled shyly. I patted her on the shoulder and said, "No, it won't close down, Anhar. And even if it did, where would Hilmi go? He will not go back to Cairo under these circumstances and I am here with my husband until who knows when. The Iraqi government has said the Egyptians and their jobs here would not be affected. If worse came to worst we can always open a press agency or a private press office."

She sounded resigned as she said with tears glistening in her eyes, "Dearest Nora, I don't know where to go."

I am puzzled by the sudden reversals in moods that I have noticed in many Iraqis: from total or near total self-confidence to withdrawal inside and fear, then a pleading tone that sends shivers to my body. And the opposite is also true: from calm docility to obstinate confrontation with no chance of reconsideration. I remembered the Egyptian saying that once Sa'idi scissors closed, they never reopened. I guess I was wrong; Sa'idis did not write the book on obstinacy.

Hatim came and he accompanied me to Rashid Street. We were surprised to see the long lines at the post office. He suggested that we reserve our turn in making telephone calls, and then go to do our shopping and come back, thus saving some time.

We went back and sat for a long time, not understanding why the line was not moving. I went to the reception desk and asked to go in to see one of the employees that I knew. I was allowed to go through. I heard one employee saying, "The National Council has taken over the line to Cairo. There's no way anyone can make a regular call tonight. We must tell people that we have to cancel their calls."

Another employee said to him, "Don't announce anything. If they want to wait, let them wait."

Abu Wisam turned toward me and asked, "Can I be of help, Sitt Nora?"

I laughed, "The line is out."

He smiled. I went out to Hatim with shock and sarcasm all over my face. I said, "We're going home."

He said, "You're always hasty. What happened? We've wasted the day. It's over, but at least we are together. Let's go for a walk in the open air, then come back. Don't you want to hear your mom's voice?"

I said, "I do want to. But come, let's get out of here first."

As soon as I was out the door I burst out laughing. I struck one palm against the other in utter disgust and disbelief and said, "The sons of bitches, they are talking with each other and they couldn't care less if we go to hell. Everything is going on as usual. They are having a blast together. Their own relationship has not suffered one bit and our lot is to be insulted as treacherous lackeys. I don't know why we have to pay the price of their messes."

"I don't understand what you are saying, Nora. What happened to you inside? What relationship? And what messes?"

266

"The National Council has taken over the line. It means that the presidential palaces in Egypt and Iraq are talking to each other, contrary to the public posturing about cutting off relations. Ever since Sadat announced his accursed visit, they have been referring to him as 'Abu Righal,' about whom I had heard absolutely nothing except here. Abu Righal is the one who led the army of the Abyssinian king Abraha to Mecca, then died of the plague. They say that pilgrims stoned him. My relatives make the hajj every year and I have never heard that name. I thought they stoned Satan. That means that the cutting off of relations is part of the pressure they exert on people to cause them disruptions and hardships and get them kicked around from one airport to another. Maybe it's an attempt to impoverish the Egyptian people so that it will revolt against its rulers. It's a stupid way of thinking and we are paying for it!"

"Calm down, Nora."

"They transmit the broadcasts of *Sawt al-Uruba* (Voice of Arabism) which calls upon Egyptians to rise up in revolt. And even though some Egyptians, about whose patriotic feelings I have no doubt, take part in writing its programs, this idea of exporting revolution is a stupid idea, Hatim. And it smacks of an arrogance that I don't like, and which they themselves would never accept and would never imagine anybody applying to them, even non-Ba'thist Iraqis."

"You are against Sadat's act and you know its consequences on the region. It is natural for there to be confusion and desperate attempts to get out of the international trap that has been set and which appears shiny and attractive from the surface. I am not talking about Sadat's right to do what he did. My analysis of the situation might be much gloomier than yours, but what I object to is taking measures against the Egyptian people who are repressed by their rulers and who pay the price for the foolish decision of Egyptian and Arab rulers together under the guise of revolution and unity."

I said, "Those who supposedly want to help us should help us resist, not weaken people by making them too busy trying to make a living."

267

I sat at the conference roundtable. Today we had a full schedule of presentations in the morning session and celebrations in the evening. The only time I could visit my old house in Dora was in the break immediately after lunch. I realized that someone was talking to me: "Sitt Nora, there's someone on the telephone for you. Come with me, please."

Tariq Mandour sounded overjoyed to hear my voice. "I miss you, Nora. How long are you staying?"

I said, "Tomorrow at dawn we leave for Basra and I'll be back in two days. Most likely I'll extend my stay in Baghdad for two more days."

He said, "I'll come to Baghdad. How's Mom, and Salwa, and Uncle Hatim, and Yasir and the baby?"

I said, "They're all fine and they say hello to you. I have a letter for you and some small gifts, but not a fattened duck."

He said, "Good. I hope nothing like your mom's duck. Do you remember it?"

I said, "How could I forget? It was such a scandal."

"I'll call you at the hotel in Basra. I have many stories for you. I know you're busy."

I said, "I'll be waiting for your call. Bye."

I went back to the conference session. I thanked God that the presentation underway was pure propaganda, so I didn't miss anything. I opened the notebook in front of me and began doodling.

I remembered Tariq when he came to Baghdad for the first time looking for work. His older sister, Salwa, was my dearest and closest friend since childhood. When he called us to tell us he was in Baghdad, Hatim was overjoyed. He has never forgotten that it was thanks to Salwa and her fiancé, Hashim, that he and I met at Salwa's birthday party. We went to see him at his hotel and took from him copies of his credentials to circulate in government departments in Baghdad. Hatim told him, "Accept any job in a restaurant or a store.

The hotel meter is running every day. Or find work with the laborers. Go in the morning to Tahrir Square and wait for a contractor to come by. Try everything. If you do that from the first moment you won't be laboring under any illusions about how things work here. It's just until we can find you a job suitable for your qualifications."

Tariq looked visibly shocked and disappointed. He had grown up in a well-off family. Both his father and his mother were radio and TV announcers and it had never occurred to him that he would do menial work. I looked at his fancy clothes and imagined what could happen. I asked him, "Do you have any other clothes, besides these? Something of a different level?"

"Of course not," he said, surprised by the question.

I said, "Nothing is cheaper than clothes in Baghdad. Why don't you buy an Iraqi pullover and pants so you won't stand out in your trendy clothes?"

Tariq began to sweat. I could sense the tension that he tried to hide. He looked at the floor, not quite sure what to do, then he looked at me and at Hatim and said, "Nora, what's happening?"

I said, "Tariq, what was the first thing I said to you? Come, live with us. Work in government departments and factories right now is quite hard to get and the jobs are filled. Commissions go to Egypt to finish hiring procedures for jobs that had been advertised in the papers. Iraqi officials prefer to go to Cairo, of course, where they interview dozens of young applicants and they come back with official contracts. As for getting employed from within the country here, it is subject to other conditions. First, local hires are treated exactly like Iraqis and at a regular salary. Monetary transfers are allowed only for minute percentages. And don't forget: an Iraqi lives at home with his family and enjoys many benefits that you cannot get. What you don't know is that their appointment procedures might take a whole year before they are finalized. That is, if there is a post to begin with, because you're an accountant and not an engineer or a doctor. Even they are having a hard time now that thousands of them have descended upon Iraq."

Hatim said, "I think that working with contractors is the only way for you to go. Iraqi contractors are very shrewd and you won't get experience in project management without first knowing how a worker works. I know it is hard for you, but that's the only thing I can say to my younger brother. I would like you to go tomorrow to the Square and to take the first labor truck, until I can find one of the contractors who work with our factory for you. First, I want you to see other contractors and get firsthand experience on the ground."

Sounding very dismayed, Tariq said, "I have enough money to last me for at least two months at the hotel, during which time I hope to have found a job. I'll do my utmost to write applications to all departments. I hope I don't have to do what you're saying."

Hatim stood up, saying, "Where have you gone in Baghdad? Have you seen Abu Nuwas Street?"

He said, "No."

We took him to Abu Nuwas. It was a marvelously sunny day. We had a lovely time and ate masgouf, a large river fish whose body is quite fatty. Iraqis call it benni and they roast it over a slow wood fire. It's a purely Iraqi dish.

We took Tariq back to his hotel, assuring him that we would be there to help at any time. We told him about the Murabba' Café on Rashid Street. He laughed and said, "I know it. I went there in the evening and met some Egyptians."

Hatim said, "That's where it starts."

On our way back home, I didn't feel sure that Tariq would make it in Baghdad. I asked Hatim about the possibility for working in hotels here. He said, "What hotels? Four-star hotels are already overstaffed and the rest you know. As for companies that build world-class hotels, they take specially trained workers. His English is good. We can find some training for him in tourism. Why don't you talk to Engineer Ali? He might find something for him in an airline company. Besides, you shouldn't worry about him. True, he has had a sheltered life so far but he is not a softy. The best in him will come out when he is put to the test."

270

We got home. I took off my street clothes quickly, feeling happy and energetic because of our talk with Tariq. I turned on the radio to the Monte Carlo station and the playful voice of Hayam said, "This is Radio Monte Carlo news bulletin. An Egyptian judge has issued a historic verdict acquitting defendants in the recent riots in Egypt which Sadat called a thieves' uprising. The judge faulted the Egyptian government, which has starved the people who demonstrated for their right to eat. There was a state of general relief at the verdict and at this proof of the well-known integrity of the Egyptian judiciary. It is worth mentioning that this is one of three state security cases in the aftermath of the uprising."

I let out a shout that brought Hatim, naked, out of the shower. I found him in the middle of the living room still dripping with water. I was dancing and shouting, "Long live Egypt! Sadat will drop dead of vexation! What a coup! They acquitted the people!"

I started singing joyously, holding Hatim's hand, and we began dancing like little monkeys happy with the sunshine.

"You're crazy. I love you."

We heard knocks at the door. Titi was outside, asking, "What happened!"

We discovered we weren't dressed. I said, laughing, "One minute."

I put a robe on and Hatim ran to the bathroom to get dressed. I told Titi the story and she said, "I'll tell Mahmoud Isam and we'll come and drink tea with you." Then she paused a little and said, "Are we interrupting anything?"

"You couldn't interrupt anything, could you?"

We both laughed and we stayed up talking about the recent events and the impact of the verdict on the Egyptians who were going through hard times.

Hayam came on again with the news from Monte Carlo: "Counselor [Chief Judge] Ibrahim Fahmi of the State Security Court in Egypt handed down a verdict that shall remain a bright spot in the Egyptian judicial system forever. The chief judge used the famous saying of Abu Dharr al-Ghafari: 'I am surprised that a man who, not finding sustenance in his house for his family, does not go out brandishing his sword.' The government has made a deliberate policy of keeping the people hungry. It must reverse its decisions and must look after its people who have sacrificed life and livelihood in many wars and spared no effort for the advancement of their homeland."

Hatim and I screamed, "Father!"

Titi and Mahmoud shouted, "Your father! Your father!"

We kept screaming and shouting that this was my father's work, it was his wonderful style and courage.

Our guests left and I rushed into Hatim's arms and we had a quickie.

Back at the office, Hilmi Amin opened the door for me with open arms and seemed ready to go out at once.

I said, "What's the hurry?"

He said, "We have errands and then we have appointments here at twelve. What has your father done!"

The news had reached everyone, including, of course, the leading figures of the Egyptian national movement living in exile here. We finished our urgent errands and returned to the office, where many of these expatriates had started arriving. They spoke to me as if I were the one who handed down the verdict. They began to relate incidents in Egypt's judiciary system and the names of certain outstanding judges. They knew by heart the names of judges who took courageous stands. Most of the visitors had themselves been either detained without trial or had received prison sentences. The long list of visitors that day included Saad al-Tayih, Saad Zaghloul Fuad, Fathi Khalil, Abd al-Ghani Abu al-Aynayn, Galal al-Sayyid, and Ahmad Abbas Salih. Then Abd al-Rahim, Suhayla, Atef, Sawsan, Mahmoud Rashid, Samia, and Hala El Badry also came.

On that day the sentiments of most women of the political movement toward me changed. They used to think of me as part of the decadent bourgeoisie who hadn't paid a price for her opinions, hadn't been jailed, and didn't have the right to speak about Egypt or the student movement or the future. They felt that they were the ones to make the future and not the students, or the uncaring and unorganized youth. Sometimes they would be surprised at how educated and well-read I was. But we always clashed violently when they, both men and women, said that all the rich were thieves or that a rich merchant or a rich farmer was an enemy of the people, or that the rich were authoritarian and exploitive and that peasants were of no value, that the workers were the ones with organized minds and sound opinions because they dealt with machines. That picture was the opposite of what I had seen and experienced all my life in my family. And despite my love for Abdel Nasser I could never accept these views from Nasserists and, more violently and profoundly, from the communists. One evening I told Sawsan, "No dictatorship of any kind, even the dictatorship of the proletariat. I love Abdel Nasser but I hate his dictatorship. Freedom and democracy are not antithetical to socialism or social justice. If Karl Marx was right in pushing the working class to govern itself, he did not have the right to give it the same rights by which the aristocracy exploited it."

The situation got out of hand. Sawsan said, "You are tearing things down without knowing the history."

Hilmi Amin intervened, "Karl Marx was not thinking of dictatorship in the sense that you, Nora, understood, when he said that. The question here applies to the ruling of the whole class and not an exploitation of another class, in the sense that the interests of the working class, which by nature are in contradiction with the interests of feudalism, once socialism is applied across the board, would be identical with the interests of society as a whole."

I thought of the big difference between older communists and my generation and the older generation's realization that other modes of thinking existed. Was it difficult for the younger generation to understand that they didn't have a monopoly over patriotism? I thought it must be foolishness of youth, enthusiasm, and the obstinacy of a sheltered young woman, and perhaps some female jealousy that I could never understand. Mervat drew my attention to it one evening when Ragya was being unpleasant. She whispered to me, "You intuitively dress with a style that would take years to learn, even if they had the money."

The conversation led to a discussion of what had come to be known as the "the massacre of the judiciary" and of Yehya al-Rafi'i and my father. I said, "My father never forgave Abdel Nasser for the massacre of the judiciary or his lack of respect for the law, which he never acknowledged. It was my father, as public attorney, who cross-examined President Muhammad Naguib. And because my father was a dyed-in-the-wool Wafdist, we always disagreed because of my love for Abdel Nasser."

Saad Zaghloul Fuad said, "The Wafd was a patriotic party and its members were brought up as liberals."

Saad al-Tayih said, "A liberal judge giving people the right to a life of dignity. This is Egypt."

I said, "Someone like my father could not understand the reconciliation between Egyptian communists and Abdel Nasser."

Hilmi Amin said, "This is case number three. The two other cases are still before the courts and they involve instigation to overthrow the government. Leftist lawyers are taking care of these cases. This ruling will help them a lot. Among the lawyers are Nabil al-Hilaly and Ismat Sayf al-Dawla, who got out of jail and joined the defense team."

Abu al-Aynayn said, "All the syndicates and unions in Egypt are holding rallies and following up on the political prisoners, because the roundup detained anyone who was politically active."

Sawsan, laughing, said, "I've fallen in love with your father. Why don't you lend him to me? He would teach me how to be free and make me wear a bathing suit and defend the downtrodden."

We laughed a lot and it seemed to me that a new page in my relationship with the generation that I came to really know only lately was opened to me. It was my father who gave me the gift of that page.

*

I came to when I heard the applause. I thanked God that I was not paying attention. I couldn't stand listening to propaganda any more. Anisa, the Pakistani woman, spoke about illiteracy in her country. I was quite impressed by the precision of her data and the amount of research she had put into it, even though her appearance, her coquettishness, and the love story she was living with Jon, the camera man, left one with the impression that she was not a serious woman. I chided myself for this thought, saying that she didn't have to look ugly and tough. I liked surprises of that kind. I also came to the conclusion that work was work and play, play. Anisa explained the experiment of combating illiteracy in the fields among poor peasant women, under simple canopies of bamboo with the help of a basic movie projector that Jon helped operate. We saw a comprehensive summary of the results of her experiment. But, oh my God! All that poverty! I looked at the sari she was wearing, natural Indian silk. I noticed how Jon was moving as he caught her movements on his video camera. We all smiled when he applauded enthusiastically. All our hearts blessed the love story that started with the first glance. Shahira said loudly, "Bravo, Anisa, bravo!"

The lights were turned back on and we moved to an adjacent hall to have tea in a short break. I ran to the bathroom to empty my breasts, which had filled and were hurting. I had forgotten the milk completely and in spite of squeezing the last drop out, I felt dejected and left for the hall feeling miserable. Such swings of mood. I saw my friend, the journalist Imad al-Bazzaz, and I headed for him right away.

He said, "Before 'good morning,' I'd like to tell you that Anhar's mother, together with her son Abd al-Razzaq, have moved to a new house on Filastin Street. She does not have a telephone at present, but I asked how to get in touch with Abd al-Razzaq at work and I'll find that out this evening. There is information, almost certain, that Anhar is in Brazil. God is generous."

275

I said, "Thank you, Abu Nasir. I put you through so much trouble, but I wanted to make sure that Anhar was all right."

He said, "I know, sister Sitt Nora. I think the session is about to begin."

From a distance I saw a lady who visited us frequently at the *al-Zahra* office and caused us many problems. She was embracing Siham Fathi and Mona Abed. She looked happy and cheerful. It seemed she had finally settled down in Baghdad and maybe had grown a little wiser.

Dahlia entered our life one midafternoon with Ragya, the doctor. She had a fair complexion, was short and somewhat plump. She was looking for a job. She had friends in Baghdad who prompted her to come. She had a college degree in science and was one of the close followers of Ismail Fikri, the well-known leftist. They laughingly referred to their party as the party of missiles. She found work quickly in a hotel and rented a house with an Egyptian bride who had come by herself to make the arrangements for her groom to join her. I found out that Dahlia was married to a colleague of hers from the same college and political group and that they divorced after less than a year. She wasn't thinking of marrying again. Life for her after work meant parties and trips with groups of friends. We all agreed that she loved to argue, obstinately but in a calm voice, and she spoke all the time about how men were trying to seduce her.

In Dahlia's eyes there was an absent glance that represented for me a challenge and psychological burden for some unknown reason. I told myself, "Why can't you unlock that absent glance, even though you keep saying that a writer is a good reader of character and can go deeper than the invisible crumbs that come to the surface?" Perhaps because it was a complex glance, a mix of extreme recklessness, indifference, and coldness, and a muffled vexation with life. But usually a person who felt vexed was someone impetuous and excitable, not a slab of ice like her. She was not beautiful but talked a lot about the effect her beauty had on others. Was it one of those women's mysteries that nobody had bothered to explain to me? Was it the result of a certain upbringing? That glance left me uncomfortable.

Whenever she came into the office, moving in a suggestive manner, several questions came to my mind: how could she, within three months of arriving in Baghdad, get acquainted with all those families whose members were active politically in Egypt? Why was she anxious to work in a hotel despite the risks that an Egyptian woman in her twenties would be exposed to in a city like Baghdad, which looked suspiciously at Egyptian women? Why insist on continuing to work at the hotel even after Hilmi Amin got her a job, after great efforts, at the Ministry of Health, a natural career path for a College of Science graduate? If the reason for Dahlia's migration from Egypt was not political, then it must be economic. Why then was she still living in Baghdad if her income there barely met her expectations? I couldn't find a satisfactory answer except that Dahlia wanted freedom of movement. I shared my questions with Hilmi Amin, who said, "No, this is the network she knew partially in Egypt. She is a type of personality that you haven't met before."

Dahlia complained about her work at the hotel and decided to apply to the Ministry of Education, so she would have a long vacation. She went to the Ministry to apply on the same day that she found out that she got approved for appointment in the Ministry of Health, pending submission of the rest of her papers. I noticed that soon thereafter she stopped following up on her application. That brought all my previous questions back to my mind, especially when I found out that she deliberately made a habit of coming to the office after I left and before Anhar arrived. I decided to talk with her in the hope of changing my mind as I did, to a certain degree, with Ragya.

I was patient as I listened to her obstinate views and did my utmost to understand. I discovered that her way of thinking was a bundle of contradictions. And even though she was a member of a small communist party, as I found out by chance, I heard her say,

"The poor and the working class in general are the most corrupt of the social classes, even more than the aristocracy."

I came to the conclusion that she was just a lost woman, one who fit the stereotype of a devil-may-care woman I met in the real world, not in books or movies. It didn't occur to me at that time that her coming to Baghdad may not have been because of political reasons or to look for a cushy and lucrative job. It could have been to run away from a failed love story or some other reason that I couldn't think of.

We got involved in a discussion about a presentation given by the president of the Moroccan Women's Union and we left the conference hall still talking about the subject. We made our way to the restaurant. I sat with Rajaa, Ilham, and Sajida from *al-Mar'a* magazine for the first time since the conference began. We began to reminisce about our friendship and laughed quite heartily.

On my way to my room, I met Dahlia, who said, "I can't believe it! Nora Suleiman? Long time no see!"

I said, "Hello, Dahlia. So, you still live here? I didn't expect you to stay after the war."

She said, "Where would I go? Did you see Ragya in Egypt?"

"Yes, once. By chance."

She said, "Tonight let's go together to the theater. When you come back from Basra, I'll have a party for all of you in my house. I hope you can come."

I said, "God willing. Pardon me, I have an important errand."

I ran to my room and finished all I wanted to do quickly. The taxi took me through the streets that I knew by heart. Then it stopped at a traffic light before the Iraqi Museum, which I loved very much and where, sometime in the past, I had discovered an Assyrian mural of two kings, one of whom had the features of Gamal Abdel Nasser while the other looked like Umm Kulthum. Unfortunately I didn't have enough time to visit it this time. I kept watching the people through the taxi window and windshield: men wearing very baggy pants, tied with belts at the waist and round turbans, men wearing the latest fashion in suits, women with loudly dyed hair and very pronounced makeup in spite of the war, black abayas side by side with miniskirts, a mix of different ethnicities alerting me to aesthetic diversity. With time I had been able to identify the features with their ethnic groups. I could also tell from their body language at a distance and also when they spoke, because dialects here were very distinct.

In Allawi Square we passed a mosque whose architectural design I loved because of its flowing lines. I followed with my eyes the simple mix of turquoise and white in its minaret. I remembered the golden domes that dazzled me when I saw them for the first time. I asked myself, "How have things changed so quickly and in such a cruel manner?" It was the stupidity of war. I was not convinced by all the justifications that I heard for it. The road turned. I saw Zawra, at one time housing English army barracks, and now turned into a beautiful park with many swimming pools, amusement spots, and small motels and restaurants from which you could smell the aromas of fresh samun bread and hamburgers. In it you could find small shops selling salted yogurt drinks, black grape and orange juice, and you could hear in its pathways, as you would in many Baghdad streets, people hawking chilled water and cold yogurt drinks.

I remembered the mid-afternoons that I lived in the park as I pushed Yasir to play and ran behind him on winter days, or during the evening in Baghdad's hot summer. I also remembered my picnics with Hilmi Amin's family, my long reading spells under the trees to escape being disturbed by the intrusion of Sabah, my neighbor, and her family. I wondered whether they were still so sociable or whether the war had changed their ways.

The road turned toward Dora. We passed the neighborhoods of Bayyaa and Sayyidiya and came to the intersection. I told the driver to turn left on the next street.

I saw Abu Samira's grocery store. The man had passed away several years ago while Umm Samira lived by herself waiting for the return of Samira, her goddaughter who was also her niece. Samira had gone to study in Spain and married one of her colleagues there. The store was kept open and run by a family member. I wondered whether Umm Samira was still there or had passed away during the two years that I had been away from Baghdad. I asked the young man minding the store about her and he told me that she was at home.

I ran toward her. She embraced me and showered me with the kindness I was used to all the time we were neighbors. She tried to open the door of the salon so I could come in. I said, "I am not a guest. I'll come in through the kitchen door."

I took off my shoes and went into the living room and sat near her on foam rubber cushions on the mat.

She said, "Where have you been all this time? How are Yasir and Abu Yasir?"

I said, "Now I also have Haytham. Where is Samira? And how is her husband?"

She said, "They are well, thank God. Samira had twins and she is almost done with her studies. They will come next year, God willing, to buy a house here and live near us."

She got up to pour tea for me. I remembered that Iraqis would give a niece to a couple who did not have children of their own; the couple would use her name as if she were their own child and they would be responsible for her throughout their lives. This would give them happiness and would give the girl a different kind of life, more comfortable in most cases. Umm Samira tried to make me stay, but I apologized because of my tight schedule. She came with me to my old house. We knocked on the door of Abu Dalaf's house and that of his brother, Jamal. The women and girls of the family came out to welcome me. The men were either still at work or in the army. Umm Jamal used to take my son Yasir from the nursery school bus before I came back from work and feed him with her children and let him sleep in their midst until either Hatim or I came home.

Umm Dalaf said, "Abu Dalaf will never forgive you if you don't stop to see him before you go back to Cairo. You should at least go to his office."

280

I said, "I will try after I come back from Basra, even if I change my departure date."

News of my arrival spread through the houses on the street. My women neighbors, Umm Tayih and her daughters, Salma and Khuloud, Umm Sulafa, Umm Mahmoud, and Umm Jamal came, and they walked with me to my house. I noticed some changes in the wall of the house adjacent to it. My house occupied the corner lot. Its side door opened to a giant mulberry tree and a big garden. It had a grapevine trellis and its owners had planted tall trees around it to shield the inhabitants from the neighbors. The mulberry tree was now over eighty years old. A large Sabian family of gold merchants lived in that house until the children got married and left to live in several separate houses in modern parts of Baghdad. Old trees in the garden gave the place a sense of deep-rootedness and reminded me of the Egyptian countryside. We had been living in the Shurta neighborhood when an Egyptian engineer, one of Hatim's colleagues, invited us to visit him and he offered us the upper floor. He said that the villa was too large for his family since it had thirteen rooms, not counting the rooms on the roof. We agreed and moved there after a while. When he returned to Egypt, we had the whole place to ourselves. And that was how the second floor got to be rented by another family: Engineer Mahmoud Isam and his wife Titi. I remembered Sabah and Shukry. My eyes welled with tears when I heard Titi say, "You brought light to Baghdad!"

I said, "Where are Madu and Amina? Yasir sends a million greetings to them."

She said, "At a birthday party for my friend Hizam's son. You know her, don't you?"

I entered my house in the midst of a boisterous crowd. Everyone was asking about Yasir and commenting on the new baby whom they hadn't seen yet and news of Egypt and Egyptian actresses. I asked Titi about the house and what happened to it. She said, "The rocket destroyed some of the walls on the second floor and broke the glass of the windows and burned some trees. But we've made the repairs with the landlord's help."

I said, "They must have written 'Nora Suleiman' when they were making the rocket, because the only one who could have been there by chance during the day was me. You all have to go to work in the early morning and I am the only one who sometimes stayed home during the day."

Titi said, "The wicked live long!"

Umm Tayih said, "Abu Tariq's son died and all the women of the street were hit by shrapnel. Abu Mahmoud al-Qarasholi's house collapsed and Abu Nidal's house was hit."

They listed off the names of martyrs. "Do you know the Abu Sami family? Three of them died, and from the Abu Omar family, his only son and his daughter's husband. From the Abu Rashid family, the husbands of the daughters were killed."

We climbed the staircase inside to the upper floor. I stood in the living room now empty of all the things I remembered. I saw a large hole between the wall of the living room and the winter bedroom that was repaired with cement but not yet painted. I went into the large living room that opened to the front balcony, my favorite spot during the summer, overlooking the railroad tracks. There was a new concrete wall and visible repairs to the ceiling. The unmistakable reminders of war were overwhelming. I didn't find the grapevine that I looked after for a long time and that extended its branches to the kitchen window, then found its way to the roof. I remembered its leaves that I used to pick to make the fresh dish of stuffed vine leaves. I never cut one leaf that I didn't use. I looked at the roots of the vine and saw that its wooden stalks were intact. I said to Titi, "I think it started to green after the bombing."

She said, "How did you know?"

I said, "I raised it. The roots are healthy but it needs a lot of care. You have no idea how much a plant adapts in order to live."

She said, "It won't find someone to talk to it as you did."

I noticed the fancy mansion built behind the wall of my old house. I said, "The map has changed."

Umm Jamal said, "The neighbors sold the old Qarasholi house after it was destroyed and then many others caught the bug, as you can see."

In spite of the warm welcome and loud demonstration of love that they showered on me, and despite my keen desire to assure myself of their welfare, I wished I could sit alone for a few minutes on my terrace, to recall long days I had lived there: writing and thinking under the Baghdad sky whose clear, dry summer nights I was so much in love with. I remembered those nights I couldn't sleep while lying on my back, watching the stars and letting myself get lost in the distant galaxies that that sky opened for me like no other sky. I had come to believe that something special connected me to that sky and that my sojourn in that land was not a matter of chance. That was why I felt such pain and anxiety whenever I left Baghdad airport heading for Cairo, consoling myself that it was just a holiday after which I would come home, but soon after I arrived once again in Baghdad I began to count the days before I could go back to Cairo. When Hatim and I decided to go back to Egypt for good, I didn't realize that I was leaving Baghdad and that I would need an invitation to visit it, and that attachment to the place depended on my being there, not to the physical city or the stones. But then again those were not any other stones or material things by themselves. They were the walls that I had painted snow white when I was bored, or beautified with some cheerful motifs such as miniature pictures of Walt Disney characters, or gave some depth to by reproductions of Van Gogh. They were the tables at which I sat to write, the chairs, my bed, the Aladdin heater that warmed the room for five winters, the space that contained Yasir's laughs and his gazelle Zuzu which we had made up and which accompanied him everywhere in the house. They were the moments of love that Hatim and I shared. They were the hours of loneliness, sadness, and homesickness. They were Sabah and the red peppers she fried with tomatoes to feed me

283

on the days of intense craving. They were the safe haven in which I had taken refuge for years, working, loving, and laughing.

Titi said, "Hey, there. Where did you go?"

I said, "I just wanted to see how the Abu Nidals are doing. I know they have sons of conscription age."

Umm Jamal said to Subaiha, "Umm Yasir is here and she wishes to say hello."

Subaiha said, "I don't want her and I don't want her hello."

I heard the sound of her mother's footsteps running toward me and saying, "Hello, rose! Hello, Umm Yasir! Please come in."

I said, "Some other time, God willing."

I left their embraces and ran to the taxi to take me to al-Rashid Hotel, recalling the incident that caused Subaiha's anger and which I had totally forgotten. I marveled at the workings of memory.

I had stood in front of my armoire, puzzled. I counted the money that I was going to put in my purse before leaving for work. I had a feeling that something was not right. I said to myself, "I don't know what came over me since I came back from Cairo. I've been off the mark in counting my money, even though I didn't have much since I exhausted our savings before leaving." I noticed that my money was decreasing and I didn't know why. I had seen in one of the stores a light washing machine that I thought of buying to wash socks and other light clothes, once Hatim decided whether it was sturdy enough. I said to myself that I would put up with his sarcastic comments. When I bought a rice cooker, he said, "The washing machine washes on its own and the cooker cooks, so why should one get married?"

Hatim liked the washer and we reserved it and promised the sales clerk that we would pick it up the following day. I took the money from Hatim and put it in a box where I usually put my money and my keys on a shelf in the armoire. I opened the box the following day and discovered that some of it was missing. I realized that it was not a matter of bad memory. I said to Hatim, "Someone enters our house in our absence."

He laughed and said, "How would he enter?"

I thought as I went through the house that there was only one way in and that was the balcony. He climbs the grapevine trellis.

I examined the door and found a little piece of broken glass between the steel bars. I looked at the telephone shelf on which I put the terrace door key and said, "It is one of our neighbors' kids and not a burglar."

"Why?"

I said, "Because he knows where the key is, and the neighbors know where the telephone is because it has always been there for years. A burglar wouldn't take five or ten dinars only from the box, but would take all the money. I left the whole amount to cover the price of the washer yesterday. The break-in happened while I was in Egypt. The thief went through the house freely and you didn't notice anything because you lock the door of the room, but I forget to. The kids are used to climbing onto the trellis to gather the berries from the tree, and it is easy for one of them to jump onto the balcony."

He said, "It makes sense. What should we do? Lock all room doors and don't forget and leave any of them open for any reason. And we can change the living room furniture so that if he enters, he wouldn't find anything to steal."

I said, "I'll wait for him tomorrow. Most likely it is Jasim or his brother, sons of Abu Nidal. I'll lock myself in my room until I find who it is. Most likely he'll come after the usual time we leave."

He said, "No, Nora. This is risky. How do you know it's not a burglar who might attack you? Please don't do it."

In the morning I got my son ready for nursery school. I heard some knocks on the door. I found Subaiha, the neighbor's daughter and Jasim's sister. She said, "Please, Umm Yasir, I need a matchbook."

I gave her a matchbook and said to Yasir, "Eat quickly. I don't want to be late for work."

Everyone left. I sat in my room waiting for what might happen. I took off the robe I had put on to open the door for Subaiha. July heat was unbearable. I picked up a book about Iraqi civilization. I loved King Sargon of Akkad! I was in awe of the layers upon layers of civilization. The deeper I got into it the more fascinated I was by Ishtar and Inanna and began to imagine that Isis had visited Iraq or was herself transformed into Ishtar before she went to Greece, all those human gods roaming God's world!

I came to when I heard a sudden movement, the sound of the spring attaching the screen door to the terrace steel door. I jumped up from the chair and opened the window that overlooked the garden and the side street. I walked to the door of the room on tiptoe and pressed my ear to the door, but I didn't hear a thing. I turned the key slowly and kept the door ajar. I didn't find any traces of anything moving in front of me. I opened the door suddenly and a cat jumped over the door in panic. I thanked God as my heart-beats raced. What if it was a burglar? There were no burglars in Baghdad after they hanged them publicly in the square and no one dared rob or burglarize anymore. It was a harsh way but its firm application worked. People left their doors unlocked and everyone was safe. I remembered that there were some burglaries and thefts since Egyptian workers entered Iraq without visas or jobs. When I asked the minister of labor how true that was, he said, "There are five million Egyptians in Baghdad. It is only natural that if some people don't have jobs right away and spend all their money, there would be crimes. Some time has to pass for entrants in a new society to adjust to their new situations."

I thought it was a very clever and wise answer, but it did not deny that thieves had reappeared.

I returned to my room without closing the door. I sat reading and got caught up in the history of Sargon of Akkad. After an hour I heard the same sound at the door: the cat again, I thought. I got out to look and was struck by the two eyes right up against my face. I thought it was Jasim. Yes, it was Jasim. The boy jumped with fright and got his hand out of the glass opening in the door with difficulty, and cut it in the process. He ran toward the terrace.

I shouted, "Thief! Thief!"

I realized that in his haste he might fall off from the relatively high wall. I noticed that I was still in my sleeveless nightgown. I returned to my room and quickly put on a galabiya and ran to the terrace. I found the boy at a distance running toward the railroad tracks. I shouted. The women neighbors came out quickly running, and so did a man who chanced to be passing in front of the house. The neighbors called the police, who arrived half an hour later while people were still milling around inside the house.

The policeman asked me, "Did you see the thief?"

I said, "I think it was Jasim, the neighbors' son. Same height and physique, but because of the distance from the door of my room and the glass between us, it is not quite clear."

"What did he take?"

"He took a small sum of money every day, five or ten dinars."

"Did he take jewelry or anything else from the house?"

"No."

I added, "Yesterday, by chance, we forgot and left the garden hose on in the garden and the soil under the trellis was soaked. So, when he jumped over the wall, his feet got stuck for a moment in the muddy soil and they left a track which is still there. Make him put his foot down, and if it is not a match, I'll forgo the charges."

He said, "Sign these papers."

I said, "Why don't you get him now and we'll finish this whole thing."

He said, "I said, you Egyptian, sign here. This is police business."

The neighbors left. In the evening, Abu Nidal, Jasim's father, came to meet Hatim, then he asked to meet with me. He sat in front of me, obviously sad. He was a simple worker who had not caused any problems as far as we knew. He had many children. I felt pity for him: events had escalated beyond anyone's calculation.

He said, "I assure you, if our son had stolen, he did that without our knowledge and I did not get a single fils from him. I've never encouraged him to steal. On the contrary, I teach them all honesty.

Dear lady, I am a poor man, but I fear God and, as you see, I work from the break of dawn until the evening. Life, for me, is a lot of heartache."

I said, "I know you quite well, Abu Nidal. I didn't want to call the police. All I wanted to know was who was the one who broke into my house, so I could stop him from doing it again. It was one of the neighbors who called the police. Ask Abu Mus'ab, he was here when it happened."

He said, "I know. But are you sure it is my son?"

I said, "I won't tell you it was him. Ask one of your sons to bring his shoes and place them in the mud which has now dried up and preserved the track. You decide for yourself. If the track is not his, then I give you my solemn word that I won't press charges. I know that he is used to climbing the mulberry tree, and I also know that he is no thief. The opportunity was there and that tempted him to take a small sum. Young men have been known to do such stupid things."

"What sums did he take?"

"I don't know, but yesterday he took twenty-five dinars."

"Take however much you want, but don't testify against my son in court. If he went before juvenile court, he won't come out alive or normal. He would be sent to juvenile prison and from there to an adult one. He is close to sixteen and he will either come out a criminal or a wreck. You're Egyptian, and you don't know Iraqi security. My son will be lost forever and it's all in your hands. We are neighbors who have never harmed you."

I said, "You are the best of neighbors and I love your son and call him to gather the berries with his brothers and friends every year. I have never thought of doing any harm."

He said, "Would you agree to tell the judge that my son was chasing a bird that fell in the garden?"

I said, "Yes, if he believes me."

Hatim said to the man, "Hang in there. It's a small problem and it will pass, God willing."

The man left and I began to cry, not believing the amount of hardship I had brought this family. Hatim embraced me and said, "You are not the one who committed the crime."

He said, "I warned you. Didn't you think for one moment that you may have miscalculated, and thus exposed your life to danger? It's a crime of opportunity, Nora. It may have been Abu Maasuma, the gardener, or Abu Mushtaq, the driver, or any worker in one of the shops nearby."

I said, "I depend on being one hundred percent correct. Therefore, it was an unnecessary risk. But one who works does not steal. Now I pity the family. Did you see the fear and sense of defeat in the man's face? He feels that his son is inevitably a goner."

He said, "Tomorrow I'll ask my colleagues in the legal department at the factory about your testimony in court and we'll find a way to get him out of the catastrophe he brought upon himself."

I slept only intermittently that night, during which I was assailed by nightmares. A few days later I received a summons to testify in court. I went early in the morning. A dignified judge, about fifty years old, came into the stately courtroom. He asked me to tell him what happened.

I said, "I was alone at home. Suddenly, I saw a boy on our terrace. I screamed and the neighbors came. Then it turned out that the boy had been chasing a bird that had fallen into our garden. After the police left, we found the bird hiding in the terrace behind the central air cooler."

The judge said angrily as he waved his hand dismissively, "Go. Go to your family."

I was taken aback by his tone and tears welled in my eyes. The court usher said, "Come and sign these papers."

I left, wondering what angered him so much. Did he find out that I was lying to protect the boy? Have you forgotten your father and how he arrives at the truth with terrifying speed? It seemed all the judges were like that, or was it because I was an Egyptian and it was wrong to accuse an Iraqi boy? I ran from the place to the street, not trying to hold back the tears. I had intended to go to the office, but decided to go home first to bring Jasim's family the reassuring news.

I knocked on the door. Subaiha opened and was surprised to see me. I asked her if her mother was there.

She said, "She's here. What do you want from her?"

The mother, whom I had rarely seen, came. I told her calmly: "Thank God, today I testified in favor of your son. I think the judge believed me and the problem has been almost taken care of."

She wiped her tears with her shawl and said, "Thank God, good lady. Thank God and may God bless you."

I cried as I took my leave.

Who knows what that incident did to Subaiha, when she is at a marriageable age, or to her family? Did I follow up on that? Of course not. I considered it a simple incident that ended well. But has it ended for them? I don't think so, given that reaction of hers.

I arrived back at the conference right on time. I ran to the bathroom to pump out the milk before going back to the panel presentations and discussions. Anticipating the discussions, I couldn't help reflecting on the contradictions through which Iraq was going these days: a war and, at the same time, a determination to carry on with the development plans. Can this really succeed? I had sensed some fear on the part of leaders of the Ba'th even though they were skilled at hiding it. Last time I saw them before the war they were acting in an arrogant manner. But it wasn't the people's fault. At the beginning they had faith in their leaders without thinking, but with time they questioned the audacious plans and decrees, first in whispers, then loudly.

My friend Umm Salah told me on the telephone, "Nora, all my family volunteered to fight in the war, even my young son in middle school!" Then she cried.

The presentations reminded us of the role played in the country by brutal colonialism and the Syrian and other Arab betrayals responsible for what was happening in the region. This got me to thinking about the relationship between Iraq and the United States and how puzzling it was. The Ba'thists frequently mentioned that a certain power had helped them take over. For us, Egyptian journalists, though we kept that a secret from Iraqi colleagues, that power was the USA, even though they publicly attacked America and called it all kinds of names. At the same time they were at war with Iran, a war that was in the United States' interest since the latter was really upset about losing the shah, its policeman in the Gulf. According to rumors, the bomb at Mustansiriya University and the attempt to assassinate Tariq Aziz were the work of Iraqi intelligence; there were also rumors that it was the United States that suggested to Saddam Hussein to escalate the conflict with Iran, and that the US made promises of monetary and military support. It was also rumored that American experts and SAVAK, the shah's intelligence service agents who fled Iran after his fall, estimated that the war would not last more than three weeks. I don't like accusations of betrayal and I don't believe the rumors, because I believe how stupid the petty bourgeoisie can get when it takes over power and how arrogant it can become. Besides, the Gulf countries supported Saddam Hussein, as did many countries, including France, Britain, Argentina, and Brazil. As for Syria, that was a different and very complicated subject.

I remembered my first trip to Syria. One day I ran into my neighbor Umm Tayih in front of Abu Samira's grocery store. She said to me, smiling and winking, "We are going to Syria. Would you like to come with us?"

I said, "Who is 'we'?"

She said, "I and a group of women neighbors. Abu Tayih and Abu Mahmoud will also come with us. Umm Sulafa used to organize these trips for us. We would have a good time and buy stuff: clothes, food, and everything. Didn't you ask me for garlic a few days ago? I'll buy you a bunch."

The morning papers, Ba'thist and others, had spoken of the resumption of relations between the Iraqi and Syrian Ba'th Party sides. The news was met in the street with great joy. Travel agencies in Gamal Abdel Nasser Square instantly hung posters adorned with electric lights about their trips to Damascus.

I told Hilmi Amin about my neighbors' trip. He laughed and said, "Let's arrange a trip to Damascus, as part of our plan for the future to cover the entire region. Let me first think of a visit on my own."

I welcomed the step, even though I was preoccupied with Iraq by itself, day and night. Hilmi Amin went to Syria and he came back happy, having concluded some press agreements there. Finally, I said to myself, today Damascus, tomorrow Beirut and maybe the whole Middle East. My dreams were getting bigger.

Hatim had promised me to spend the first vacation we would have together in one of the countries surrounding Iraq, because it was difficult for him to travel to Egypt, since getting an exit visa there took a long time. He was also subject to be called as a reserve officer in the army. He let me visit Egypt whenever I wished and postponed his own visit until such a time that he could have a vacation to have enough time to renew his exit permit. I seized upon the opportunity of the reopening of the Syrian–Iraqi borders and asked him to fulfill his promise: a one-week vacation in which I would also work on some features.

He asked me, "Is it a vacation or work?"

I said, laughing, "Both. Please, please."

Umm Tayih gave me the information about that tourist company that arranged her trip from which she had come back happy. She sent me a box of Syrian sweets and invited me to her house to show me what she had bought. I said, "You wiped out the family savings!"

She said, "You shouldn't think that, dear lady. This is Syria, not London!"

My women neighbors used to put a box in the kitchen in which they'd save any surplus in their budget of spending money for an annual summer vacation. The men would go to Cairo, most of the time without the rest of the family. One day Umm Mahmoud surprised me when I asked about her husband's knee treatment in Egypt. She showed me a picture of his in which he was shown leaning on the shoulder of a dark, young Egyptian woman. I asked her who she was and she laughed and said, "A prostitute."

We traveled on an old huge bus, which we preferred to a plane since it gave us a good opportunity for a more scenic trip. The bus filled up with Iraqi women, some of whom wore black abayas under which they had on the latest fashions. Those healthy-looking Iraqi women expressed their joy of living by singing aloud and eating together, sharing food that they had brought on the bus. As soon as they got on the bus, they took out thermos bottles filled with tea and began telling stories loudly. Before the bus stopped in two small towns on the way, all the passengers had come to know each other, including the few men who were on the bus. One of the women passengers addressed the bus driver using the name "Rashid," the protagonist of the textbook used in the literacy campaign. The passengers laughed and the driver smiled. Rashid became the go-to man in the bus who helped with small chores and the whole situation became the subject of light-hearted exchanges. One woman said, for instance, "Give Rashid two dinars to buy us some hot samun."

The driver played a cassette about al-Husayn and the women began to cry. I knew the story well, but when the singer got to the scene when the infant Abdullah ibn al-Husayn was killed while thirsty, the column of the cries rose and my own tears started coming down as if by contagion. I watched the collective sobbing in disbelief at the intensity, but when I saw one of the women beat her breast repeatedly, crying: "Oh mother! Mother! Mother!" I smiled. Hatim nudged me in the side as my grin grew broader, saying, "Watch out."

The situation, for me, turned into a comic one. Hatim realized the awkwardness of the situation and that I couldn't control myself and tried to curb my laughter, but to no avail. Then his pallid face and sharp reprimanding gaze restored my senses. I couldn't understand the pain they felt, nor the way they expressed it. I thought it was just an act. I had attended the wake of a very old man at the house of one of our women neighbors and noticed that at a specific moment, the women placed the abayas on their faces and began to wail and that they, with the exception of the close relatives of the deceased who were truly grief-stricken, were just playing an expected role out of courtesy. I didn't know why I made a connection between that scene and the present one. Then I asked myself: courtesy to whom? Martyrs who had died centuries ago?

I took me years to understand the cruelty of the events that have given the land of Iraq that tragic character and the feeling that the bleeding was still fresh. I asked myself whether Iraq was predestined to go on shedding blood forever, whether it was something beyond their control or just foolishness. Those days in Iraq, things were looking up: development, work, and political success.

We arrived in Damascus at midnight. We entered the hotel happy and holding hands. It was pouring, and the cold that our friends had warned us about was much more than we had expected. We got up early and headed straight for downtown. A worker at the hotel had told us how to get to the Umayyad Mosque and Suq al-Hamidiya. We walked and on our way stopped in al-Marja district looking for the river Barada. We recalled the poetry written about it. Hatim recited:

A greeting, more tender than Barada's east wind,
And tears that wouldn't stop, Damascus!
Red freedom has a gate on which bloodstained hands are knocking.

I stared in shock at the stream and I asked Hatim, "What is this?"

Hatim said, "I don't know. This can't be."

Hatim asked one of the young men passing by, "Where is the river Barada?"

The young man said, "That's it."

It was just a little canal of which we had hundreds in all Egyptian villages. The Nile immediately came to both our minds. We laughed and Hatim said, "That's what you get when you believe the poets."

I said, "It must have been a desert dweller who was impressed by the water. Imagine the difference between a well and a river. One of my Yemeni colleagues in college was walking with us to University Bridge in Giza and he shouted when he saw the Nile, 'All of this is fresh water?'"

Hatim said, "It is all relative, my dear. But this poetry is from Ahmad Shawqi, the Egyptian poet."

I called a Syrian journalist friend and made an appointment in the early morning to accompany me to the newspaper *Tishrin*. I asked Hatim if that would be okay and he told me to do as I liked, provided that we go together.

We toured the city and had lunch in a traditional restaurant. In the evening we enjoyed watching *Waiting for Godot* at the National Theater. We planned our schedule, divided between pleasure and work-related meetings. The first of these was with the Minister of Culture Najah al-Attar. I was met by Hanna Mina, who worked as one of her advisers. I said to him in a whisper as he was showing me in to see her, "I loved your novel *al-Yatir* and its wonderful heroine, Shakiba."

He smiled and came in with me as I met with her to have an interview. I also met the president of the Syrian Women's Union and I wrote a feature article about the return of Iraqi–Syrian relations. The editor in chief of *Tishrin* asked me to write from Baghdad about people's reactions to the resumption of relations and to send articles and features to the newspaper on a steady basis.

Hatim went to museums while I worked, then went back to the museums with me when my work was done, and in the evening we would see another play. We went to Suq al-Hamidiya to buy abayas embroidered with the famous Syrian sirma. At the shop, I could hear the Palestinian dialect. I remembered what my mother told me: "Don't forget to buy Syrian brocaded silk and lingerie, especially bras."

I heard the applause. I paid attention to the man speaking at the podium, to his words and his voice with which I was familiar. Was it really the thinker Ilyas Farah, who had been sentenced to death in Syria and who came to Iraq with Michel Aflaq to support the Ba'th Party? Or was I confused and was Ilyas among those who had been executed?

Naglaa passed in front of me. I remembered Nafi'a Othman, so I asked Naglaa about her. She told me that she was busy opening a new culture palace in Suleymaniya.

I had met Nafi'a Othman, president of the Women's Union in Erbil, one morning and heard her expounding on the Ba'th Party efforts to develop the region and encouraging women to have regular jobs as factory workers. She was a beautiful, well-educated, strong woman who believed in her role in development and displayed great energy playing that role. I went back to the hotel to get ready to go with Hilmi Amin to the house of one of the founders of the Kurdish Communist Party.

The surprise that awaited us was that Nafi'a was Abu Bakr Othman's daughter. I said, laughing, "I was with you an hour ago. Why didn't you tell me?"

She said, "I wanted to surprise you. This is my father's house, not mine."

We sat with a shriveled man whose stature was quite different from his tall daughter. We started talking about the Kurds at length. Hilmi Amin asked him, "Would Kurds revolt again despite the autonomy?"

"Yes," he said calmly.

Hilmi Amin asked, "How?"

He said, "If any Kurd took up arms, be that Mullah Mustafa Barzani or any other revolutionary, everyone would follow him."

I said, "A small country cannot stand by itself, and unity among the Kurds is impossible because they are divided among the Soviet Union, Iran, Iraq, Syria, and Turkey. Would any of those countries put up with secessions of its Kurdish part?"

He said, "No. It's an eternal struggle, bigger than the Palestine problem."

I said, "Why is rebellion in Iraq more frequent and stronger than in any of those other countries, even though you have autonomy which the other countries don't have?"

Abu Bakr Othman got up and opened the window in the room where we sat and said, "Here, come and look at the banner in the street right in front of you. What does it say?"

"It says, 'Arab oil for the Arabs.'"

He came back to his chair as calmly as he got up and said, "This is the heart of the problem. This is not Arab oil; it is the oil of the Kurds and always will be. Kurdish wealth must be returned to the Kurds. Developing their society is the only way to peace. The region needs to be truthful as it confronts the Kurdish reality."

I said, remembering what Nafi'a was saying in the morning, "Isn't the effort exerted equal to the value of the oil?"

He said, "Absolutely not. The state is interested in other things and their allocations for this area are much less than its actual needs. This is something they have to realize before it is too late. It is not a matter of Arabs and Kurds, but rather the Ba'th Party as an authority that does what it pleases with the wealth of the country."

Hilmi Amin said, "But a coalition front of five parties is ruling the country."

Othman shook his head and said, "I am not optimistic."

I said, "I like the idea of the coalition front. I hope it spreads in all our Arab countries."

He smiled as he looked at me for a long time then said, "We all wish the best for Iraq."

Nafi'a was moving among us on tiptoe, serving us drinks and pastries stuffed with walnuts that they called klisha, like any other homemaker. I wanted to ask her whether she was a Ba'thist or not, but I felt abashed. I wished that the communist father would have a Ba'thist daughter, and that Arabs and Kurds would merge. I had fallen in love with the Kurds and liked very much their women's outfits that sparkled in the sun. I had never seen such cheerful attire anywhere else.

So, Nafi'a was still working in the position of authority! But where is Anhar Khayun? Where are the other communist colleagues? What happened to that time when communists were everywhere in Baghdad? You know where they have gone, Nora, don't you? I still remember the black days of the end.

One morning, after our bureau changed status and became a private press bureau, Hilmi Amin told me, "Let's go first to *Tariq al-Shaab* before we go to *al-Jumhuriya*. Abu Ghayib did not find the newspaper in the market. We would know at least whether it had been banned or is just late for one reason or another."

We walked under the pleasant warm sun of Baghdad in the winter. We opened the bolt of the garden gate of the office of *Tariq al-Shaab*. We rang the bell of the building door that had usually remained open in the past. A young journalist, a man, opened the door for us. Behind him came a frightened, beautiful young woman and asked in alarm, "Who are you?"

Hilmi Amin said, "I am the director of the former *al-Zahra* magazine bureau and this is my colleague Nora Suleiman. Is Ustaz Adnan here?"

A journalist came from inside quickly and said, "Please, come in."

We heard the young woman say, "*Al-Zahra* bureau, now?" She left us wondering and went to the door and left it ajar as she looked behind it in apprehension. Then she came back and asked us, "*Al-Zahra* bureau? Are you Egyptian?"

The male journalist said, "She is wacky!"

She went back to the door and closed it. The room was plunged into darkness and we realized that there were no journalists except for the two of them. In the past it used to be crowded with working journalists and their visitors. Nabil Yasin came in and welcomed us, saying, "Sorry. Most of the young journalists are on assignment and the editor in chief also is not here."

Hilmi Amin said, "We didn't find the paper in the market. Was it delayed for any reason? Or banned?"

He said, "I'll get you a copy right away."

He gave us a copy as the young woman kept looking around her and from behind the window curtain, then came back to stand in a dark corner of the room. We felt that something was suspicious. We took our leave, promising to come some other day. When we crossed the threshold of the outside gate, we heard it being locked with bolts. I said, "What are they afraid of?"

He said, "Maybe the police."

I said, "Would a door stop the police? This is Iraqi security!"

He said, and I could hear a troubled tone in his voice, "The door wouldn't stop the police, but it would give one of them a chance to escape. Things deteriorate very quickly. This is not the first time the paper has been banned. It seems that Iraqi communists have entered a conflict phase with the state and that it might escalate."

I said, "That doesn't sound good, for them. Their adversary has no mercy."

He said, "It seems the Ba'th Party has been surprised by the large numbers joining the Iraqi Communist Party even though Ba'th is the ruling party." Then he added, "A short time ago, the Communist Party celebrated its anniversary and invited the central committee of the Ba'th Party to attend. Saddam Hussein himself went to the party. New members' names were announced and welcomed. It seems that demonstration did not sit well with Saddam, who was surprised by the numbers. He left, intending to punish them."

I said, "Do you think this is the only reason? There must be other sources of conflict. I feel sometimes that communists resent the Ba'th Party and the way it has been running the country."

We arrived at the *al-Jumhuriya* newspaper offices. One of our communist colleagues told us that *Tariq al-Shaab* had come out and that it contained an article defying the Ba'th Party and that it had bypassed the censor.

It was announced that a communist organization was uncovered in the army. We got news of the arrests. *Tariq al-Shaab* denied the claims of the presence of an armed wing of the Communist Party. The five-party coalition front collapsed.

I remembered what Jamal, Abu Sargon, had told me while we were at his house in Erbil: "Those underground parties worked together against the monarchy and English occupation. They know each other's every move and no member of any of those parties can escape and hide from the other parties."

We hear that communist detainees were subjected to horrible torture in jails to confess their membership in the military wing of the party in the army. That was painful to hear. We no longer knew what was really happening. I could sense the anxiety gripping Hilmi Amin to his very core: he believed the collapse of the relationship between the Ba'th and the communists would have repercussions for the communists in the whole Arab world in general and for an Egyptian communist in exile in Iraq even though he had been safe so far. He was also worried that Anhar might be arrested at any moment.

I began inquiring about my communist colleagues who worked at other newspapers. I especially liked Salwa Zaku for her seriousness and integrity. I found out that she was in jail and that her husband had fled the country. The Ba'thist journalists looked alarmed when I asked them about our communist colleagues.

Developments followed in quick succession. It was announced that some communist officers were executed. Many intellectuals fled the country and upon arriving in any other country announced their condemnation of the Ba'th Party regime, accusing it of dictatorship and abuse of power and squandering Iraq's resources and corruption.

Detentions continued and extended to all Iraqi cities. The names kept coming. Hilmi Amin would meet his communist friends in the evening and get detailed news from them, and the names of detainees and those who had fled the country. A large number of pivotal artists and writers disappeared. Some went to the Soviet Union, France, and Eastern Europe while others went to Yemen, Morocco, and the United States.

The clove necklace in my dresser's drawer turned into a symbol of Iraqi communists and I was no longer able to put it on at all, for its scent was a potent reminder of the woman who had given it to me. I wondered where Nariman was, and even though I couldn't wear it, I couldn't keep it hidden away, as if its physical presence would give her security and life and remind me every morning of my friends who had disappeared in circumstances I had never expected.

We received some news of sexual abuse of women communists in detention. The Ba'thists denied the news and we no longer knew whom we could believe. I couldn't find out what happened to Nariman. Was she still exiled in Shaqlawa? Or detained? Or did she flee the country? Those were the options for Iraqi communists now. And where is Sulafa? I remembered the day she told me that she was preparing to get married. I received the news as if it were a bolt of lightning, but then I told myself: What else could she do? Jamal is a Christian who cannot divorce his wife and she couldn't wait for him. Where are you now, Sulafa? It's not your health I am worried about now, but about the imminent danger facing you. I didn't know at the time that Anhar would disappear the same way and that Hilmi Amin and I would look for her to no avail, or that I would leave Iraq without knowing anything for sure of her whereabouts or come back two years later hoping with all my heart that she had migrated to Brazil.

The memories weighed down on me. I couldn't concentrate or think straight. All the contradictions that I had seen throughout the five and a half years that I worked in Iraq came back all at once: all the successes and all the conflicts, explosions, and failures. In the seventies, the rate of growth in employment in government agencies reached three hundred percent over ten years. Women in particular made huge strides: at least forty percent of the increase affected them. Women in education, especially medicine and pharmacology, increased their numbers by thirty percent. Daring progressive personal status laws dealt a blow to tradition. Then there was the literacy campaign, as mentioned in the papers presented and from my own experience. All these contradictions! How, in God's name, has all that happened? What kind of authority was responsible for all of that? Was it truly nationalist? Progressive? (They sometimes characterized it as something co-opting the communists.) Or was it just a dictatorship using terror to cover up its foolish acts?

Naglaa, who noticed how lost in thought I looked, asked me, "Nora, you out of all participants in the conference have your own experience in this country. Do you think we will find the right answers soon?"

I said, "Your history haunts me a lot. Can I tell you something of that history without any comment, Naglaa?"

She said, "Please do. I'd like to reassure myself."

I said, "There was an ironic Babylonian parable that goes something like this: 'A mongoose once chased a mouse. The mouse wanted to hide so it ran to a cave inhabited by a serpent. When it found itself facing that new danger, it didn't know what to do at first, then it said to the serpent: the snake charmer sent me to you with his best wishes.' Do you think this parable applies to your situation today, thousands of years after this Babylonian parable?"

Naglaa cried and got up to wash her face. I met the leftist literary critic, Yasin al-Nusayyir. I asked him how he was and how Baghdad Underground, our name for avant-garde culture that did not agree with the state's official culture, was. I hoped my artist friends and their works were all right. I told him I also wanted to go to the theater. Yasin said that the day's program included a performance of a wonderful show, *The Door*, by a new company and that I shouldn't miss it.

The conference hall was full to the last seat. Iraqis, at least on the official level, celebrated closings exactly as they did openings, and on the whole they have become dazzlingly successful at mounting and running festivals. Some poorer women in traditional garb were usually seated in the last rows and ululated every time the president's name was mentioned. I got used to the long poems they delivered on such occasions, as if they were still desert dwellers. I remembered the giants of Arabic poetry and wondered why of all the poetry of al-Khansaa only those elegies in which she lamented the death of her brother Sakhr survived!

After the closing ceremony we went to watch a one-act play whose action took place in an underground tomb. That brought back memories of how I loved to watch Iraqi actors on the stage. It also made me wonder where such important Iraqi theater figures were now, men such as Yusuf al-Ani and Jawad al-Assadi. Haytham snatched me away from the play, even though I had pumped out the milk a short while earlier. I tried to keep his image away from my mind's eye, but he kept coming back, looking for me with tears in his puzzled eyes. I tried to hold back the tears and focus on the play in front of me, but my chest felt Haytham touching it and it hurt, even though nothing physical caused this pain. It must have come from somewhere in my soul. Yes, it must be that. I was taken away from the pain by trying to keep up with the dialogue between the actors on the stage.

Baghdad Railway Station
Five in the Morning
Buses took us to the Baghdad Railway station. I hadn't taken an Iraqi train before because trains were slow. I loved that time of the morning in the winter: a breathtaking fog that lifted, revealing sun or rain. The silence was broken by an Egyptian's melodious voice as if he were hawking goods. I saw that the voice belonged to a worker wearing the official railway uniform and covering his head with a woven wool skullcap and a white turban. "A morning of cream!" he said.

"A morning of roses," I said, laughing.

He said, "May our whole day be honey!"

Layla and Sajida replied together, "A morning of jasmine, my love!"

The whole column we were part of burst out laughing. The non-Arab participants asked why we were laughing. Sajida explained the humorous exchanges to them. We got on the train, most of whose cars had been reserved for the conference delegations. For the first time I realized that I hadn't gotten close to the non-Arab guests, even though among them were several people that I wanted to interview. During the trip I had a chance to catch up with my Iraqi friends and find out what happened to them during the past two years. They were not used to venting to me that much and with such candor before. I didn't know why. Was it because I was preoccupied with my work, or was it that the tragic war had cast a shadow on their lives and they couldn't hide the pain any more? I noticed that they were no longer very secretive and on several occasions my tête-à-tête with one of them got collective comments from several other participants. I asked Lutfiya, "And how do people receive condolences on the death of a son?"

She fell silent as tears glistened in her eyes and said, "The mothers cry at home among the family members, for a martyr belongs to the whole homeland, and it is an occasion for joy, not grief."

Her broken sentences rang in my ears for hours. So, the fear of speaking one's mind was no longer as strong as it once was, but it was still there. Were the party's watchful eyes and ears still strong? Was it the party that was doing the watching or some opportunists to prove their loyalty? Was what I heard just exaggerated rumors?

Manal al-Alousi came and sat by me. "Nora, how are you today? Do you need anything? Don't let the time pass without us sitting together for a long time. I want to know all the news from Egypt and the latest jokes."

I said, "Thank you, Umm Tayyiba. I am among family here with you. In Egypt, they wanted to come up with new jokes and discovered that they had used up the Sa'idis in jokes. Someone who had just returned from Iraq said, 'Get a Ma'idi.'"

Sajida joined in and said, "Or a Kurd!" and we all laughed.

I said, "How is your sister Hind and her husband? Anything new?"

She said in a sad voice: "No. He's still missing like thousands of Iraqi men. This is her problem right now. Don't forget that we've got to get together."

I felt hot as milk filled my breasts. I did not look forward to going to the train's very cramped bathroom, but I had no choice. I decided to empty some of the milk over several trips but finish the job better at night. I asked myself whether there was a point to what I was doing, and whether I should either stay at home and devote myself to mothering my baby or do what my colleagues did and feed him baby formula from a bottle. "Until when," I asked myself, "will you continue this dance, trying to balance the role of a traditional mother and that of a journalist preoccupied with the wide world outside?" I pushed the questions aside as I remembered Yasir, who would let go of my breast to play with me, letting the milk flow all over my chest. I also remembered my aunt Fawziya saying, "Why are you so cruel, Yasir?"

I was surprised to hear that. Yasir was used to nursing voraciously for a short while, then letting go of my breast to breathe through his mouth because he suffered from a recurring blockage of his nose. When he let go of my breast, which by that time would have responded and turned on, the milk would soak my breasts before Yasir came back to it. When he got his fill he would laugh and begin to play and breathe at will. I looked at my aunt and guessed what she tried to tell me, but I was not convinced. My aunt got up and patted Yasir on the shoulder—he hadn't yet finished his sixth month, the same age as Haytham right now. Then she made me hold my breast and place the nipple in his mouth and said, "Don't take it out of his mouth while he is nursing for any reason."

I said, "But his nose . . ."

305

She said, "He'll get used to its being in his mouth and he will breathe."

Yasir learned to breathe while nursing but kept letting my breast drip. "Do you remember celebrating his birthday every year even though you were not with him?" I asked myself.

Tante Fayza and Hilmi Amin's daughters had arrived in Baghdad to spend the summer holidays with us. The office routine changed. Hilmi Amin was more relaxed and family activities dominated our schedule, which was now full of social activities. Dr. Ragya came to the apartment regularly every afternoon. Anhar said she was going to Kubaysh, her village in the marshes, with her mother to visit her family and totally disappeared.

I said to the girls: "I am going to Orosdi Bak to buy a gift for Yasir. His birthday is today."

They said, "We'll go with you."

I found a teddy bear almost the size of Yasir and happily bought it. The girls brought more joy and happiness to my life. I was used to them coming back home with me and staying for long periods of time during the summer months. This holiday, however, was different and shorter. We went back to the office and I told Tante Fayza that I was going to make a cake for Yasir and asked her to let the girls go with me.

Hilmi Amin said, "She's having a party for her son and expects him to talk to her on the phone from the party which his grandfather and the family will have for him in Egypt. Have you seen more madness than this? Okay, Sitt Nora, we will come."

I went back home. I found that the cake I had baked in the morning had cooled down. I drew a model of an elephant and began to work on the icing. My tears flowed. I had never gotten used to Yasir being away from me despite my frequent visits. I was beset by anxiety that something might have happened to him or that he was in an accident. I spent hours at the Central Post Office on Rashid Street to try to hear his voice on the telephone.

I put icing on the cake and the elephant appeared in its full glory—a splendid Indian elephant, I told myself, and began to work at break-neck speed. I finished arranging the food and hanging decorations. Nahid arrived and her daughters brought liveliness to the place. I loved that family for their simple goodness and generosity. Nahid reminded me of the families in which the wife lived just to feed the kids and the husband and take care of them, letting the man devote himself to working outside the home without saddling him with any more worries.

The girls ran with Madu, Titi's son, to the garden. Mahmoud Rashid and Samia came with Basil and the house was filled with children and joyous noise. Then Hilmi Amin's family came, accompanied by Ragya. I placed the big bear on the middle chair at the table in front of the cake and we blew out the candles noisily despite my tears. We laughed and took pictures. We heard the telephone ringing the long distance tone.

Yasir said, "I love you very much, Mama."

Hatim and I kept snatching the receiver from each other. We finished the telephone conversation with the family in Egypt. I noticed that Ragya was totally silent. I offered her some cake, which she accepted only after my insistence, then she placed it next to her. Samia, who put her up in her house when she arrived in Baghdad, tried to talk to her but she blocked every attempt to have a conversation. Nahid also tried to engage Ragya and, when she found out that she was living by herself in Baghdad, invited her to her house.

I asked Hilmi Amin in a whisper what was wrong with Ragya and he said, "She came to visit us without an appointment so we invited her to come with us."

Titi started pouring the tea and offered some to Mahmoud Isam, saying, "My husband first."

Madu ran after her trying to snatch a balloon that she had placed on her arm to save it for his younger sister.

Ragya said, "I am sorry. I want to go home."

I said, "It is early and the children haven't eaten cake yet."

She stood up and persisted: "No. I want to go now, right away." Then, addressing Hilmi Amin, she said, "You can stay. I'll go out and find a taxi."

Rasha said, "I want to stay with Nora. Stay with me, Mervat."

Tante Fayza said, "We'll come some other day."

Ragya insisted on not waiting. She sat down for a few minutes until the girls had some cake, then she left with Hilmi Amin and his family.

Nahid asked me, "Who is that sourpuss?"

I said, "Poor woman! She had some tough circumstances."

Samia said, "I noticed that she was tired and sad. It seems she has many problems. I didn't ask her because I didn't want to bother her and she hasn't told me anything. It is obvious that Tante Fayza likes her a lot."

I said, "She performed an abortion on herself just one day before coming to Baghdad."

Nahid said, "Dear God!"

I had noticed that Tante Fayza sympathized with her, but the two girls were detached. I understood how someone like her found it difficult to get along with them.

Hilmi Amin's family's holiday was drawing to an end, quickly as usual. I woke up one morning realizing that we had to have a farewell party for them. I agreed with Hilmi Amin to have it in the office that evening. I quoted the Egyptian proverb: "A wolf's den is big enough for a hundred lovers."

He said, "We have no choice. During the day we have a lot of work and official appointments and Anhar has run away. When she comes back, I'll have a talk with her. This mixing up of things is not acceptable."

I looked at him for a while without saying anything. He said, "What do you want? Say whatever you want. I am listening."

I said, "Nothing."

Dahlia came in with Abd al-Rahim. Her face was quite pallid. We had agreed to help her find a place to stay with an Egyptian family. Her appointment with the family that we had approached was yesterday but she didn't turn up, putting Hilmi Amin in an awkward situation. We had interpreted her not keeping the appointment by assuming she had solved the problem with her neighbors, of whom she complained bitterly.

Tante Fayza asked her what she wanted to drink and she said, "Tea."

Abd al-Rahim said, "Dahlia has a problem with the police."

Dahlia said, "The neighbors objected to my guests, and my having parties at home. They got insolent and we had a quarrel. There were several complaints from many neighbors to the vice squad. They wanted me to leave the house. I was going to leave it anyway but now I am reluctant. They have no right to kick me out with an accusation like that."

Abd al-Rahim said, "This is not the first time. The problem is that that has happened at a previous residence. The police came at three o'clock in the morning and took her along with her female roommate and investigated the complaint."

Hilmi said, "But an arrest warrant cannot be issued because of a problem with your neighbors."

Abd al-Rahim said, "She is right in front of you and she is not saying anything."

Mervat brought the tea. Dahlia said, "I want milk with it. I don't drink tea without milk."

I said, "Oh, persnickety!"

We all laughed. Hilmi said, "What happened exactly? I cannot help you without knowing the details."

Dahlia said, "The man claimed that we received Kuwaiti and Saudi men and that I go out at ten in the evening and don't come back before three in the morning and that the visitors came at this time before dawn. But the officer reassured us that there were thousands of lawsuits because of the housing shortage and that landlords resort to these kinds of complaints to build cases for eviction. Then he said, 'We are sorry for what happened, but the person who filed the complaint is one of you and we cannot do anything to him.'"

We all said at the same time, "Is the landlord Egyptian?"

Dahlia said, "No. But we've sublet part of it because it is huge."

I said, "If we had an Egyptian association we would have taught him a lesson. Five million Egyptians and we can't have one association?"

Dahlia said, "We left after Atef called the company where he works and the company lawyer said he would sue for libel. I had a discussion with the officer about liberation for Iraqi women, who disappear from the streets at a very early hour whereas women in Egypt enjoy greater freedoms."

I exchanged glances with Hilmi Amin and I said, "That's all they need!"

Dahlia said, "But the officer said he had visited Cairo and discovered that Egyptian women are not seen in the streets after seven in the evening."

Hilmi said, "How observant!"

"I vehemently denied that," Dahlia said.

Hilmi asked, "Okay. So, what have you decided?"

Abd al-Rahim said, "We met at my house yesterday and decided to come to you. Maybe you can solve the problem and maybe Dahlia can pledge to simmer down a little."

Dahlia turned to Hilmi and said, "As for the new house you were going to move me to, please don't tell the family with which I'll live what happened."

Hilmi Amin got up, saying, "Wait for me. I'll be back right away. Nora, come with me."

I followed him hurriedly as he descended the stairs, while lambasting our rotten generation, permissive upbringing, and the consequences of irresponsible behavior. I remained silent, not knowing where we were going. We stood in front of the apartment building, thinking how we would handle the situation, especially with respect to the family that we had asked to put Dahlia up. We discussed the matter and decided that it would be unfair not to tell the family what happened, for they would be surprised when the police descended upon them one day and they found themselves saddled with a problem they had nothing to do with.

Hilmi Amin walked into the supermarket and I followed him. He called an Iraqi lawyer friend of his and explained the situation to him. He took out a piece of scrap paper and a pen and wrote down the lawyer's name and telephone number. Then he hung up. I stood waiting, afraid to ask him why we were waiting. He redialed the same number and said, "Thanks a lot. We'll be there shortly."

He turned to leave the store and said to me, "Finish what you've started writing, then go home. I'll cancel all our appointments and deal with this bimbo, even though I wish she'd just leave Baghdad. Instead of getting respectable people, we get this one. She wanted milk in her tea! Here's a woman, implicated in a vice case, and she wants milk in her tea?"

I couldn't help but laugh, without making a sound though, for fear of the whole situation turning against me. He said, "Go up and send her down with Abd al-Rahim. I'll wait here."

Tante Fayza and the girls asked me, "Is she really going to jail? Is she going to be deported? What did the two of you do?"

"I don't know. I think Ustaz Hilmi has made an appointment with a big lawyer. If there's nothing to it, as she says, and if it is proved that she has done nothing wrong, she'll get off. But if there are things she's hiding, that would be a different story."

Tante Fayza said in exasperation, "That's all Hilmi needs. More problems!"

In the evening we had a party for the family since they would be leaving in two days. Many friends came. When Hatim and I arrived, Dahlia was already there. She looked composed, so I assumed the problem had been taken care of. I breathed a sigh of relief and didn't ask her anything. Abd al-Rahim and Suhayla arrived and a short while later they were trying to convince her to go home with them to protect her from her neighbors. I found out that what Dahlia had said, that the whole problem was just a tempest in a teapot, was not exactly what everyone thought. It turned out that the lawyer had spoken at length about the police report in a manner that was not in Dahlia's favor, nor did it do her image a lot of good.

We were surprised to see Fathallah and Maha show up unexpectedly. We were happy to see them, as always. Fathallah had been awaiting the verdict in a political case and he was acquitted, but the fact that the verdict was published in the newspapers bothered him because he had kept his political activities in Egypt to himself. He said, "I want to lead a quiet, simple life here, to make enough money to rent a bigger apartment for Maha's sake because we were married in a small apartment quite far from my work. I don't want any political discussions here nor any invitations to join the party. When the verdict was published, my cover was blown. One of my fellow engineers asked me and I told him it was just a case of mistaken identity."

Hilmi Amin said, "No one should be ashamed of his political activity. The fact that you were part of the student movement calling for liberating Sinai and that you had been arrested because of your political activity is quite normal. You have every right to do what you are doing here. Your present job has nothing to do with politics. I'd say 'good job.'"

Maha was the exact opposite of Dahlia and Ragya. She was a model leftist woman who understood politics properly as a means for struggling for justice and propagating ideas of brotherhood. Her study of engineering made her more focused and more guided by logic. That was also what I noticed in Hatim and his engineer friends.

It was Maha's model behavior that prompted me to think of all the women I had met and dealt with in Baghdad. Some were types that I had never dealt with before in my life: contentious and quarrelsome women intent on picking fights with me after my first book came out, even though they were not working journalists. The one thing that really surprised me was Tante Fayza's transformation during her current visit to Baghdad. Previously, in earlier visits she refused to go out on visits or to travel to other cities for recreation. She accepted our invitations only after earnest pleadings, and often Hilmi Amin would take the daughters by himself on social occasions. But when she met this group of leftist youth, she opened up, welcoming them at home and fostering close relations with them despite the great age difference. I don't know whether Ragya was behind all that or not, but I was happy that she became more outgoing.

The party was over and friends said goodbye to the family since the days remaining before their return to Egypt were workdays when no one had the time to visit again. Dahlia went back to her old house with no prospects of moving to a new lodging.

On the train going to Basra, my fellow women journalists and writers were singing a famous song by Nazim al-Ghazali. When I began to join in singing the Egyptian version of the song, Naglaa cried out, "You've totally ruined the tune, Nora!" and went back to the Iraqi version.

I said, "Isn't this one of our songs?"

Laughing, she said, "They are all Arabic songs and the words are the same all over the Arab world."

I said, "Not exactly. You've changed 'battikh,' the word we use for watermelon, to 'raggi,' and our word for melon, 'shammam,' you've changed to 'battikh,' and so on and so forth. You use Kurdish words, Persian words, and Turkish words. You even use English words."

"What English words?" she asked in alarm.

"Well, you say 'glassat' for 'glasses' and 'tankaji' for 'metal worker'."

"And you? Don't you have the same thing?"

"We say 'merci' and 'bus,' but you have many more loan words."

Naglaa laughed and said, "Come on! Tell us the latest joke. Our dialect is much easier."

We all laughed. A beautiful voice began to sing another Nazim al-Ghazali song and soon many other voices joined in.

The train whistle sounded intermittently, then the train stopped moving. We all looked toward and through the windows, but there was no movement and no sound and no one knew or told us anything. One of the passengers said, "Maybe a military train is moving. But trains carrying troops and military equipment usually travel at night, not in broad daylight."

I said, "That's not necessarily true. Egyptian soldiers crossed the Suez Canal at 2:00 p.m. to surprise the Israeli troops in the middle of the day rather than the usual night attacks everyone had expected."

A mood of anxious waiting prevailed on the train. Some women journalists stood in the aisles, others changed seats. I took out my recorder from my handbag and looked for Manal al-Alousy and went over to her. "Do you have time for a short interview?"

The president of the Moroccan women's union moved to give me space and said, laughing, "Work, work, work?" I'll have you know that I am watching you!"

Manal said, "Nora is a dear friend. Whatever she wants."

I asked her about the conditions of Iraqi women at the present time and the losses they suffered in the family laws that women throughout the Arab world had hailed when they were first announced. She said, "Necessity forces us to detach ourselves from our own feelings and to give the homeland sons to defend it. A martyr's widow deserves special considerations and society adapts to changing conditions. Marrying a martyr's widow is a national duty and noble ideas are always costly."

She knew her figures by heart, listed them calmly, and spoke of the union's role, saying that the whole Iraqi people were voluntarily ready to defend the homeland and build the country, keeping the factories and the farms running. Then she winked at me and said, "With the help of the Egyptians, no?"

I went back to my seat full of sadness over the time when laws banned bigamy except under extremely extraordinary circumstances and gave women rights that infuriated men.

I took my mothering tools out of my bag and headed dejectedly for the bathroom. I didn't want to reach for my breasts but my bulging veins forced me to empty them. The conference was over and I had gotten used to the emptying process, keeping it up regularly, but I felt tired. I told myself that I should be thankful, but I felt very tired. I remembered how easily Haytham nursed. I felt cold even though I had dried my chest thoroughly with the towel. I was in great need of a cup of tea from the samovar. I couldn't believe it when I found Naglaa waiting to give me one as if she knew exactly what I needed. Then she distributed hamburger sandwiches, the ever-present magic Iraqi solution for everything. We sat down to eat our sandwiches. It was neither breakfast nor the usual English lunch. It was what my mother-in-law would call "Getting your mother-in-law's goat," when the young daughter-in-law shirks her housework before lunchtime, claiming to be hungry. The train started moving again. I opened my notebook and jotted some brief comments so as not to forget what was said or what I thought at the time. I remembered my friend Nahid, who insisted on feeding us every time we went on a trip, and how we used to try to run away from her, saying, "If we keep eating what you are pushing on us, we'll end up being like sheep fattened for Eid."

I remembered the last time we met before everything was turned upside down. I think it was a birthday celebration for Basil, son of Mahmoud Rashid and Samia.

We had gone in the morning to the central post office to send our weekly letter from Baghdad to *al-Zahra* in Cairo. We had kept our working relationship with the magazine even though the bureau had ceased to represent it officially and became a private, independent press office. I bought some postage stamps. Hilmi Amin said, "Why all these stamps? Are you corresponding with all of Egypt?"

I said, "Tomorrow is Friday. That's when Hatim and I write our letters to family and friends."

We found in our mailbox a letter from Tante Fayza and the girls. Hilmi Amin sat on the wooden bench to read it. It seemed he was pleased. I didn't ask. I waited for him to tell me. These last few days he has not been quite himself, given to different moods.

He said, "Thank God the transfer was made and Fayza solved some financial problems. This gives me some respite."

I said, "Thank God. I'd like to stop at a photography supply store to buy some film for the camera."

"Well then, let's go through the other door," he said.

I had hardly taken three steps from the door to the street when I stopped in disbelief of what I saw. Tariq Mandour was sitting in front of an upturned wooden box on which were displayed packs of Baghdad cigarettes and matchboxes. His hair was long and he hadn't shaved in some time. His shirt was negligently not tucked in and he looked exhausted, and it seemed that he hadn't been sleeping well. I said to him reproachfully, "You are here and I have been looking for you all over Baghdad? I thought you had gone back to Egypt. I was going to write to your mom tomorrow to ask her."

He said, "Sorry, Nora. I didn't want you to know where I was. My circumstances have changed completely. I moved to a very bad hotel and I've been doing my best to make enough money for a plane ticket to Egypt."

I said, "Why didn't you come to our house or to the office and tell me what was happening to you?"

"Did Ustaz Hilmi tell you? He saw me yesterday and I asked him not to tell you. He tried to give me money, but I refused."

"No, he didn't tell me. I came here by chance. Come on. Get up and come to our house."

"I am sorry. I can't. I have to sell this carton and pay the owner. I'll drop by tomorrow."

"Take this money. Pay the hotel and move into our house."

"No. I have enough. I'll come by tomorrow. Say hello to Uncle Hatim."

We returned to the office, Hilmi Amin and myself. I wanted to wait for Hatim to come and take me and Hilmi Amin to celebrate Basil's birthday. Anhar came. She asked Hilmi eagerly whether he had received the letter.

He said that he had. I said, "He is so happy about it. Don't you see how cheerful he looks?"

She waited for me to leave the room to bring tea and asked him what was in the letter. I heard a few muffled sentences in a whispered exchange that sounded angry and full of worry. I wanted to just get away from there. Their relationship these days was not a calm, relaxed relationship, but one that created tension and unhappiness all around. What good are such relations? Why don't they make up their minds? To go on? To get married? To get a divorce? To break up? To move ahead? What good could come out of this vacillation? What should I do now? As I crossed the corridor, I sang out loud the comic singer Shukuku's song about the "love taxi" that moves faster than pigeons and trains, without wings or engines, and which brings distant lovers closer. I made sure they heard me singing.

"Here's the tea. I'd like to go now to buy the cake from Karrada Maryam, so we can save some time. It is much closer from here to Waziriya."

I went out to the street. I walked on Saadun Street. I loved to look at shop windows in the afternoon, a time that had a feel all its own, quite different from rushed mornings and slow nights. It was the very heart of the day and its emotional center, filled with happiness. Why haven't I noticed that before? I thought about how much I loved Mahmoud Rashid and Samia, for whom I also had great respect, maybe because they were the closest couple to me. Mahmoud had problems with his eyes that required several surgeries, which he preferred to have done in Egypt despite the recent advances in medicine here in Baghdad.

We arrived at Mahmoud and Samia's house, followed by Adel and Nahid. We stood around the cake and candles and sang an Egyptian children's version of "Happy Birthday." Then the children left to play in the garden. Mahmoud went into his study and brought out a new book by Noam Chomsky wrapped in gilded foil, saying he did that with all his political books so as not to attract attention to them, and when one of his colleagues asked him what it was he would make up a novel's title.

We laughed and Hilmi Amin said, "Ask Nora about her story with *Autumn of the Patriarch*."

I said, "I was walking down Saadun Street when the owner of a bookstand recommended a novel by a Colombian author, Gabriel García Márquez. I held it in my hands, and because I hadn't heard of the author before, I thanked the owner and returned the novel to the display and left. That same night I heard it had been banned. So the following morning I went back to the book-stand but the owner told me apologetically that the police had confiscated all copies of the book. I told him to please try to find me a copy, saying that since I was Egyptian, I was not subject to those banning and confiscation orders. He laughed and said he couldn't do anything about it. I made the rounds of all bookstores I knew, even communist bookstores, but I couldn't find a single copy. Then Ustaz Hilmi obtained a copy for me from a friend of his, secretly of course. It's a beautiful novel in which the author uses Latin American mythology to poke fun at dictatorship. It's a novel full of vibrant life that captures Colombia, redolent with its scents. I fell in love with it."

Adel said, "But why was it banned?"

I said, "They do not admit that their regime is a dictatorship. They should have left it available on the street so that people would know that all Third World regimes copied each other."

Hilmi said, "A dictator believes that he is right in whatever he does, that he is surrounded by secrets that would elude even those on whom he is imposing his dictatorial rule."

We all laughed and Nahid said, "Why don't we think of something more pleasant on this birthday?"

Samia said, "May it all be for the best. When are you leaving, Nora? Hatim's told me that the doctor has finally agreed to let Yasir come to Baghdad."

I said, "Early summer so Hatim and I would have a long vacation during which Yasir would get used to us. I don't want to cause him any psychological disruption by taking him away from his grandpa and grandma before he gets to know us well."

Tariq did not come to our house. I looked for him all over Baghdad to no avail. Then, out of the blue, he called me from Suleimaniya to tell me that he had gone to work for a contractor, then quit his job after a while and settled down working at a tourist tea and beer garden.

After lunch everyone on the train was singing and dancing, and that helped time to pass more quickly than before. Most of the women gathered in the car where I sat and a Moroccan lady got up to dance in the aisle to the music of the train movement. There was a lot of shouting and merriment and Moroccan colleagues told me that they usually danced to entertain their guests. The Egyptian women in the car admitted failure in that department, perhaps to defend the reputation of Egyptian women, about whom the other Arabs said we each had a belly dancing outfit that we put on for our husband's pleasure every night. I smiled as I remembered Hilmi Amin's article, "Arabs and Egyptian Women," in which he refuted the idea that Egyptian women awaited Arab men at Cairo International Airport, chanting and welcoming them with open arms. I thought of the adolescent way Arab young men behaved vis-à-vis Egyptian female movie stars and their naïve fantasies that behind every door in Egypt was a Suad Hosni, a Naglaa Fathi, or even a Hind Rostom. And for Arab women, especially impressionable young women, there was, of course, Abd al-Halim Hafez and all the fantasies created by Egyptian cinema's portrayal of drug gangs and guns and macho men like Farid Shawqi.

Awatef Wali stepped forward in the aisle, moving her neck right and left and forming a bow with her hands above her head. Everyone laughed and Aziza Husayn shouted: "Long live Egypt!" Iraqi ululations and very loud songs rang out and hands clapped noisily. Then all of a sudden an Iraqi tabla drum appeared from nowhere and non-Arab women got up, dancing in an arrhythmic but beautiful way. The Iraqi women organized themselves in a dabka dance formation in the aisle, swaying with their long hair and statuesque figures, shaking their shoulders up and down, forgetting their anguish. I imagined that each of them was trying to forget a loved one on the war front or a missing brother. Bitterness gathered in my throat at the thought. Then I began to feel milk lightly streaking on my chest. I automatically reached for some Kleenex as I caught a whiff of the milk curdling. I said to myself that it could be turning into yogurt. Lutfiya, who was nearby, understood what was happening on her own and asked me, "Your chest again?"

I told her, "By the time we get to Basra, I'll give you a piece of cheese!"

We both burst out laughing as she said, "I want a lot of cream."

I got up, wading through the dancing crowd on my way to the bathroom. I closed the broken window with great difficulty. Earlier in the day I was not bothered by it but with the sun waning I felt cold, and together with the heat I felt coming from my chest, the desert wind gusts were unbearable. I looked through the window at the road, now totally empty except for reddish trails and purplish clouds. I removed the wads of tissue that had accumulated in my bra. I've always loved to travel outside Baghdad. I remembered the rhyming saying about Basra and how those who hadn't seen it would regret that until the day they died. I also remembered the shanashil, or the latticed wooden windows, crafted by Arab artisans and adorned with lace, which helped to hide the faces of young women from prying eyes while permitting these women to look out at the street, exactly like mashrabiyas in Egypt. I tried to fill in from memory the rest of the picture: scattered tents and Bedouin women

320

sitting in front of their spindles and carpet looms, with camels grazing in the distance and savanna reeds rising like aimed arrows on the river banks. I remembered my exasperation and my desperate cries to myself: "All this red soil and all this water and no one sowing or reaping? What's wrong? Where are the Egyptian peasants? This is our land! Our land!"

I noticed in the distance a long line of camels, chewing as they moved forward with a lone boy following. As the train came closer I saw a donkey moving ahead of the boy, an unusual sight in Iraq. I remembered the day I went to al-Khalsa village and saw a number of donkeys. I smiled.

I told Amm Ahmad Wadie, "The donkeys have come!"

The agricultural supervisor said as she laughed, "Egyptian peasants are spoiling the donkeys, giving them chewing gum and soda pop!"

Everyone laughed. The children stood around, happy to see their old friends, the donkeys. Every boy rode a donkey as big as a mule and started racing.

I said, "What's the story?"

They all said at the same time gleefully, "A donkey for one dinar, Abla!"

I said in disbelief, "One dinar?"

Amm Ahmad said, "Yes. Donkeys here wander about in the desert, lost, and no one feeds them."

The engineers smiled and Shadha, the agricultural supervisor, said, "Iraqi peasants have little use for donkeys. They prefer Toyotas."

I said, "You don't know how fond we are of donkeys. They are the only creatures with enough patience and fortitude to stand with our peasants and bear up under all the hardships and oppression they have to live through."

Hilmi Amin said, "Well, here they are, reunited with their old friends!"

I said, "Did you know that we have in Egypt a society that supports donkeys? Do you remember Tawfiq al-Hakim's donkey?"

They laughed and said, "No!"

Hilmi Amin said, "Of course you don't. This is a topic for intellectual talk."

I felt relieved and pleasantly relaxed after I emptied both breasts. Now I can go to another car instead of the noisy one I left behind, but I've never been able to make such decisions: leaving company, even to get some rest. I usually exhaust my energy, then collapse all of a sudden. So I found myself going back to the car I had left and to my seat. It was now a different scene. They were distributing sandwiches, soda pop, and fruit. Each one withdrew to their seats and the boisterous mirth subsided. The car was now quiet except for whispering voices here and there. The train seats suddenly became isolated little islands. I could hear a few words here and there about being late in arriving because of military trains. The train stopped. One woman tried to open the window next to her but someone ordered her to close it. The lights were turned off. Silence prevailed. I began to observe my colleagues, some of whom were sleepy while others were fast asleep. I kept looking at the guests of the conference while aware of the Iraqi young women who were watching us carefully and who knew much more than they revealed to us. I imagined how difficult it must be for them. I pondered what it meant for us to go to the front lines and also what it meant to carry on such noisy activity in the thick of war. I asked myself, "Was propaganda so important? And how exactly was it useful?"

I heard Layla calling out, "Zubayda! Zubayda! Over here!"

I turned toward her. I saw a very beautiful young Iraqi woman carrying water bottles and handing them out as Layla tried to draw her attention to an Indian lady who wanted some water. I remembered Zubayda and smiled.

*

I had gone to the office with ideas about several features I wanted to research and write. I told Hilmi Amin that I wanted to locate the burial site of Zubayda, wife of Harun al-Rashid, and also al-Hallaj's resting place.

Hilmi Amin smiled and signed the papers I needed. I found out that Zubayda's tomb was in the Karkh area. I knew that the Tigris divided Baghdad into two major sectors, al-Karkh and al-Rusafa. I was surprised that Hilmi Amin wished to come along to visit Zubayda's tomb. He gave me a book about the Abbasid era in Iraq. From a distance we could see a tomb that stood out with a design that resembled a dovecote. The taxi waited in front of the door. A plaque on the white structure adorned with turquoise mosaic said it was the tomb of Zumurrud Khatun. So, where is Zubayda's tomb? No one knew. We walked around for a little while and were informed by some locals that that was indeed the tomb of Zubayda, wife of al-Rashid.

The following day I made several visits to the ministries of Tourism and Information, and the Antiquities Department. I also pored over what historians had written about Zubayda, the enigmatic beauty who was given the name by her grandfather, Abu Jaafar al-Mansur, the founder of Baghdad, because of her white skin and her plumpness. Then I went back to *One Thousand and One Nights* to fill in the gaps in my knowledge of her image as created in the popular imagination. Hilmi Amin helped a lot in my work and gave me new suggestions every day. I followed his recommendations happily and kept working on that feature and he kept encouraging me and pushing me further. One late afternoon as I was going home I heard children of the neighborhood playing along the fence and singing, "Kash, Kish safran, Sitt Zubayda ran."

I did not understand their words but I figured out that Zubayda's memory lived on after all the years since Abbasid times. I concluded there must be a reason for that.

I wrote my feature with great love and went to the office filled with pride. I found on my desk beautiful drawings in a folder. Hilmi

Amin came in, smiling, and said, "Here, young lady, are line drawings for your story: splendidly beautiful pencil sketches of the tomb
that we have visited: The tomb of Zumurrud Khatun, signed by Dia
al-Azzawi, the Iraqi artist who visits us regularly."

I was overjoyed and exclaimed, "When did that happen?"

Laughing, he said, "I went with him to the tomb one afternoon
and let him do his work his own way. And there it is: your feature is
all ready to be sent, with line drawings that are perfect for *al-Zahra*'s
style, and it incorporates an Iraqi component. We must distinguish
ourselves from other newspapers and magazines, proving that long
experience and history in the field is worth something. Right?"

I couldn't shower him with kisses, so I shook his hand very warmly,
saying, "Thank you! You are the most beautiful Hilmi Amin!"

He got up, smiling, the cigarette partially turned into ashes still
stuck to his lips. He read the title: "'Sitt Zubayda in a Dovecote.'
Okay, young lady. Carry on with your successful work! We'll stumble
along. Send it."

The train stopped in the city of Amara. The posters on the walls of
the station inveighed against the Persians, calling them "fire-wor-
shipping Magi." In the faint light we read slogans trying to arouse
Iraqi zeal against what they characterized as "wars to eradicate the
Arab race." I remembered Anhar and what she told me about the
marshes and the book on Kubaysh that she had given me as a gift
when I wanted to learn more about that region. I remembered what
she told me about the boats that women used in that region: the
slim balam and the larger shahhat and all the trouble and toil that
marked their lives in the midst of the reeds and the artificial islands
built in the water.

I once asked Amal al-Sharqi, managing editor of *al-Mara* magazine, "Labor liberates a person since it makes one economically
independent. An Iraqi peasant woman works day and night while
her husband is idle most of the time. Why doesn't work liberate the
Iraqi peasant woman?"

"Because she is a serf," she said.

My memory took me back to that night we celebrated Suhayla Bezirgan's surviving the decree to deport all Iraqis of Iranian descent. Hilmi Amin invited us to his apartment and when Suhayla came in, followed by Abd al-Rahim, Sawsan sang Sayyid Darwish's famous song "Salma ya Salama," celebrating coming home after a long trip away from home.

Abd al-Rahim said, "Thank God we didn't go on any trips."

Atef grabbed the lute and began to sing an Abd al-Wahab tune, but Maha said, "What's with all these serious songs, people? Let's sing something cheerful!"

Anhar arranged various fruits and glasses full of juice on the desk and said, "I'm going to let you in on a family secret. My brother, Abd al-Razzaq, works for an insurance company. He had a very beautiful love affair with a colleague of his, the daughter of a tycoon who had Iranian affiliation, and my brother decided to propose to her. You know Abd al-Razzaq, my only brother, who came after a long wait and hardships. But my father asked that they get to know each other for a long time before announcing the engagement because of Shirin's family's huge wealth. Before I tell you the rest of the story, you have to know that that forced emigration of Iraqis with Iranian affiliation was not the first such emigration during the Ba'th rule, but rather the second one. The first one was in the years 1970 and 1971 and that was a blow aimed at big merchants just as it was this time."

Sawsan said, "Big merchants? I thought it was all political, because of al-Da'wa Party."

Anhar said, "It is very complicated and full of details. In 1951, Iraqi Jews immigrated to Palestine. Before that they controlled the bazaar."

Maha asked Anhar to explain the word "bazaar" and the latter said it simply meant "suq" or market. Then she went on, "The second force controlling the bazaar was made up of Shi'i Arabs and Iranians. They were so strong that they could make or break governments. So, when the Jews emigrated, these Shi'i merchants took their place and controlled the market from 1951 to 1971. That period witnessed several military coups: in 1958 Abd al-Karim Qasim toppled the monarchy; in 1959 the nationalist officers staged a coup against Abd al-Karim Qasim, then came the coups of al-Shawwaf and Rifaat al-Hajj Sirri. In February of 1963 came the first Ba'th coup, and in September the coup by the nationalists against the Ba'thists led by Abd al-Salam Arif, and in 1965 the coup by the nationalists against the nationalists, and in 1967 came the second coup by General Arif Abd al-Razzaq against the government of Abd al-Rahman Arif. Then, finally in 1970 came the coup by General Abd al-Ghani al-Rawi. In other words, we had eight military coups in twelve years."

I asked what the merchants had to do with these coups.

Sawsan said, "Nora, let her tell us the story."

Anhar said, "One way or another, with the blessing or outright support of the Shah of Iran, it happened that Abd al-Ghani al-Rawi, despite the fact that he was a Sunni Islamist, was looking for support, so he coordinated with Iranian intelligence. Therefore when his group was arrested and when he ran away, the first forced emigration took place. But it was on a very small scale."

I handed Anhar a glass of yogurt drink, saying, "You've earned it."

She added, "During the crackdown on Islamists in 1977, Shi'i merchants had strong connections with the old-school religious establishment. At that time religious authority was in the hawza which was in the hands of the men of religion, because a Shi'i man of religion had little to do with the government at that time."

I said, "Am I the only one here who doesn't understand? What is a hawza? And what does it mean that a Shi'i man of religion has little to do with the government? Does a Sunni man of religion have a lot to do with the government?"

They all laughed and Abd al-Rahim, Hilmi Amin, and Hatim all said in unison, "We also don't understand."

Anhar said, "A Sunni man of religion is an employee of the ministry of awqaf or religious endowments. He gets a monthly salary. A Shi'i man of religion takes a fifth of zakat money. People pay canonically mandated obligations in the form of zakat or khums, which amount to one-fifth of the profits of a business, in other words, twenty percent. For a millionaire or a tycoon, this amounts to a huge sum. Those merchants are beholden to the men of religion and they are fulfilling their religious obligations."

I said, "God's mercy! Please, what are these canonically mandated obligations? Do you know what these are, Ustaz Hilmi? Do you know them, Sawsan? Oh, but of course you don't, since, as Nazim al-Ghazali sings, you are a brunette from the Jesus people!"

Sawsan said as she laughed, "I swear by the Prophet, I know it better than you!"

Hilmi said, "Of course I know what she means. Go on, Anhar."

Hatim, Fathallah, and Atef shook their heads.

Anhar went on, "These canonically mandated obligations are greater in value than zakat. The injunction came in the Qur'anic verse: *and whatever you take as a spoil of war, a fifth of that shall be for God and his messenger.* (God has indeed spoken the truth.) The Muslims used to pay that to the general treasury or bayt al-mal. When the Prophet, peace be upon him, died, some schools of thought, in this case, rites of jurisprudence, deemed those obligations to have lapsed, while other rites believed that they remained in effect. The Shi'i believed that while it was true that the Prophet had died, he had left an offspring entitled to that share. This is the strong tie between the Shi'i merchants and the religious establishment, because they pay large sums of money to it. Therefore, and because of their strong influence, governments fear them and think a thousand times before alienating them.

"After the problems with Iran started, the Baghdad Chamber of Commerce sent invitations to about one hundred of the most prominent tycoons, all with Iranian affiliations, to an important meeting with the president of Iraq."

Maha asked, "What are tycoons, Anhar? Please go easy on us."

Anhar laughed and said, "It means big rhinoceroses, or what they call in *al-Zahra* 'the fat cats.'"

I said, "You mean 'whales of commerce'"?

She said, "Yes, Sitt Nora. They went without knowing what the meeting was about or why they had been invited."

I cried out, "Don't tell me it was another citadel massacre like Muhammad Ali!"

She said, "Exactly. The doors closed and they were ordered onto buses that took them to a plane bound for Tehran. They told them that the Iraqi authorities considered them personae non gratae and that their families would join them in a few days. Then they confiscated their money and their possessions, and Iraqi intelligence raided their homes at the same time and informed the families that they had only six hours to pack their bags and clothes and put them in cars under heavy guard. Then they took them to the Iraqi–Iranian borders. This all took place quickly and simultaneously with the expulsion of the fat cats so that none of them could take their money out of the banks or dispose of it in any way, shape, or form."

Hilmi Amin said, "I had heard some rumors about some of these details, but for me they remained just that: rumors. This is your fault, Anhar. I didn't know the extent of it. But we know that it didn't stop at a hundred or a hundred and twenty tycoons—it extended afterward to ordinary people."

Anhar said, "Yes. They started with the fat cats, then went on with the next level and so on."

Suhayla, her face turning red and her eyes tearing, "Until they reached the poor."

Fathallah said, "What happened to your brother and his fiancée, Anhar?"

Maha said, "First, I'd like to understand the story of 'affiliations.'"

Anhar said, "That's a long story concerning the Shi'a in Iraq. The Shi'a during the Ottoman period did not consider themselves subjects of the Ottoman state, because of their sectarian difference. Therefore many Arab families were registered as Iranians, so as not to be conscripted into the Ottoman army. All Iraqis were supposed to have Ottoman 'affiliation.' This was determined by the father's ID and his original nationality. But if the father belonged to a nationality with another affiliation, he was not considered an Iraqi and as such not entitled to an Iraqi nationality certificate, the most important document in Iraq.

"What happened with my brother a few days before the wedding was that his fiancée called him and asked him to come to her house right away. There he found her father and brothers in a state of extreme panic and the whole household in chaos. She told my brother that they, meaning the government, had given them six hours to leave Iraq. 'I want you to take this tin can in which we have stowed all the family jewels and whatever cash we could get our hands on. I will leave it in your safekeeping until we settle down somewhere, because we'll go to Iran first and from there most likely to Paris or Beirut, depending on my father's or brothers' jobs.' Abd al-Razzaq was at a great loss about what to do and said, 'Why don't you leave it in safekeeping with one of the husbands of your sisters, some of whom are Iraqi with Ottoman affiliation?'

"She said, 'I don't trust anyone but you.' Abd al-Razzaq thought for a little while then said, 'I am sorry, Shirin. I cannot guarantee the safekeeping of these assets. Iraqi security forces might come and take them by force. How would I look then, to you and your brothers? And what if your father or other members of your family did not believe me? What would I do? Security men might confiscate it, then the officers would later on deny it. I am sorry. I can't do it. I want you, not your money or your family jewels.' She cried and said, 'The officers and policemen will seize it now. Please, help us. Maybe no one would know about it. I've put it in a cooking butter can that you can hide anywhere you wish. If all goes well, then our property would be preserved. If they seize it, then at least we've tried, because if we keep it they'll take it anyway since the departure order permits only what we need on the road to the borders.'

"Abd al-Razzaq said, 'I am sorry. People lose everything for much more trivial reasons. I hope you understand my position. We will meet in Beirut when things calm down, God willing.'

329

"Shirin then opened the can and took out a gold miniature Qur'an on a chain and a ring and got him to wear them. Abd al-Razzaq went back home despondently. And naturally they haven't met again yet and he doesn't know if they ever will. Shirin's father was the biggest fruit merchant in Iraq and owned several import and export companies. He had been spared the big deportation operation with the other tycoons because he was sick that day. Shirin's older brothers were in Beirut, where they still are, and none of them had gone to that meeting."

A deep sadness enveloped us. It was the tragedy of love and hatred that Iraq was constantly experiencing over again. I thought to myself, "Why is it that Iraq is so hard on its own people? Why?"

Sawsan whispered, "Doesn't it remind you of Inji and Hasan Abu Ali in the movie *Rudda Qalbi*?"

Maha lightly struck Sawsan on the thigh. I got up to prepare tea in the samovar and to try to break the sad mood that had settled on us. A few moments later I heard some loud laughter. I said to myself, "Thank God," and asked them to tell me what they were laughing about. I saw tears in Anhar's eyes despite her smiling face. Suhayla said, "Anhar must tell the story. No one can tell it as well as she can."

Anhar said, "The deportation continued in descending order according to the status of the deportees. It even got to the point that some people made false accusations about people that they knew. Most beggars were either Iranians or Indians, especially near the shrines. An old lady whose husband had died rented a room in my uncle's house. This uncle is a very old man who lives alone with his wife after marrying off his children. Their relationship with this ajami woman was very strong and it grew stronger because she checked on them every day until, with time, she became part of the family, especially since she didn't have any children. Suddenly they arrested her and put her on the military truck and told her she could only take a bag, a blanket, and a bathroom pitcher. The old woman was frightened and had a panic attack that left her with a case of acute diarrhea. My uncle and his wife could not help her in any way. Kazim begged them to let her go, but they threatened him harshly. Faced with the cruelty of the soldiers, the poor woman got on the truck, crying the whole time. Throughout the drive, the driver refused to stop so she could go to the bathroom. The diarrhea persisted and she couldn't control herself. The other passengers and the soldiers escorting them couldn't stand the stench. One of them said, 'What can this ajami woman do and what difference would it make if she stayed in Iraq or left?' He ordered the driver to stop and rid them of her."

Anhar then stood up, imitating the soldier and saying loudly, "Go, go. You're so disgusting!"

"My uncle and his wife were surprised when she returned after a few days in a pitiable condition."

Everyone was touched by the sad story, but when Atef grabbed the lute and began to sing a serious, melancholic song by Abd al-Wahab, Sawsan asked him to stop and to sing a more cheerful popular song.

Naglaa gave me a banana. I told her, "The way you're feeding us, you'd think you're fattening us for the Eid!"

She said, "I am sure you're hungry."

Then she placed her hand on her mouth to whisper, "You are nursing and you need food."

Abd al-Razzaq never met his fiancée again—the war made that impossible. I remembered asking Anhar a few months after that whether the deportation of Iraqis with Iranian affiliation had stopped, and she said, "Yes. Some of those close to Saddam said to him, 'Why do you give Iran the gift of an army of angry young men who resent being forcibly deported from Iraq, when they know Iraq inch by inch and could come back as spies or carry out terrorist activities without arousing suspicion?' So Saddam ordered the deportation of girls and the elderly and the detention of young men at Abu Ghraib. I understand there are thousands of young men between the ages of eighteen and forty-five being detained now. The catastrophe is that now that war has broken out, it's become impossible for them to be released. And nobody knows the true facts or exact figures."

I looked behind as I heard a girl singing in the back of the train car, "Tarry, tarry, sun! Sun, tarry, tarry!"

The Iraqi women on the train joined in and started singing the rest of the song. I tried to keep track of the boisterous singing even as I kept hold of my thoughts. The singing rose so loudly it engulfed the whole car:

> The morning bird passed by and greeted me.
> It said "good morning" and wished me well.
> It fluttered its wings and sang to me.
> It dispelled the clouds and revealed the light;
> It took me to my house and gave me a mare, two robes, and a kerchief.
> It said to me, "Congratulations, a thousand congratulations! You're now free!"

My tears flowed. Where is that freedom now, Anhar, Abd al-Razzaq, Shirin, Suhayla, and Naglaa? Who else can I think of, and where is that freedom? Why was the picture so different when I lived among them? Why were Hatim and I so happy for Iraq, thinking that it was prospering? Why did we, along with so many, love Saddam? Oh God!

The train stopped in the Nasiriya station. We were getting very close to Basra. Will Basyuni keep his promise and come to our appointment at the hotel? I remembered his baby face and his excessive zeal, his sense of humor and his sudden fits of anger. I asked myself: What tempted him to join the Iraqi army in the war against Iran? Did he really believe it was a national war in defense of Arabism? Has the war changed him just as prison had? Nora, what does prison do to a boy who finds himself among veteran political prisoners? Undoubtedly they spoiled him and he took on the role of a revolutionary without fully understanding what the word meant. But it also points to a sort of suicidal character, the makings of a Greek tragedy: from prison to Iraq and from a clean bed to laborers' tents to war in one fell swoop? Why does life choose certain people to test by fire from so early on? I don't think it's mere coincidence. If you keep running, you are bound to stumble at some point.

We arrived at Basra at two-thirty in the morning. We went directly to the lattice-covered Sheraton hotel. I took a hot shower and quickly emptied my breasts without bothering to measure the outcome. I just wanted to go to sleep.

I woke up at five in the morning as usual. I opened the window and turned the radio on, filling the room with soft music. I conducted a thorough examination of my body. I noticed that the milk in the glass came only to the half-way point. I counted the days, using my fingers, and held on to hope. I took out Hilmi Amin's memoirs from the bag and started reading. Maybe they could shed light on Anhar's disappearance, even though he described the memoirs as the body's journey that he couldn't record for me. And why not? Anhar is his beloved even though he hadn't mentioned her in the pages I had read so far. I continued reading:

The First Pick

All these experiences with women and now, the only woman I've ever wanted with all my being, I find myself unable to plunge into her body. I know that body from the outside, I desire each of its cells, yet I am content to stop at its threshold, at these outer pulsations that fall with the overpowering turnings in my hands. When your body twists, Anhar, and when I hear your moans, breathless with desire, filling the whole room, and when you cannot contain the desire pressing you for completion, I get aroused to the point of madness, I call on my iron will and long experience in self-control to prevent our becoming one body. It had become quite a knot, and I don't know how we will untie it in the coming days.

Do you remember the first time I saw you naked? I began to kiss you as you twisted sweetly, melting like an ice cream scoop in my hand, and abandoned resistance at the threshold of your lips and lifted barriers one after the other as I undressed you?

I remember all the details very well. They say that women are best when it comes to details, but I say that I see the picture so clearly and in vivid colors in my imagination's eye, because of the many times I have recalled it on the lonely nights since you left. I removed your wool vest first, then you smilingly gave me your blouse as you waited for my next step. I raised your slip and you slipped out of it, laughing as you reached for the clasps of your bra, undoing them and handing it over to me in a gesture of acquiescence. How strong you are, Anhar! You left me facing your breasts as perfectly shaped as pomegranates anxious to leave their tree, calling out to me, inciting me to pluck them. Oh God! Are you really mine? Are you really standing, half naked, like a goddess, head pointing to the sky, delighted in showing off what you've got? I must admit that you are really consciously proud of what you have and that I would one day realize that your pride would be our biggest problem. I got lost in my reflections until you got me out of them by asking, 'Where have you gone?'

You had sat up, resting your knees on the mattress, leaving your legs bent behind you, naked except for black netting stockings through which your skin appeared even whiter. You also wore black lace panties. I pictured you as Venus, standing on the water's surface, defying the world, time, and the gods. It got to the point when all that was left was for me to remove the last piece of clothing. I reached for your shoulders and began to feel them, reverently worshiping the body open before me. I wanted to touch its pores, get to know its minutest details, in reality and not just fantasy. I sat a short distance away, my fingers seeing what my eyes could not. It was as if I had realized that all my senses were aching to know you. I kissed you and my lips wandered all over your smooth and firm complexion. Did you know that I loved the taste of your skin? That it had a flavor all its own, which left me at a loss for a long time to figure out where it came from and why it so captivated my mind? Was it some kind of perfume? I knew your perfume quite well. It exuded a totally different fragrance when another body wore it. Was it a special kind of soap? Was it the food you ate? When my tongue made the acquaintance of your skin I realized you had a rich, deep flavor resembling the rich scent of the alluvium of the Tigris after a rainy winter afternoon. My desire to kiss you all over grew stronger and I gave in to that desire. When I reached the dimple of your navel, I moved my head back a little and began to devour with my eyes the deep mark of your birth and said to you, 'Maybe I should place a colored bead there to protect it from both devils and gods!'

I inserted my tongue into the navel, feeling that I was having intercourse with you. Your skin trembled. Have you ever touched the neck of a horse and felt that lustful tremor under your palm? Your tremor tempted me to kiss your whole body, which I started doing until I stopped just outside the gate of paradise. I kissed you there and wiped my forehead on it; perhaps it would grant me entrance. I removed the black lace fabric and was surprised to see the red crest of the rooster alertly standing guard, armed with the banners of two lips filled with blood. It was overcome with desire so it shouted its readiness. I couldn't prevent myself, before taking any further step forward, from going back to look at your eyes. But you had closed them and withdrawn to a different world to which I had not been introduced yet.

You had stretched out on the bed in front of me, naked and available, beautiful and lustful, having lost all control of your body as my fingers moved freely, squeezing the nipple like a soft yet firm red grape which put my whole body on fire when it slid to my palm. I saw happiness washing over your face with holy prayer water, drawing me into the prayerful mood, causing me to forget time and place and defeat. But you automatically reached for my shirt buttons, taking it off, not knowing that at that very moment when you were signing the deed of the union of our flesh, you awakened my mind and made it possible for it to confront me and to remind me of my fear for you and the fact that you were my daughter's age. I started feeling torn between my overpowering desire for you and my responsibility toward you. I did my utmost to escape and to come back to our present moment and to cling to you as much as I could, so I embraced you tightly and began to rub and squeeze your back and your breasts fervently as you also rubbed and squeezed me, as if each of us wanted relentlessly to take the other deep inside. I sank my teeth into your neck and heard you screaming, thinking it was an act of lust and its fire, whereas I was seeking protection from the pain of my trying to stop my runaway desire. Then you surprised me by moving under me as if I had plunged into you. You made me feel as if I were on top of a mare galloping rhythmically and moaning, seeking my help to free you of the pain of waiting. I stole a glance at the rooster's crest and found it changing color from red to maroon to violet and getting darker and darker. My palm clung even tighter to it and it began to devour your lips, my pleasure increasing as my hand felt the fanlike movement and as I held myself back from ravishing you while desiring to contain all of your organs at the same time. My eyes were still fixed on what was under your eyelids, trying to pry them open and get into your innermost depths. Then your screams exploded so loudly I feared the neighbors would hear them in the quiet of the night as your hand reached into my pants, freeing my penis, which had been awaiting your hand's move. I felt your fingers hesitating as they felt the effect of age. But it was too late to stop or go back. Your own movement had begun to reach a crescendo. Then my hand felt the rhythmic movement subside. I stayed with you, patting it gently, until I got the message of your desire to withdraw.

I got up and sat before your body outstretched and totally available to me, and began to kiss you as you sank back into blissful rest. I took my time, enjoying your being so close at a leisurely pace. I saw your netted stockings still covering your legs. I held the end and began to remove it little by little. I heard you laughing and saying, "The Graduate." I said, "I thought you were too young to have seen the movie."

You began to relax again as my lips roamed all over your soft, supple legs. Then you sat up just so you could reach for a cigarette, which you lit and placed between my lips. You lit another cigarette and began smoking it as you kept your eyes on my prayerful watch over your body. You reached for my clothes, trying to take the rest of them off of me. I involuntarily recoiled, but you gave me that look of anger and defiance that I knew quite well and I also knew what followed. I turned off the light and took off the rest of my clothes. I came back to you in the dark to spare your eyes the shock of seeing what time and age had done to my body. You opened your legs and I hid my face, feeling the pleasure of tarrying and stretching the moment that you, at your impatient age, did not understand. I did not need you to overheat at this moment. I wanted a calm arousal of desire, wave after wave, to savor the journey rather than the destination. I didn't worry about what you might be thinking at the moment for you were still in that phase of innocent not knowing, and it is I who will teach you loving. I reached with my tongue to the sacred portal, to the heart of the jewel that I had never had the privilege of penetrating for the first time before, as my wife was not a virgin. She had a short unsuccessful marriage before we met. I stared at it, then I felt it with the tips of my fingers: it was strong and well protected by layers of soft pink flesh. I had a strong desire to break it open, knowing that you would have no objection at all. But I desisted. I was content with pushing apart the lips guarding it, and licking it. You trembled again and you slid out of the bed and embraced me and began to kiss me all over as your feelings rekindled the fire, changing the quiet pace of the calm enjoyment that I had imposed on the whole situation. Your fire started to engulf me even though I just wanted slow, quiet loving and cumulative emotional fulfillment. The battle raging on the bed revealed the intensity of your feelings and your extraordinary joy as you relentlessly tried to break my slow deliberate rhythm and to bring back to life my dormant volcano, not yet ready to erupt.

I kept calling on all my strength to set the fire of desire to my body that had succumbed to inaction. I was anxious that the touch of your hand should not change course from lustful eagerness to pitiful pats. But I saw you rising and flying higher and higher to the sky while I was still on my way to reach full ignition. Then your escalating tremors overwhelmed me. You got up strong and happy, as stunningly beautiful as ever. You put on your clothes and kissed me as I was fighting off sleep. I asked you to close the door gently behind you.

I remembered Basyuni's appointment. I took my camera and got down to the lobby. I discovered that I was the earliest guest to come down, with the exception of the organizers. Then the other member guests began to arrive one by one. The restaurant came to life and the smell of fresh baked bread permeated the hall. Delicious dates started finding their way to the tables, where guests helped themselves to European-style continental breakfast or an Iraqi breakfast of date molasses and hot bread. I remembered the smoke coming out of the carts serving turnips and molasses in the squares of Baghdad early in the morning and the restaurants for pacheh, made from lamb's head and feet, which to my surprise served their meals at five in the morning. I also remembered the kahi pastries that were served with cream and syrup in stores that closed at seven o'clock in the morning. There were scenes and experiences that stood out and were noticed mainly by the eyes of non-natives. The first thing that drew our attention was the great attention Iraqis paid to food. Hilmi Amin once told me as he pointed to the many tikka carts dotting the street that he had an explanation for this phenomenon: "The Arabs in the Arabian Peninsula after the revelation of the message of Muhammad, peace be upon him, began to dream of gardens underneath which rivers flowed, quite different from their arid desert that had only a few springs and some palm trees, goats, sheep, and camels. So, when they came to Ard al-Sawad, the rural areas of Iraq, and when they saw the Tigris and the trees and the vineyards and the fig and olive groves and the fruit orchards, they settled down and started eating and haven't stopped till now."

I sat down eating the hot bread, which brought back the memory of the aroma of clay bread-baking ovens that arose out of the houses all at the same time as the noon prayers. I remembered my good neighbor women who would send me gifts of bread from time to time, knowing that no one could turn down hot bread. I put a dried date in my mouth, of the kind they call "dijla nur" because of its luminescence. I had a hard time chewing it because of the copious salty tears of remembrance.

I did not believe my eyes when I looked up and noticed one of the hotel workers pointing in my direction. He was accompanied by a young man who looked as if he was looking for me. It was Basyuni in the flesh. But where was the flesh? When I first met Basyuni he looked like a body builder, with bulging muscles, a broad chest and shoulders, a chubby face, and a very fair complexion. How did he become so brown and emaciated? I remembered Shahira al-Asi saying as she commented on the appearance of the Iraqi cabinet ministers, "Dried and mummified, scrawny, miserable ministers!" So, what happened to Basyuni? What did war do to people, Nora? He approached, all smiles, extending his hands. I welcomed him very warmly. He said, "How are you, Abla?"

I smiled. So, he has kept his innocence despite the brutality of the war in which he was plunged; he still thinks of me as his big sister. I said, "The war has consumed you, Basyuni. Tell me, are you all right?"

He said, laughing to hide his bashfulness, "What could I do? Things are so hard here. I came today only by a miracle!"

I handed him his family's letter. He opened it eagerly. His face changed color and he didn't say a word.

I said, "While you wait for them to bring you tea, tell me what has happened to you since you left for Mosul and how you ended up in the war."

Laughing he said, "All of that before tea? We might need a whole breakfast first. To begin with, Engineer Fathallah took me to his house. And even though Maha is not much older than me, they both treated me as if I were their son. I was appointed to work in the highway department. I discovered that he is held in very high esteem in Mosul. I don't know the reason for that: was it the letter of recommendation that he brought from Khalid Muhyiddin? His gentle nature and his skill as an engineer? Or for all those reasons?"

"Most likely, all those reasons," I said.

"I found out that Fathallah was the official in charge for managing the highways in the Nineveh governorate, even though I am certain that he hasn't joined the Ba'th Party. He gave me a monthly salary that, with incentives, came up to five hundred dinars, a sum that I couldn't spend in a year even if I tried. Let me tell you that the difference between my salary and Fathallah's was only forty dinars. He took me to the shop as an assistant to the mechanic, Amm Sayyid al-Mursi, and said to him, 'Teach him everything.' Amm Mursi is a very capable mechanic usta, even though he is illiterate. But he can read the catalogue for the parts. And yet I got a salary higher than his. They appointed me to the Mosul–Sheikhan road that connected Mosul with the Yazidi Kurdish towns. I befriended the Kurds and came to like them a lot. They were overjoyed that the government made it possible for them to get loans to build new houses. So, any young man who wanted to get married would get a three-thousand-dinar loan, one-fourth of which would be forgiven when they had their first baby."

I said, "All Iraqi young men had that same right to the loan and enjoyed the same privileges."

He said, "Yazidi Kurds enjoyed greater privileges than other Kurds and far greater than those enjoyed by the Arabs, since they got the loans as soon as they applied and needed nothing more than their own ID cards to finish the procedures."

I asked him to which party the Yazidi Kurds belonged to, the Kurdistan, Democratic, or . . .

He didn't let me finish. "Neither. They don't join the Kurdistan Workers Party. But some had joined the Ba'th Party right before the

340

war in view of the steps taken to improve their living and economic conditions, for they had been totally marginalized before."

I said, "You got an unusually high salary. What tempted you to enter the war?"

He said in great alarm, "No! And I swear to you. I didn't enter the war as a volunteer soldier. An administrative order was issued to transfer the group working on the northern Mosul highway to the south to keep the roads in repair to serve the movement of the army forces. So I moved with my unit to Abu Ghurab al-Sharahani. When I went the fighting was still ferocious and shelling went on day and night. Sometimes I got up in the middle of the night terrified, finding myself up in the air, half a meter away from the ground. Amm Sayyid al-Mursi was also transferred there. He was a miracle worker, I swear. He could repair any equipment that had been blown up even if one half of it, and sometimes more, had been a total loss. I assisted him and he encouraged me, always saying, 'Have no fear. You won't find better conditions to learn.' That was why I acquired great technical skill."

He fell silent for a moment then said, "Believe me, I'm not bragging."

"I know, Basyuni. Go on," I said.

"That's it," he replied.

"Where is that area?"

"I don't know where it is on the map exactly. It's one of the first areas to be occupied by the Iraqi army. The cars took us to the Amara Highway and from there to a road leading to Iran."

I said, "Why are you fighting in this war, Basyuni? Your family is worried sick about you and they want you to go back as soon as possible."

He said, "I am not fighting. I was transferred in my job from one place to another in a country that is fighting a war. I will soon go back to Egypt."

"When?"

"I can't tell exactly, but in a few days."

Then he added, laughing, "I might arrive in Egypt before you."

"Can you get out of the army that easily?"

"With God's help."

"What are you going to do, Basyuni? Don't do anything foolish or crazy. Request permission to travel, legally and officially. You know the system here."

"This is not my war and my blood will not be shed in it without rhyme or reason."

"You are saying that now? You should've known that from the beginning, before you got embroiled. Wouldn't your leaving now be considered desertion? Running away from the war? Wouldn't that be grounds for a court-martial? What made you change your mind?"

"I asked my Iraqi colleagues: 'Why are we fighting?' They said, 'To regain our land which had been taken from us in the 1975 treaty.' I told them, 'Didn't Saddam Hussein himself sign it?' They said, 'He had no choice. He had to sign it so that the shah would stop aiding Mullah Mustafa Barzani. The Kurdish insurgency was at its worst, so Iraq was forced to give up that territory.'"

I said, "Iran's problem is that Muhammara and Ahwaz have a commanding view of Iranian oil sources. For Iran that's a strategic position that it won't give up easily. But I still don't understand what made you change your mind."

He bowed his head lightly, then bent forward, clasping his hands together, then letting them drop between his legs, and didn't say a thing.

"Talk to me, Basyuni. You are talking to your older sister. If you believe that you are helping Iraq because you consider it your country and that you are responsible for any war it enters, I will not argue with you about it. But I don't feel that you believe that."

He said, "They told me that they were fighting the Shi'i Iranians. I didn't know what the word 'Shi'i' meant. I thought they were infidels, but when I asked them if the Shia were Muslim, they said, 'Yes.' So I said, 'Do they say, *There is no god but God and Muhammad is the messenger of God?*' They said, 'Yes.' So I didn't understand. Believe me, I tried to understand. So I asked them, 'Why do you fight the Shia when they are Muslims?' They said, 'It's a long story.' As time went by, I realized that the historical battle between the Sunnis and the Shia in the land of Iraq since the family of the Prophet was killed was still going on. I realized that it had been a political battle from the beginning, and that Islam had nothing to do with it. When I figured that out, I decided to leave."

I said, "You needed two whole years in a war to understand? I also want to understand a few things. Please bear with me. You have gone to Abu Ghurab al-Shirhani and other places deep in Iran. As far as I know, Iraq continued to occupy towns in the south such as Muhammara, Qasr Shirin, Mehran, and Dezful, rough terrain that is difficult to fully control. You were near that region and took part in what was happening there. One day those territories were in Iraqi hands and another in Iranian hands and so on. Describe for me what happened in the first major defeat of the Iraqi army in the battle of Taheri last October."

He said, "I was not in the battle itself, of course, because the Iraqi army at the beginning of the war, in September 1980, had crossed the Karun River in Iran. It's a big river like the Tigris and Euphrates and it ends in Shatt al-Arab. Then after almost a year, Iran launched an effective large-scale offensive that the Iraqi forces had not anticipated. The Iraqi forces tried to retreat, but they found the river behind them. So, they fell into the trap. Thousands of officers and soldiers were killed, as I heard, and Iran took more than twenty-five thousand Iraqis as prisoners of war. Didn't you get the news at the time? A profound sadness descended upon the whole of Iraq. I don't think they have gotten over it yet. Have you not noticed a difference in the Iraqi personality which you knew and dealt with during the years you worked here?"

I looked at him for a while before answering him. I was amazed at the profound change that had come over Basyuni. He seemed to have grown mature during the hell fire of the war he had gone through. I said, "Yes, Basyuni. I've felt that Iraqi grief was now more profound, that they no longer try to hide it like before. It is now bigger than them."

I noticed in his eyes the beginnings of a suppressed tear that wanted to come out without his permission. I went on to say, "Yes, we got the news in detail, but the killing of Sadat consumed all international media and so the news of that defeat and its massive casualties did not get the attention it deserved, even though there was no deliberate attempt to conceal it. In less than an hour I am going to meet some Iraqi army commanders and I am going to ask them the same question that I wanted your opinion about: Why did Iraq change its military strategy from offense to defense? We were all surprised by Iraq's political initiatives to withdraw from Iran's territories to the international borders. Do you have an answer for that? How do the Iraqis around you explain this position? Or are they afraid to talk?"

He said, "You know that Iraqis don't talk until they are totally reassured that you are not a government spy. That's what the Arabs are like. You can imagine how it would be with the Kurds. They are doubly afraid. And yet when either the Arab Iraqis or the Kurds get drunk they lose control over their feelings and their words, so they say whatever they like. According to rumors, there have been many detentions because of words said at the bar."

He paused, so I asked him, "Yes, and then what?"

He looked at me long before speaking. I looked behind me. One of the Iraqi women organizers, actually a friend of mine, was on her way to where we were sitting. I heard her saying, "Am I interrupting anything? Is your friend an Egyptian?"

I said, "Khuloud, this is my friend Basyuni who works here in Basra."

She said, "It's time to get ready. The bus will be leaving for the front in fifteen minutes."

I said, "I'll catch up with you whenever you're ready."

She went over to the other tables to alert the other delegates.

Basyuni said, "She will immediately report this meeting of ours. I am going back to Egypt, I promise you, Abla. I heard that the change in strategy from offense to defense came about after the Iraqis realized that the war had gone on longer than expected—two whole years, during which the Iraqis lost a lot of money and men. It also came about after the realization that a soldier fighting to defend his own land was a better fighter, especially after the great loss in the battle of Taheri. This point of view became known after leaks picked up by soldiers from conversations among the officers in dining halls at officers' quarters. As for ordinary people, they had grown tired of the whole war. But Iran doesn't believe that and doesn't trust Iraqis' intentions. So their mobilization continues. We even heard that they are now mobilizing fifteen- and sixteen-year-old boys."

I said, "This explains the big brouhaha accompanying this conference of ours and all this talk about Iraq's desire for peace and return to the international borders. This is all so unusual and new, at least to me, especially after the earlier noise they made about regaining Shatt al-Arab."

I heard movements in the tables around us and I realized that members of the delegations were getting up and moving toward the door. I got up to say goodbye to Basyuni and told him in the Iraqi dialect, "For your mother's sake, please put an end to this story and go back home before you get injured in a war that, the way I see it, you are not convinced about. If you were to tell me that you are fighting so that Iraq would regain its land, I would just leave without asking you to go back. Please listen to reason and put an end to this."

He gave me a big hug and kissed me on the cheek, holding my shoulders so hard it hurt my muscles. Tears rushed to my eyes and I felt dispirited. I was afraid for Basyuni as if he were my younger brother, even though I had met him only once before. I prayed to God, as the bus was moving and as he waved to me, that he would go back safely to his family, for he was not even twenty years old yet. So young, I thought, but also, so rash.

A number of high-ranking officers welcomed us warmly and they escorted us to very large pavilion-like tents with large posters condemning Iran's aggression against Iraq and declaring the right of Iraqis to their occupied territories. They pointed out to us that that was the furthest we could go for fear for our safety. We found a chart showing where the forces stood on both sides. They explained to us details about the deployment of the Iranian forces and the positions they occupied. The commander of the forces in the region told us that the Iranians left behind bodies of twelve-year-old boys who had undertaken suicide missions. The officers kept using the words "Persian" and "Persians" in almost every sentence. I knew that the roots of the enmity went back a long time over the history of the battles between the Arabs and the Persians up to the triumph of the Muslims against the Magi Iranians and their conversion to Shism. I remembered the visit Hatim and I made to Iwan Kisra in Salman Pak, so close to Baghdad, and saw how ancient and modern history intermingled. I thought of the enigma of the ordeal of Barmakids, when Harun al-Rashid summarily got rid of his Persian allies and his grand vizir, Jaafar the Barmakid. He had just formally married his sister Abbasa to Jaafar, so she could attend their literary gatherings with both of them—her brother and her "husband"; but when the two lovers, Jaafar and Abbasa, consummated the marriage, Harun al-Rashid flew into a rage. The love story was still reverberating everywhere and the river of blood was still flowing underground, and whenever its waters dried up, they flowed again somehow. It was a long history of merging and separating, an eternal neighborliness, quiet at times, then erupting again with conflict over power.

I came to as the Iraqi officer was saying, "Even though Basra, thank God, is not occupied, yet one half of it is, unfortunately, within range of Iranian artillery. We want peace and our position is clear in our goodwill initiatives for ceasefire and conciliation and a return to the international borders."

I said to myself, "What international borders?" I got dejected and prayed that Basyuni would not do anything stupid! A refreshing breeze gently stroked my hair.

I remembered what happened in Baghdad when the Iranian revolution broke out. Saddam Hussein was still vice president. He took over five months later, during the July celebrations. He announced the resignation of President Ahmad Hasan al-Bakr, for health reasons. Then he executed two-thirds of the regional command of the Ba'th Party after aiming a blow at the left and finished off the Iraqi Communist Party. He now held sole power in Iraq. Did he bet on playing the region's strongman in the absence of the shah? It was a foolish move. He didn't give Iran its full due. He began applying pressure to regain half of Shatt al-Arab. He sent a message to the new regime in which he said something to the effect: "You are an Islamic government that knows the true meaning of fairness. We were forced to sign the Algiers Treaty because of the role that the shah had played in supporting the Kurdish insurgency in our country." The Iranian government replied, "These are international agreements. We have inherited the shah's regime for better or worse. International logic dictates that what the shah had taken was now gone. We are obligated to pay his debts." The slogan for regaining Muhammara and Ahwaz was raised and displayed all over Iraq. Then there began a wave of attacks against Iraqi political Islam, and the fear that Iran would export the revolution grew stronger. That threw a monkey wrench into the workings of all branches of the Iraqi government. We began hearing of the Organization of Islamic Action and al-Da'wa Party, whose president and founder, Ayatollah Muhammad Baqir al-Sadr, had considerable charisma and great popularity. Oh, how I need your opinion now, Ustaz Hilmi!

An old memory jumped to the surface of my mind. I remembered asking Hilmi Amin, "Why do Arab governments make carbon copies of their fascist experiences in dealing with the opposition rather than their good experiences in democracy, if they have any? Don't they understand that by aiming their blows against the communist party and the left in general they allow political Islam to expand and take over the vacuum like a mindless cancer, that it will turn against them one day? Is that so hard to understand?"

347

Hilmi Amin said, "It is not hard to understand at all, but there are two reasons for that to be so. First, hubris, in that a dictatorial power believes in its ability to control that cancerous expansion since it has the key to power and the key to prisons; second is its real desire to support that tendency for some unknown reason, perhaps because of external support or orders from abroad. In all cases the West benefits."

I said, "The journalist Hadya al-Jaafari has asked me to buy her books in Cairo that deal with the Muslim Brotherhood in Egypt. It is obvious that fundamentalists are a cause for concern to experts everywhere."

He said, "I want you to go to *al-Thawra* newspaper and spend two hours there every day gathering all the material you can get from the archives about the relationship of the Ba'th Party with Islamist movements in Iraq since 1970–71, that is, since the execution of Sheikh Abd al-Aziz al-Badri, one of the leaders of the Islamist party, and since the beginning of the liquidation of political Islam. I'd like for you also to look into and gather information about the death sentences handed down in the years 1977–79 and, of course, any information about the demonstrations that Muhammad Baqir al-Sadr tried to organize last year; as you know, those demonstrations were aborted and he was placed under house arrest. We've written about this. Go back to our stories and study the file closely, then write me a detailed report that I could use should any further developments occur. I will personally review your report."

I said, "I need books that analyze the relationship between the Ba'th Party and Islamist parties in earlier eras so as to develop a deeper understanding of the experience. Would I find anything in the bookstores?"

"I don't think so. You'll find nothing, Umm Yasir."

I gathered the material, feeling that I was under surveillance that whole time. I would tell laggards that we, in *al-Zahra* magazine, depended on scientific reference books in compiling our information so that our journalistic reports would be correct and well documented. In practical terms we used most of the material we had gathered as background material rather than directly in our features. It helped us understand the publicly declared Iraqi political position, for Hilmi Amin was extra careful in maintaining a working relationship with the state agencies, which used extreme caution when dealing with Arab or foreign correspondents. Then there was a huge surprise right before the war with Iran. Ayatollah Muhammad Baqir al-Sadr, the man who was loved and revered by all the Shia, was executed. The Iraqi government within the previous few months had clamped down hard on Shiʻi organizations that had clear appeal in the Iraqi street. We also found out from numerous sources that Iraqi security had been sending warning signals to Muhammad Baqir al-Sadr, cautioning him to stay away from politics, especially since he had issued a fatwa at the time of the Iranian revolution, forbidding, on religious grounds, joining the Baʻth Party. They sent someone to interrogate him and, being a religious man, he did not lie. They asked him, "Are you the one who issued the fatwa declaring it to be religiously forbidden to join the Baʻth Party?"

He said, "Yes, because the Baʻth Party is antithetical to religions and to people of faith."

They tried to persuade him to retract the fatwa or deny that he issued it. But he refused. They tried again several times to no avail. So, getting nowhere with him, they ordered that he and his sister be executed on April 9, 1980 after long and unimaginably horrific torture whose reverberations echoed with the Shia, tormenting them and igniting revolt in their hearts while they did not dare to speak out.

How romantic and revolutionary and truthful that man was! Why was Iraq destined to pay all of that! Oh, my God! I felt tears gathering up in my throat. I inhaled deeply to keep them from appearing on my face and calmly wiped the ones that got away. The officer was now telling the members of the conference delegations sitting in front of him in the pavilion on the Basra front, "We are a peace-loving country. We don't want war. We want to liberate our land."

I said to myself, "What peace?" I wanted to raise my voice and ask the officer, "Have you looked at the eyes of those around you? Have you observed all this Iraqi sadness? Do you need hundreds of years of waiting, slapping of faces and self-mutilation and bloodshed, to realize that what is happening now is foolish?" I was suddenly aware of the sadness in his eyes. I realized that he was not that far from the sadness around him.

I remembered my neighbor Umm Samira telling me in whispers, "You know something? I can assure you that the troubles in the north between Mullah Barzani and the government are the result of preventing us from performing our religious rites. God is great! Why don't they let people do what they want? God be my witness! It is all because of God's anger. My beloved al-Husayn!" She spoke looking around in fear.

When I came to Baghdad for the first time in 1975 an order had already been issued banning the performing of Ashura rituals, during which Shia went out on the streets practicing self-flagellation and shedding bitter tears for the killing of al-Husayn, in a violent spectacle in which they beat their backs with iron chains. Some of them would strike their own heads with long sharp knives that looked like machetes and that they called qamas. And despite the police's strict enforcement of the ban in Kazim and even in Najaf and Karbala, the Shi'i strongholds, Shi'i resentment was strongly simmering. I bought some cassette tapes recording recitations of the bloody epic of al-Husayn's killing. I wept as I listened to the folk epic verses retelling the battle of al-Taff and realized that the sadness around me had deep roots that could not be ignored, even among the educated, who realized that self-flagellation would never bring back what was gone and would not acquit them of killing al-Husayn or of not defending him.

"Please, Ma'am."

"Nora! What's wrong? The man is talking to you. Do you want some tea?"

"Yes, please."

The officer was saying, "Our land. We want nothing but our land. But Iran doesn't want peace."

I went back in my mind's eye to the garden in our house in Dora.

Assembled with us were Adel, Nahid, Titi, and Mahmoud. Hatim gestured to their children, who were playing nearby, to be quiet, as Radio Monte Carlo was broadcasting important news.

Nahid said, "What's with Monte Carlo all the time? Get us another station."

"Ten-thirty in Monte Carlo. A sudden storm disabled the American helicopters that had come at a late hour today to Tehran to rescue the hostages."

We all shouted, "Hooray, praise God. The planes fell down! The planes fell down!"

Nahid asked, "What are you cheering about? What planes?"

Hatim said, "Wait. I'll look for another station."

We spent two hours arguing and shouting, then we retired to get ready for the following day. Early the following morning I was getting ready to go to Habbaniya Lake with Hilmi Amin and Anhar and the Egyptian screenplay writer Hafez Abd al-Rahman, who was visiting Baghdad and who wanted to meet the director Samir Abu Tayf, who was shooting the movie *al-Qadisiyun* around the lake.

I went into the office still filled with last night's joyous news. I rushed to congratulate Hilmi Amin, and asked him about Anhar. He said, "Let's go wait for her outside the building. The car from the Ministry of Information will bring Hafez. We should get there early."

She arrived. I said, "What a great occasion! A trip to the desert."

Laughing she said, "Rather a trip to Susan Hilmi, Omar Awni, and Samir Abu Tayf."

The car arrived. The escort got out and said, "We are too many for this car. We have to get another one."

Hilmi Amin said, "It's big enough. You sit in front and the back seat will be enough for us."

The escort waited until we sat in the back. He didn't seem convinced of the arrangement. Baghdad sun was shining and everything looked promising for a pleasant trip. Hafez asked how far it was to Habbaniya. The driver said, "About a hundred and twenty kilometers."

Hafez said, "Congratulations on the fallen American planes!"

I said, "They are cowboys. What were they thinking? Did they think there are no laws? They want to do whatever they want to do and they don't like it when people defend themselves?"

Anhar said, "They must understand that this time it is serious: The Iran of the shah is different from Khomeini's Iran."

Hafez said, "America has lost its mind. They have now lost Iran, from which they used to spy on the Soviet Union."

I said, "God will punish the extravagant oppressors!"

Hilmi Amin laughed loudly and said, "Women will be women!"

The atmosphere in the car grew warmer. Hafez was an old friend of Hilmi Amin's. We exchanged the news that each of us got from different broadcasts. We spoke quite freely. We noticed that our public relations escort and the driver, as usual, never took part in the conversation except with a polite word here and there or to answer very direct questions. But we didn't care. We were full of the spirit of adventure and felt patriotic pride that the USA was a loser against one of our countries.

Hilmi said, "The Iranians will teach them a lesson they won't forget!"

The car stopped suddenly, causing us to hit the front seat. We looked at the driver, before whom the road was clear, and there was no traffic in the middle of the desert. We didn't understand what happened. The escort said, "We took a wrong turn. We'll back up."

For the first time we noticed that the driver had indeed turned on a small side road in the midst of the sand. We wondered why he had done that but we didn't say anything. The main road was quite straight and clear and there was no sign indicating any right or left turn or pointing to any other direction to Habbaniya. He returned to the main wide road.

My eyes met the driver's eyes. He fixed me with a steady, hostile glance in which I read defiance and arrogance that I was at a loss to understand. I didn't like the glances of drivers of official Iraqi cars, especially the younger ones. They conveyed some sort of accusatorial attitude that I got right away. Maybe they were just suspicions that had accumulated over the long time that I had spent as an Arab correspondent in Baghdad. But that was the first time that I saw an Iraqi government driver who couldn't control his angry feelings, even though he did not speak a word.

The main road took us toward a sign that said, "Habbaniya: 80 kilometers." We started talking about the movie and the Egyptian artists and the huge sums allocated by the Iraqi Cinema and Theater Organization for the production of the movie. We also talked about Susan Hilmi's recent cinematic activities. Baghdad at the time was a haven for Arab intellectuals and artists. Some settled there as professors at the universities and the arts academy. Some formed theatrical troupes or worked as experts for Iraqi troupes. Baghdad was rising like a great, beautiful, albeit arrogant, giant.

We spent the whole day with the movie crew, who warmly welcomed us. I discovered that some other Arab artists had roles in the movie, as did many younger Iraqi artists whom I had seen on the stage performing in wonderful plays. They took us to Saha where they were shooting the war scenes. We were introduced to the Italian expert who was brought over to oversee the production at the highest technical level. We sat to watch the tumult of war as if we were in the midst of real battles that had just come out of history books with shouts and cries and the clanging of swords. The scenes were shot several times, tiring the extras to exhaustion. I saw Hilmi Amin taking out a white handkerchief and giving it to Anhar to dry her sweat instead of using a facial tissue. His face was filled with indescribable kindness and affection. Anhar took the handkerchief gratefully and thanked him with a long loving glance. The scene needed to end with a long kiss in which these two lovers would forget that we were there with them. But they returned to a more formal mode.

We went back to Baghdad at night after the movie crew promised to visit us in the *al-Zahra* magazine office. In the morning I learned from Hilmi Amin that the driver's behavior the day before was not random or a coincidence.

He said, "The driver wanted to send us a message. He didn't like what we said about Iran."

I said in disbelief, "What did we say that he took such offense at, that he acted so threateningly?"

"We said what we actually felt. They live in a world different from ours. They are not used to our kind of freedom," he said.

I said, "I noticed that Anhar did not talk much in the car. She knows her people better."

Hesitantly he said, "To some extent. Sometimes I fear for her because of our outspokenness."

I said, "But it is not an Iraqi concern."

He laughed for a long time, then said, "Who said that? It is at the heart of Iraqi concerns."

I broke out of my reverie as the Iraqi officer, using a pointing stick to draw a large circle, was saying, "This is the Arabian Gulf, not the Persian Gulf. Thank you."

The Iraqi Women's Union cars took us to a desert road that had no greenery. Then there appeared green shrubs that had thorns, and tumbleweeds were blowing in the wind, flying here and there in front of us. I noticed that there were tents opened on all sides as if they were desert hats for playful women. Under the tents were long, thin tables at which sat many soldiers and Bedouins eating together. There were huge pots of food cooking on basic woodstoves and dozens of bread rolls heaped on the tables. There were long lines of these tents along the road. I asked Layla about them, and she said they were open around the clock to feed the soldiers and offered free meals to any Bedouins or travelers who happened to pass by.

We stopped at one of the tents. They prepared for us dishes of tharid, which is bread sopped in broth topped with rice, and young lamb meat on very large trays, and hot bread. In front of us were pitchers of yogurt drink and teapots that they passed around. Zulaykha, the Russian woman, said to me, "I can't believe I ate all this food!"

Anisa, the Pakistani woman, said, "I am so stuffed, I'll die."

Jon said, "You're a glutton!"

I said, "It's the desert climate and the company. Both quite appetizing!"

Layla said, "Enjoy it in good health!"

Tea glasses and Arab coffee pots made the rounds. Bedouin men danced a beautiful dabka to salute the president commander. Some foreign women journalists got up and danced with them, mimicking their shouts and patriotic songs in shrill voices that made us laugh.

I went into the hotel, eager for a hot bath. My breasts were almost jumping in pain in front of me, even though I had gone to the bathroom twice on the road to empty them, but I did not have enough time to finish the job. I didn't think of Haytham all day long. Oh, my God. What was happening to me?

Yasir's face came to me as he did from time to time, with his calm eyes that radiated serenity and confidence. I think he got that from Hatim, either through genes or mimicking. I began to prepare a real bath that might be the only one possible before tomorrow night at the earliest. I turned the television on and watched the president commander meeting workers at a factory. Then there were many shots of him taking a car ride through the streets in Baghdad with people cheering. Then there were some meetings with cabinet ministers and Ba'th Party meetings, all interspersed with patriotic songs by various choirs. I kept looking for a channel that might have songs or dabka dances, but the best I could do was an Egyptian movie starring Farid Shawqi and Mahmoud al-Meligi. I remembered my Iraqi women neighbors asking me innocently if I knew Farid Shawqi or whether Naglaa Fathi lived in our neighborhood. I also remembered how Iraqis were fond of hearing the Egyptian dialect. I changed channels and came across one that featured classical Arabic music. I gave in to the water and held my nipples and massaged them with cream as milk flowed from them, little by little. My muscles began to relax and I calmed down, almost dozing off, still half awake. I suddenly noticed the steam permeating the whole room. I wrapped bath towels securely around my body and succumbed to deep sleep. I came to as the alarm clock rang and the president commander peered from the screen, wearing his military uniform, tall and extremely self-confident, with all that old charisma that made the masses fall so madly in love with him. But this time there was something different about him, something that I couldn't quite figure out, perhaps because, for the first time, I was hearing him talk about his desire for peace, without the old rhetoric of power. I wasn't quite sure. Then I found myself wondering: was he really a lady-killer as rumors would have us believe? Or was it the old habit of turning leaders into legends, even when it came to sex? There came to my mind many stories about his love affairs. I laughed. They were all crazy.

I was quite surprised by how energetic the various delegation members were: younger and older women chatting merrily or poring over papers or books, reading or looking up things. Some were also looking at items that they had purchased: woolen kilims and popular costumes. They showed no trace of fatigue after the long trip. I told Sajida, "Go visit your mother. You don't have to attend the panel discussions today. I'll do the work on your behalf."

She laughed and said, "Thanks, sweetie. My younger brother will come to the train station and tell me how mom is doing. I'll be coming back next week, God willing."

"Why? It doesn't make sense!"

"Well, please. Work is work."

We gathered at the door of the hotel holding our small bags, like fragile beings afraid of getting our clothes wet in Basra's torrential rains. We ran to the buses that took us to the theater to meet leaders of the Women's Union and some local leaders. During the panel we found out that families were afraid to let their children go to school because of Iranian artillery shelling, and that the city had severe shortages of foodstuffs.

The Basra musical ensemble appeared on stage and I gave myself over to the Iraqi maqam, to take me into its heart and bring me closer to the Iraqi people whom I had come to know over a long time, and who had not revealed themselves to me right away but began to open up to me very cautiously, like a flower shying away from the dew, opening its petals only in the full light of day. Knowing Iraqis fully still seemed to me to be somewhat fantastical. The distance between us and them was still great and barriers all too real. Many of the ideas formed by a twenty-year-old woman still fell short of true understanding, no matter how much of a cultured woman she imagined herself to be and no matter how much history and politics she tried to immerse herself in every day. Such a person would still fall short of grasping the keys to the Iraqi character. Now, seven years later, I still felt at the threshold, still not understanding that character despite my many sincere attempts. All I knew and all I cared about really was that I loved the Iraqi people. All these musings came to my mind accompanied by fragments of popular Iraqi music and songs.

It was now midnight when we sneaked on to the train in a manner and mood quite different from yesterday morning. Was it only yesterday that we took the train from Baghdad to Basra? We settled in our seats to a long interrupted sleep. I felt thirsty and saw Layla's hand extended to me with water, as if she was attached to me by an umbilical cord. I was awakened several times by the discomfort of the wooden seat and the monotonous clanking sound of the train's wheels as they hit the ties on the railroad tracks. Before me, on an imaginary screen, I saw a picture of women, some wide awake and some fast asleep, different in age, nationality, and garb, all gathered under one roof and unified by one feeling: an ability to love life. Trips like this one have taught me that we, cultured, intellectual women (and men, for that matter), represented one class throughout the whole world, regardless of nationality, environment, or even political identity, preoccupied with the whole of humanity, constantly seeking human freedom and social justice. The fellow women travelers on this train and other trains and planes that I took to any part of the world have always been ready to catch the spark of friendship. As soon as we caught glimpses of each other we knew that we shared a common history, one that we did not put into words but carried on our shoulders even if we did not speak about it. We could broach any subject, at any point, and come to know it and each other intimately.

I fell asleep and woke up at nine o'clock in the morning to Naglaa's broad smile as she handed me my box breakfast. I stretched or at least tried to, and in so doing I leaned my whole body on Layla, who cried out, laughing. We all got up, made cheerful by the new day. I saw some of the women standing up in the aisles and soon songs began to ring out. And even though I knew we still had nine hours to go before we arrived in Baghdad, our general feeling that we had covered half the distance added to our overall cheer. Our day was filled with chitchat and side stories, and friends vented their pent-up feelings and shared some sad stories. It was my first time to be with them behind the scenes and not right on the stage, as if the two years I had been away gave me the right to enter their private world as the doors to their hearts lay wide open to me.

We arrived in Baghdad in the late afternoon, and even though heavy rain was falling, we were happy to get off the train and into the white marble halls of al-Rashid Hotel with our very dirty shoes. They told us that the evening was free, so, if we liked, we could hit the markets. I thought of going to the office today instead of tomorrow as I had planned.

I apologized to my colleagues for not accompanying them to the market, and we all dispersed like a flock of sheep whose shepherd had left us. I went up to my room and turned off the telephone until I finished my bath and slept for two whole hours. I noticed that the rain had stopped and Baghdad appeared at its best, as it usually did on a clear winter day. I went down to the lobby of the hotel and heard a rhythmic beating of drums. I smiled. An Iraqi bride would have her honeymoon in this hotel. The Iraqis usually had their bridal processions in the late afternoon and not at night as we did in Egypt. I found that the procession was ending and the families were taking pictures with the couple. I cried out, "Naglaa? I don't believe it!"

Naglaa rushed toward me. She had just come back with me on the train from Basra.

I said, "What a surprise? Congratulations, my darling! Congratulations, bridegroom!"

She embraced me, laughing demurely, "God bless you!"

"I can't believe that you had to go to all this trouble on your wedding day. Why didn't you tell us? At least we would have spared you our silly requests and many demands on your time."

"We were busy at the Union and thank God it all ended well. Tomorrow we go north and after a week we'll come back to our house and have a celebration. I wish you'd stay in Baghdad."

I said, "We begin by celebrating the wedding whereas you keep the celebration till later. What matters is that we rejoice for you."

The bridegroom said, "You know the circumstances in Baghdad." Then, looking at his bride, Naglaa, he said, "Come on, darling."

She extended her hand to him and shrill ululations of joy rang out all around. I tried to mimic their ululations but my attempt sounded thin and funny. I stayed there, watching the couple as they disappeared and the drums with their beaters withdrew. I left the hotel and walked on the just-washed asphalt of the road. I finally got a taxi just as silent clouds were gathering, hiding the wan lights of the small, scattered stars that attempted to come out. The almost empty streets were quiet and the corners were dark.

On top of the Ministry of Planning building I read: "One Arab nation with an eternal message." The taxi turned on Abu Nuwas Street. I didn't find the yellow, red, and blue lights that used to shimmer on the fronts of the bars, taverns, and restaurants that were named after their colors. Then I could make out the Farabi Bar, the White Rose Restaurant, Bahmadun Bar, Harir Drinks. Wasn't that the Cellar Bar? The Gondola Restaurant? That one, as I remembered, was an Indian restaurant. That one was al-Sadir Café where chess players gathered. There was a faint light coming from one of the establishments. I could read the sign: Umm al-Jarra Restaurant. I asked the driver to stop there.

I could see the embers glowing through the holes in the grate as the attendant was busy fanning the air right and left. I remembered that Hatim and I had seen Anhar at that very restaurant with a young man whom I had never met or seen afterward. I sat down, trying to wipe away from my memory a green moss and red rust that had grown in the dark recesses of my soul. My days appeared clearly to me like a clear blue sky in which there lived an all-powerful siren tempting me to keep traveling, to keep following her, and to get lost in an endless, eternal labyrinth. I remembered Ragya, the doctor who disappeared suddenly from the office and from Baghdad and from the center of our attention when she left for Beirut to work there after causing a lot of anxiety for the Iraqi security services by her free and wide-ranging movements. I met her only once after that.

I had been invited to a movie shown at the Cinema Club in downtown Cairo. At the exit I saw her carrying a very beautiful baby girl that she introduced to me, saying, "My daughter, Merit. This is my husband, Hisham."

Ragya looked full of life with her captivating Egyptian beauty: light brown complexion, red cheeks, big black eyes, and long eyelashes, which we could finally see as she did not have those strange dark sunglasses on. She was moving naturally and spontaneously among a group of friends. I was about to ask her about her lawsuit and how it was resolved or not and what she had done, but I didn't. When I told Tante Fayza afterward about meeting her, she was surprised and said, "You met her here in Cairo, Nora?"

"Yes. And who knows? She might have solved her problem with Iraqi security."

"That's very strange!"

*

Ragya came back to my memory together with her friend Dahlia.

I remembered that she had come to visit us two days after that famous evening when the police interrogated her about a vice complaint. She had not, as usual, bothered to inform us she was coming beforehand. We were writing the Baghdad letter to Cairo, working on important news that we had only gotten with the morning bulletin from the Iraqi News Agency. We welcomed her to the living room and not the office, and Tante Fayza came to keep her company, since Mervat had gone out with Rasha to do some last-minute shopping before returning to Egypt. We finished what we were doing and I got up to ask her to join us. Then I heard someone knocking merrily on the apartment door. When I opened I saw Maha and Fathallah. They had just come from Mosul and they looked very happy. Fathallah said, "Maha's application to the college of engineering has been accepted."

Mervat and Rasha, who had just come back, and I kissed Maha and sang a line from a famous song by Abd al-Halim Hafez. We all went into the office and I brought out a bottle of black grape juice in place of the usual Egyptian red sharbat served on such happy occasions. We started chatting about pleasant subjects. Then we were surprised when Dahlia got up suddenly and said in an angry tone, "I am leaving!"

We turned our attention to her. She stood there with tears in her eyes, even though she was not crying, not yet anyway. She headed quickly for the door and didn't give any of us a chance to talk her into staying. She ran down the stairs. I said to myself: "Wow! The mountain has finally moved and the snow has melted! Dahlia's feelings have come to the surface." The rest of us began to talk about Dahlia.

Maha, with that calm demeanor of hers that we all loved, said, "She actually does finish work at three o'clock in the morning and that was ascertained and included in the police report, and that was a point in her favor. One of the Egyptian men who worked with her used to give her a ride home. The car he drove had a 'Kuwait Export'

361

license plate because it had not cleared customs yet. This is what made the landlord somewhat suspicious, despite her innocence. But the real problem was: she partied until the morning."

Then she added, "I'd like to tell you all that I am very surprised that a young woman should behave this way. I don't mean the morality aspect, for she was indeed proved innocent of those charges, but I mean her irresponsible behavior!"

I looked at Maha, so young and yet so clear and decisive in her judgment. Then I heard Tante Fayza asking, "Is she in an organization?"

Maha said, "Yes, she belonged to an organization that is now defunct. Dahlia was with Sawsan in the detention camp and she and her group caused many problems. Sawsan has declared that she wanted to have nothing to do with Dahlia because of their history together."

Hilmi Amin said, "Actually it was her sister who belonged to that organization."

I said, "How is that, Ustaz Hilmi? I know she was in Ragya's organization, 'the rockets,'" and laughed.

Fathallah nodded, smiling. "Yes, even though Ragya left the organization, with her husband, even before coming to Baghdad."

I said in alarm, "But Ragya . . ."

Fathallah reluctantly said, "She collected some contributions for the party before her departure, then she took the money and left the country. It was a strange organization that caused us many problems. It had uncalled-for clashes with the prison authorities and when we sided with its members against the prison administration, they withdrew to their wards, leaving us to face the wrath of the jailors. As a result of their behavior I was wounded and had seven stitches in my head."

He then bowed his head for us to see the deep scars on a spot on his head that had no hair.

Sometime later Hilmi Amin noticed that I was writing about Dahlia in my new novel. He asked me why I was doing that.

I told him that she was a unique dramatic character.

He said, "Nora, I don't like what you're writing in the novel. You will indict a whole movement involved in the struggle for the sake of the homeland because of the irresponsible behavior of some members or their petty acts!"

I said, "But the greatest revolutionaries are ultimately human beings."

He said, "Yes. But set that aside until you've understood life and the human psyche at a higher level. Postpone the novel. Maybe you'll come to see in these characters aspects that you don't see now. Write about any other subject."

I began reading about Egyptian expatriates and understood what Hilmi Amin was after. I liked his calm demeanor and his ability to convince me. I knew he was very interested in my writings. I stopped writing what I had started and picked up a new blank page and a pen and started writing every day tirelessly. One morning I surprised him, saying, "Here's my first novel!"

After all these years, has my attitude toward those characters changed? Yes. It changed a lot. Now I have greater appreciation of them. I've grown more tolerant and more understanding of the price they had paid. I came to from my reverie, confused, regretting the fact that I had not kept writing and recording the raw emotions of those days regardless of whether I published what I wrote or not. Memory is traitorous. It burns down certain parts and leaves behind certain other parts as ashes mixed with grief.

I became aware of the waiter standing in front of me, asking whether I wanted something to drink before dinner. I said, "Tea, please."

I followed him with my eyes as he walked away lightly. I saw in the corner behind a latticework partition dozens of beer bottles arrayed on young people's tables. I remembered the old routine: each patron naming the number of beer bottles that they wanted to consume which would then be placed in front of them on the table. In that river of memories a fish came to the surface. I tried to catch it, but it turned and looked at me, blankly but deeply. My whole body shook when I saw that it was a blind fish.

Hilmi Amin said, "Salah Abd al-Subur is in town and he is waiting for us at Hotel Baghdad."

We accompanied him to al-Kazim Mosque. We spent an enjoyable day with him. He was a beautiful, polite man. I adored his poetry. I told him that as soon as I met him, as I gave him my book on al-Khalsa village. Then I asked him, for an interview. He told me his schedule was very tight but that if I were to write my questions, he would answer them at night. I tried to dissuade him, since questions and answers bred other questions. He said, "I am sorry. I can't." Hilmi Amin intervened, saying, "You can fill the gaps with a short interview the following morning." I had no choice, so I agreed. Then I dropped in on him at the hotel to pick up the answers and took them to the office to read them.

Hilmi Amin said, "They don't give him an appropriate welcome here. They don't like his politics and they prefer to have dealings with Ahmad Abd al-Mu'ti Higazi."

I said, "Higazi wrote for Iraqi newspapers before going to Paris, and he is still writing for them from exile. Is it necessary for each intellectual to engage in a battle with authority?"

"No. But in the end, it boils down to attitudes and positions. Salah is a conventional Egyptian bureaucrat."

I said, "Salah Abd al-Subur is not Yusuf al-Siba'i, nor is he Tharwat Abaza. He is the greatest living poet. Is that not enough?"

"A poet is a stand, Nora. No one can cast doubts on how patriotic Salah is, but Arab authorities use intellectuals for their own ends and whims."

"I am going to go look for al-Hallaj's tomb and write about Salah Abd al-Subur and his poetic verse drama that will live on in people's hearts forever."

I had learned from my earlier visit to the tomb of Zumurrud Khatun where to get information that I needed to get to Iraqi monuments and shrines. But there was no trace of al-Hallaj's tomb in any Iraqi publications. Some fellow journalists told me that I had to search among the traditional tombs in al-Karkh. Hilmi Amin decided not to let me go by myself to the cemeteries this time also. We made an arrangement with a cab driver to come and pick us up at six in the morning before Baghdad's August temperature reached its highest degree. That temperature, usually not spelled out in forecasts or announced, was usually above fifty degrees Celsius. I was fasting. We met some visitors at the tombs and each gave us different directions. The taxi kept going around in various directions for four hours. The driver would let us off at one of the side streets, then we would go on foot, then go back without finding anything. A man working in the vicinity met us by chance and we asked him for directions after we had given up and decided to go back. The man pointed forward and gave us the name of a street. He said to keep walking until we found a sign with his name on it. I stood looking at the scene in front of me. Graves extended to no end as the horizon lay open before us. I couldn't believe what I was seeing. The heat must have created a mirage of stones rising and moving in their color of dust under the burning sun. We kept walking until we were swallowed up by the dust and the graves, and no one could tell us from the endless expanse of holes in the ground. It was only a minor difference in time that let us walk steadily above ground rather than beneath it. Finally we found the sign with al-Hallaj's name on it. We followed the arrow until we stopped and stood before a short, one-room building on one of whose walls was written, "The Tomb of al-Hallaj."

I stood before a grave marker covered in green cloth of very dirty, frayed satin and I cried. Hilmi Amin asked, "What's the crying for?"

"Poor in his life. Poor now and forever poor."

"He was an ascetic."

"He was a revolutionary philosopher. This is the aspect we love in him and this is what Salah Abd al-Subur looked for."

We made our way back to the office. I was resisting fainting from the heat of the sun in the gray, desolate desert, without a single tree or a flower. Oh God! My tongue was more silent than a tombstone! I could still smell the dust and the ancient history. I smelled death and oppression and the scent of my sadness burning with the fires of impotent anger. I wanted to tell Mansur al-Hallaj how much I loved him; I wanted to hug him, just hug him. I withdrew inside myself, hiding my dejection lest it escape and drown the whole world. We arrived at the office, my lips encased in solid black layers of dust and sweat. Hilmi Amin tried to dissuade me from going home but I left and braved August's heat again.

Under the shower I shook off my body the red layers of vexation mixed with the black poison of oppression and the blue bitterness of impotence. I kept looking at the different colors, intermingling in circles and uniting in one ugly gray color that the walls of the shower stall absorbed gradually until it totally disappeared, leaving behind in my heart a profound feeling of loss, as if al-Hallaj had just died. I started crying in silence until Salah Abd al-Subur's big, clear eyes paid me a visit. I said to myself that the intellectual's battle with the authorities would go on forever. And I began to wonder about Iraq's turbulent history and why I was there. Was it my good luck or bad luck? I thought how impossible it would be for any Arab journalist to really know his or her own country without studying Iraq. Was it a matter of journalism then? No, no! Absolutely not. In the evening Hatim came over to where I was sitting, holding Salah Abd al-Subur's play, and started reading with me the following part of the dialogue:

He says it is love: the key to redemption. Love and you shall prevail,
Perishing into your beloved, becoming one with the worshiper, the prayer,
The faith, the Lord, and the mosque.
I gave myself over to love so completely there was room for nothing else.
I kept imagining until I saw
I saw my Love and He granted me perfect beauty
And I granted Him perfect love

Hiding myself into Him!
Abu Omar: Hush! This is total abrogation of faith!
Ibn Surayj: No, this is just one of the states in Sufi practice!

Hatim walked me to bed, pointing to my head and saying, "What should I do with this mind of yours? The whole world is in there. Don't you get tired of all the crowding? You need a traffic cop! Have mercy on yourself."

"Hold me."

"Why all these tears? He died a million years ago."

"He hasn't died. Read the rest of the scene."

Ibn Surayj: Did you corrupt the populace, Hallaj?
Hallaj: No one corrupts the populace but a corrupt ruler who enslaves and starves them."

Hatim held me by the waist and said, "I want this and this. Hallaj has lived his life and now it is our turn to live ours."

A wind escaping from the dark road into Umm al-Jarra restaurant on Abu Nuwas Street blew and I heard the door close as someone came in. I remembered how cold it was outside and dark days from the past kept coming back.

The glow of the first few years of life in Baghdad began to fade despite Hatim's successful career in the factory and my venturing into new areas in my writing and getting Yasir back to live with us. With the passing days I acquired new traits, which I learned from the silence imposed on me. I learned contemplation, digging deep inside myself and building forts and castles to protect me from the vicissitudes of time. I got deep inside myself for the first time and tried to explore it, and in the process I inflicted on it dark stains that required running rivers of joy to wash them away. Hatim tried to pull me to safety from drowning inside myself with his simple lifesavers but his placid soul couldn't give me security. The storms had started to blow and sweep away everything that had not struck deep roots within the good earth. Oh my God! I feel so lonely. I took up knitting and began to make a jacket for Yasir, then for Hatim, then for myself. I chose other colors and started all over again, filling the armoire, but I could not stop the howling of the emptiness inside the darkness of my soul. I looked around and saw Hatim outside my well-fortified castle, playing all the required roles and living in peace, having set his goals without getting involved in what I got myself into. He understood me without lifting a hand to change me, as if I were moving behind an invisible glass wall. He saw me but he also didn't see me. He spoke with me but did not light a fire in my bones, nor did he put out the fire of joy that sometimes ignited within me. He was just there. I shouted at the long line of ants that had taken up residence inside my throat and started creeping deeper into me: "What more do you want, Nora?"

I got no answer. I couldn't ask my women friends who were busy with their own lives. I couldn't ask my friend Hilmi Amin about what I was going through for I could see that he was like a lion held captive in a small cage, going around in circles looking toward the far horizon, seeing nobody, then circling some more, tirelessly testing every inch of the cage walls and realizing that there was no way out. I felt the whole time that he was suffocated and I wished Anhar Khayun would come back to him, for she had given him a life that was full, even if with pain. Tante Fayza and the girls' visits sometimes helped him but he became even more miserable again when they left. He had changed considerably from what he was like when I first met him. He used to be quite optimistic even when things got really bad. He knew what he wanted without fearing consequences. The years of exile had cast a veil of gloom over him that kept him company until he couldn't take it any more. One day he said to me, "I want to go to Beirut, meet my friends, and breathe the air of the Mediterranean."

One week later I was climbing the stairs of the Sheikhaly Building, not knowing whether he had come back or not. For, even though Beirut was such a short distance from Baghdad, he hadn't called me as he usually did when he traveled. I didn't know when he was coming back. I saw a light under the door and rang the bell. I heard him clearing his throat.

"Hello, Nora."

"Thank God for your safe return. Any news from Beirut?"

"There were many surprises. Do you remember Sulafa, the beautiful Kurdish woman, Jamal Abu Sargon's colleague who came to visit us a few times?"

"Yes. What about her?"

"She is a fugitive in Beirut. She had been arrested and detained for a few days, then was released, and ran away with her fiancé."

"I can't believe it! What a strange turn of events! Who would believe that this sweet, lovely girl is living in exile? And in Beirut, in the midst of all this tension?"

"She invited me to her house and cooked a kibbeh dish for me and told me the story. It's so sad! I also met Hadya Haydar, remember her?"

"Yes. She's the Lebanese journalist, wife of Jalil Haydar. She has a lovely face."

"They're both in Beirut now."

"Did you see Ragya?"

"Yes. She is working there and has been trying to go to South Yemen, but the South Yemenis insisted on her getting an approval from the Egyptian Communist Party. And since she belongs to a different party, the comrades are still reluctant to give their approval. Before leaving Baghdad, Ragya had contacted the Yemeni consulate, which gave her an appointment. While waiting for the appointment, the Yemeni chargé d'affaires was arrested and relations between Southern Yemen and Iraq got very tense."

I laughed and said, "And that was the end of the Ragya story?"

He shook his head, "Not quite."

I said, "Please tell me what else happened."

369

The waiter brought a pitcher of salted yogurt drink and a pitcher of water and poured a glass from each. I picked up the milk glass, unable to keep away the memory of the days that were assailing me and completely taking over my mind. I remembered a period of time when the numbers of Egyptian intellectuals in Baghdad, especially the stars, had dwindled as they departed to other countries.

Ahmad Abd al-Mu'ti Higazi left for Paris and shortly after that Mahmoud al-Saadani joined him there and started publishing a magazine that he named after the July 23 Revolution. Amin Ezzeddin left for London, where he established a center for Arab studies. Ahmad Abbas Salih traveled frequently to London as a prelude to settling there. Abd al-Ghani Abu al-Aynayn left Baghdad for some other place.

When things changed in Baghdad, when the Front collapsed, Tante Fayza suggested to Hilmi Amin to leave for Paris or London. Then she began to pressure him to leave. I felt that I, somehow, was responsible for her apprehension, but I had no way to assuage her fear except to stay close to her and reassure her through the example of my little family that it was safe in Baghdad, that she had nothing to fear. I couldn't tell her that the threat to her had been removed when Anhar Khayun disappeared, God only knew where. Some friends said they had met her in Hungary. Others said they had heard that she was in California. Nothing definitive. I could feel Hilmi Amin's pain and his bitterness and fear for her. Sometimes he would say a few words about her, then fall silent and say, "Who knows?"

I would try to change his mood by making references to lines from characters in comic programs and he would laugh but fall silent again. We didn't know whether she had actually left Iraq or whether she was in jail. We did not get any news that she had been arrested and that in itself was somewhat reassuring. But questions remained.

We got a hand-delivered letter that Abu Ghayib gave to me. Hilmi Amin read it, then he handed it to me.

Dear Hilmi,

I had to leave. I am in a safe place. When I settle down I'll let you know. Don't ask about me and don't worry. I left this letter for you to reassure you.

Anhar Khayun

I said, "This is her handwriting indeed."

He said, "Before her departure. Is there one guarantee that she actually left safely?"

I said, "No. But we should assume the best."

I couldn't tell that to Tante Fayza, of course, even though she had learned of Anhar's disappearance. I found out from Mervat that her mother was often suspicious of her father and that Tante Fayza intervened between the two of them in spats concerning young journalist interns that he was training. I told Mervat, laughing, "My mother has suspicions about my father even though he is the last person you'd call a womanizer. It seems that mothers are always afraid of young girls for no reason at all."

Mervat looked at me, laughing and squinting. She knew that I was in on all her father's secrets and that I wouldn't say a word. We both laughed. We were true friends.

That day there was a big flare-up between Hilmi Amin and Tante Fayza. We had organized a picnic for Zora Park. My son Yasir enjoyed the company of Hilmi Amin's daughters and Hilmi Amin loved running after his daughter Rana on the green grass. We took a toy pigeon that had a spring that enabled it to fly. We noticed that the turns and durations it took hovering depended on the number of turns we applied to the spring. We began to turn it more and raced to reach it before it fell to the ground, and we kept a score of who got to it first. Then we got tired and returned to the table where the adults were sitting, while still laughing. We could hear them arguing from a distance and we could sense the tension, but there was nothing we could do to stop it. Hilmi Amin and Tante Fayza paid no attention to us, even when we tried in vain to get them to change the subject.

He was saying, "I won't go to Paris. The writer Medhat Kamal is playing the violin on the streets. Do you know how much it costs to live in Paris? Just getting an apartment? Ahmad Abd al-Mu'ti Higazi is teaching Arabic at the university because he is a well-known, major poet, and he left Baghdad early. *July 23* magazine cannot afford my salary because its budget is based on funding donations rather than distribution. Its advertisements still do not cover the cost of publication. The maximum they can give me is the price of one article, which wouldn't be enough to cover one week's expenses in Paris. Here I get a modest salary from *al-Jumhuriya* newspaper. True, it is not much, but it pays for the rent and for your expenses in Cairo. Whatever is left over from my freelance work you can save for the girls and their marriages."

Tante Fayza said, "We have enough money for you to live in Paris for a few months without work until you find a job in an Arab newspaper. I don't like London, but Ahmad Abbas Salih told me about the possibility of your working at the center opened by Amin Ezzedin with a good group there. Mahmoud Amin al-Alim is in Paris: there you can continue to write for *al-Jumhuriya* newspaper and so you can continue to get the same salary. The only difference would be the rent of an apartment in Paris and that you can get from the articles you write for *July 23*."

Hilmi Amin replied, "They won't cut off my salary so long as I am here in Baghdad since they consider it exile pay, even if I did not commit to writing my weekly article. But if I move out of here they would cut off my salary right away. They'd pounce on the opportunity. I am an Egyptian communist. Don't you understand? Things have changed. If things here didn't work out, you'd all starve to death."

She said, "Baghdad will always be unsafe. And I'll be afraid you'd be arrested for any reason or that Sadat would get you one way or another. In Paris, it is different. There you'd enjoy quasi-international protection. If you don't like living in Paris, go to the Soviet Union or to any socialist country."

He raised his voice, saying, "Iraqi communists have taken up all available places in all communist countries. They have descended upon Europe in huge numbers, making it almost impossible to accommodate even a single additional Arab intellectual. And the Iraqi communists open their homes to fellow Iraqis and take them under their wings until they find work. Where would I go?"

She said in anger, "Aren't they your friends?"

In a tone of resignation he said, "Yes. But they hardly have enough to eat themselves."

She said, "I am not convinced. Why do you insist on staying here? This is not our country. And it is not safe."

Then she started sobbing. The girls got up and stood around her. Mervat said, "Mom, don't you get tired of this? Every day?"

Fayza said, "I won't give up on this demand until he leaves. I want him to get out of this place."

I took Yasir and Rana by the hand and asked Rasha to come with us to buy some sandwiches. As I was moving away I could hear him screaming so hysterically that people noticed and stopped to watch the two of them.

The quiet in the park amplified the sounds of the argument despite the isolation that we had assumed would insulate us from the crowds. I began to cry in silence. Yasir said, "Are you crying because Rana took the pigeon?"

I said, "No. Because we forgot to bring the ball."

Rana said, "Let's play with the pigeon, Tante."

I hugged Rasha, telling her: "Don't be afraid. Tante Fayza is afraid that your father would be arrested here. He is not engaged in any political activity that would get him arrested. The only problem he might face is that they would ask him to leave Baghdad. She has every right to be afraid and suspicious because she hears every day about the arrest of one or another of his Iraqi friends. These are regimes that should not be trusted at all."

Mervat came over and said, "She's calmed down a little."

I wondered whether Hilmi Amin was trying to secure a permanent place that Anhar could reach at any time, so that they wouldn't lose each other forever if he were to move somewhere else. But after all, he was a journalist who signed his articles, and if he moved to work for any Arabic newspaper the news would spread and Anhar would undoubtedly find him. Why was he so attached to Baghdad? Was it just financial security or was there something else that I didn't know which he had not revealed? Maybe I'd find the secret in his memoirs. Why didn't I give the memoirs more time? Why was I reading them at such a slow pace? Was I afraid? Yes. Why? I didn't know. Perhaps it was because I didn't really want to know. Perhaps because I wanted everything that happened to us to remain mythical, and that would be lost if it were revealed; it would be turned into something ordinary and everyday, even if it were the everyday of a valiant warrior.

The waiter placed before me a plate of tikka, tomatoes, grilled onions, and hot bread, and said, "Enjoy it in good health."

I thanked him and reached for the sweet onions and began chewing in silence, staring at the distance, absently following indeterminate figures standing up or sitting down and going about their business. I wished I could go back to my house in Dora and sit in the garden on the metal swing and its cushions that knew my body well, next to the charcoal grill, and hear its crackling sound, following Yasir as he ran after Hatim who held onions in his hands, shouting, "Let me put it on the fire," and Hatim answering, "The fire might burn your hand."

I could hear a voice in the distance singing. It was a recording of Nazim al-Ghazali singing about love between a Muslim man and a Christian woman. I asked the waiter to turn up the volume a little and let the song make its way to my ears as I remembered buying the same cassette for the second time.

A long time had passed since Tante Fayza and Hilmi Amin's daughters visited him. The arrival of any letter from the family gave him joy and rejuvenated him. I would know it right away when I saw him smiling in the morning instead of that frown that gave his face those deep furrows over the last few eventful months. When I arrived at the office that day he hadn't gotten ready for work yet. He hadn't shaved in days, leaving coarse white straggling hairs on his face, wearing the same pullover and shirt that he had on when I left at four in the afternoon the day before. The only difference was that he had slippers rather than shoes on. The effects of staying up late showed on his swollen eyes and his reddened nose that looked as if a professional boxer had dealt him a knockout blow. I noticed that his lips were pale. I said as the surprise tied my tongue, "Good morning."

He said, growling as he removed with his stiff hand the remnants of a cigarette, the ashes of which had fallen onto his chest: "Hello, Nora."

I went into the office and found the ashtray overflowing with cigarette butts that bespoke his wounded solitude and the bitterness of his watchful wait. I noticed a number of empty beer and vodka bottles. There was no trace of any food. On the desk there was a letter whose edges were burned and which lay opened next to an envelope. I thought to myself: Oh dear God: how did it catch on fire? From the cigarettes? Could that be?

I heard the door to the bathroom closing. I took out the article that I had started writing the day before. But I couldn't begin to work, given the mess all around me. I looked at the high waves in the painting hanging on the wall in front of me and the sailboat visible on the horizon at a distance. I got up and carried the empty bottles and threw them in the garbage can. I gathered the ashtrays and glasses on a tray and carried it to the kitchen. I cleaned the place quickly before Abu Ghayib, the office messenger, could come and see what happened the previous night. Hilmi Amin had always taken pains to keep the office separate from his living space, even after hours. I felt pity toward him. I didn't know what happened exactly nor what was in that accursed letter. Ever since he came back from Beirut his affairs had been in disorder. He had been talking about exile the whole time. I closed the letter and put it in the desk drawer and sat down to finish my article. After a short while I got up to make some tea for myself. I noticed that the window in his bedroom was open. I realized he must be lying down or asleep, as two hours had passed without my hearing any sounds at all. I prepared the papers that I would take to the Iraqi Ministry of Information. I called out his name and knocked on the door and went in. He was fully dressed in his business garb, resting on the back of the bed, with a totally burnt-out cigarette butt dangling from his mouth. The room looked like a battlefield.

"What happened?"

"Nothing."

"Please tell me. I'll make you a glass of tea or get you some milk with a piece of cake."

"Go to work."

"Please, for my sake."

"Nora! Go. Let me sleep for a little while."

"It's obvious you haven't eaten anything since yesterday. When did you last eat?"

"With you at noon."

I took him some cake and milk. He pushed the tray forcefully. The milk spilled on the bed and the glass found its way to the window pane before reaching the floor in smithereens. I was taken aback and stood there transfixed after retreating two steps.

"What happened?"

He said, with sparks flying from his eyes that by now were bloodshot, "I told you to go. Go to your work and come back quickly."

"Did you write your article for *al-Jumhuriya*?"

"Yes. Take it with you. It's in the desk drawer."

I took the papers and closed the door behind me. I thought of knocking on the door of the neighbors next door and asking Dr. Michael if he had seen him the day before. I stood hesitantly, then Tante Violette opened the door.

"Hello, hello. Where have you been? We hardly ever see you even though we're so close."

376

I said, "We've been very busy the whole time. How's Dr. Michael and Abuna Hydra?

"They are well, thank God. We don't see Ustaz Hilmi much these days. Where is he?"

I said, "He's around. I just wanted to say 'good morning.'"

"Good morning."

So, Tante Violette didn't know anything despite the strong friendship between Hilmi Amin and Dr. Michael. I didn't think Ustaz Hilmi told the doctor anything about his political circumstances. For him and his family, he was just the director of an Egyptian newspaper bureau. I thought of getting in touch with Abd al-Rahim or Atef, but I realized they would be at work by now. I thought, "Why don't I call Sawsan and arrange to meet with her under some pretext or another?" I recalled the events of the last few days. His loneliness must have gotten the better of him and increased his sense of exile, his feeling that he was on a boat waiting before his island but forbidden to enter it. He was thinking and talking about Sinuhe, the ancient Egyptian exile, all the time and writing with great pain as if he were a prisoner.

"But you are not a prisoner."

"Exile is worse than prison. I am away from my beloved."

When he came back from Beirut, his cheeks rosy, looking happy, I jested with him, "All this joy from such a short trip?

"No. It is the sea breeze and its smell that filled my chest. I sat on the beach, following the waves with my eyes, as they traveled to the coast of my town and brought me its fragrance from there. They were well-behaved, obedient waves that gave me all I've asked for."

"And I am supposed to be the poet here?"

"It's Egypt that makes poets of us all."

"Tell me the truth. I won't tell Tante Fayza about your escapades."

"It's not about young women and, as you know, if I wanted women I'd find beauty queens here."

"Daughters of Ishtar, temple priestesses! They're all around you!"

But since he returned he had been feeling sorry for himself. And even though the Iraqi Ministry of Information had appointed him at *al-Jumhuriya* newspaper with a regular salary close to his previous salary at *al-Zahra* magazine since he was an exile, and even though all he was required to do was to write a weekly article for the paper, he was thinking a lot about his freedom and his inability to write what he really wanted to and his being unable to go back to Egypt. He was thinking about Rana, who had been born unexpectedly, late in his life. I wondered what he had written in his article that day. I opened the envelope as I sat in the minibus I was riding and began to read the article. I was surprised by its title, "Sighs for Rana." The article was a piece of literature filled with bitterness and despondency, written by an Egyptian intellectual in exile, pained by his separation from his homeland and family. Tears filled my eyes as I entered the building housing *al-Jumhuriya* paper in al-Bab al-Mu'azzam. I met Muhammad al-Jaza'iri, editor in chief of the Literary Supplement. I gave him the article. He asked me, "Where is Hilmi Amin?"

I said, "He has a cold."

The editors and journalists there asked me to convey their greetings. One of them asked me, "He is your uncle, right?"

I said as I smiled, "Yes."

I ran back to Tahrir Square, then to the Ministry of Information. I delivered the papers and went to the cafeteria. I bought lunch for him and myself, praying to God that he had gone to sleep and gotten over the crisis. I had never seen him drunk before. When he sat down among people who drank, he would drink a little till he got a little high and became merry in a reserved way that was different from the way young people in my age group overdid it, not that he noticed.

I arrived at the office. It was about one o'clock in the afternoon. I rang the bell. No one answered. I opened the door with my key. I couldn't believe what I saw. The apartment was full of broken glass. The woolen kilim was piled up in a corner in the office, with the pillows scattered on the floor and the chairs overturned in the hallway. He was slumped over the desk, his tears flowing. I stood in front of him in silence. Then I took him in my bosom and wiped his tears. He gave in to a spell of crying, sobbing loudly. Then he got up suddenly and started pushing me outside, saying, "Everyone is a traitor. I don't want anyone. All are traitors!"

"What happened?"

"Go home."

"Should I call Abd al-Rahim or Atef?"

"No. Go home. I don't want you here."

"What's in the letter?"

"None of your business."

"Did anything bad, God forbid, happen to Tante or the girls?"

"It's none of your business."

"Where's the letter from?"

He started screaming again and breaking everything he got his hands on and pushing me out.

"Okay. I'll get my bag. I'll just get my bag. Whatever you say."

My tears ran down my cheeks as I tried to keep our voices from reaching the other apartments in the building to avoid a scandal. I remembered that Tante Violette was getting ready to go out when I saw her earlier. Abu Ghayib was not sitting in front of the building, and the other inhabitants were at work. I walked to Saadun Street to look for a telephone far from the office. I called Hatim at the factory and told him what was happening briefly.

He said, "If you want me to come, I won't arrive before two hours at the earliest."

I said, "No. Go home for Yasir, because I am going to be late. I'll go to Abd al-Rahim in his office which is closer, and if I don't find him, I'll go to Sawsan and stay with her until Atef comes back and then I'll return to the office with him."

"Why didn't you call Mahmoud Rashid?"

"He is his wisest friend, but I think Abd al-Rahim Mansur is his closest friend."

I asked the man at the front desk to put me through to Abd al-Rahim. A colleague of his, a woman, told me he was out of town on official business and was not expected back in the office that day.

What could I do? I started walking aimlessly in Saadun Street, with which I was quite familiar. I stopped absently in front of a bookstore. But it was not a day for books or bookstores. A store clerk smiled and came over to shake my hand. I scanned the book titles without thinking. I just wanted to kill the time until Atef came. I wanted to go back to the office to make sure that Hilmi was all right. He might not open the door for me or he might make a scene again. Was it not better to let his angry fit run its course? But perhaps he would hurt himself: he could fall, injure himself, or his heart might even stop. Dear God, what should I do? Tears ran down my face and I just let them flow. I kept walking in the general direction of Atef's house in Karrada Maryam. I got tired. I looked around for a café catering to families. I found one next to the Babel cinema. I went in and ordered tea. The waiter asked me as he placed the tea on the table, "Are you Egyptian?"

I said, "Yes."

He said, "What's the matter? Do you need money?"

I said, "No, thank you. It's just a little crisis that will pass."

He said, "We should help each other. If you have a problem, yours truly is at your service."

I said, "I heard some bad news from a friend. I just need to rest for a little while until the time of my appointment comes."

He said, "Just as you wish. I am ready to help. My name is Ahmad Abd al-Mawla. You can ask about me anytime. We are all good Egyptians ready to help at any time. Do you work?"

"I am a journalist."

"Well, in that case, we are the ones who need you. You know all the problems about money transfers and the like."

"Sure. Any time."

He let me drink the tea, then brought me another glass, saying, "This one is on me, a gift."

380

I sat for a whole hour looking at the clock and at the increasing traffic on the street, as people scurried during rush hour and engines roared. Then I noticed that the crowds were beginning to thin and the hubbub to subside. The waiter Ahmad Abd al-Mawla placed another glass of tea for me on the table. I drank the tea, then hailed a taxi and gave the driver Atef's address.

Sawsan opened the door for me. I heard loud laughter coming from inside.

"Hello, Nora. What a nice surprise! Come on in. Where are you coming from? We hardly ever see you. Whenever I ask Ustaz Hilmi, he says you rush home in the evening to Yasir. Ever since Yasir came to Baghdad, we no longer see you. Hello, my darling. I miss you very much."

She introduced me to a middle-aged Egyptian man, Hagg Abd al-Mawgud, "My cousin who came from Egypt especially to visit us. We've been trying to convince him to stay here and look for a job anywhere so we would be a big tribe here. What do you think? Can Engineer Hatim get him a job?"

I said, "We'll try. Just get him to stay here by any means."

The man welcomed me warmly. Atef came and was equally demonstrative in his welcome. I gave them a few minutes to finish the hospitality routine and then asked Atef to speak to him alone. I told him the story and that we had to go back to Hilmi. Atef explained the situation briefly to his wife and asked her permission to take me to Abd al-Rahim. Sawsan tried to come with us to make sure that Hilmi was okay, but both of us refused. When we got to Abd al-Rahim's place he was still in his work clothes. Before leaving the apartment building's main door we found Sawsan in front of us, still insisting on coming with us. I pleaded with her, "Please, he does not want anyone to see him in this condition. You know how proud he is. I only want Abd al-Rahim alone to come with me. You, Atef, and Sawsan, join us after an hour."

Sawsan gave in and said, "You go with them, Atef. She's right."

We arrived at Sheikhaly Street. When he saw me getting out of the car, Abu Ghayib said, "Abu Mervat is not in the office. I knocked on the door to give him the bread, but he didn't answer."

I said, "Maybe he was asleep. Thank you, Abu Ghayib."

I opened the door with my key. We found him sitting on the chair at the desk. All the lights in the apartment were turned off and the mess was exactly as I had left it. He welcomed us very calmly and gave me a long reproachful glance.

He said, "You inconvenienced people for no reason. Why did you do that?"

I said, "I was worried about you."

"No need to worry. It was just a passing crisis, and now it's over. What would you like to drink?"

His speech was slurred and his eyes unfocused as he tried to speak with us, then his head would fall forward. Abd al-Rahim said, "Nora, come with me."

He took me to Hilmi Amin's bedroom, opened the armoire, took out a large bath towel and clean clothes, and took them to the bathroom. He made sure the water heater was working, then we went back to the office and he said, "Please, Ustaz Hilmi. Will you come with me?"

Atef got up and he and Abd al-Rahim helped him up, as he presented a feeble attempt to resist, saying, "Where to? I am all right. Let me go."

I went to fix some food for him. I thought of calling Abu Ghayib to help tidy up the place, but I quickly changed my mind. Atef came out of the bathroom and started helping me to put the chairs in their place and pick up the broken glass. Then Abd al-Rahim came out of the bathroom with Ustaz Hilmi and took him to the bedroom and helped him to lie down on the bed. Then he began to feed him like a young child. Hilmi was responsive in a manner that I hadn't expected. Then he fell asleep. Abd al-Rahim joined us in the office, which we had tidied up. He said, "Thank God. What happened?"

I said, "I don't know anything. Obviously he has heard or received some news. Maybe a letter from his daughters aggravated his sense of exile. It must be that, because I was at the newspaper today delivering his article. I was also at the ministry and everything was normal there also. To my mind, it is something personal and the Iraqi authorities have nothing to do with it. I don't think he was facing a termination of contract or an order to leave the country or anything major."

I left to call Hatim and make sure Yasir was all right. Two hours later I left with Atef, he to go back to his guest and I to my house, and we left Abd al-Rahim to stay with him overnight. When was that? It was the day that Yehya al-Mashad was killed. I will never forget that day nor the events accompanying it and their fallout for as long as I live. The temperature in Baghdad that day, June 13, 1980, had reached its cruelest peak. The French police announced that they had found the respected Egyptian scientist Yehya al-Mashad, who was working at the time on the construction of the Iraqi nuclear reactor, murdered in his apartment in Paris where he had been spending his vacation. The newspapers claimed that the murderer was most likely a woman with whom he was spending the night, a prostitute who robbed him, then killed him. We were all incensed by the news. All indications pointed at the Israeli Mossad that could not tolerate the fact that an Egyptian nuclear scientist was using his expertise to build an Arab reactor. But the police couldn't prove anything. It was one of the strangest coincidences that he was killed in France, which had exported the nuclear reactor to Iraq; in other words, it was a French reactor employing French, Iraqi, and Egyptian experts. What a black comedy! The murder investigation, according to the police report, concluded that it was committed by a person or persons unknown. The investigation was not reopened, even though Israel bombed the Iraqi nuclear reactor the same month, one year after the murder of Yehya al-Mashad. The F-16 dropped tons of explosives on the site and returned safely to its base in Tel Aviv.

A few days later, Hilmi Amin had the breakdown. Was that the only reason? Of course not.

I gestured to the waiter to get me the check.

He said, "You haven't eaten."

I left.

At the hotel I checked for messages but there were none. I was waiting especially for a message from the man who bought the office. I decided to go to the old apartment first thing in the morning before he left, since it would be Friday. I took the room key and wondered why everything was so eerily quiet and for a moment I felt dejected, lonely, and at a loss. Then I quickly shook off the creeping depression and swept the lobby with my eyes, and I saw Layla and some of her coworkers sitting not far away. They were busy, poring over some papers. Layla saw me and beckoned. When I got to where she was, she asked me, "Where've you been? The other women wanted to say goodbye before leaving for the airport."

I said, "I thought they had some time. I thought they'd leave from the guesthouse."

"Well, no. This is wartime. But you'll all meet in Cairo," she said.

"You think it's that easy? Everyone is busy," I said.

"So, what are you going to do tomorrow?" she asked.

"Tomorrow, all of it, is for my friends, near the hotel. The day after tomorrow I'll go to al-Khalsa village," I told her.

"I'll send a car to pick you up."

"There's no need. I know the way quite well. I'll hop in a car at the Uqba ibn Nafi' Square," I said.

"No, no. First of all, you're our guest and second, I'd like to come with you because I haven't visited the village," she said.

I went up to my room, totally exhausted, but I decided to resist my fatigue. I turned on the hot water in the bathtub, then walked over to the radio and turned it on, letting the music fill the room. George Zamfir was playing one of his famous pieces. I liked the smell of my clean underwear as I followed the white bubbles when I stirred the gel with my hand. Then I slipped into the tub and let the pump do its task, emptying my breasts. I missed Hatim's fingers to recharge my love of life. I've always wondered about the magic that the hands of a man can make in the body of a woman in love. Would the result be different if the woman didn't love the man? I thought it would, despite the tyranny of the body's needs. I decided that love is the most important ingredient for lasting pleasure.

I made a mental to-do list. I still had many things I had to do even though I extended my visit by two days. I decided I had to look for Hilmi Amin's remaining articles that Tante Fayza had not collected. I needed to visit the office and the *Alif Baa* magazine office, *al-Jumhuriya* newspaper, and the village al-Khalsa, and meet some friends. How? When?

Haytham's voice woke me up at five in the morning. I turned in the bed, fighting off laziness, leaving the tingling sensation free to tickle my breasts. Then I was fully awake and alert. I jumped out of bed, drew the curtains, and turned on the radio. Dalida was singing "Helwa Ya Baladi":

Memories of all the past,
My sweet country!
My heart is full of stories,
Remember, my country?
My first love was in my country.
I can never forget it,
My country.

I finished my morning routines quickly, then I arranged my papers and notes and sat down to write my first article about the war. I finished it quickly. The fresh material I had gathered in Basra helped. I looked through Hilmi Amin's papers. One title gave me pause and I started reading.

Thresholds of Love and Jealousy
Before your overpowering beauty I feel old. I feel the unevenness of love between us. I rejoice in your beauty even as I see the envy in the eyes of friends and lifelong companions encircling me. They think you are nothing but a beautiful body that I use to awaken my old, cold body. They don't know that I am content with just an

approving smile that might light a spark of hope in my life hastening to start its final voyage.

O single spark
In the dark of a night awaiting a distant dawn.
I tirelessly try to kiss the spark,
But I never get my chance as the spark keeps flying away.
My breaths race, eager
Like a man on death row, waiting for reprieve,
One last stroke of luck before it is too late.
Hold me long and close in your embrace,
The sadness at my core can be dispelled only in your loving arms.
A mountain vast, extending from Cairo to Baghdad, lies heavy on
    my being that alone I can see while the world expects a smile
    every morning from me.
Be my smile, then.

I take delight in your youth, in the fresh vitality that your presence imparts to the place when you come into my house and throw yourself into my embrace, or when you prance before me, showing off your new haircut or a dress or a shawl or even a pair of shoes. I stand transfixed before the expressions in your eyes and the smile on your face as you talk to people in the middle of a party where I cannot get too close to you. I watch you from afar as your eyes tell me: be strong and patient. I am with you and I love you despite all the distance, the people, and the repression. We have our own heaven.

I give in, losing myself in your gaze. My old eyes relentlessly keep you in sight until I see you giving in to a friend's hand inviting you to dance, and you, smiling in joy accepting his invitation. You stand there in the midst of those young people, swaying with the music. I can read your body calling out to him, getting close then slipping away, turning with him with intimate familiarity, leaving me nothing but the echoes of brazen laughter, an invitation to intercourse that stabs my inner core, makes my gray world even darker, uncovering hidden fires. I try my utmost to put out the shooting, constant flames as your angelic looks change in front of me into the features of concubines of light that only blood will sate. Then in the midst of this dissipation you send me a glance of approval that feels like a cold drink that puts out my flames. And before I realize how heavy is the burden of being crushed under your fickleness, I see you coming, having picked up from the table of drinks a glass of whiskey which you offer me, saying, "Hello, Abu Mervat. A thousand welcomes."

I realize the enormity of the sacrifice you are making as you hold the glass. I have never seen an Iraqi woman intellectual holding a glass of liquor in a public place before. You fix me with a long stare in defiance of the world. I ask you, trying to hide my anger, "What are you doing?" You say in a whispering voice, using the Iraqi dialect that you seldom use with me, "What? I can't do anything without an order from his majesty the king?"

You sit before me following what is going on in the party, your whole body transfixed, mesmerized by the dance and the youth. I follow your eyes as they rest on the face of that young man with the thick black mustache, stealthily seeking communication with him as that puzzling smile transforms your face. The waiter serves me one drink after another. Then you excuse yourself and go back to your gathered friends Saadun, Yas, Niran, and Qays. I figure out that something must be going on. Emboldened and made reckless by the drinks I go over to you. I hear you saying in that Iraqi dialect, "What a mess! I don't know how it will end!"

Qays says, "Come on, Anhar! What's bothering you? It's not that bad! Look on the bright side."

You are surprised to see me after you tell them or one of them, "I won't stand for it, even if a palm tree grows on the top of your heads!"

I ask you anxiously, "What's wrong, Anhar?"

You take off the angry mask instantly and smile, saying, "It's just work."

I say, "Can I help?"

Niran says, "Would you agree to start all over again?"

Yas says as he walks away, "These two are inseparable like two peas in a pod."

I hold your hand and take you outside, I try to understand the words you are whispering, "These are just punks! What can I say?"

I want to take you into my arms and protect you, but I can't. I hear you saying decisively, "This is Baghdad and we know it best: you can't trust what you see at the moment."

I say, "Go home now. Tomorrow you'll explain it all to me."

Of course you don't broach the subject again, Anhar, and I don't pressure you. I go back to my apartment confused and frustrated. I thought life and prison had given me enough experience to understand people. I remember Nora hesitantly telling me, "Ustaz Hilmi, even though you've had a vast experience in life, your experience of people is still shaky. I always picture you sitting behind a desk as if you had never been involved in matters of this world!"

On the wall of my bedroom stands Anhar's shadow twisting in lust before a young man without features. The shadow grows bigger; it fills the ceiling, the glass window, and the walls. I cannot sleep. I feel helpless before her burning youth. My years become a burden bending my back. I feel even more crushed. The hours of the night flee away from the vexation whose sparks fill the room. I come face to face with the new day with my eyes bloodshot and my features clumsy. I cannot look at the mirror to shave, so I ask Nora to go alone to our appointments, then go back to bed. I try to sleep but I discover that I am lying in a heap, recalling Anhar's towering live figure, and I beseech myself to be saved from this love as I suffer a relapse into fever. When she comes I burst out in her face, cursing the day I saw her entering this door.

She rushes into my bosom. She pulls my arms and kisses me on my cheeks, screaming from the thorns scratching her face as I push her away. This mad woman runs outside after failing to calm me down. She runs away leaving me to face my need for her.

I went down to the restaurant. Gone were the cheerful noises and laughter of the women in the conference. I didn't hear the clicking of the spoons, forks, and knives, nor the gentle sound of tea being poured into small glasses. It was as if I were looking at a placid lake under the glow of a hot sun. I walked into this still-life painting and broke the stillness. The waiter said, "Hello, Sitt Nora. What can I get you to drink?"

I said, "Orange juice."

I got some food on my tray and sat down and ate quickly. Then I went out and took a taxi to Bab Sharqi, then to Mashjar Street, until it stopped in front of the Sheikhaly Building. I saw Abu Ghayib sitting on his bench as usual. He looked closely at me as I got out of the cab, then ran toward me, "Welcome, Sitt Nora. I can't believe you're in Baghdad!"

"Yes, thank God. How are you? And how are Umm Ghayib, Dia, and our friends and neighbors?"

"They're all well, thank God. Did you see Hilmi and what happened? How are Sitt Fayza and the girls?"

"They're all well and they send their greetings."

"Are you going upstairs to Abdallah or to Dr. Michael? He and his family left a while ago. Dr. Ali Abu Dahlia is upstairs and so is Abuna Hydra."

"Good. Thank you, Abu Ghayib."

I knocked on the door of the office. A young man, about thirty years old, came to the door. I said, "I'm Nora Suleiman. I used to work for *al-Zahra* magazine. The owner of the apartment has sent me to look at some of what she has left behind as the two of you had agreed."

He walked ahead of me after introducing himself, "Abdallah al-Sharbatli. Please come in."

I sat on the first chair I could find. The room had not changed. The lighting and the desks were the same even though the owner of the desk was gone. I looked at the half-empty bookcase and said,

"Sorry to arrive without an appointment. I left you a message but you did not call."

He said, "I am sorry. I was out of town and came back only today. I understood from your message that you'd come back from Basra at a late hour."

"Tante Fayza told me that she had shipped most papers except for a few files that she didn't know what to do with. She asked me to go through them and to keep important ones and dispose of the rest."

"I kept everything safely as I promised her. Please, feel free to open the drawers and feel at home. What would you like to drink?"

"Tea, please."

I found an archive of information, including photos of Egyptian and Iraqi artists, thinkers, and politicians. It seemed that Tante Fayza took only Hilmi Amin's writings and left the rest behind. I found copies of my three books about women, al-Khalsa village, and Egyptian peasants, and some folders of material that we had prepared for publication, some official releases put out by different Iraqi ministries, and some Iraqi and Egyptian magazines. There were various books on history, art, and politics. It seemed that Tante Fayza took some books at random.

He brought the tea and asked me, "What are all these folders? I wondered why you focused on certain artists, the Kurds, Egyptian peasants, the October War and Sadat and poetry and novels. Do you need all of that?"

I said, "Suad Hosni was shooting a movie here called *al-Qadisiya*, directed by Salah Abu Seif. Karam Mutawi' and Suhair al-Murshidi were teaching here in the Art Academy in Baghdad. They and many journalists came to us to help them find Egyptian material. As for the Kurds, we were preparing a book about them. And Baqir al-Sadr was the founder of an Islamic political party, an important subject here. This book about Egyptian peasants has actually been published. If you would like to keep the books, they are yours, or you can ask Dr. Michael to take them to the church. Disagreement with Sadat about the October War, the Corrective Revolution that came before it, and then Camp David after that meant many people wrote their points of view and their memoirs about these issues and published them outside Egypt. Hence their importance."

He said, "Please leave them. I'll decide what I want to keep and give the rest myself to Dr. Michael."

I said, "I'll take the folders to the hotel and stay up sorting the papers. I'll ship what we need and leave the rest for our Iraqi colleagues. As for copies of my book, I'll take them all."

I opened one of the books. It was a copy signed by me for Hilmi Amin. Tante Fayza had left all my books that I had signed for him. My tears flowed against my will. The man was taken aback and said, "God grant you strength."

I asked him permission to wash my face. I went into the bathroom and found that nothing in it had changed one bit. I could even hear Hilmi Amin coughing and clearing his throat. I almost believed it was the same towel that used to be in the bathroom. Then I realized it was just another Egyptian towel made in Mehalla. I knew that I was going to start crying hysterically. I began to drink water directly from the bathroom faucet and wash my tear-covered face. I calmed down and went back to the room where the man was. I called Abu Ghayib, who brought me large cardboard boxes and twine, expressing sadness for the good old days. I gathered the folders and tied the boxes, thanked him, and took them back to the hotel.

In the hotel I emptied the boxes on my bed and began to open the folders. Memories of writing the material assailed me: there were Iraqi women talking to me, photos of us in the north, Kurds returning home after the defeat of Mullah Mustafa Barzani, the house of Jamal, pictures of Sulafa, copies of my Kurdish-language articles in *Hokari* newspaper, pictures of the airport explosions and Father Hydra, the visits of Fathi Ghanim, Salah Abd al-Subur, and Naguib al-Mistikawi, the Egyptian soccer team, the visit to Habbaniya with Hafez Abd al-Rahman, an interview with General Saad al-Shazli, economic conferences, art festivals, an interview with Vanessa Redgrave, a whole album of photographs of Anhar;

by herself everywhere we went together, then pictures with me or with Hilmi Amin or with the girls and Tante Fayza. The pictures made me laugh, then cry. I got up and walked away from the papers then went back to them. There were records of interviews with the peasants, their pictures with Iraqi women agricultural experts, women in the factories, Bedouin women at their prettiest, the shanashil window lattices of Basra that I loved, the Iraqi historical fashion shows that I adored, our pictures in Kufa and Najaf, the photos of our Egyptian friends in comic poses in the office, Hilmi Amin and Tante Fayza next to Rasha riding a donkey in al-Khalsa, Mimi leaning on my shoulder on Mount Saffayn, Hilmi sitting at his desk or on the sofa with his daughters, and Abd al-Rahim and Suhayla. Then there was a picture of Vladimir.

I remembered the day I went into the office as usual and found Vladimir drinking coffee with Hilmi Amin. I was surprised he was there so early. Ustaz Hilmi said, "Nora, please wait a little bit in your office."

I took out my papers and began to arrange the news items and placed them into a folder. I heard some movement, then the door to the office opened and Hilmi Amin dashed out like a stray arrow to the door of the apartment and opened it. He then stood aside to let the correspondent Vladimir out. I noticed that both of them were frowning and totally silent. I looked at Ustaz Hilmi's totally pale face and the cigarette, burning on its own on the corner of his lips. I didn't utter a syllable. Hilmi Amin closed the door calmly and returned to his desk and said to me, "Come. The son of a bitch thinks he can recruit me and milk me for information."

"What?"

"Stupid intelligence services that understand nothing. He thinks that just because I am an Egyptian communist he can . . . I kicked the bastard out. When this bureau opened, before you joined it, I was subjected to very strict surveillance by the Iraqis who, of course, planted some eavesdropping bugs. I think they came back and removed them later. They were within their right to check what sort of activity the bureau was engaged in. I know they realized the bureau was on the up-and-up. But this jackass thought that he could use the bureau's respectable reputation and start some kind of relationship that he assumed was possible. The only way to deal with his offer was to kick him out."

"That's unbelievable! Are you sure? What kind of information was he after? Why us?"

"It doesn't matter what kind of information. The most important thing is to nip his efforts in the bud and make him understand exactly where he stands."

"Do we need more problems with correspondents?"

"This all comes with the territory. The main thing is to know how to deal with it."

I put the photograph aside. Why did we keep it even though the man never came back and avoided us in public gatherings afterward? Then I sighed deeply when I saw the photos of Chen and Yang, the Chinese correspondent couple who invited me to visit their country. I told myself when I received the invitation that I wouldn't have the patience to wait until Hatim came back from work to tell him that the Chinese invitation had arrived. I ran downstairs and kept running until I got to the Ramses Hotel telephone service desk. I called Hatim at work and said to him, "Hatim, I am going to China."

He said, "Wait until I come back to talk about it."

I said, "Are you so busy we can't talk now? I am sorry but I couldn't wait to tell you."

He said, "See you in the evening. Bye."

I said, "Bye."

Then I wondered why was he so cold?

In the evening I was surprised when he said, "Nora, we never agreed that you'd travel outside Iraq by yourself. I am very busy right now and can't leave the factory while we are setting up a new production line."

"But the trip is for me alone. It's a work trip and there is no need for you to travel with me."

"Postpone it until I can go with you."

"That's impossible. It's an invitation to a conference about the Chinese media and their relationship with the Middle East. You know how austere the Chinese are and the fact that Yang was able to get this invitation for me meant that he exerted an extraordinary effort, and that it won't happen again. He and Chen will conclude that I am not serious and they will not think of dealing with me ever again."

"I'd be worried sick if you travel alone. I also need you here these days."

"I don't understand your position."

So, the trip was gone. I shuffled the photos. I really liked Chen. Later on I told my father in passing that I had declined an invitation to travel to China. He asked me, "Do you think such an opportunity will come your way again? I doubt very much that you'll ever see China. You decline an invitation because Mister Hatim did not approve? Are you crazy? Why didn't you put up a fight and insist on going?"

"It wasn't worth all the trouble, and he really was busy."

"You tie your movements to his? You're a journalist. Is this the daughter I raised?"

"It wasn't all that bad. I also was very busy covering conferences in Baghdad."

"I don't want to interfere in your life, Nora, and you know how much I love and respect Hatim, but there are rules you should observe in your work just as you observe rules in your house."

"Hatim agreed to my traveling alone to other countries afterward. He realized how much I needed to go on those trips. Maybe also he felt guilty. I don't know."

I wondered where Chen and Yang were now. I said to myself that perhaps I should correspond with them when I got back to Cairo.

I gathered all the important papers about Iraq in a box to take with me. I put the rest in other boxes that I asked the front desk to keep until a colleague from the Iraqi News Agency came to collect them.

And, now: what should I do with Anhar's notebook? I had tried since arriving in Baghdad to call her house or find out anything about her to no avail. Of course I wasn't going to give her diaries to her colleagues. I also couldn't leave them in the post office box. Imad al-Bazzaz was still trying to find her brother's address. I wished I had an address for her, anywhere to send the notebook to her. The only solution was to take it with me. As for Hilmi Amin's notebook, I knew that he had left it up to me what to do with his memoirs. I opened a folded sheet of paper taken from a school notebook. I read:

Cairo, 5/10/1978
In the name of God, the Merciful, the Beneficent
Dear, respected father Abd al-Salam Muhammad Hasan:
After greetings and best wishes:

It gives me pleasure to write this letter to you, expressing my love and longing for all of you. Now then, dear father Abd al-Salam, I have received your precious letter and the letter of my wife Fadiya. We praise God for your good health and ask the Almighty to keep you and preserve you always and forever.

My dear father, I miss you just as plants miss water and the sick miss medicine, and the child misses his mother's loving embrace.

Dear father, I would like to tell you that the writer of this letter is Mr. Abd al-Basit Ali Shukr, from the house of Ali Shukr who send their greetings, especially Ramadan, Muhammad, Gum'a, Eid, and Ustaz Ahmad, and Sitt Umm Ramadan. A thousand greetings to you and to all the people in al-Khalsa, Diyali, and al-Kut. I would also like to tell you that we are all well, thank God, and we lack nothing except seeing you. From here we send greetings from brother Qurni and his wife and brother Rabie and the esteemed mother, a thousand greetings, and brother Auf and all the brothers old and young. My own greetings to Sitt Fadiya, my wife, and my dear son. A thousand million greetings. May God make it possible that I come to you very soon, God willing. By the way, I would like to tell you that this is the third letter I have sent.

Writer of the letter:
Oweis Ali Shukr

I had taken that letter from Fadiya, daughter of Amm Abd al-Salam, to include it in the book on al-Khalsa. She was visiting her family and hoping that her husband would join her at the project.

I felt a sting in my chest. I remembered Haytham. It was the time for his first nursing of the day. I looked at my watch. It was close to dawn. I got up and opened the window. A cool breeze sneaked into my room. I stood watching the thin threads of daylight as they were making their way to the Baghdad sky that I loved. The city in the distance was awaiting an Iranian rocket or a shell, ending one era and beginning others. I remembered reading how the Mongols overran Baghdad and the rivers of blood and the Tigris that was filled with books and manuscripts and the palaces that were razed to the ground. I asked Baghdad: What's your story, Baghdad? Could this land really be accursed?

I said to myself, "Impossible. This is the land of Sumerian writing, of the Hammurabi code, the land of Akkad, Ashur, and Babylon. I remembered the Iraqi mawwal that always began with "Yawayli" or "Woe is me." So, was it the land of tragedy? But tragedy is a human construct, here or in Greece or India or in Karbala. It is man who brings misery upon himself and others.

I looked at the huge mess in my room. Books and papers were everywhere, plates of food that had not been touched since yesterday, tea cups, a juice can, an almost empty glass of milk on the nightstand. I arranged the books that I would take with me to Egypt and packed my clothes together with the important papers in the big suitcase. I left space in the smaller bag for what I would be using the day before my flight back as well as things I'd need during the flight.

After a warm bath I felt I could face my long day at al-Khalsa, then the trip back home—God knew how that would go.

Tariq Mandour arrived. I told him about the trip to al-Khalsa and took him to the car and introduced him to Layla.

On our way I told Layla, "I hope the war has not affected the village. I am optimistic especially if Engineer Mahdi al-Mu'ezzin is still in charge of the project. I think he is old enough to be past the age of conscription."

She said, "They are conscripted wherever they are serving. The village is still receiving the attention and care of the party and I know that its inhabitants have been settled there for a long time."

I said, "Yes. The village was inaugurated in 1976. It is entirely inhabited by Egyptian families, each of which has been given twenty dunams and a house, plus a monthly salary of thirty dinars that they get for the first few years until they have managed to reclaim the land and live off it. Then land ownership for each of the families was raised to twenty-two dunams and, as the project expands each family's holding will rise to thirty dunams."

She said, "I know that you've published two books on the subject."

I said, "They considered it an experimental model of Arab economic integration: land and money from Iraq and peasants from Egypt."

Tariq Mandour said, "Why has the project stopped? I thought it was just the beginning, that it would be followed by other villages?"

I said, "That was the idea. The target was fifty thousand families, with five members in each. But despite the success of the peasants and the prosperity of the village, the Iraqi and the Egyptian sides did not agree and so the project came to a standstill. As I learned later on, the Iraqis tried duplicating the experiment with Moroccan peasants but the project failed quickly. Who knows? Maybe in the future, after the war is over, we will make an effort to revive it."

Layla said, "I feel so lazy today. The sun is so beautiful we really needed a trip."

I told her, "Come on, get some shut-eye. We have an hour before we get there."

Tariq told me how he ended up settling in Suleimaniya. He said, "A friend took me to a restaurant whose owner he knew. One week later I had decided to leave it, but the bitterness of my experience with unemployment in Baghdad convinced me to be patient. One evening I went with my friend to a cafeteria on a mountaintop. There I got to know the owner. I don't know how we became friends so fast. I visited him frequently, then he offered me a job. I discovered that he owned several cafés. As time went by, he gave me financial supervision of most of his businesses. Here when they trust someone they give him everything. And here I am: successful and happy and I work night and day, especially after the beginning of the war and conscription of the young men."

I said, "That's the Tariq I know."

The news of my arrival at the village traveled fast as usual. Engineer Mahdi and the young women working at the agricultural unit came to meet me. I went into Amm Wadie's house and many people from the village followed me. I learned that the young bride had given birth to two children. I also met Abd al-Hayy and Zaynab and learned that they had finally settled down after he bought a Toyota in which he hauled his produce to the market. She told me that Abu Ahmad was helping them in farming the land. Amm Ahmad insisted that his wife bake some fitir mishaltit for us to eat with them. His son, Gamal Abdel Nasser, came with his sister and greeted us. I said, "Do you know who Abdel Nasser is?"

He said, "The president."

Layla said, "Bravo!"

I finally took my leave saying that I had a tight schedule and promised them to come back to Baghdad at the next available opportunity.

On the way back Layla said, "I had no idea!"

I said, "The dream stays alive so long as people like that are still there."

Tariq said, "I have to go to the train station to catch the train. Please reassure the family that I am fine and that things couldn't be better."

At *al-Jumhuriya* newspaper we were received very warmly. Friends came and gathered around us asking about details of life in Egypt and reminiscing about Hilmi Amin. I asked the editor in chief to tell me where I could find Hilmi Amin's articles. He said, "That's an impossible task. Leave it for scholars studying the press of this era."

I said, "But his family wants to keep them and perhaps reprint them in a book."

He said, "Try to save the articles he wrote for *Alif Baa* magazine, since they were published over a short period. I'll send one of the colleagues with you to help you get them from the archives."

After great effort we were able to find most of the articles. We left exhausted as the night was chasing away remnants of the day.

Layla said, "You don't have time to pack. You must get some rest. I'll leave you now and come back at 10:00 p.m. to arrive at the airport in time."

I threw myself onto the bed and was soon fast asleep. I woke up feeling sharp pain in my chest. I found that I was soaked in sticky milk. I ordered a room service dinner and got into the water in the bathtub. The milk I pumped out of my breasts came to only three centimeters. I must be tired, that's all. Tomorrow there will be more milk, God willing. I made sure my suitcase was closed well and the box of books was sturdy enough for the trip. Hilmi Amin's memoirs were still on the nightstand next to the bed. I picked them up and stretched out on the pillows and began to read before putting the notebook with Anhar's memoirs in my carry-on bag and taking them to Egypt.

The Bitter Honey of Full Maturity
The ultimate love,
Flowing from my heart
To the tips of my fingers,

The love that mixes with blood
In the arteries, veins, and all the cells
Resting and coming to with the pulse,
With inhaling and exhaling,
With reveries and dreams
Accompanying the beats of the heart
Turning into percussion beats
Of the song of our love.

I take refuge in writing to you to alleviate my sadness over my family's departure, a departure that reminds me of my inability to go back to Egypt. I ask myself if I will see my daughters again. And that young bright girl that came to me as I prepare for my last journey from this earth: how many years that I don't have does she need to grow into her own as a young lady? Will Rana recognize me next time after long months of separation? I wait for the hours, and bleeding, count the seconds until you knock on the door and I open it, having dimmed the light just as you like and prepared the nest of our love after a long deprivation. You come in, opening your arms to embrace me, and give me a long kiss as you lead me to our room, telling me while laughing, "If you betray me, that's how I'll kill you." You move your clenched fists pretending to break my neck. You push me onto the bed, forcing me to lie on my back. I laugh and gasp as I cough, shouting, "The cigarette, Anhar!"

You shower me with kisses and you squeeze me passionately. We spend minutes wriggling and twisting on the bed. I reach my hand between your thighs and feel a sticky liquid. The surprise stings me. I ask you to calm down until I light a cigarette. I ask you where you've come from, and you tell me a long story about guests who have come from Kubaysh, your village, cousins who are staying at your house. You complain about your fiancé who no longer leaves your house, claiming he has to keep the cousins company, you tell me you've tried many times to end that story by breaking the engagement, but you can't because everyone is taking his side.

I lick my wounds and slowly swallow my pain as you keep talking and talking, placing your head on my belly, which I didn't bother to cover despite the light filling the whole room. You bring me tea. I ask if we can drink it in the office, but you refuse adamantly and persist in rubbing against my body and touching and feeling while I am away, far away, being consumed by jealousy whose fires put me face to face with a reality in which I see nothing but betrayal.

Then I tell myself: Wake up, Hilmi. Enough. Get up from your fall. She is not yours. She is not yours regardless of all the passionate love she professes for you. You've lost your compass and you no longer know where you're going. A young girl has played you for a fool: all she wants is to get through you to the elite circle around you. You are her ticket to society and her password to rise to the top. Get up, old man. Stop this farce, protect your dignity and your status! Don't fall for it! Don't fall!

You finish the tea, then you begin to take off your clothes. You reach for my shirt, trying to take it off. I cling to it, but you don't give me a chance. You sing the line from Umm Kulthum's song, "Except that the fire of longing keeps burning brighter day after day."

You hold my palms and guide them between your thighs, twisting, announcing a desire that has gone out of control. I lose control over my body and my organs. The bitter taste in my mouth turns into sweet honey as your tongue plunges into my mouth. I start looking for the rooster's crest and I find it oozing like a flowing river, wetting your upper thighs. I jump from the bed, cursing you loudly.

"Clean yourself of . . . of him. Two weeks? You couldn't bear to wait two weeks? Fifteen days, my friend? The one I thought was the most pure?"

I swallowed with difficulty as I coughed, "Where've you come from now? You were with him?"

"With whom?"

"You sleep with him in your house, in the midst of your family? You seized the opportunity of him being there and you invited him to your room. It was you who invited him, right? It was you!"

401

"Who?"

"Your lover. The lover you say you can't stand. You come to me with his vestiges still on your body?"

"Have you gone crazy?"

"No. I just woke up."

"You accuse me of betraying you when I haven't slept one minute since yesterday because I missed you so much! You're hiding your own satiation after the days of love you spent with Fayza."

"Look at your body: what's all this wetness?"

"It comes from my own desire and nobody else's."

"You are a liar. You lie all the time. You've deceived even me, the experienced old man. Yes, the *old* man. But now I say no. I can kick you out of my life, banish you."

"Please. This is all untrue. I love you. So why are you pushing us into this abyss? You'll regret what you're doing."

"So, now *you* are threatening me. Has it come to this? I don't want to see you again. Go, there is no work for you today."

You went to the office. I heard you crying for one whole hour. I clung to my bed, lighting one cigarette after another. I heard your footsteps going toward the apartment door. I got up in alarm, saying, "You'll come tomorrow on time, your regular time. Work is work. Otherwise you know I know how to get you."

I heard you saying in a dejected voice, "I'll be here." I wanted you to stay, but you, in your naïveté, opened the door, then looked over your shoulder at me in humiliation, and left.

My rage lasted for four long days in which I turned into a nervous wreck. Illusions dispersed and I found out how fragile I really was despite my strength, which was legendary among my fellow prison inmates. I turned into a shadow of my former self before a young girl my daughter's age racing toward her future while I was preparing to leave my years on death's door. Then I was surprised when you knocked on my door one day. It was Friday, the evening I spent with friends at the Writers Union. You came into the office. You said, "For days I have been trying to understand, but I couldn't. I felt too shy to tell you that before even taking off my clothes, my desire had risen to such heights that I couldn't handle it. So it had an orgasm while you were kissing me. That was my own water. I thought you knew. That was my mad love for you. You forget that I am a virgin. All I know is what you've taught me. Please don't open the door to hell."

I wanted to believe you. I waited for you to extend your hand and touch my face, to embrace me. But you just sat before me, humiliated, with tears running down your cheeks. Then you suddenly got up and ran downstairs and disappeared into the Baghdad night.

When you came the following afternoon, I, the fool up to his ears in love with a girl his daughter's age, took you into my bosom as if nothing had happened.

I closed the notebook and got up to wash my face, wondering what I would find in Anhar's notebook. Would it give me the other side of the story I'd just read? I told myself that maybe I'd read some of its pages while waiting for my plane at the Amman airport, even though they told me it was going to be a three-hour layover, rather than seven hours as happened on the way to Baghdad.

I left the hotel with Layla with tears that I tried to hide. I had slept only two hours after spending the previous night sleepless until the morning, sorting the papers from the office. That crazy night will remain etched on my memory as long as I live. I didn't know for whom I should cry: for myself, for Hilmi Amin, or for our people in Iraq and Egypt, for our children or for other people's children. Should I cry over knowledge or ignorance? Impotence or fulfillment? Steady balance or falling?

Traveling to Cairo alone apart from the official delegation was not safe. No one would wait for me at Amman airport. The authorities there might force me to wait outside as they did with ordinary passengers. No, Layla actually checked the arrangements carefully. But even if things went as arranged, the waiting time depended on other plane schedules. Waiting could take from three to seven hours. Only God knew. It was also a time of war.

I left the hotel that I never liked even though it was my only way to stay in the city that I loved, from which I couldn't imagine being completely cut off. I looked over my shoulder as the car sped away and I saw the snow-white hotel, the ground washed with rain, the small green bushes, and the flowers on both sides of the road, and I asked myself, "Will I come back to you, Baghdad?"

I answered myself, "I don't think I will. Not for a long time, at least."

I was afraid of being seized by another crying fit and I struggled to keep the potent scent of longing from assailing my nose. From the bottom of the river the memories erupted a plethora of intermingling sensory fragments: the smell of overripe dates, fragrant anise, bitter coffee and cardamom, cracked wheat cooking, the din of drums, taps of feet dancing dabka, gunshots fired in joy, the breaking of glass, the shushing sound of the rain falling on various parts of the house, the rustling sound the wind made through the palm tree fronds, the yellowness of an expansive desert, the indifference of towering trees, very high green mountains, the grayness of stagnant ponds, cities in clouds of sand, suitcases and a necklace made of clove buds, drunken bodies and kisses. I shooed away those fragments as I prepared to be forcibly dissociated from the city. I was overcome with the trembling silence of anticipation. I felt Layla's hand patting my hand. Her understanding touch gave my heart a promise of security. She saved me from the trap of wallowing in pain. We passed roads that I knew by heart and the outer shell of my solid will cracked. Images of friends whom I have lost, by death or long separation, came tumbling down on me, breaching the wall of my soul: Hilmi Amin, Anhar, Engineer Adel, Nariman, Sulafa, Jamal Abu Sargon. I looked at the towering, giant picture of Saddam Hussein hanging on top of Salihiya Gate before Gamal Abdel Nasser Square. My memory was overcome with pictures of the vice president's morning fieldtrips to factories and government schools to make sure everything was working properly as he was preparing to become president. I recalled his sweeping popularity, with people crowding around him screaming for more. I recalled when he was declared president, and his proud, self-confident parade in an open car and how he waved to the masses. The memory brought another one: Gamal Abdel Nasser, waving to us on the Alexandria Corniche during the celebrations of the anniversary of the July 23 Revolution, and how people crowded to shake his hand as the car moved slowly. What a difference between the two!

I wanted a few moments of peace and closed my eyes and tried to stop the assault of the images and memories on my consciousness. I sought refuge in Layla who was sitting next to me. I held onto her arm. She patted me. I was still having a hard time freeing myself from the captivating city even though I realized that those last few minutes belonged to Baghdad and should always. I burned the incense of my memories in places I walked, played, ate, slept, grieved, sang, breathed, and met people.

Layla said, "I'll miss you very much, Nora. Don't forget us. Try to come to Baghdad whenever you have a chance."

I said, "That's not so easy. I am going back full of wounds. Seeing is not like hearing."

She said, "Are you crying?"

She hugged me hard and didn't let go of my shoulder until the car stopped in front of the airport.

I said as I got out of the car, "Please pardon the excess baggage. You know how crazy we are about books."

She said, "Come to the guest hall. Leave everything for the driver."

I tried to say goodbye at the airport gate but she insisted on staying with me until the plane took off. She took my passport and ticket to finish the procedures. It was the same beautiful glass-covered airport that I had arrived at and departed from dozens of times. But now it was dark and looked a little desolate, having lost the joyous feeling of Iraqi pride and security. I was used to traveling and moving around since childhood. I was also used to passing through airports lightly and dealing with them in a very practical manner. I would be touched by tears of reunion and farewell, but I would also shake them off quickly, so they wouldn't slow me down. On my first visit to Iraq the airport was small and simple. Hatim told me that they were building a brand-new airport in the latest, ultramodern style. Security was conventional until that explosion which was blamed on the Syrian government. After that, security procedures were changed totally in Iraq. For the first time, buildings learned about and used metal and weapons detectors. My first trip after the airport explosion turned into a catastrophe.

I was going to visit Yasir for the first time since I left him in Egypt. I couldn't sleep the night before my departure because I was worried. I hadn't seen my son for quite some time and I was scared. Would he recognize me? I tried to convince myself that he hadn't forgotten me, that he was fine as they told me several times on the phone. I tried to visualize him. What had changed in him? Would the doctor agree to my taking him with me to Baghdad? Did he really get better in Egypt's milder climate? How have Iraqi babies survived if the climate was behind his health problems? It wasn't his problem but yours. You could have rejected the doctor's opinion or sought a second opinion and brought your son to Baghdad, enrolled him in a daycare center during your workdays like all mothers here. My God! I should stop this guilt trip. What has been, has been. Tomorrow I would see him and make sure he was fine.

My joy anticipating seeing Yasir outweighed my fear. My enthusiasm for going back to Cairo was quite overpowering as Hatim was driving me to the airport. But I remembered that I would be leaving him alone during my absence. I felt bad about that. Hatim smiled as he kissed me and pushed me to the passport control area, commenting in the meantime on how good I looked in the new rose-colored woolen dress with the high collar that I was wearing. He said, "Come back quickly, you and Yasir, otherwise I'll cancel the contract. You have one week."

I pleaded with him, "Two weeks?"

"One week only."

He pushed the suitcase onto the scale and stood with me until I finished checking in and moved to the "passengers only" area. The female officer standing there motioned me to go to a security booth for women. I turned to Hatim, and laughing, I said, "Goodbye."

I turned to face the officer. I raised my hands so that she could pass the metal detector security wand that I was seeing for the first time, around my body. I detected some anxiety in her movements. I tried to respond to her gestures to give her an opportunity to move around me more easily. For one reason or another that I couldn't figure out she became more tense and said in a loud commanding voice, "Don't move."

I said, "I didn't."

"Stay in place."

Then she pointed at the dress collar and said, "What's this?"

"A high collar."

"Open it."

"It doesn't open. This is a one-piece dress."

"What are you hiding inside it?"

I laughed, "A rabbit."

"I asked you: what are you hiding inside it?"

I said in surprise, "Nothing. The money is in my purse and I have the change voucher."

"How many dinars do you have on you?"

"Not more than a hundred dinars for expenses on my return trip from Cairo."

"Are you returning? Where is your passport?"

"Here it is. I am a journalist in the Egyptian *al-Zahra* magazine bureau here in Baghdad."

"Turn around. Raise all your clothes upward and take off your underwear."

"Why?"

"Take off your clothes."

She placed her hand quickly between my thighs before I knew exactly what was happening. I cried, gasping as my tears coursed down my cheeks.

"Bend over forward."

"I will not bend over. I want the representative of the Ministry of Information right away. You are making a big mistake."

"Stand up straight."

"I want the ministry representative or the director of the airport."

"Put on your clothes."

My tears flowed as I remembered. Layla, who was coming toward me, thought I was crying because I was leaving Baghdad. She put her hand on my shoulder. I got a hold of myself and forced myself to smile. She accompanied me to a security partition. Now the security was much more complex than before. I entered the women's booth with a beautiful woman with the rank of captain. She passed the wand over my body while smiling gently. I looked at her shapely figure in the military uniform and remembered the arrogant manner in which that woman who insulted me with her crude search and her rigid demeanor, despite her beauty and her curly blond hair, and the hunter–quarry game she played on me. I remembered my father saying as he laughed, "Write an article demanding gentler handling of women. You, as a journalist, should know that she is just doing her job. You yourself admit that the security situation in Baghdad has changed greatly since last year. What should the Iraqis do to combat sabotage? Security is the most precious thing in life."

Yes, father. I understand it quite well.

I sat with Layla waiting for the call to board the plane. I looked with my eyes for the monitor indicating departure times. I found that the flight was on time. I remembered Fathallah and Maha and their inability to come to Baghdad to meet with me. So I thought I should call them to say goodbye. I asked Layla, "Where can I find a local telephone?"

She pointed to a wall to the side nearby and asked me, "Do you have change?"

I said, "No. I only have dollars. I'll change them at the bank."

She laughed as she reached inside her purse, saying, "Here. Take this. Keep the dollars. They'll come in handy if you want to drink tea at Amman airport."

I put the money in her hand saying, "Here. Let's spend the last penny. Why don't you buy some gifts to your liking while I make a call."

She laughed, "You Egyptians don't give up! I'll buy you some snacks you might need in Amman."

I dialed the number. Maha answered. Her voice sounded worried. Maha was Maha: her feelings as clear as the sun. I said, "What happened, Maha? What's bothering you?"

She said, "All I said was 'hello.' I didn't say a single word that would tell you I am upset."

I said, "Maha. I don't have the time to explain everything to you. Give me Fathallah."

She said, "To tell the truth, Basyuni disappeared suddenly from work and took with him a Land Cruiser belonging to the Roads and Logistic Support Authority. No one knows if he had been injured somewhere or just ran away. Security has been looking for him all over, but has turned up nothing so far. They interrogated Fathallah today at work but he knows nothing about him since he visited us in Mosul last month, with the exception of that message he left for him to meet you and his telephone call to confirm that meeting. He never mentioned any plans. He was laughing and telling us stories about the war. I am very scared that he might be injured somewhere or another, God forbid. Fathallah wants to talk to you."

I felt a hidden anxiety in his voice. He said, "Nora, where exactly are you now?"

I was quite alarmed and felt as if I had a sudden drop in blood pressure. I also felt the milk drying up in my chest. I said, "I am boarding the plane in a few minutes."

He heaved a deep sigh of relief, saying, "Thank God. I hope you get out all right before security can give you a headache. The scoundrel did it. He ran away."

I said, "Do you think he took the car and escaped from Iraq?"

He said, "No, he definitely left it somewhere. True, it's a half-million-pound car but he couldn't have done it, because, number one, he is not a thief and two, he wants to cross the borders and he doesn't have any papers to prove he owns it."

I said, "Are his belongings still in Mosul? How would he leave Iraq without obtaining an exit visa from the Residency Department? No Iraqi exit point will permit him to leave without such permission."

He said, "I think he'll look for a secret route to cross the borders and this is what I am afraid of, for him. On the whole he knows a lot about Iraq now. I hope it all ends well and he doesn't fall into the hands of a swindler or someone who tempts him to do something foolish that would cost him his life. Anyway, say hello to everyone in Egypt."

Layla noticed how pale my face was as she gave me a bag of candy and cookies. I took it from her without thinking and sat down next to her absently until I heard the call to board the plane. I kissed her and proceeded to the gate without any expression on my face, waiting to be called at any moment and taken to one of those places about which I had often heard, about how brutal and frightful they were. Places like "the Palace of the End." I smiled. I said to myself, "Don't be silly. Nobody will know anything about me now that Layla has left me. Security would not dare arrest one of Iraq's guests at a time when they need their efforts to win the world over to its side. Anyway, that won't be an arrest but a cross-examination, a right to which the Iraqis are entitled. I met Basyuni in front of many witnesses hours before he disappeared. Arresting a visiting journalist would create a big scandal that they couldn't afford to have."

I climbed the plane ladder in the midst of a very cold and dark night. The scene brought back to me what Iraq had done to itself. What have you done, Basyuni, you poor fool? That was all we needed!

To get Iraqi security involved! What kind of trip is that? I leave my nursing baby behind and come to a country at war where I could die for no reason at all except the so-called struggle. What kind of struggle? Search for the truth? Did I find any truth? Or was it just one-sided information? I sat on my seat praying to God that the plane would take off. I followed the sound of its engines, inserted all my being into that sound; my veins expanded, reaching out to the cold metal parts as I welded my consciousness to them, pushing them to fly, willing them to fly. My body began to vibrate as the engines turned and the blood in my veins whirled in small eddies rising with the speed of the engines.

The stewardess came, smiling coquettishly. I fixed my gaze on her. She asked me, "Can I get you anything? Your face is pale."

I said with a forced smile filling my face, "I have a stomach ache. I am afraid I might throw up."

She said, "I'll get you something for that right away."

I began to hum, trying to get the engines to hurry up. I was afraid the man sitting next to me might hear my humming. I tried to muffle my voice, but it began to sound hoarse. The man will imagine that I am singing. He definitely won't realize that I was gripped with terror. But it didn't much matter, anyway, as he had fallen asleep the moment he sat down.

The stewardess brought me a glass of water, saying, "Here, please: this is medicine for motion sickness. We will take off right away."

I heard the usual roar of the engines as the stewardess turned and hurried toward her own seat and fastened her seatbelt. The man sitting next to me smiled, then closed his eyes, as the plane raced at top speed on the runway, then ascended to the sky with its wings up and the roar of its engines that felt like a cool spring rain. I smiled even though my ears were throbbing with pain, almost jumping off of my head. I noticed a hand offering me chewing gum. It was the man sitting next to me. I took it from him, thanking him as my face radiated with the most beautiful smile I ever experienced in my life. I put the gum in my mouth and closed my eyes. In a short while the seatbelt sign turned off and the lights were turned on. I went to the restroom and washed my face. I felt refreshed. When I went back to my seat I relaxed and felt comfortable. I also felt how small I was and how little I understood about the world. I was happy to hear an Iraqi song and the Iraqi captain's voice. I said to myself, "This is another face of Iraq." I remembered Basyuni and wondered where he was now. I recalled his laughter as he repeated, "I might arrive before you, Abla." Abla? The jackass! Could he have learned from what Fathallah did when he smuggled some of his Iraqi communist friends? It's impossible that Fathallah might have lost all discretion and told him how. But why not? He might even have used him in his operations. But Fathallah is wise and intelligent and it is inconceivable that he would trust such a child, no matter how brave he seemed. Because Basyuni is reckless and rash.

I heard the story about smuggling by sheer coincidence when Fathallah was visiting us at the office after the blow to the Communist Party. Hilmi Amin asked him for news about Muhammad Aziz, a cadre of the Iraqi Communist Party. He said, "He's flown."

Hilmi said, "Are you sure?"

Fathallah said, "Yes. I saw him myself as he flew."

I gathered the papers I was working on and went out to welcome him. He was startled to see me.

Hilmi Amin said, "This is my daughter, Fathallah." Then, laughing, "My beloved Nora."

I said, "Did they arrest a military wing of the Communist Party or is it just a story that they fabricated for some reason or another?"

Hilmi said, "It was an organization of eighteen officers, according to official announcements. Military intelligence arrested them and after torture they confessed to being the military wing of the Iraqi Communist Party."

I said, "They made a mistake. In 1973 they joined the ruling coalition and were the second strongest party in the country. It was decided that they would be represented by three members. The agreement, after the release of dozens of detainees, was that communists would not enlist in the army."

Fathallah said, "Everyone lived up to the agreement, from 1973 until the end of last year, when those officers were arrested and they discovered their affiliation with the communist party. And, since they had formed a military organization, naturally they were thinking of staging a coup d'état. But why hit the lower ranks, the second and third tier rather than the leadership who were not subject to even a simple interrogation?"

Hilmi said, "This is quite an intelligent move. First, the military members who were convicted were executed. Do you remember vice president Saddam Hussein's visit to Moscow, then Yugoslavia, then his meeting with Castro in Havana later on?

Fathallah said, "Yes, of course. It was immediately after uncovering the organization."

I asked Hilmi Amin, "You mean Saddam Hussein got the green light from the Soviet Union and the Eastern Bloc before handing down the death sentences, even though they were legal and part of the coalition front protocols? Didn't Castro, Tito, and Brezhnev try to get the sentences commuted, especially as Iraq and the Eastern Bloc were on a political honeymoon?"

Hilmi said, "According to the theory of non-capitalist transformation advanced by some theorists, it is all right for developing countries to be led by non-communist parties and nationalist leftist parties may lead the transformation process."

I said, "That's what Samir Amin, Khalid Bekdash, and the Egyptian Communist Party say."

Fathallah smiled and Hilmi said, "These theories were advanced first by Gramsci and also Jean-Paul Sartre when he wrote *Critique of Dialectical Reason*. Lenin approved of national liberation movements against colonialism even if such movements were not communist. He supported the 1919 revolution in Egypt led by the Wafd Party. What happened recently was the result of an article written by Yevgeny Primakov: "Joy on the Banks of the Nile," and that's where all those you mentioned got their idea. When Saddam Hussein went to Brezhnev with documents indicting the participants, of course Brezhnev would say to him, 'If you have an agreement, that's all there is to it.' The same thing happened with Castro. This way Saddam Hussein would be blameless. And that proves that Ahmad Hasan al-Bakr was quite smart: not taking any action before sending his deputy to consult, and this way the move to strike the left would be seen as legitimate."

Anhar arrived, earlier than her usual starting time. She looked merry and welcomed Fathallah and asked him about Maha. Then she sat next to me and said, "How's the Egyptian journalist today?"

I said, "Never better."

Hilmi said, "What we have here is a forty-year-old political party, secret for thirty-five years. All its printing presses and organizations are underground. It's a well-established party with street support and subject to repression throughout its long history. When it clashes with the authorities, its leaders are arrested or executed. The second tier then moves to the front to keep it going. That second tier is not known to the authorities. The party is fully functional again, keeping its strength despite the blow dealt to it. When the Ba'th Party leaves the base alone, arrests the mid-level leadership, tortures or even executes its members, then leaves the door open for the top leadership to get away, the result, as the Ba'th Party predicts, is a psychological blow to the members of the Communist Party and resentment of the base toward its leadership, as you hear from the comrades in this office every day, Nora."

I kept shifting my gaze between Hilmi Amin and Anhar and got worried. "Why does Hilmi trust her so much, when he is usually so careful?"

Anhar said, "Yes, the disappearance of the midlevel leadership finished off the organization."

The stewardess brought some snacks. She was moving quickly between the seats since it was a short flight between Baghdad and

Amman. I took the food tray from her. The pain I felt in my soul seemed to move to my body. I began to munch the cookies absently as I told myself: "It is not plausible that Fathallah had told Basyuni of any help he had extended to the comrades. If they have executed the Iraqis, what would they do to an Egyptian who smuggled them out of the country? But Hilmi has told us that they had left the door ajar for the top tier leaders to undermine the reputation of the party among the youth. Did they know what Fathallah had done but left him alone, free to act under their watchful eyes and ears until he overstepped the mark they had set for him, when they would arrest him? That way Basyuni's case would be the straw that broke the camel's back. But Fathallah didn't know where Basyuni went." Now my worry shifted to Fathallah. My head was about to explode.

The captain announced that we'd arrived at Amman airport, asking us to fasten our seatbelts and return our seats to the upright position. I closed my eyes. I wanted to put a piece of chewing gum into my mouth and offer the man sitting next to me another piece. I looked for the bag of chocolates but discovered I had left it in Baghdad airport. I waited for the plane to land. Thank God I had three hours in Amman. That would give me a chance to go to the bathroom to empty my breasts first, then get some rest in the transit lounge before boarding the Cairo-bound plane, God willing.

I got into the small airport at midnight. I remembered my trip with Hatim and Yasir and how we got so bored after the three days that we spent in Jordan that we decided to go to Syria to spend the rest of our vacation. I asked an officer where the transit lounge was and he said, "There's no transit lounge. Stand in the passport control line."

"I was here a few days ago with an official delegation and they put us up in a lounge."

He examined my passport, then looked closely at me, then asked me, "Whose picture is this?"

"It's mine."

"And the baby?"

"He's my son. But he's not with me. When I got the passport two weeks ago I planned to have him accompany me, but I changed my mind at the last moment."

"The photo is quite faded."

"It's one of those instant pictures that I had to use to make it on time to a conference in Baghdad."

I reached in my handbag and took out my Egyptian and international press IDs and the letter of invitation to the conference and presented them to him.

He pushed them aside and said, "Take your passport and check with Jordanian intelligence tomorrow."

I said, "I am going to Egypt. Why should I check with Jordanian intelligence?"

He said, "Your name is similar to someone wanted by security."

I said, "I don't have any money, so I can't enter Jordan, book a room in a hotel and check with intelligence. That might take God knows how many days. Isn't there another solution?"

"There's nothing you can do except enter Jordan and check with intelligence."

I said, "I am not going to enter Jordan and you have no right to make me enter against my will. I am just a transit passenger and where I am standing is an international zone. I am very sorry. I am a member in an official delegation. I was told in Baghdad that a protocol official would wait for me in Amman to facilitate my travel. Please let him know I am here."

"As you can see, there's no one."

"Please inquire."

"Look around you. There's no one. If an official from the Iraqi embassy came, he would've come before me or my colleague."

Another officer came over to find out what was happening because our voices were tense and loud. He took the passport from him and looked at it, spoke to the other officer in a low voice then told me, "Get out of the line and wait a little while."

Other passengers around me said loudly: "Don't enter Jordan."

An Arab passenger said, "I am a man of the law. He has no right to make you enter Jordan. Insist on staying in transit. Don't give in in any way. You are young and you don't know what it means to be a suspect. You'll be lost if you enter."

"Thank you. But what will he do to me if I refuse?"

"He cannot force you. Believe me."

I got out of the line and moved toward a wall to lean on since I couldn't find a seat. I felt a stinging pain in my chest. The veins throbbed hard even though the milk had decreased considerably. I had not pumped the milk in hours and whenever the tension increased, I felt sharper stinging. But it had not started flowing out yet. I was terrified when I began to think about my situation—Jordanian intelligence, without anyone knowing a thing about it, as happened with Musa al-Sadr? And without money? Why did I spend the last of my money yesterday? Books. Have I read all the books I bought before? Was it just the lust for buying? Okay, now I reap the fruits of mindless spending. What exactly was the story? Somebody's name similar to mine? Who? My name is purely Egyptian. "Nora Ibrahim Fahmi." As for Suleiman, Hatim's name, it was not listed on the passport and had no Palestinian connection whatsoever. He asked me if I had visited Jordan before and I said, "Yes." He said, "Why?" I said, "As a tourist." And is that not the truth? But how could someone like him believe that some crazy people like us spend their hard-earned money to see the rest of the Arab world? All he wanted was the money of the poor Egyptian workers who paid fees to enter and exit Jordan for no reason.

The hall I was in was now quiet. No new planes had landed in a long while. Two hours had passed and the officer who went to inquire had not come back. I didn't want to go back to the first passport control officer who had been adamant. I preferred to wait for the other one. Finally he came and signaled to me, saying, "I regret to say that you have to enter Jordan and to check with intelligence tomorrow, because you won't be able to enter this airport without checking with them."

I said, "Why?"

"The picture is quite faded and the officer has every right to doubt the authenticity of this passport."

I said, "My ticket is from Baghdad to Cairo. I have nothing to do with Jordan. The law gives me the right to be in transit whether you, sir, like that or not. If you kept me here for ten days, I wouldn't enter Jordan. I am a journalist and I'll raise hell. If you want me to wake up officials at the Egyptian embassy, I can do that by using this telephone here." I pointed to a public telephone attached to the wall. "So, there's no need for this obstinacy."

He said, "Order is order and it will apply to you just as it applies to others."

He pointed to the new lines of passengers that had begun to form in front of passport control.

I said, "You exploit Egyptian workers by charging them fees. This is your order that you are trying to apply to me. This is also the fault of those passengers who did not object to an illegal order and did not refuse to enter. The fact that there might be a problem with my passport, that has nothing to do with you. So there's no need to apply this order to me for a few lousy dollars."

"Why are you shouting?"

"Because you know full well that I am in the right and you don't want to understand."

"This will do you no good. Your passport is not valid."

"Okay. Do what you like. This is not your concern. This is an Egyptian matter. My country will hold me to account."

A number of officers gathered around the line of Egyptian and other Arab passengers. Many said emphatically after they heard the story: "Do not give in. They can't do anything to you. Do not enter Jordan." They spoke loudly in defiance of the officers. Someone said, "These are humorless people. A Jordanian would not show happiness even over a hot loaf of bread. This is a young woman. What do you want from her? She's said she doesn't have money."

The officer left after I refused to stand in the passport control line. Another hour passed. I went to the public telephone and tried to inset an Iraqi coin but it did not fit. One of the passengers gave me a Jordanian coin. I inquired about the Egyptian embassy number and called it. A recorded voice said to leave a message. I left a brief description of the situation and hung up. I went back to the wall to lean on it. Another hour passed that exhausted my attention span. Another officer arrived and asked me about the story. I told him. He said, "Come with me. Come here. Do you have your passport?"

"Yes."

He opened a side door and from it I could see another hall facing the runway directly. I saw the exit gates. I couldn't believe my eyes. I followed him like a blind person. Then I looked at my watch and asked him, "Has my plane departed?"

"Yes."

"Did it depart on time?"

He laughed, saying, "Yes, regrettably. Please accept my apology." I said, "For God's sake! Why all of this?"

"Well, he's within his rights to resolve any doubt. For what newspaper do you write?"

"For *al-Zahra* and *Rose al-Yusuf* magazines."

"Great publications: with Salah Jahin, Salah Hafez, and Ahmad Bahaeddin."

"You're quite knowledgeable about the Egyptian press. But most of those writers are now writing for other publications."

"We've all been raised on Egyptian culture."

"Please, for God's sake, what would become of me if I entered Jordan with a passport I cannot use to leave Jordan?"

"You should be thankful to God that you are here now. Do you have enough money?"

"Unfortunately, just some change."

He ordered some sandwiches and tea for me, then left saying, "A plane will depart for Egypt at three in the afternoon. We'll get you on it, God willing."

Then he added, laughing, "I hope it also departs on time. Good-bye. If you need anything, I am at your service. I'll be around."

"Thank you."

The food came and I sat down to eat, rearranging in my mind what happened, not believing that I got out of it by a miracle. Jordanian prisons? My God! Drops of milk flowed from my breasts. I just let them trickle down my body, tickling me. I could smell the fresh milk but I didn't care what was happening to me. I said to myself. "I'll soon have a cold; thank God my carry-on bag has lots of underwear, towels, and cleaning supplies. I will deal with the place as if it were a hotel and may everyone go to hell." Jordanian prisons! I remembered the story of my friend, the poet Hilmi Salim, who entered Jordan in 1981 and they told him to check with Jordanian intelligence. From there they took him to jail for no reason that he knew of. His ordeal lasted for fifteen days until they deported him to Syria with several other detainees. That was last year, and to this day he hasn't found out why. But why prison? Shouldn't the embassy intervene in cases like this and give me a new passport? But who said it was a matter of passports? The man said: check with intelligence because of suspicions about the name. Could one of them come now and say: "We've changed our mind, you have to enter Jordan now"? Why? It's finished now, Nora, daughter of Fahmi. You shouldn't worry about it. I wondered how my son was doing. We didn't need such events to separate me from him even longer. Why didn't I return with the official delegation? The country is at war and my younger son is only six months and the older is five years. You're a mother, and in charge of a family. I hope that what happened has taught you a lesson you won't forget.

I carried my bag and went into the bathroom. I was met by an attendant other than the one who had helped me before, on my way to Baghdad. I didn't bother to explain my behavior to her. She was looking at me from afar with inquisitive eyes, so I figured out she had heard about my story with passport control. I placed my things on the sink counter and went into a stall, leaving the door ajar so that I could extend my feet. I sat, exhausted, and tried to pump the milk remaining in my breasts slowly. Then I buttoned my blouse and went out of the stall. The attendant was still sitting on her seat. I told her, "Good morning. Would you kindly close the door for five minutes so I can wash, because I am nursing. Things are quiet now."

She said, "Pregnancy, mothering, and nursing! That's our life, daughter. Where's your baby?"

I said, "In Egypt."

She said, "I'll be outside if you need anything."

The hot water made me feel human again. I changed my clothes, then went out to the lounge. I chose a seat away from other passengers and the television. I was overtaken by sleep for a few minutes during which I quickly lost touch with everything as I slipped into a black pit. Then I awoke fully aware of every movement around me: footsteps, clanking of cups, sips of coffee, the incessant announcements of planes departing or boarding, children crying, and passengers chit-chatting. Waking up usually came to me like a sudden flash after which my mind became fully alert, as if I had not been deprived of sleep for the third day in a row. Then the whole trip would come to my mind arranged neatly as if it were offered to me on a tray, or I would remember Hilmi Amin and Baghdad, whereupon my tears would flow uninvited. I could smell espresso, so I got up to get a double shot. The server asked me, "Anything else? A sandwich, cookies?"

"Cookies."

I said to myself, it should be a bar of chocolate to make it as it should really be! I smiled as I realized that I was regaining my sense of humor. I sat on the high stool at the bar for a change. I remembered Basyuni. I wondered where he would be by now. The night hours would not be enough to get to the border before they would discover his disappearance with the car in the morning. He must have chosen a car under repair in the garage, so the officers would not notice it was gone. Would such absence easily escape the notice of Amm Sayyid? He must have delayed reporting it for some time to give Basyuni a chance to cover the longest distance away from the unit. But it was a war and any mistake would result in the poor man being accused of collusion and all kinds of problems with the military police. He must have protected himself, on paper at least. Would Basyuni hide somewhere until security quit looking for him? Would security quit? Why don't I call Fathallah and ask him if he had new information? No. His telephone would be wiretapped and my question would bring upon him problems he didn't need. Why should I give them the chance to seize upon a sentence that might be straightforward and innocent for me but have a different meaning for them? I was still under the authority of Jordanian security, which of course had strong ties with Iraqi security. All this time everybody believed I was in Egypt. Okay, now are you convinced that Iraqi intelligence had made a connection between your meeting Basyuni and his escape? Have James Bond movies twisted your brain? Buthayna, the woman in charge of the logistics of the trip, must have reported the meeting, as would be expected. Besides, it was only natural for Basyuni to have told his fellow unit members that he was going to meet an Egyptian journalist who had a letter for him from his family. Maybe he had also disclosed to Amm Sayyid or to one of his Kurdish friends his intention to escape. His words to me hinted at something like that but I was not paying attention to that at the time. No need to call Fathallah today. All the trouble with the passport in Jordan was quite enough. You are still under the thumb of Jordanian intelligence. One intelligence service is quite enough—I smiled—one here, let alone the one there.

Song of the Falcon
I took out Hilmi Amin's papers. I found a carefully folded sheet with the title: "Song of the Falcon." I started reading:

> Today I finished reading Gorky's collection *The Birth of a Man*, even though I had read it many times before in Egypt. The shrieks of the falcon resounded throughout my apartment in Baghdad, combining the agony of pain, the strength of the will, and the lust

for life and triumph. I went to bed as the falcon hovered in the ceiling of the room, shouting at the snake: if only I could ascend to the sky one last time, I would squeeze an enemy on my wounded chest, making it choke on my blood. Oh, how sweet fighting is!

High up in the mountain a snake had ascended and curled up and began to stare at the sea. Suddenly, in the crevice where it curled, there fell a falcon with a broken chest and feathers stained with blood, emitting a piercing cry, crushing its chest against a rock, in impotent anger. The snake was frightened and crawled backward, but soon realized that the bird was dying. It thought that life in the sky must be so comfortable, judging by the falcon's laments. The snake suggested to the falcon to move to the edge of the cliff and throw itself downward, so that its wings might lift it upward to live for a little while in the air it loved so much.

Gorky said, "The falcon shuddered and with a loud, proud cry, proceeded to the edge, its talons slipping on the slippery rocks. It made it to the edge, spread its wings, inhaled deeply. It looked with its flaming glare, then fell downward. It rolled on the rocks, tumbling down and quickly breaking its wings and losing its feathers. The waves swept it away, washing off its bleeding and, foaming, rushed back to the sea. The sea waves crushed the stones with a melancholic roar. The corpse of the bird was never seen in the vastness of the sea.

"The snake contemplated the death of the bird, its eagerness to fly in the sky. It curled into the shape of a coil and flung itself, falling onto the rocks. But it didn't die."

I said to myself, "The artist has intervened here to give life meaning when he made the waves crash and crush the rocks and the sky shake and roar like a lion singing of a proud bird!

"We sing the praises of the glory of the brave dreamers!

"O falcon! Come and talk to me. We are all alone now: what crossed your mind as you lay dying? Were you afraid?"

The falcon said, "The sky knows nothing except thirst for freedom and light."

I said, "What did you feel as you were flying for the last time? Are those few moments of flight worth a whole life? Didn't you think of a truce, even if that meant being deprived of flying high in the sky?"

The falcon said, "What good is an impotent life? Death is preferable to terrible times. It is a longing for revolution. Dreams shorten distances and transcend the boundaries of time."

I said, "O falcon, don't condemn your lips to impossible silence. Crying would lighten your burden greatly now. We are all alone, together. Even the snake has disappeared. There's no one besides you and me and an old man that I have summoned from the novel by Hemingway who was merciful enough to invent the boy who was taking pity on the old man. Life frequently forgets to give a touch of beauty and warmth."

The falcon said, "We've loved freedom to death!"

I said to the old man, "You and I, what have we reaped? Our adversary is the same: tempests, waves, whales, and bloody sharks, monsters of land and sky."

The old man said, "The snake did not see what the dying falcon saw in that bottomless and endless desolation as Gorky described it. Nor did it find out why those like the falcon are so puzzling to the soul as they die for love of flying in the sky. What do they see so clearly there? People gathered around my skiff, watching the backbone of the huge fish, did not understand why I fought the monsters of the deep."

I said, "Fate defeated you but did not kill you. There's still some time left for you to go back to the sea, just as the falcon did by flying in the sky even if only for a short while."

The old man said, "Who has just come in?"

I looked at him for a long time. Then I heard him saying, "Don't you recognize me? I am Saroyan, companion of your youth. I am the one who made those difficult Latin lessons bearable. It was I who made it possible for you to cope with Aristotle, al-Farabi, Ibn Rushd, and Sheikh Ibn Sina. It was I who helped you when life was not so easy. I demanded that you take the first right step, because if you did, no force on earth could stop you. All you had to do after that was just to live."

I said, "Now I recognize you. You're the one who wrote about America, the virgin. Young Egyptian writers fell madly in love with you. I have read your obituary recently. Why this surprise visit? Do you feel my need for you now?"

Saroyan said, "Just like Hamlet and the ghost, I came to you evoked by Baghdad's night hours. I brought you the words of your old friend, the fisherman who used to grill little fish for you in front of the nets set up to catch quails on the beach of Anfushi in Alexandria. Remember that? He said he sensed your loneliness and boredom and felt that you hadn't lost your faith in and love of those old days, the love you used to tell your friend Salah Hafez enslaved us. Salah would then laugh and say, 'We die and come back to life for our love of life.'"

I said, "That's Sheikh Sam'an. What did he tell you was happening in Egypt right now?"

Saroyan said, "He said that Egypt, in times of trials and tribulations, gives birth to monstrous freaks whom it disavows; as soon as they come of age, they also disavow it. Dislodging these freaks from Egypt's good soil, he said, requires extraordinary effort and it insists on attributing their ancestry to the times of trials and tribulations."

We heard a laugh. The snake slithered out from under the bed. We all turned into birds flying and hovering high up in the room. The snake said sarcastically, "So, this is the pleasure of flying in the sky? Silly birds that have no knowledge of the earth, so they get bored and fly away to the sky, seeking life in a searing emptiness filled with light but no food and no support for the living. Who needs such a boring existence? And, why taunt others? Is it to cover up the madness behind their desires and their uselessness in life? Silly birds! But I will not be deceived by their idle talk again! Now, I know everything. I've seen the sky, flown in it, got to know it quite well! I've even experienced falling but I did not break; rather I got more confident in my own abilities. Let those who are incapable of loving the land live on in deception. But I know the truth and I don't trust their calls. I was created on land and on it I shall live."

We all flew around and hovered. We opened the windows overlooking the Baghdad sky and took off, flapping our wings, happy with freedom and light, as Gorky said, "We sing the praises for the valiant craziness of the brave."

I closed the folder and put it in the bag. I decided it was autobiographical musing that I could read at leisure in Egypt. Maybe they would solve for me the riddles that I haven't been able to comprehend so far: Anhar's disappearance and also his own departure.

I noticed that a new batch of passengers had come in. They were mostly Egyptian, but there were some other Arabs and Iraqis and very few foreigners. Was it time for the Cairo plane? How could that be? I looked at the sign close to the gate and saw that it indicated it to be Alia Airlines flight to Baghdad. I thought to myself: "One man's poison is another man's meat!" Egyptian daily flights between Cairo and Baghdad and also Iraqi Airways flights had been suspended and now Alia has taken their place.

I heard a gentle voice asking me, "Is this seat taken?"

I looked up and saw that it was a pregnant woman, about twenty years old, the same age I got pregnant with Yasir. She looked quite healthy and cheerful.

I said to her, "Please, go ahead," pronouncing my words the Iraqi way. But she didn't notice.

She sat down after she placed her bag on the floor in front of her and looked around. I had goose bumps and began to sweat suddenly, something that happened to me every time I saw a pregnant woman. She asked me, "Are you Egyptian?"

I said, "Yes."

"Are you going to Baghdad?"

426

"No. I am going back to Cairo."

Laughing, she said, "So we are trading places. I am coming from Egypt to give birth in Baghdad in my family's house. My husband works at the Iraqi embassy. There's only a few of us left there after the closing of the embassy."

I asked her, "Are you comfortable in Egypt?"

"Yes. And Egyptians are lovely people."

I said, "Why didn't you give birth in Egypt? You would get the same kind of care."

She said, "As you know, family is something else. This will be my first baby."

We heard the announcement for the Iraqi Airways flight. She got up and took her leave.

I remembered the conversation between me and my Iraqi women neighbors when I decided to travel to Cairo to give birth to Yasir. But things did not go as planned, even though I had packed my bag and booked the ticket. The eve of my departure, which I had eagerly awaited, came and my women neighbors at the Shurta neighborhood, Umm Allawi, Umm Saadi, and Umm Safaa, came to visit. Samia, Mahmoud, Adel, and Nahid also came to bid me a safe trip. Besides packing my bag I had been cooking a lot of food and putting it in the freezer for Hatim all week long. I went to bed totally exhausted, but not really feeling it until my head hit the pillow. Hatim came and embraced me hard, but was surprised when I started giving in to sleep. He let go of me, saying, "I miss you." I told him, "I'll wake up early for you."

I was awakened by light blows to my side. I tried to ignore them and go back to sleep, but the blows kept coming and getting harder. I tossed and turned a few times and got up, went to the bathroom, then back to bed, as the blows kept increasing in frequency and intensity. I went downstairs and paced in the hallway. I sat on the first chair I came across. Then I stood up again but that didn't provide any relief either. The blows were now quite hard and painful.

I held my sides to give them some support. Then I kept whirling around until I almost fell down. Tears flowed down my cheeks. I heard Hatim saying, "What's wrong, darling?"

"I don't know. Hard blows in my back."

"Should I boil some cinnamon for you?"

I laughed, "Again?"

Hatim, whenever he noticed my discomfort in the early months of my pregnancy, boiled some cinnamon sticks for me and insisted I drink it. His sister saw him making a cinnamon drink for me during her visit to us and she screamed at him, "This would expel the embryo!"

He said, "I used to see you women doing that whenever any of you felt a stomach ache."

Hatim took me in his arms and sat me on the bed. The pain increased and he could feel my hot tears on his chest. He got up, put on his clothes, wrapped me in my robe, and took me outside.

Sabah and Shukry heard us going out at two o'clock in the morning. They opened the door and asked us in alarm, "Where are you going? What happened?"

"Nora is in great pain. It seems she's about to give birth."

Sabah said, "No. She's still at the beginning of her eighth month. Wait for me. I'll come with you."

"Thank you. I'll make sure she is all right in the hospital, then I'll come back, God willing. You're pregnant yourself and shouldn't strain yourself."

We left Sabah in a state of sincere anxiety, a state of true tenderness that she surprised me with from time to time.

I went to the hospital. The doctor on call asked me to lie down on a table and started listening to the fetus with her stethoscope, then said, "You'll be admitted to the hospital. This is a case of premature delivery."

I said, "But I am going to Egypt tomorrow."

She said, "Before the morning comes, you'll have a beautiful baby, an Iraqi to boot."

I said, "But a baby in its eighth month doesn't live and is usually weak."

She said, "This is a common mistake. An eighth-month baby has a better chance of survival than a seventh-month baby because it spends more time in the womb."

I asked her in tears, "What should I do now?"

Patting me on the shoulder she said, "You'll have a natural birth. Have no fear about the baby who, God willing, will be a strong healthy child. What did you do today?"

"I had a lot to do: I received a number of guests and packed. Could what I am feeling now be the result of exertion and if I rest the birth would be on time?"

She laughed and said, "You cannot postpone birth. If the baby decides to come, nothing in the world will stop him. Go to the maternity ward. And because this is your first, delivery will take a long time."

She wrote out the admission forms and ordered a wheelchair for me. Hatim accompanied me to my room and whenever I had a contraction, I held onto the back of the bed. At five in the morning another doctor came in and examined me.

She said, "The womb is dialated almost four centimeters. Do you feel any pain?"

"No."

She looked at Hatim and asked him, "Why are you here?"

"I am waiting for my wife."

"Are you a doctor?"

"No. I am a mechanical engineer."

"A mechanic does not assist his wife in giving birth. She still has some time to go. You're not allowed to stay here."

"But she's all by herself."

"That's natural and we're all with her."

Hatim gave in after desperate attempts to get the doctor to let him stay. He went home first to reassure Sabah and Shukry. After a few hours, Sabah arrived carrying a clothes bag for me and the baby. They allowed her to visit for a few minutes after she pleaded with them. The doctor ordered an X-ray for the fetus, and when she examined it she said, "Why the tears? The baby's weight is excellent and he is very normal and poised downward. You are in labor but you still have some time."

Hatim came in the evening, directly from work, without eating anything. He looked exhausted and worried. He told me that he had called my father, who had waited for me at the airport in vain, and reassured him. We both went to the doctor in charge and asked him why I hadn't given birth yet. He said, "It's labor: the womb is open and I cannot discharge you. I don't know when the contractions will increase and when the baby will come out. All we can do is wait."

On the third day, when the first doctor came into the room I asked her to let me go home. She said, "The baby is coming. If you put your feet on the ground, you'll give birth right away. Every hour the baby stays in your womb is good for him. Sleep on your back until contractions come again."

Hatim took me home and prepared the room, providing everything I needed. He said, "I'll give the key to Sabah so she can come to you without your having to get up."

I sat on my bed, not believing that I was back at home. The telephone brought me my mother saying, "Don't be afraid. Hundreds of babies are born every day and you are brave, even though your son is impatient."

My father took the receiver and said, "You cheat at everything, even giving birth? You want to rob us of two months. May God be with you. Listen, it's your mother who is going to be a grandmother. Your father is still too young for that. Listen to the doctors' instructions."

Hatim brought the television set to my room and moved a sofa there and a small table and two chairs.

I said, "Why all this trouble?"

He said, "I want you to feel comfortable and to sit on the sofa to read if you get tired of the bed."

"Are you happy I didn't travel, darling?"

"Of course, I cannot bear the separation. But I wanted you to have mama's help as you give birth. Before, you were complaining that you didn't have enough time to read. Now is your big chance."

I started getting bored after the second day at home. I left the book on the pillow and opened the window to let February's soft sun come to my bed. I had a strong desire to get to the refrigerator to put meat on the grill and have it ready before Hatim came home. But I was afraid. Hatim used his own practical shortcuts. He would marinate the meat in the evening and when he came home he would shove whatever vegetables were on hand in the oven, and make some instant soup. After dinner he would sit next to me to read.

I heard someone knocking on the door and when I looked I saw Fathiya coming into the room carrying a little baby wrapped in a blanket. I cried out, "Who is this?"

"Ali. Abla Sabah gave birth during the night. She wanted to spare you the excitement."

"I heard a great commotion last night. I thought you had guests."

I held the baby's hand and kissed it. Fathiya placed him next to me on the bed so I wouldn't carry him. I asked her, "Why does he look so old?"

She laughed, "Abla says that just before he was born, he lost some weight. Babies change fast. In a week he'll be as beautiful as the moon."

Two days later, Sabah and the children came up to visit me and life went back to normal. Three weeks passed, feeling like three years. My belly was distended and I was as swollen as a balloon, feeling that I was a bomb about to explode. Then my belly curled like a ball and began to creep downward. I felt as if it was going to fall off. I awoke, bored, then went back to sleep after Hatim left. I sat next to the window overlooking the garden. I saw Fathiya picking up the children's toys. I said to her, "Please tell Sabah I want to see her."

Sabah was surprised to see me all dressed up. She asked me, "What's up? Why are you so dressed up?"

I said, "I want to go to the market with you. I am tired of lying down. I'll walk next to you slowly. Bear with me."

"But the doctor has warned you. And, thank God, we've gone a long way into the eighth month. Be patient."

"I am tired."

"Okay, I'll change clothes and call out to you."

I applied light makeup for the first time in a long time and put on a wig as I smiled. I'll ask Sabah to take a picture of me, round as a ball in my present condition. Suddenly a bucket of water gushed between my thighs all at once. I cried out, "Help, Sabah!"

Sabah ran up the stairs shouting, "What happened?"

She was surprised to see the large puddle of water in which I stood. She said, "You're giving birth. Fathiya, get a taxi right away. Where's the baby bag?"

"In the armoire."

"The doctor told you not to put your feet on the ground."

"I only walked three steps. Thank God we didn't go to the market."

We got in the taxi. I was full of shame not knowing how to hide the water gushing out of me. I told the driver, "Please excuse me. Yarmouk Hospital, please."

He said, "God is generous, honored lady. May He grant you safe recovery."

I had never seen an Iraqi driver driving so fast and also so calmly. He took us directly to the maternity ward and checked me in himself. I tried to ask him not to go through all the trouble, but he insisted.

The doctor examined me. The she asked me, "How long between contractions?"

"There are no contractions and I don't feel anything."

She led me into a room and said, "When contractions begin, tell the nurse."

Sabah sat with me. Two hours later I began to feel intense pain. They took me to an operating room alone. I cried, "Don't leave me, Sabah!"

The nurse said, "It's forbidden. No one is allowed to come in here."

I saw a woman in her fifties stretched out on the next table. The nurse whispered in my ear, "Umm Ali. She will be signing papers for a caesarean section. She'll be moved to a surgery room now. She is fifty-four and this will be her fourteenth birth, all natural up till now."

I looked at her after the nurse left. I saw her lying down calmly, her gray braids stretching on her body like a snake slithering coquettishly and her long white galabiya rolled up revealing two very white legs contrasting with her wheat-colored face covered with brown spots. She was staring at the ceiling murmuring a soft prayer of which I could only distinctly hear, "Ya Ali." The nurse came in holding a sheet of paper and said to her, "Your son has signed the papers. This is the last baby, Umm Ali. Did you hear me?"

"It's enough. Thank God."

The nurse looked at me, saying, "You want a boy, of course."

"No. A girl."

She said in alarm, "A girl? Umm Nisrin, whom we've just admitted, was told by her husband that she would be divorced if she had a fourth daughter. Umm Sherweet is also under the threat of divorce. Umm Mahmoud has three boys and wants a fourth one. You are the only woman in this hospital who wants a girl."

A very beautiful doctor came into the room, wearing surgical gloves. She inserted her hand to examine my cervix as she smiled. Then she asked me, "What would you like?"

"A girl."

She repeated in alarm, "A girl. Why?"

"You're a girl. Aren't you?"

"Delivery, right away."

I cried out, "What did you do?"

She paid no attention to me and left together with the nurse. A strange quiet prevailed. Then I heard Umm Ali shouting, "Ya Ali! Help me! Ya Ali!"

She shrieked in a high, shrill voice. And I saw a dry baby rushing out between her thighs, as she bent forward and clung to it with her palm, her body not helping as the baby tried to get loose onto the floor. The nurses and the doctors came in running. One of them miraculously caught the baby. The room was filled with merry shouts: "Umm Ali had a natural birth!" I heard the sounds of scissors and feet coming and going. Then I saw a beautiful baby swaddled in white cloth like a little mummy. My tears flowed.

I heard a nurse saying, "She's Egyptian. See how she has contractions like in the movies!"

The room became quiet again after everybody left. I began to feel anew the painful blows coming from my lower back. I called out to the doctor but no one came. Then after a while the doctor came in and began to pat my head calmly. I said, "Any chance of delivery, soon?"

"In a few minutes. It will come soon."

She left me then came back with a nurse pushing a gurney on which a woman of about thirty was lying down, writhing hard and trying to muffle her groans. They stopped in front of me. The doctor got busy delivering the baby. The woman's screams got louder. I myself had difficulty breathing and my tears flowed profusely down my cheeks.

The doctor ordered the woman, "Push. You're strangling him. Push."

I heard a baby crying. The woman asked, "A boy? Right?"

"No. A girl."

Silence prevailed again. I saw the woman's face covered with tears. A nurse brought the baby to the woman after taking her outside to show the father. She said, "Her father named her 'Kafi,' Umm Sherweet."

"Did he say 'divorce'?"

"No."

"Thank God."

My contractions came faster and were more painful. I let out a scream that must have scared all creation and gradually lost consciousness but soon came to with piercing pains tossing me back and forth like a racquetball. I waited for the doctor to do something, but she just said, "Push. Push now."

I felt a tremendous release and calm. The doctor said, "You have a frizzy-haired boy."

"Is he all right?"

"Perfectly so. A true Iraqi boy, quite strong. Was he not conceived on Iraqi soil?"

I smiled and said, "Yes."

I tried to sit up to see him, but I couldn't. She patted my hand, saying, "I'll give him to you right away."

I lay back, giving in to the sounds and voices around me, feeling that I was on top of a wave carrying me to an endless horizon. I wished to sleep and let the wave take me wherever it wanted to, but it forced me to wake up. I longed to see my son. I once again tried to sit up, but my attempt was feeble. Then I saw the nurse bringing my son to me, a brown boy with a forehead covered with smooth thick black hair. I embraced him and kissed his head and lay down again. I realized they were washing me with water. I felt pain whenever they touched my exhausted body. The nurse pushed the gurney outside. In my room I found Sabah picking up my boy from another nurse. I said as I laughed, "He undid the baby blanket. He knows he is Egyptian."

They bound his body in a white cloth, tied each arm to a leg, and rewrapped his body, turning the swaddling cloth into something like a tube from which only his head appeared.

My life changed when Yasir arrived. I was constantly reminded of my being a mother and of his right to a normal life. I had wanted to work in Beirut to follow closely what was happening there. I realized that the experience of working with the Palestinian resistance was a must for anyone who wanted to live a life like that. I told my husband and he said, "Don't worry about anything. I, together with your mother, will look after Yasir until you come back safely."

His ready acceptance pushed me to confront the question, "Doesn't Hatim have the right to live with a conventional wife and to secure for his son a mother who would watch over his schooling, even if she were a journalist?" I went back with both of them to Egypt. I didn't know if that was the right decision or not, but it has changed my way of life forever.

I chose to be a mother first and then a journalist. I gave birth to Haytham one year after going back to Cairo. But am I really a mother first? I left my son in the care of his grandmother and a wet nurse. My breasts have almost run dry in order to attend a conference. But it was Baghdad, calling after a year and a half of absence. And it was in a state of war. What mattered now was for this crazy trip to end well. I needed to sleep. If only I could, just for one hour, O God! Why don't I go to the bathroom, empty my breasts, give myself a sponge bath? I might fall asleep or at least feel clean. I got up heavily, trying to do what I had been doing for a whole week. I went behind a small and narrow door, hearing the steps of women coming in and going out with their children. I could hear them cleansing the children or taking them into the toilet stalls, calmly cajoling them. Where did we get all this patience to look after our children? It is the child who is the dictator and not the husband. No other creature besides us mothers would understand that. My body began to feel refreshed. The scent of the fragrant cream soothed me some more.

A family, all clad in black, came into the lounge. It was an Egyptian mother holding three children, walking in staggering steps. I had seen a similar scene before, and in fact I was deeply involved in it.

Hatim told me, "I am going to tell you a sad bit of news. Today at the factory, Adel had a heart attack and we took him to intensive care at Medical City Hospital. He will be in critical condition until tomorrow. If he survives until then, he'll live. We should go to Nahid at home. She needs you. Please get Yasir ready quickly."

I said, "This is shocking! Adel is still in his early thirties. How did that happen? True, he is overweight but his face speaks volumes of health and vitality. Why the heart? Does he have a family history of heart disease?"

436

He said, "The real problem is that Adel is profligate and, as you know, he likes to live as if there is no tomorrow."

"I know he comes from a well-off family."

"He owns some agricultural property, but what good is that now? He should've put it to good use rather than travel so far from home to find a better life."

Yasir pulled me by the hand as he sang. I was not in the mood to play with him. He loved to visit Adel's house. We found Nahid in a terrible condition. She couldn't stay by her husband's side in the hospital. Hatim promised her to stop at the hospital and call her from there and give her the latest doctor's reports. She agreed, nodding in resignation, and got up to prepare food for Yasir and the girls.

I said, "Let me do that, Nahid. This is not the right time for you to be working."

"Aren't they going to have supper? They have to eat."

We went to the hospital. They would not let us go in. We called Nahid and told her that he said hello but that he was not supposed to move until the following day at noon.

The crisis was over and Adel survived, feeling revived. He ignored doctors' orders completely even though they told him clearly that a heart attack at such a young age was worse and more dangerous than if an older person suffered it, because a young person's strong body would trick him to move about normally, taxing his heart, and because the arteries would be so strong they wouldn't let the blood through if a clot blocked them. Adel's illness brought us closer to his family and we accompanied them on picnics to Zora Park and the bank of the Tigris.

Hatim called me at home as soon as I went inside and, without any preliminaries, said, "Adel has died. Leave Yasir with the neighbors and go to Nahid at home until I arrive."

I found all the friends surrounding Nahid. I hugged her while tears flowed down our cheeks. She kept asking us, "What am I going to do?"

She called her daughters, one after the other, and her baby son, who had begun to run and stumble behind his older sisters. "What am I going to do?"

We tried to calm her, but we didn't know how. We remained silent until the men came into the living room.

They told her, "We have taken care of all the preparations concerning the shroud. Right now, he is in refrigeration until we finish the shipping procedures, get the necessary papers, and book a flight."

Hatim said, "Tomorrow, Nora, you will go to the hospital and get the forms listed here, because that can only be done in the morning. Then you will go to the Egyptian embassy, I mean to the chargé d'affaires, and get the papers signed also. From there you will go to the passport department in Karrada. If you can, please also go to the Iraqi Airways office or get in touch with Engineer Ali to find out if he can expedite travel. It is not easy."

Mahmoud Isam said, "I will finish the procedures of end of service at the factory and get the pay and find out if he had accumulated vacation days or shares in profits or any compensation for the children."

Nahid said, "My dear Adel has turned into figures and compensations. O my love!"

Hatim said, "Your sorrow over him will never end. But let's first make sure you all get back safely to Egypt."

We spent a whole week chasing the paperwork in the morning and taking our children and going to Nahid in the afternoon. Nahid surrendered herself to her women friends, letting them take care of the kitchen. She said, "Adel has filled the freezer with meat and chicken. Take everything out and distribute it to the neighbors."

No airline would agree to transport the body. I was so surprised by that refusal. Engineer Ali said to me, "The pilot must agree. I will try with the Dutch plane coming at the end of the week."

We no longer knew who was responsible for the delays. Was it the company management or the central bank, which every day demanded new forms and papers, or the airline and freight companies? Nahid tried as much as possible to lighten the amount of items to be shipped, but it was to little avail. She told us, "Each of you take what you want."

We cried. Nahid clung to the electrical appliances, saying she would take them all, even if shipping cost more than double their price, because Adel was happy to buy them. The house was almost empty except for things necessary for her and the children for the few remaining days. Relief finally came. Engineer Ali was able to arrange for the body to be shipped on a plane going to Cairo via Cyprus, and booked tickets for the family on a plane going via Damascus.

Nahid asked him, "Will I arrive with him?"

"No, actually you will arrive a few hours earlier. Sorry, you will have to wait for him at Cairo airport."

"What matters is to attend the burial," she said.

On the way home, Hatim told me that Nahid would not attend the burial because her trip would take two days, and he would arrive before them, but that they agreed not to tell her or else she would refuse to take the trip. Nobody knew when another pilot would agree to transport the body. This information created a transparent barrier between me and Nahid. So I kept silent until it was time for them to leave. We stood at the gate bidding her and her children goodbye in a somber funeral-like group. We gathered outside the airport gate in circles that made us look like the flock of black ravens that I had seen from the window of my country house one morning. We suddenly heard shrill loud cries. I opened the balcony and saw more than a hundred ravens landing in circles while shrieking, then flying up together, fluttering their wings. At the same time lines of ravens stood in front of a dead raven. After several times of flying up and landing, they shrieked in unison, then descended upon the body, carried it off, and disappeared. I remembered that it was the raven that gave Cain the idea of burying the corpse of his brother Abel. I haven't heard of another bird having a funeral for one of its kind.

Nahid said goodbye to us, then fell silent and dried her tears even though we were all crying. She had suddenly turned into a

439

typical peasant woman, one of those widows I've often met, devoting their whole lives to raising their children, stern and firm and strong, shedding many of life's little details and in the process coming to look alike, with the same austere features. I had always thought that such women acquired such features with the passage of time as they faced problems of pensions, family courts, and the complexities of inheritance, all on top of raising their children alone. Mahmoud al-Saadani's famous dictum, "as dizzy as a widow in Egypt," came to my mind. Furrows of sadness, despair, and loneliness suddenly appeared to occupy her face as if she had been born a widow. I accompanied her to the furthest point I could go at the airport with the help of my colleague Imad al-Bazzaz. We said our goodbyes in the hope that we would meet again soon in Cairo. When I came back to the lounge most families had left. Hatim took me to another building. I asked him, "Where to?"

In a chagrined tone he said, "I want to make sure everything is okay with Adel's own trip."

We went into the office of the dispatcher. He looked at the papers and said, "No. Unfortunately the pilot took eleven bodies. Two others, one of whom is this name, couldn't make it."

We both cried at the same time: "Where is he? What should we do now?"

The dispatcher said, "I am sorry. We are doing our best with an Austrian pilot who will fly out tomorrow. There's also another plane from Italy which had come earlier and taken some bodies. It will come in the evening of the day after tomorrow and then depart right away."

I said, "Do you have such a big problem with Egyptian corpses?"

The dispatcher said, "In Iraq now there are five million Egyptians and nobody is immortal. If each Cairo-bound plane carried the body that arrived, there would be no problem. That explains why the bodies travel in groups."

The door opened and a man in his fifties came in. He moved around with the confidence of a high-ranking official. The dispatcher said as he pointed to Hatim, "The engineer wants to make sure that one of the two remaining bodies would travel."

Looking at the papers, the official said, "We have the same interest. I'll lean on the very next pilot."

Hatim said, "He's a young man. The head of a family that has already left today."

The official said, "Death is death and I know more than anyone else what dying away from home means. Get in touch with me tomorrow after three in the afternoon. I'll have good news for you."

We left the office, our tears now completely gone and our minds incapable of thinking any further. I said, "Does that mean that Nahid would arrive before her husband?"

"Maybe she'd arrive exactly at the same time, if Adel takes tomorrow evening's flight, or she might arrive before him if he takes the noon flight because it is also not a direct flight."

My eyes welled up with tears at the memory. I had read in an Egyptian newspaper that Iraq was sending back to Egypt corpses of Egyptians that had been shot in mysterious killings and that Cairo airport was receiving dozens of corpses. I realized that the sight of multiple funerals contributed to that particular narrative. When I explained what I had experienced in the case of Adel, no one believed me. They would say things like, "You're only saying so because you love the Iraqis." Then some people said they were Egyptian soldiers taking part in the war against Iran. One Iraqi officer had told me, "There are no Egyptians in the army. We have a brigade of Arab forces directly under the national leadership, but they are not permitted to take part in the war. There are Egyptians in logistical support: equipment and truck drivers, or people paving roads and the like." I remembered Basyuni and I sighed deeply at the painful memory.

I remembered Anhar's notebook that had come into my hands for no reason except perhaps that our paths crossed with that story that was born under exceptional circumstances. I pulled the notebook out of my bag to continue reading. I had stopped at her mother's unfortunate marriage circumstances and Anhar's insistence on not accepting an unjust fate similar to her mother's and her pledge not to repeat her tragedy.

I turned the pages quickly as images passed in front of my eyes as if they were a long reel of our lives. Anhar did not leave any of the events of our lives without commenting on them. I wanted to ask her, "Why did you go away? I needed you just as you needed me. We were not competitors in anything—work, love, or whatever." Who knew how much she carried in her heart? All this sorrow, Anhar?

My hand stopped at a page on which was written "Erbil." My eyes passed over the words until I got to that night on which I saw Hilmi Amin entering her room at that new hotel that had not offi-cially opened yet and in which we were the only guests. She wrote:

I was surprised that someone was knocking on my door. I thought it was Nora, needing something or another, for she had suddenly had a fever today. I asked, "Who is it?" But there was no answer. I opened the door and was surprised to see Hilmi before me. Before I could say anything he had come into the room and closed the door behind him. I felt embarrassed for being alone with him behind closed doors. I feared that some other guest in the hotel might find out. I was more afraid that Nora might realize what was going on. I took pains to hide our relationship from her, especially after I realized her profound closeness to his family, since I did not want to place her conscience in an awkward position. He didn't know that every-thing in Iraq was under surveillance and that this move of his would be held against me and my future. I said to myself, "We're together alone in the office most of the time, so what's the difference?" But we are in the bedroom. He had sat on a chair in front of the bed and kept looking at me without saying anything. When the silence grew longer, he said as he pointed to his thigh, "Come here."

I went without thinking. We had exchanged a few quick kisses before. He put his arms around me and buried his head in my chest.

I didn't say anything as I felt his breaths moving upwards and touching my ear. A tremor ran through my body. I got up.

"You'll be uncomfortable like this. Would you like to drink something? There's cold water. There's milk."

He held my hand without a word and pulled me onto the bed without any resistance on my part. Our feelings escalated at a speed that left me dazed. His hands extended, reached, and imparted heat to all the heretofore inert inlets into my being, then doing it again with a persistence that kept escalating and pushing my desire to explode even as his hands massaged my body, pulling my mind into an endless zone of imbalance. I almost demanded that he enter me, but I was too shy. I forgot I was a virgin and that losing my virginity would mean being deprived of marriage all my life long. I began to ready myself to receive him with an insane longing that I had never felt before in my life. He was pressing on my lower mouth and moving his palm on it at such a fast speed that I thought sparks were coming out of it and that a fire had started in my clothes, which I had not taken off. Suddenly my body contracted hard, then it relaxed and felt like a fan bringing a cooling breeze on a very hot night. I heard a hissing-like sound demanding more ecstasy. I opened my eyes and saw two very large eyes strangely trained on me. The pained looks in the eyes pierced my heart like arrows and began to awaken my absent mind. But they got there too late. My body had spread its sails and raced into an internal space. It opened for me the gates of paradise and hell in one fell swoop and began to deliver what delight it had, lighting the room with phosphorescent stars. Then it subsided while his hand still held my lower mouth tightly. Then I felt his palm relax and come out from between my thighs. Sleep started caressing me without permission. I longed for a kiss from Hilmi but I couldn't raise my head to kiss him. I saw him from a distance sneaking out of the room on tiptoes until he disappeared in the dark.

In the morning I stumbled along as I walked between him and Nora, preoccupied with what had happened at night. My mind lost its ability to give orders or coordinate the parts of my body. It gave a signal to my right foot to move to the right, so I turned to the right. Then it gave my left foot a signal to move forward, but it got twisted around my other leg and I found myself tumbling onto the sidewalk. Nora extended her hand to help me up. I saw in her eyes a question which I ignored for the time being. Then my mind started again: what will the next step be? If we could control our bodies yesterday, would we be able to control them tomorrow? I felt weak. I felt I was going to be the one demanding that he go all the way. At midnight he sneaked in in the dark. We both jumped into bed without thinking. We each started feeling each other's bodies, exploring. He didn't waste time and grabbed my breasts, squeezing them as he wound the sheet around his body. I extended my hand to remove the sheet but he pushed my hand away. I pulled the sheet again but he held my hand so hard it hurt. He turned off the light and let his hand sneak to my thighs and massage them until all my organs came to attention. He said, "How beautiful you are!"

I felt my ears catching on fire and turned my face to the other side. He said, "Are you bashful?"

"I am a virgin. Don't you know virgins' shyness? Please keep mine intact."

"I forgot it a long time ago. I won't let you down."

He got up and squatted next to me. He began to fondle my body which was all open in front of him, burying his face in my chest, licking me like a cat. I found myself having an orgasm under his palm again.

Our relationship changed completely. We could no longer stop fondling each other's bodies. But I noticed how he loved the dark and how he hid his body the whole time. I didn't ask. I sometimes felt that he was shyer than me, so I didn't ask him to give me more than he already had. And he gave me to excess. I enjoyed a sexual pleasure that was beyond my ability to resist, and that erased from my mind all questions about the future. I came to know what it meant to love an old, generous man who spoiled me no end and

444

who took care of my body's needs with a patience that only added to my love for him every day. I asked myself one day: can a young man love me as Hilmi does? Or give me the tender affection that Hilmi gives me? Impossible! A young man pursues his desire and enthusiasm quickly. If such a young man remembered me in that pursuit, that would be nice. That's what my married women friends told me anyway.

I closed the notebook and listened to a call that I thought was from Egypt Air, even though the time for its plane's takeoff had not come yet. I went to the counter where I found a Jordanian woman with a white complexion. I asked her whether she had just made an announcement about the Egyptian flight to Cairo. She said, "Yes. There is a two-hour delay."

I said, "O God, the whole world is intent on tormenting me today!"

She said, "Pray to God that the delay would not be longer."

I said, "You're absolutely right!"

My eyes got glued to the board with its many numbers and various cities. I saw the numbers changing, indicating that a Lufthansa flight was scheduled to take off for Germany in half an hour. A great number of passengers came into the gate area, most of them Palestinian. Then quiet prevailed a short while later. I remembered Anhar. What else will you reveal to me, my beautiful friend? And why me? Who are we? Mere stories walking on two feet! Involuntary birth, involuntary death, and in the middle a cruel game that life plays with us! I picked up the notebook and once again I began to turn the pages. A sentence saying, "I got more depressed," caught my eyes. I started reading again.

I could no longer bear what was happening between us. It got so hard I feared being alone with him. I tried to change my work schedule, to work at the Agency in the evening and go to the *al-Zahra* office in the morning when Nora or Abu Ghayib would be there. My boss at work said that was okay with him that week until Zabiya came back from her wedding leave, and after that we would wait and see. Hilmi did not like the change, saying to me angrily, "The bureau circumstances need you to be there in the evening shift and not in the morning. I cannot change Nora's schedule since she is a wife. Besides I need her to make the rounds in the morning, especially al-Khalsa village."

I said, "These are my work circumstances."

I didn't give him a chance to be alone with me. He got angry and flew into a rage at the least provocation. My body had gotten extremely tired of what was happening between us. The ecstasy resulting from the element of surprise was gone. My body wanted the natural, normal release. The long time we spent in bed turned into an onerous burden. I would climax quickly and then wait for our encounter to end, but it would not end. With time I learned to postpone my climax as I noticed that my tolerance increased as long as I hadn't reached my climax, but I had little tolerance after that. My body needed rest and sleep, while Hilmi wanted to stay awake. I came to fear being close to him and the more desire I had, the more pain I felt until my body betrayed me suddenly and I gave in.

He told Nora, "Today the rounds are all yours. I will take Anhar with me to an appointment at the Ministry of Industry."

As soon as Nora left, I found him confronting me, "What's the matter with you?"

I said as tears flowed down my cheeks, "I am tired."

He said, "Why? We are on an island in the midst of a tumultuous sea. It is much better than our wildest dreams. What more do you want?"

I cried. "I don't know. I am just tired. We've got to stop right away."

He took me into his bosom and began to squeeze me hard, "I missed you."

He pulled me inside, kissing my face and neck. I found him on top of me. Once again, preliminaries that led nowhere, for me. His hand reached between my thighs. I held on to the back of the bed and kept pressing it, gritting my teeth as his hand's movements got faster and his body writhed next to me. My body exploded with its rising crescendo. Then it came to a standstill and his hands kept moving while his whole body was lying on top of my chest, writhing ceaselessly.

I cried out, "Enough! Enough!"

He came to and said, "What happened?"

"I can't. My body can't. Why don't you . . . ?"

"Why don't I what?"

He sat up next to me, "You want a complete relationship?"

"Yes."

"But you're a virgin."

"So be it."

"You know that I . . . that my body . . . that my long imprisonment has affected my . . . that . . . that . . ."

"It is not a matter of virginity. My friend's fiancé takes her from behind."

"Please forgive me. My health conditions make it impossible and I wouldn't do that."

"What should I do?"

"Bear with me for some time."

I cried. He brought me a glass of tea and took me to the office. He said, "Please don't mix your work with me with our private relationship. You are free to stay with me until I recover completely. You know I was imprisoned for a long time and I was tortured."

I said, "I love you more than you imagine, but I don't understand."

He said, "You're too young to understand what ails a man my age. Your life is still ahead of you, while mine is heading for the end. Please don't leave me. Light will disappear from my life if you do. Can I call you Anwar, 'Lights,' Khayun, rather than Anhar Khayun?"

I smiled. He got up and kissed me then said to me, "Go now. We'll talk about it calmly tomorrow."

I couldn't get out of the trap I found myself caught in. I dreamed one night that I was lying stretched out in a hole in the ground, my legs wide apart as they would be on Hilmi's bed and my head in a deeper hole. There were many ravens standing next to my head, pecking at it every time I tried to raise it. When I moved my head back, my neck hurt very much and I felt as if I were going to die. Then some ravens alighted on my thighs and began to peck me as they calmly crept closer between my thighs. I screamed. I found myself on my bed. I cried and decided never to go back to the office. In the morning I went to the agency at my usual time and refused to receive any telephone calls from outside the office. On the following day Nora called me. I said my mother was sick and that was partially true, because it was my brother who took my mother to the doctor's office. I told Nora to apologize to Abu Mervat and to get me a two-day sick leave. I traveled to Mosul and there I sat at a café on the hill in the woods. I remembered the first time I met Hilmi. Why do I love him so much? Why all that mystery he surrounds himself with? My friend Maysa tells me he is exploiting me. I reject that completely but I can't stand it any more. I've got to find a solution. I searched in the midst of the trees, in the paths where we had walked and disappeared, where we had talked a lot about ourselves. I knew back then that he had entered my heart, but I also knew there were still many barriers between us. I imagined that he had caught up with me here in Mosul and said to me, as they did in the movies: "I was sure I'd find you here." "How did you know?" "Don't cry and don't waste time. Come with me."

But I was not in an Arabic or a Kurdish movie. I am living in a reality that I couldn't accept any more. One evening he found me standing in front of the office door. He took me by the hand and accompanied me inside and said to me without any preliminaries, "I know I have been unfair to you. But before I tell you why I am doing that, you must know what I am suffering from exactly. I didn't promise Fayza anything. It's just a matter of honor. The honor of being responsible for the woman who has been taking care of me and my daughters after their mother died."

"But she hasn't previously agreed to marr . . ."

"Please, don't interrupt me. Let me tell you first what I feel and what is tearing me apart. Fayza was like a tender butterfly who was so much in love with her lover that when he died, she couldn't see anyone else. Time stole and captured her. Believe me. Her self-image and the image she had created for herself in front of people stood as a barrier between her and going back. It was not faithfulness as much as weakness. That's something you won't understand, because you're still young. You don't think of death or old age. Faithfulness has a much deeper meaning than fear of marrying another, for when love has united two parties that makes the other external to them both. She is well-educated and sufficiently mature to understand that, and to understand that she would never forget her first love ever, even if she married another man. She is now about forty and I am her brother-in-law. I have been forbidden to her until recently. It would be difficult for her to look at me in that special way that would spark love. But, all of a sudden, she has found herself taking care of my clothes, my food, and my daughters. There is between us, right now, a young girl who has known no other mother and who calls her 'mommy' and calls me 'daddy.' It is hard to snatch her away from her, for neither of them has known any other mother or daughter. They are now and will remain forever, together. I don't know if she loves me just as I don't know if I love her."

"What? Love her? How about me?"

"Please let me finish. The cost of what I am saying is too much for me and I am an old man. My strength is waning just like my days."

"I am sorry."

"I was saying, if Fayza meets a man now, she will have to choose between him and Rana because it doesn't make sense for her, or so I imagine, to take Rana to him when she is not biologically her daughter or to leave her to me to give her another mother and introduce her to the experience of loss a third time, even if she doesn't remember her own mother. Fayza and I are victims of fate. We did not choose our present situation, believe me. And perhaps Fayza doesn't want me, but it's a duty. She also wants me to save her. Do you know that she got an unpaid leave from the exhibitions authority where she worked, without consulting me? Suddenly she found herself giving up her salary, which was more than she needs, and living on her late husband's pension. All I can do now is to take Nora with me to buy her a gift of gold from Suq al-Nahr or to buy certificates of deposit in her name and make the girls give them to her on her birthday. All of that of course amounts to measly sums that don't compensate her for the loss of her regular monthly salary. Please dry your tears so I can finish what I have to say."

"Okay."

"Together we, she and I, are bound to one wheel of life from which we cannot free ourselves. Many have told me to marry her, even my own daughters. But I told them all that I couldn't, because my wife is still alive within me. She understands that. But, and the truth must be said, immediately before you appeared in my life, I had begun to give the matter some serious thought and perhaps to ask her, after Rana became two years old, to marry me. This way she would be free to refuse my proposal and Rana would no longer be in such dire need of her."

He sighed and added: "But I was surprised to find myself falling in love. I resisted at the beginning, because you're young and beautiful while I am at this age and my daughter Mimi is about to finish college and she is almost the same age as you. Please wipe your tears. I cannot bear to look at you crying."

"Then what? What made you change your mind? What made you love me this love that you've just made forbidden? If only you were married to another woman! If only you loved your wife! If only you were a miser or a drunkard or both! If only you were anything other than what you're telling me now! You've killed me without showing me any mercy!"

450

"You. Your youth. That challenge that your body imposes on my soul. That vigorous vitality that you have without knowing it. You're like the sky that doesn't know how vast it is, the sea that doesn't know how deep it is, the sweet orange that cannot savor its own taste or realize how much it quenches the thirst of one who eats it, the nectar of the flowers, like this wanton nature that plays with our hearts and our fates without knowing what it is doing to us. I am going back to what I started telling you at the beginning! I know I have not been fair to you. I know that you have the right to have me. But, until this moment, I cannot make a decision except to love you. And whether you leave me or stay with me, I'll go on loving you. My consolation will be that I, at the end of my life, have found the love I have been seeking. I know that many people will imagine that I am chasing a young body to give my body a renewed sexual drive, but you are the first to know that that is the most awkward part of it, that it does not give me strength. On the contrary, it has posed for me a challenge I cannot handle even though I have been with other women. I do not deny that. I see Mimi when I come near you. I am overtaken by fear that I am not permitted to touch you. I wish I were a heretic or the kind of person who can exploit others, then I would be able to accept a complete relationship with you as you sometimes push me to do. I cannot do that because you are my beloved, you are my daughter, and I will not approve of a bridegroom for my daughter who would die in a few years, leaving her in the prime vitality of her life or turning into a tottering old man before you are thirty."

I screamed, "Enough, enough! What do you want from me? You don't love me. You are a devil, just a devil. You are a Humbaba! You are Gilgamesh's ghoul Humbaba himself! What do you want to say? That you cannot marry me and hurt that poor woman who is raising your daughters for you and you cannot marry her because you don't love her, but love me, but you don't let her live her life, but dump your daughters on her? Are you saying that you cannot marry me because you are on your way to the grave and I am on my way to live and because this body of mine is too much for you? What can you do? Just to love me? Okay. I accept. I agree that you can love me as much as you do, but you'll never touch me. Is this clear? Do you understand? As for this heart of mine, I'll tear it to pieces if it even glances at you."

He said, "Is that all you understood of what I said? Is it really?"

My screams got louder as I said, "You wanted me to work with you, so be it with these conditions. If you want me to disappear from your life, I will do it. You choose now what you want."

"I want you to stay with me. I'll never talk to you about love again. Please, calm down; the neighbors will hear us."

He extended his hand and embraced me. He started patting my hair on that night like no other night. His lips looked for my lips and he gave me a long kiss. I felt heat on my face. I opened my eyes and saw tears washing both our faces. I cried out, "No, no," and ran out. I walked on Abu Nuwas street until I got tired. I didn't know where to go. Should I go back to him and force him to take the only right step: to be together? Should I go home and to my work and leave him forever? In the morning I went back to work and then to him and to my life exactly like before, knowing deep down that there will come a day when I will not go back.

I was tired and unable to move. My chest felt heavy and hard. I went to the bathroom before my breasts decided to unload, dragging my feet listlessly, preoccupied with Anhar Khayun. If only I could submerge my head under water until I feel awake again! But why do I want to wake up? Why don't I give in to sleep? Washing my hair might give me a cold. I washed the towel in the sink, refreshing its fabric. Then I went to the small stall with my equipment. The attendant asked me, "Do you need help? You look as if you haven't slept in days."

I said, "Thank you. This is exactly what happened. I haven't slept in days."

I finished my business and left the stall. The attendant said, "Maybe it's better to leave the towel on the top of the dryer. You'll need it on the plane."

"It is a very good idea, even though the remaining time is not that long. But only God knows. Thank you."

"We're all women and we understand our problems. God willing, you'll go back safely to your baby."

I said to myself: our problems come from our governments, not our people. I sat down feeling unexpectedly alert. A group of foreign travelers came and some members of the group sat beside me. They were elderly Americans. I wondered what tempted them to visit Jordan. A stout white woman asked me, "Are you Jordanian?"

I said, "I am an Egyptian journalist."

She said, "Oh, from Sadat's country. You love him, don't you? He's the champion of peace."

I said, "No."

She was taken aback and said, "You don't like Sadat? Why?"

Suddenly my internal energy that I thought had crumbled a few hours ago came back. I said, "It's difficult to make peace with a thief that has entered your house, occupied a room in it, and said to you: 'Write a peace treaty with me.' The thief has to get out of your house first, then if you agree to talk to him after he gets out, that's a different story."

Her face turned completely pale and she said, as members of her group began to follow our conversation, "You want to expel Israel? That's impossible."

The man sitting next to her said, "What Sadat did is real magic! The whole region will change completely after peace."

I realized what I got myself into. I said to myself, "You want to change the minds of elderly Americans who don't know whether Egypt is in Asia or Australia? End this discussion before you get a headache and before they accuse you of being a fanatic or an anti-Semite."

I said, getting really exhausted, "It is a complicated subject. Sadat is not a popular hero for us. There is disagreement about the Camp David agreement and I believe that the change in the region is not in the Arabs' favor, by any means. Israel is occupying part of

Syria, part of Jordan, and another part of Lebanon. Getting Egypt out of the war now does not mean the end of the conflict."

I nodded as I made a faint attempt at a smile and started reading a paper that I suddenly saw on the seat in front of me without understanding a single line of what I was reading. I sensed that they were moving shortly after a call to go to the gate. They left, waving goodbye to me, but still visibly shocked at what I said. They stood in line with their athletic shoes and brightly colored clothes, their short hair, awkwardly overweight bodies, and the heavy burden of their years.

The television was rebroadcasting news of the battles in Iraq and Sadat was still on my mind. I hated him from the very beginning in appearance and substance. After Gamal Abdel Nasser with his irresistible charisma and overpowering popularity, Sadat appeared with his ugly face and his pretentiousness. I never believed him.

I was telling Hilmi Amin that whenever I saw Sadat with one of the new sheikhs who had recently become popular in Egypt, I would turn off the sound and watch wonderful comic scenes.

He said, "That's true. I would like you, whenever you analyze any of his positions, not to forget the trickster side in his personality, and also the actor aspect. Why did he invite the shah of Iran to come to Egypt?"

I said, "I don't know. Perhaps to do America a favor and to declare his loyalty. Or perhaps because he is an exhibitionist and a show-off, surrounding himself with kings and the nobility that he lacks in his own lineage. If he were proud of coming out of a modest class like Gamal Abdel Nasser, he wouldn't have done that."

He said, "No. It is because of the shah's wealth. He is the richest man in the world and he is providing for him, in Egypt, a secure life of luxury, making him feel that he is still a king. Then he begins to convince him to spend money to help him get his throne back and get from him billions of pounds under the pretext of funding a coup against Khomeini."

I burst out laughing. Hilmi Amin said, "This is not a joke. Your analysis of a situation should be through reading characters in motion. Simply speaking, Sadat wants money. The shah with his wealth is an easy prey."

I said, "The whole region is afraid of Iran exporting its revolution. Saudi Arabia, Egypt, and Iraq are afraid. The shah who played the role of America's policeman in the region was easier to take than Khomeini."

He said, "Any imbalance in the region will have repercussions on the balance of power. The region will not achieve stability without this balance. When America lost Iran, it threw its full weight into Afghanistan, on the Soviet borders. The Soviets will not accept that because these are their borders and they have strong, direct relations with the cities of Soviet Asia, close to the borders. America is far away, separated by an ocean. That is why the conflict in Afghanistan will be violent and there will be more weakening of the left in Egypt and the Arab region, so that the Soviet Union would not have its old influence in the region and so that the whole region would turn to a market economy and all socialist gains would collapse: the huge factories owned by the state, iron and steel, textiles, and everything that has anything to do with that industry and the workers because they are, of necessity, amenable to being organized and educated. All of that would be just for the region to once again be a mere market for their goods."

I felt hungry and cold, despite the heavy coat that my mother had given me. I am still your child, mother. What should I eat? Roast duck? A cheese sandwich and some tea, if possible. I reached in my handbag looking for any money that I had left and began to read the price list. I gave some money to the waiter. I still had enough for another order. They should have provided me with meals, because it was they who delayed me from my flight. But I didn't want any conversation with them. As a matter of fact, I didn't want to see them at all. The shift of that officer who brought me to this place might be over and I might have to deal with some crazy officer who wants to start the whole story all over again. Let me stay here in hiding until the plane arrives safely. And whoever comes again to this country deserves what happens to them. A ball came rolling toward me. I looked up and saw a beautiful child coming to retrieve it. I kicked it toward him. He stood there clapping, then picked up the ball and pushed it toward me.

I said, "That's nice."

I opened Anhar's notebook and started reading again.

Sadness is My Companion

I said to Hilmi in alarm, "Why are you so sad?"

He said, "It's loneliness. You don't know how sad it is for a man who doesn't have a god. Sadness is my companion."

I said, laughing, in an attempt to cheer him up, "If sadness is your companion, then you have a companion."

He said, "Gods are humanity's greatest inventions. Do you know how desolate life would be without gods?"

I said, "I love God. I see Him in all living creatures and in inanimate objects also. I don't see anything wrong with my economic belief in Karl Marx and my belief in God at the same time."

He said, "How lucky! At least you can ask God whatever you want."

I said: "But that's an opportunistic point of view. Do this and this and you will have a palace in Paradise. A relationship with God is much more lofty."

He said, "I didn't mean that, of course: you could be asking for forgiveness and security, hope for the future or keeping in touch. But a man without a god is a lonely, sad man."

I said, "Why don't you have a god?"

He said, "I wish I were like that primitive man who worshiped whatever he feared: fire, wind, the sun, the moon. But I cannot worship that which I fear."

I took him in my arms. I didn't hide my tears. His sadness was pure, like a blue flame.

Sleep assailed me suddenly. Anhar Khayun's notebook fell from my hands. I felt my whole body trembling despite the change in the temperature. I put the notebook in my bag for fear of losing it and stretched on the seat after bringing another seat closer to my feet. I covered myself with the coat and decided to yield to the angel of sleep, but I couldn't. I went once again to Anhar's papers. I made a guess where I had stopped earlier and began reading again.

A Battle

Angry words came rushing out of his mouth. His ears quivered. The color of his eyes changed and I felt that the hair on his chin and face got longer whenever the hurtful words came out of his mouth. Those were words that had come from the black depth of his soul. It was obvious that he had been awake since yesterday. I do not know how he interacted with the office employees or how he handled his day's work.

I asked him in great alarm, "What's wrong?"

He said, "Don't play the game of the good angel and the accursed devil."

I didn't say a word. I knew I was now standing at the gate of hell's circle. He went on without waiting for my reaction, "I don't want to hear your words. It's up to you to choose the solution. The story is over and you have to pay the price. The only thing I am thinking of right now is revenge. So, don't push me there."

I said, "I . . ."

He interrupted me saying, "I hate you. I have never hated anyone in my life but you."

I said, feeling a very bitter taste in my mouth, "So, what is required of me now?"

He swallowed, placed his feet on the small table in front of him, lit a cigarette, and said, "You are the stupidest person I've known. So, don't let foolishness take you down a dead end. One of these days you'll suddenly find yourself no more than a leaf tossed by the wind."

I suspected he may have had too much to drink, something he wasn't used to. I became obsessed with just one wish: to get it over with and go away.

I said, "Tell me and I'll do it."

He said, "Don't play the smart woman. Be brief."

"I will be."

"I've made a star of you. You were just one of hundreds of women journalists. Now, you are writing for five newspapers, you're on TV every week. And yet, you're still at the beginning of the road. One kick from me will bring you down. But I am postponing my revenge for the time being."

He fell silent and kept smoking and darkening the room with smoke. I waited to understand what was twisting his features, what event he was still hiding but which was causing him to lose it.

He asked me, "Did you go to the studio today?"

"No," I said.

He said, "Why not? You should have seen the remaining shots."

I said, "I didn't have the time. I can go directly from the agency."

He said, "I warn you. The movie is over. You won't work with him again. One adolescent here and another there! Abd al-Rahim, heh?" His voice became louder and sharper, "He's just a party candidate."

"Who are you talking about?"

"I advise you to hide from view for some time. Everyone's figured you and your game out. Everyone hates you. Do you hear? Everyone hates you. Go to them now and you'll find out for yourself."

"You say that I'll pay the price. Fine. I will. But please raise the price and tell me what happened and I'll pay that too."

"I am done. I am not adding another word. You have to find a way of paying your debts."

"Agreed. So, what do you want me to do, now?"

"You want to go, but I'll wait for you tomorrow. You know that I know how to get you."

"Agreed. And this is my word of honor. You know how to get to solutions quickly and that's great."

"Keep your advice for yourself. You are so very self-confident, I can see. I will not allow a mere adolescent to . . . to . . . I told you that one day you'll destroy yourself, but you didn't listen. I told you what your weakness was, but you didn't pay attention. You are in love with that weakness and you will pay with your life for a whim. I am not stupid. I've given you all my life and you will pay for the way you squandered it."

"Are you talking about giving? I won't discuss what you've given, but if all I had was a single piece of bread and I gave that, it's all I had. And yet, I'll pay and you won't know the reason why."

"I told you not to play the angel to my devil."

"You're living in delusions and I'll leave you to your delusions."

I ran toward the stairs. I don't know how he could change from the wonderful, intelligent, bright intellectual that he is to that primitive, ill-tempered human being. What did I do yesterday with Abd al-Rahim? Just a few innocent laughs, a few photos of the whole group on the occasion of the visit by Fathallah and the rest of the gang. Had it not been for this accursed jealousy, I would have become his wife. Inside me the word "wife" echoed, but I ignored it and started thinking of the barrier that has been building between us, tirelessly, stone by stone. But today's stone has made me feel weary and suffocated. I stood in front of the blue building on Sheikhaly Street. I cast a glance, then crossed the street. I stopped thinking. I didn't want to face all the disquieting questions and I did not want my heart to experience that fear of loss. I found myself at Nasr Square. I got on the minibus but before it started moving I discovered that I had forgotten my bag, in which were some articles that I had to deliver to *Alif Baa* magazine the following morning. I got off after some hesitation and went back to the office and rang the bell. There was no answer, even though I was sure he was inside. I opened the door with my key. The whole place was pitch dark. It seemed that Hilmi had gone to sleep as soon as I left. I noticed a faint light coming from the direction of his residence. I knew he was awake. I took my bag from the office but when I opened the door to go out, I couldn't just go. So I returned, and moved toward his bedroom just to make sure he was all right. I knocked on the door, then opened it. He was lying down on the bed, smoking, letting the cigarette burn without returning it to the ashtray. I saw the ashes extend, still in place.

I said, "Hilmi, can you please tell me what I've done? What's upsetting you?"

Without removing the cigarette from his mouth he said, "Nothing."

I don't know why he looked older than any time I had seen him in my life. I took one step toward him, but he said, "Please go. I want to rest."

I said, "I won't rest as long as I am so much in the dark."

He said, "My nerves are tired. It's not your fault. Come tomorrow."

I suddenly caught sight of a glass of water on the nightstand, on the bottom of which was a rose-colored object with white edges. I looked more closely at Hilmi's wrinkled face and his lips tightly pursed around the cigarette like a petticoat on the waist of a ballerina. He had taken off his dentures and placed them in the glass. I realized why he was so taciturn and why he didn't want to speak with me. I felt pity toward him and said, "Goodnight."

I left, greeted by the street's hot air. I still didn't know why he was so mad at me, even though he mentioned Abd al-Rahim by name. For the first time I felt his real weakness, his inability to confront me. I realized the age difference. I knew he was twenty-five years older, but he was the only one with whom I felt secure, and who gave to me without expecting anything in return. That's not true. He was giving you in return for your work and enjoying your body to boot. But I also was enjoying it. What kind of enjoyment, my dear? He was sucking life out of you, your youth and your beauty. Are you able to stop the pain that tears you apart as you postpone reaching your climax? Do you realize what this is doing to your body? Didn't Umm Abed tell you that he had left his imprint on you forever and that you would not be able to be a wife, because you were no longer a virgin in the true sense of the word? That virginity meant newness in feelings and in your body receiving your first man. Right now you are not a virgin even if your body has kept that gate intact. But couldn't a woman marry twice because she was widowed or divorced? Yes. But she would not be a virgin and her new husband would know that. Can you tell your husband of this experience that you had? Would he be able to go the distance that Hilmi went with you until you reached your climax? You've killed your feelings with him without knowing it. No. Stop. Weren't you scared by his toothless face? Yes. I was. I suddenly realized how old he was, as if he had just come out of a tomb. And I want that young man who can run with me, dance with me, travel, play, eat, and get hungry. I want a normal life. He has alerted you to the joy and ecstasy you feel when you are among the young, unlike the feelings you have when you are among his friends. Do you remember the last time you met with that group of Egyptian journalists, Saad al-Tayih, Saad Zaghlul Fuad, Fathi Khalil, Galal al-Sayyid, and Ahmad Abbas Salih? Do you remember how they talked and talked with their wives and about their illnesses? The hours passed slowly until midnight without you uttering a single word, looking from one to the other as they told stories about symptoms and diseases with which they were all familiar: diabetes, hypertension, slipped disks, and heart problems, then talking about glaucoma and cataracts. Didn't you feel stifled and bored with those assemblies and look for ways to get out of them? Didn't you always make sure that Nora would be there because she was your age? Did you think he hadn't noticed that? Have you figured out why he was so mad at you during the trip to Basra, when he noticed that Kazim was interested in you? His anger at you today is very much like his anger back then, nothing more. Believe me. I indeed feel more optimistic among younger people, chatting about things that make us laugh, not because we are Iraqis, but because we are all the same age. If Hilmi keeps behaving like that, I won't

461

be able to live with him. Tomorrow I'll tell him that our fights have gotten to be so frequent and so bad that they have outweighed the moments of happiness we have together.

I had a restless sleep, waking up in fright only to find that time was not moving forward. The hours conspired to prevent the morning from coming. I spent the worst day of my life at the agency, grouchy, not wanting to have anything to do with anyone, replying to my colleagues in such an unfriendly manner that everybody got mad at me. I headed for the office after loitering on Saadun Street, looking at the shop windows of the bookstores without buying anything. I found him waiting for me calmly. I gave him the latest agency bulletin and pointed out my remarks on its contents. Our work was done.

I said, "I want to tell you something."

He said, "I also want to tell you that I am sorry. It wasn't worth all this anger. We have an invitation to the presidential palace and we must go now."

I closed the notebook and let out a long moan. I was afraid that those sitting nearby, passengers like me traveling from the Amman airport, had heard it. So, Fayza was not the only obstacle between you two! Jealousy played the leading role in the scene. But could jealousy play such a role without the presence of such a formidable, irritating obstacle as Fayza, pushing the story to hopelessness and frustration? Maybe. I had noticed during one of Hilmi's family's visits that Fayza was miserable even though she was carrying Rana and playing with her, while her mind seemed to be totally somewhere else. I told myself at the time: why shouldn't she be miserable when she was torn between two worlds: neither a wife nor an in-law, but a woman lost completely, sharing Hilmi's life in the midst of the storm? Oh, dear God!

Three men took the seats right in front of me. Their Palestinian dialect was unmistakable. They looked like big businessmen. That brought to my mind the never-ending Palestinian diaspora.

462

*

As soon as I came into the office, Ustaz Hilmi Amin said to me, "We are going to meet some Palestinian intellectuals at Dar al-Salam."

I asked him who they were and he said, "Writers, journalists, and students who have been expelled from Cairo suddenly. One of them is a political analyst, another a poet, the third one is a story writer and translator, the fourth is the head of the features section at the Middle East News Agency. There are some students with them."

They welcomed us very warmly. Hilmi Amin introduced them: Abd al-Qadir Yasin, Mourid Barghouti, Ahmad Umar Shahin, and Muhammad Ahmad Ramadan.

We sat listening to the story of their deportation from Egypt. They looked distraught and unfocused and were startled by the slightest movement anywhere near them. Thousands of questions could be seen in their eyes.

Abd al-Qadir Yasin said, "On the first day of Eid al-Adha, before Sadat carried out his promise to go to Israel, and before his plane landed at Ben Gurion Airport, the four of us were arrested as part of a list of nine writers and journalists who were the leadership of the Union of Palestinian Writers and Journalists in Egypt. But two were not included because they belonged to Fatah."

I asked, "What happened to the other three?"

He said, "One went to make the hajj, another was in Beirut, and last was Radwa Ashour, who is an Egyptian, so she could not be deported."

I asked, "Was the reason for the deportation that you had participated in the demonstrations protesting the visit?"

Ahmad Umar Shahin, the calmest and shyest of them, said, "Yes. The students gathered to protest against Sadat's visit and they read a strongly worded statement in the name of the Union of Writers and Journalists."

Hilmi Amin asked, "Who wrote the statement?"

Abd al-Qadir Yasin said, "We had decided not to take a stand, because the issue was still quite hot, and to wait until the situation

463

was clear for the masses, because we could not stand against the people whom Sadat had attracted by convincing them that it was an attempt to stop the war, the sacrifices, and the bloodshed. So, the whole thing about the statement was a conspiracy by Fatah and the security forces to get rid of the four of us."

I asked him, "Why?"

He said, "Because the Union of Writers and Journalists is the only union not in Fatah's hands."

Hilmi Amin asked, "Were you deported right away?"

Muhammad Ahmad Ramadan said, "First they arrested us at the Mugamma' and there, in the passport security office, they asked us if we had money for the tickets. Three of us said, 'Yes,' and Abd al-Qadir said, 'No.' So they took Abd al-Qadir home to get money and they took the three of us to the plane. And when we actually sat down, they got us off the plane and told us that the deportation had been postponed until Sadat came back from Jerusalem. Then they took the four of us to the Khalifa lockup at the Citadel, where they detained us for three days, after which we were deported."

I asked, "Did you choose to come to Iraq or was that imposed on you?"

Mourid Barghouti said, "We requested to go to Syria or Lebanon to be with the PLO, but they told us that Iraq was the only country that didn't require a visa, even though the plane ticket to Baghdad was the most expensive."

Abd al-Qadir Yasin laughed and said, "While we were sitting in the plane, Mourid said, 'Now Abu Nidal al-Banna will capture us and behead us.' I said, 'It's not so lawless, my friend.' A short while later a handsome blond young man came to us on the plane and asked, 'Where is Ustaz Abd al-Qadir Yasin?' Mourid said, 'Didn't I tell you?' The young man, the one who was one of the Arab Nationalist leaders, what's his name? Yes: Amir al-Helou came closer to us, saying, 'I am the chief of staff of the minister of culture. I have been sent to welcome you. Please come to the VIP lounge.'"

Muhammad Ramadan said, "Tell them about Samaan."

Abd al-Qadir said, "Something strange happened yesterday, brother Hilmi. I met by chance at the hotel the communist journalist and poet Alfred Samaan, whom you know. He apologized that the newspaper *Tariq al-Shaab* did not publish the news of our arrival in Baghdad and said that that had happened because they feared that the Ba'thists might turn against us. What's the story, Hilmi? Isn't the government in the hands of a coalition front?"

Hilmi laughed, saying, "I know you are a very judicious and patient man. You haven't rested enough after the trip. But let me tell you that the front is one for the struggle rather than for the spoils of battle."

Ahmad Umar Shahin said, "What will the Iraqis do with us? Will they have us as guests until we make arrangements somewhere else? Will we work in their newspapers? I can't live away from Cairo or away from my apartment in the Sayyida Zaynab neighborhood."

None of us had an answer even though we knew that several Palestinian organizations had opened offices in Baghdad. Hilmi Amin said, "The situation will be studied according to relations with Palestinian organizations. As for working in newspapers, that should not be difficult. They have extended their hospitality to you, so await their decisions. You know that it's all political."

We said to them, "Welcome to Baghdad, and please feel free to visit our homes at any time. The hotel is right in the center of town; try to acquaint yourselves with it. You won't be bored and don't worry about anything. We'll stay in touch all the time."

Baghdad during that time had turned into a marketplace that attracted Egyptian political entrepreneurs. Some of them got money on the pretext of starting Ba'thist cells in Cairo. Others got money for secret political opposition parties in Egypt. None of the money ever made it to the "parties." Even women got into the game. I remember one woman who asked for Iraqi funding for the party to which she belonged, then transferred the money to a cultural organization bearing her name. News spread fast all over Baghdad and many of the players felt no shame talking about their real aims. I sighed in sorrow as the pictures came before my eyes. At the end of 1978 Ahmad Abbas Salih asked Amin Ezzeddin, who was close to Saddam Hussein, to intercede on his behalf to publish an Egyptian opposition newspaper outside Egypt to be funded by Iraq. When Amin Ezzeddin went to the Ba'thist official in charge and asked him, the man said to him, "Why didn't you come before? Only yesterday we gave Dr. Yusri al-Kamil three million dollars to publish a newspaper."

Of course the newspaper has not come out to this day, four years later. What really infuriated Hilmi Amin was the sycophancy of such Egyptian politicians in their dealings with the Ba'th Party. Some of these politicians were considered friends by Hilmi Amin. One of those was Abd al-Samad al-Kholi, who shouted slogans in support of the regional and national leadership of the Ba'th Party, and who took part in establishing a regional leadership for the party branch in Egypt. Hilmi Amin told me in sorrow, "Abd al-Samad needed delicate, complicated eye surgery, which Iraq paid for. But is this enough for him to sell out his history of struggle in this manner?"

Hilmi Amin got caught between a rock and a hard place: sycophants currying favor with the Ba'th Party, on the one hand, and his inability to look the other way when it came to Sadat's government, on the other. I think that was the real reason for his furious rage when I brought him Abd al-Rahim and Atef.

We left the Palestinians and started walking on Saadun Street. I noticed how sad Hilmi was. I said to him, "Iraq has opened its doors for the Palestinian splinter groups, what is called 'the front of the forces rejecting surrender solutions,' and is supporting them to spite Syria, but to this day I don't understand why."

Hilmi Amin said, "I think it was Iraq that called for the forming of this front. When the Syrian forces entered Beirut last year, 1976, to support the Maronites, the leaders of that front and their members fled to Baghdad and opened offices to be against Fatah."

I said, "You mean the Abu Abbas group and Wadie Haddad who split with George Habash?"

Hilmi said, "We are living in hard times, Nora. Hard times."

I wondered where they were now.

A month after that took place, we heard that Abd al-Qadir Yasin had gone to Romania for medical treatment and from there to Beirut. Hilmi Amin told me that he met him there. Mourid went to Hungary and I think he is still there. As for Ahmad Umar Shahin, he couldn't stand Baghdad's summer heat and traveled to Cairo where he stayed at the airport for two weeks before they let him in. They couldn't find anything they could hold against him. Muhammad Ahmad Ramadan left for New York to work as an interpreter for the United Nations. Hilmi Amin wrote a wonderful article in *al-Jumhuriya* newspaper about Abd al-Qadir Yasin with the title: "I Still Remember Your Smiling Face, Abd al-Qadir Yasin," in which he related the story of their detention together in the Oases detention center.

Oh, my God! How could I forget Hilmi's screaming voice in a public telephone booth talking to someone I didn't know after he came back from Beirut, "I am not going to let Iraq turn the national movement into a copy of the Palestinian organizations in which every group speaks on behalf of the country giving them shelter. The Egyptian opposition in exile are not going to be a pawn in the hands of Iraq or Libya to express its point of view or speak in its, or anyone else's, name. We will not be so fragmented."

I asked him in alarm after we attracted the attention of the passersby on the street, "What happened?"

He said, "Do you remember Herman Melville?"

I said, "Yes, of course. He wrote *Moby Dick*."

Then I laughed and added, "The Don Quixote of the sea."

He said, "Melville says that when the whale is surrounded by whaling boats and sailors, and when the harpoons attack it intensely and pierce its skin, and when the sea is filled with its blood, it becomes very quiet and motionless, so much so that the whalers think that it has died and happily come close, ecstatic about their catch. Then it surprises them with a fatal blow of its tail, splitting their boat while it goes back to sea, victorious. That's what we Egyptians engaged in struggle are like!"

I said, "I don't understand anything."

"The time will come. The time will come," he said.

I dozed off. Then I woke up feeling pain in various parts of my body. The lounge was lit but outside it was pitch dark. I heard the call: "Egypt Air announces its flight to Cairo."

I went to the gate. I saw people had gathered in a long line. I recognized some of the faces I had seen at passport control. I asked about the flight even though everything was written clearly on the board in front of me. I went back to the bathroom after I asked the man standing in front of me to keep my place behind him. It was stupid and naïve but I did it. I washed my face and retrieved the dry towel and thanked the attendant. I presented my passport to the officer. He looked at me closely, then signaled to one of his colleagues who was standing at a distance. His colleague gestured his approval.

I couldn't believe that I was at the very last gate while the plane was standing there right in front of me. I moved forward confidently and with a perfectly neutral face, even though I could blow up at any moment. I handed another officer the ticket mechanically. I got on the bus, climbed the plane ladder, then took my seat, without hearing what was happening around me, and I slept. I awoke to the flight attendant's voice as he was giving me a food tray. I ate semiconsciously and started trembling again even though I had not taken off my overcoat. I felt my ears almost exploding as the plane was landing at Cairo airport: I was about to scream as I tried to swallow, to no avail. I placed my palms on my ears. I wanted to wrench my ears off. The plane came to a stop. I dragged my body outside with difficulty. No one would be waiting for me because they didn't know my new time of arrival. The airport limousine would solve the problem. Tomorrow I go to Maghagha to bring my son home since going now was impossible. I presented my passport to the passport officer and told him what happened in Jordan. He looked at the picture and the papers I had just filled out and matched them with the passport, saying: "There's no problem. The photo is a little faded, that's all. Go back to the passport office at the Mugamma' in Tahrir Square and change the photo. Is the baby with you?"

"No. Do I need to check with the Jordanian embassy?"

"I don't think so. It's just that the passport officer there was not sure about the photo. I don't blame him. Welcome home and thank God for your safe return."

"Thanks a lot."

I waited for my luggage to arrive at the carousel, fidgeting in exhaustion. The book box arrived first. I started sobbing as I read on a big board: "Enter Egypt safely, God willing." I began to look closely at the streets from the window of the taxi. It was a whole separate world. I needed an hour to arrive at my house. I was here only ten days ago. Does it make sense for all these events to have taken place in ten days? Ten Days That Shook the World. People here are clueless. They don't realize that what is happening in Iraq will actually affect them. But what can they do? The prices they have paid in the Arab–Israeli conflict are exorbitant and the experience they had dealing directly with the Arabs is totally different. The Egyptian worker likes the way the Iraqis do business and he likes Arab Gulf money. How would that impact Egyptian society? I've often asked myself: why does the Arab Gulf accommodate such large numbers of Asian workers? Are they afraid of the concentration of large numbers of Egyptians?

Why isn't the taxi moving? Has everybody come out on the street just to delay my arrival home? Finally, my friend, the Nile, the Corniche, the Balloon Theatre. Turn here, please. Stop right here to the left. I gave the driver Egyptian pounds as I wondered why they did not take Egyptian money at the airport in Jordan. I looked up. I saw on the balcony an indoor clothesline with wet, small clothes. Those were Haytham's clothes. Has he come here? How and when? Did my mother-in-law send him to meet me? Is Fattum with him or did they feed him infant formula? The doorman came. I left my belongings with him and ran upstairs, extremely apprehensive. I opened the door as I rang the bell using my other hand. My mother came to welcome me.

"Thank God for your safe return. Why did you miss the plane?"

"Is Haytham here?"

She said as she kissed me, "Slow down! Yes, Haytham is here and he is fine."

I got out of her embrace as I looked for my son. Then I asked her, "What's he eating? Is Fattum with him?"

She said, "Patience. Have no fear. Everything is all right. Sit down first. Come, Haytham."

The young servant girl came in carrying Haytham, whose face lit up with a big smile when he saw me. I burst into tears when I saw that my son was all skin and bones, having lost almost half his weight. I asked in alarm as I extended my arms to carry him, "What happened?"

My mother said, "Just a simple intestinal problem and he's over it, thank God. Right after you left he had a mouth infection and refused to nurse. Your mother-in-law called and we brought him to the doctor. As usual he said to give him carrots and apples and to stop giving him milk. Today he put him on baby formula. He got only one bottle and would go back to normal gradually."

I said as tears covered my face, "Poor baby, poor darling son. It's all because of me."

My mother said in a gentle rebuke, "Didn't he get sick before, while you were with him? How was your trip, first of all?"

I replied as my eyes were glued to him, looking at his thin neck that miraculously supported his head and at his complexion that was no longer its usual rosy color, "Thank God. Where are Yasir and Hatim?"

My mother said, "Yasir went to buy candy and Hatim is in Alexandria. He'll be back tomorrow."

I dried my tears and opened the blouse, giving Haytham my left breast closer to my heart where he liked to nurse first. He took it with a big smile and started sucking slowly, his eyes fixed on my eyes, which were now apologizing to him in all possible ways and telling him how much I loved him. He, in the meantime, was trying to make sense of what happened, with his laughing eyes and without a single look of reproof, as if I had never left.

My father, who had been performing his prayers in his room, came and saw my son nursing happily. He said, "Of course, the cow has arrived, you little pig! Thank God for your safe arrival, daughter."

I couldn't look at my father as I returned his greeting, for fear of confusing my son. "May God keep you safe, father."

Yasir came in with my brother and flung himself in my arms. Haytham raised his face, then began to suckle again. My father told Yasir, "Let her alone until she feeds your brother." Yasir shook his head and refused to move away, holding on even more closely to my waist. I said, "Let him be, father." I patted him on the shoulder and kissed him.

I felt Haytham's legs moving in my lap. He kicked his little blanket away, left my breast for a few seconds, and started singing a beautiful "aaaaa," his face lighting up with a wonderful smile, then hastened to grab my nipple again. I thanked God for the miracle of my baby accepting my breast after being away for so long. I saw looks of surprise in my father's and mother's eyes. I felt the milk gushing forth anew. I moved Haytham to my right breast, fondling his hair with my hand as he resisted falling asleep. Then he was fast asleep. I moved him to the crib as Yasir followed me closely. We returned to the gathered family with Yasir still in tow. I hugged him hard, then placed my palms on my face, trying to stop all the images racing around in my mind and the sense of guilt gripping my heart and all the bitterness and anger. I gathered all my strength in order to ask about their news. My mother came carrying a glass of fruit juice.

My father laughed, saying, "I didn't know you were so weak. Today's piglet will grow up to be a big pig tomorrow. What happened?

I said, "I will never travel and leave my baby again."

My father said, "Don't be so hasty in your decisions. What matters is: was the trip worth the adventure?"

I said, "What adventure? The adventure was not here, father. It was there."

My tears came flowing down. My mother ordered a glass of water for me and insisted that I drink it, saying, "Be steadfast in your faith! Babies are a lot stronger than you think."

I remembered Basyuni. I asked, "Where's the telephone?"

My mother said, "Where it's always been. You've been here only a few minutes. Have some patience."

I said as I dialed, "No. This is important. I must do it right away."

Thuraya's voice came to me, happy and ebullient, "Thank God for your safe arrival! Basyuni has arrived safely in Lebanon and said several times to make sure to call you to reassure you. I called yesterday but your mom said you hadn't come back yet. We were all very worried about you. We were afraid Basyuni's escape was the reason you were late. But we didn't tell your mom anything."

I said, "Thank God. But why did Basyuni leave one country at war to go to another country at war?"

She said, "What can we do? The PLO is in Lebanon and he'll find someone to help him there."

I said, "Didn't he try entering a country for political reasons? Wasn't the Iraqi experience enough for him?"

She said, "With no college degree or any expertise he thinks he's a revolutionary fighter."

I said, "How did he escape?"

She said, "He told the story of his leaving from a town called Zakhou with some sheep. Thank God for your safe return again. I hope we meet soon, after you are rested."

I went back to my family, who were anxious to hear details of my trip. I started telling them some of what I had been through, but all the time, all I really wanted was just to get some sleep.

A few days later I received a letter with a Lebanese postage stamp. I opened it and read:

Dear Abla Nora

Warm greetings. Now then:

I write to you from beautiful Beirut, land of Arab struggle now,
to reassure you about myself. I wish that when I saw you in Basra
I could tell you when I was planning to leave Iraq. I had noticed
while working there that roads were being tamped in a way that
I had never seen in my life before. I asked my colleagues about
those specifications and they told me they were paved to the international specifications H1, H2, and H3, which applied to airport
runways. I said: "Why go to all this expense?" They said: "They
would be considered spare or reserve airports in war situations."
I followed the work of the prisoners and learned a lot from their
precision work. But at the same time I wondered why preparations were being made for war at a time when all was quiet on the
Iranian front after the Algiers Accord. Please bear with me. These
are things I have to tell you before I go on with my story. When
the department where I worked was moved to the region of Abu
Gharb al-Shahrani, I told Engineer Fathallah that I didn't want to
comply with the move order. He exerted great efforts to keep me
in Mosul. One of my Iraqi bosses said to me: "You are a mechanical
technician. If we keep some tamping workers here, we won't give
up any Egyptian technical workers. So, don't get Fathallah involved,
because it wouldn't do you any good. You will not be recruited into
the army, but, together with your team, you will continue the same
kind of work that you were doing there to directly facilitate the
movement of the armed forces."

I went on the same evening to the bar, tired and angry even
though he had told me that my salary would be tripled. There
I saw an Egyptian engineer named Salah whom I had met earlier
by chance. His story was very strange. He had graduated from the
College of Engineering, electronics department, and served in the
Egyptian army in the missile division. He had just arrived in Mosul
two weeks earlier at his sister's house to look for work. To his mis-
fortune he sat with an Iraqi friend of his sister's husband and told

him his whole story. So the man told him to worry about nothing. A few days later he was surprised when that Iraqi man, together with a man from the Ba'th Party, knocked on his door. They told him that he was wanted to work for the Iraqi army. When Salah apologized, telling them he had had enough war and that he thanked God that the war with Israel was over and he had gotten out safely and gone back to his family, they told him that he was not going to fight, but that he would serve with the technical support division in the engineer corps. They induced him with all kinds of temptations. But he refused. So they threatened him, telling him it was a matter of life and death, that they needed him and that he wouldn't get out alive. I met him in the bar in the evening; he was extremely perturbed, and cried as he told me his story. He told me that he had given in, that he had done so under duress. When I asked him why he hadn't gone back to Egypt, he said to me, "How can I go back? I borrowed money from all my friends to come up with the price of the ticket and got a one-year leave from my job. Besides, my sister and her family have done nothing wrong. They were living in peace until I came."

I told Salah of what happened with me and we both decided to accept facts and we each went where we had been ordered to go. I waited for an opportunity to escape. I had my eyes on the car that had come to the shop for repair and I had to go the following day to another unit to secure the extra spare part for it. I chose the time carefully so that no one would miss me or realize I was gone. I traveled at night, covering a long distance, driving the car for thirty-six hours without anyone suspecting anything. I stopped at every checkpoint and crossed it with the papers that I had, which were considered military orders, having amended the route miraculously. I entered Mosul to take my passport and some important papers and photos and letters from my mother, my fiancée, and my family. Then I left the car at a far distance from Mosul and headed for Zakhou near the Syrian and Turkish borders. I had heard from my colleagues that the Bedouins who moved among the sheep markets to sell them to butchers were the ones in charge of smuggling, especially since they belonged to nomadic tribes and had relatives all over the place. I met a sheep merchant and made a deal with him to travel the following day. In the morning he got me a driver, who gave me Bedouin garb and made me sit with the sheep in the back of the truck, in place of the attendant who usually helped him unload the truck upon concluding the sale. I kept telling myself that I had been through worse things: I lived for two years under constant shelling, that life and death were matters that God alone decided, and that I should not be afraid, that fear would give me away. The wind got quite brisk so it helped me cover up half my face with the kuffiya they called yashmagh there. I discovered that the driver was well-known to customs officials, that they greeted him and his attendant all the time since he and his car crossed the borders twice every day, morning and evening. When I heard him saying to the soldier on duty, "May God help you, brother," and heard the soldier say, "Go, in God's peace," I breathed a sigh of relief. We crossed the Syrian borders, from Zakhou to Qamishli and other points with the same routine. It was then, and only after a hundred meters, that I danced for joy, not believing that I had gotten away. But I did it thanks to my parents' prayers, thank God. I entered the very first hotel I came upon in Syrian territory and I slept very soundly for twenty-four hours, after which I went to Damascus and took the first service cab to Beirut. I called Mom to tell her everything was fine. Then I contacted a friend who knew Engineer Fathallah, so as not to cause him any problems. Then I wrote you this letter to reassure you and also so that you'll forgive me.

My utmost love,
Your younger brother,
Basyuni Abd al-Mu'in
Beirut, February 1982

Glossary

Abaya: A long, loose-fitting overgarment concealing the shape of the wearer.

Abla: A child's respectful form of address to a female teacher or older sister; sometimes used by adults as a noun to refer to a female teacher of children.

Abu, Umm: Father (of), mother (of): used in combination with the name of a firstborn son (or daughter, if there are no sons). The use of such a name shows respect, and some familiarity or affection.

Abuna: A title used by Coptic Christians to refer to a priest.

al-Ahali: "The Population;" opposition newspaper published by the socialist al-Tagammu' party in Egypt.

Ajami: A term used to designate non-Arabs, especially Persians.

Amudi poetry: "Columnar poetry," i.e., poetry written in the classical style according to specific meters and with a single rhyme. The division of each line into two hemistiches creates the appearance of columns.

Balam: A boat used by the Marsh Arabs of southern Iraq.

Dabka: A line dance popular in the Eastern Mediterranean.

al-Da'wa Party: A Shi'i religious party founded in 1957 in Iraq.

Dunam: An Ottoman land measure; approximately 1,000 square meters or about one-quarter of an acre.

Fitir mishaltit: A thin, layered pastry with a sweet or savory filling.

Halawa: "Sweet"; a homemade candy mixture used like wax for hair removal.

al-Hallaj: An Iraqi Sufi (mystic) and teacher, executed in 922 for heresy.

Hawza: A center for training Shi'i men of religion.

al-Jumhuriya: "The Republic;" official Iraqi newspaper, founded in 1976.

Kahi: A breakfast dish of thin pastry drenched with syrup after baking; sometimes eaten with cream.

Kaka: A polite form of address to a Kurdish male (although some Ba'th Party members used the term in a derogatory way.)

al-Khalij: "The Gulf;" newspaper published in the United Arab Emirates.

Kibasha: Small, artificial islands or platforms made of reeds on which the Marsh Arabs of southern Iraq live.

Majallat al-Mar'a al-Iraqiya: "The Iraqi Woman's Magazine."

Majlis: "Place to sit"; used to designate the house of Ali (the first Shi'i imam) in Kufa.

Maqam: A specific melody type in Arabic music, which provides a framework for improvisation.

Maqamat al-Hariri: A virtuosic work of fifty anecdotes in art prose, written by the eleventh-century Iraqi author al-Hariri.

Masgouf: Seasoned, grilled carp; sometimes considered the national dish of Iraq.

Mashuf: A canoe used by the Marsh Arabs of southern Iraq.

Mawwal: A genre of Arabic song which often includes improvisation, and is frequently mournful.

Mugamma': A very large government office building at the heart of the Egyptian bureaucracy, located in Tahrir Square in Cairo.

Mumbar: Stuffed intestines (a kind of sausage).

Pacheh: A dish made from the head and feet of a sheep.

Rose al-Yusuf: A woman's name, used as the name of a magazine (and later, also a newspaper) founded in 1925; originally it was progressive.

Sa'idi: Someone from Upper (southern) Egypt. Sa'idis are proverbial for being strong and clever but simple, and they are often the butt of ethnic jokes.

Samun bread: Traditional Arabic flat bread.

Sawt al-Arab: "Voice of the Arabs"; an extremely influential radio station during the period of Abdel Nasser, broadcasting from Cairo to the rest of the Arab world.

Sawt al-Fallah: "Voice of the Peasant"; an Iraqi radio station broadcasting from Baghdad.

Sawt al-Uruba: "Voice of Arabism"; an Egyptian opposition radio station broadcast by Iraqi radio during the period of President Sadat.

Sayyida Zaynab, Shubra: Lower-class neighborhoods of Cairo.

Shabka: The groom's gift to the bride, from a simple wedding band to a collection of jewelry, sometimes very expensive.

The Shahada: The attestation of the oneness of God and mission of Muhammad; reciting it is one of the five pillars of Islam. Used colloquially in many different contexts, not all of them serious.

Sharbat: Akin to sherbet; a sweet fruit drink served chilled.

Sirma: A form of embroidery characterized by a satin stitch in gold.

Sitt: "Lady"; a polite form of address to a woman.

al-Tagammu': An Egyptian socialist political party.

Tante: "Aunt," in French; a respectful form of address to an older woman.

Tariq al-Shaab: "The People's Path;" newspaper published by the communist party.

al-Thawra: "The Revolution;" Ba'th Party official daily newspaper.

Usta: A form of address used for a foreman or an overseer, or for someone in a lower-ranking job, such as a mechanic or taxi driver.

Ustaz, Ustaza: Respectful forms of address to a professor, teacher, or other professional (respectively, to a male or female).

Zaghruda ululation: Women's long trills of joy, marking happy occasions such as weddings.

Zakat: The "alms tax" required yearly of all Muslims, the payment of which is one of the pillars of Islam. It is roughly 2.5 percent of one's assets held for more than a year.

Zamalek: Upscale neighborhood of Cairo.

Zifta Repubic: A town in Egypt that declared its independence after Britain expelled Saad Zaghlul and other leaders of the 1919 revolution.

Modern Arabic Literature

The American University in Cairo Press is the world's leading publisher of Arabic literature in translation.

For a full list of available titles, please go to:

mal.aucpress.com